ALSO BY

TEGAN E. ARMSTRONG

PORT ARBOR SERIES:

The Home We Make

The Rule We Keep – Coming Fall 2026

the Home *we* Make

Book One in
The Port Arbor
Series

Tegan E. Armstrong

THE HOME WE MAKE

Copyright © 2026 by Tegan E. Armstrong

Contact: www.teganearmstrong.com

Front Cover Design By: Tegan Armstrong

ISBN (Paperback): 979-8-9946041-1-3

ISBN (eBook): 979-8-9946041-0-6

First Edition: February 2026

10 9 8 7 6 5 4 3 2 1

Content Warnings

Dear Reader,

Your mental health matters and I want you to feel safe and supported while reading this story. The Home We Make deals with mature themes that may feel triggering or distressing to some readers.

This story includes:

- **Child abuse and neglect** – shown on page in flashbacks and discussions.

- **Narcissistic parental behavior**

- **PTSD symptoms**

- **Parental hospitalization and subsequent death** – shown on page.

- **Mentions of suicidal ideation and self-harm** – referenced in flashback.

- **Explicit sexual content between consenting adults** – shown on page.

- **Strong Language**

the Home *we* Make

For the little girl who only wanted to be loved,
and the woman who finally learned she was.

Chapter 1

Tiffany

THE ECHOING OF HEELS clicking against the vinyl floors chases me down the quiet hallway. Our meeting ran over, and now I'll be scrambling to get out of the office on time tonight.

I shake my head, trying to sweep the loose hair out of my face, huffing as it falls back against my cheek, and picking up my pace as I hurry toward my office.

The stack of papers in my arms wobbles haphazardly, my laptop sliding across the top with each step. Somewhere between my chest and the stack, my phone buzzes, pulsing like a second heartbeat I don't have time to deal with.

I shoulder my office door open, nudging it shut behind me. The mess in my arms thuds onto my desk as I set it down, chaos barely contained.

I collapse into my chair and flip over my phone.

It's my older brother. The one person I regretted leaving behind.

The notification lights up my phone again. I reach for it, but the desk phone rings and it's my boss...again.

Clenching my teeth, I ignore my cell and answer the ringing phone.

"Yes, sir?"

Wedging the phone between my shoulder and cheek, I bite back a groan as he launches into a monologue that could've been an email.

Or God forbid, he could have covered in the meeting we just left.

I hang up and reach for my cell again before anything else can interrupt me. Swiping open my brother's text message, I choke on the air I'm breathing.

I read it.

Then again.

The words blur, and my ears ring. And for a moment, there's nothing but the weight of the message. It's not anger, not grief. But the knowledge of what this means overwhelms me.

I have to go home.

It's an angry drumbeat in my brain.

My eyes cinch shut, and the echo of an angry shriek rends through my mind. My heart races as I'm dragged through the years back to the house that holds my nightmares.

Dragged back to the bright whitewashed brick siding and the impeccable - if outdated - interior hiding the monster roaming inside.

My mother.

I survived Port Arbor. And I don't want to go back to the place that still haunts me.

Lowering the phone, I place it face down onto the desk.

A shudder runs down my spine, and the memory of fast hands across my cheek flashes behind my eyes.

My hand shifts to cradle my face as her words echo in my memory, voice surrounding me and threatening to take me under. It digs out the pit in my stomach, looking for corners it hasn't breached yet.

"You fat, ungrateful bitch. How could anyone love me with your shitty attitude hanging around. I'll never have anything good in my life as long as you breathe. It's all your fault!"

She lunges for me.

And I fall back.

The drumming of her beating all her rage into my body presses against my ears.

My eyes flash open with the boom of a door slamming in the hallway. I stare at the deep mahogany of the desk under the glass, and the fluorescent light flickering.

My heart hammers in my chest.

I inhale the sharp scent of melting plastic drifting in from the operations floor and pluck at the soft fabric of my sleeve.

Anything to pull me back to the office I'm in.

Dad is in the hospital. It's serious.

Come home.

My jaw clenches. I'll have to leave the safety of my hours-long distance between me and my memories. Partially because my brother's coping mechanism is to disassociate, which makes him terrible in an emergency.

Partially because I'm guilty of not having answered any of his attempts at contact in weeks.

Jason or Dad's.

I'm busy.

I'm always busy, keeping my head above water.

Another text dings through.

Anger flares through me. Because why didn't he call me? Is this what he considers appropriate for a text conversation?

The anger fades as a heavier weight settles on my shoulders.

Because it's not his fault.

I've been avoiding them.

Jason

> **He's been here for days. Where have you been?**

I study the office around me again.

The sleek, impersonal office I've been sitting in for the last two years. The distant sound of my coworkers' voices drifts through the too-thin walls. Someone's braying laughter grates on my nerves.

My hands drop, tapping irregularly on the glass. Everything is bare except for the work I dropped on the desk when I entered, and a small, half-hidden photo tucked neatly between my monitors of my daughter.

Come home.

The itch to run pummels against me, and my knee starts to bounce.

Come home.

My chest rises and falls faster as each memory I've spent years holding back floods my senses.

Come home.

Back to the place I swore I'd never go again.

3

To the tiny, idyllic Port Arbor, Ohio, town. Where nothing bad happens, and everything is safe.

Except for the house I grew up in.

The tiny town that I ran from all those years ago.

I lift my phone to my ear to call my brother, but his phone rings and rings before dumping me over to voicemail.

"Jason, call me." I swallow the heavy lump in my throat, coughing to clear it. "I need to know what exactly is going on with dad? I didn't know anything was wrong with him. I'm assuming the worst, but I would like confirmation before I upend my life to come home."

I pause as the coldness in my voice hits me, and the strain cuts my usually steady tone to pieces. "I need to know as soon as possible so I can figure out what I'm going to do."

A knock at the door interrupts me. It opens before I can answer.

"Ma'am?" My assistant's shy voice calls out.

"Call me back." I grind out before I hang up.

Exhaling sharply as I stand, I adjust my shoulders and motion for her to come in.

"Evans is asking for you. He wants you to come directly to his office. Something happened out on the floor."

Come home.

The words repeat a deafening clamor in my mind, echoes of slamming doors and fear so thick you could taste it threaten to unravel me again. My chest tightens, and my fingers begin a staccato rhythm on the desk now level with my hips.

It's an SOS no one will ever hear.

Lisa clears her throat, gently drawing my attention. "Ma'am?"

I blink, slamming the gates back down against the swarming memories.

"Right, sorry." I motion for her to go, following her to the door. She doesn't stop to look back, but I do.

I let my cell ring.

I take a deep breath, clenching my teeth so hard my jaw cracks.

Then I walk away from the last two years of my life.

Because if I don't, I'll be just like them – the thing I swore never to become.

The setting sun floods the room as I glance around the beautiful two-bedroom, Georgia apartment I finally finished decorating just weeks before Jason's text shattered the calm.

The paintings we found at an estate sale last fall hang behind the loveseat - their soft colors warm against the harsh, white apartment walls. The long navy curtains frame the room with quiet drama.

Everything here has been carefully chosen and collected over the years we've lived here.

I look around the place that has been my home for the last 3 years as my foot rubs over the soft lump of dog who lies beside my curled legs on the couch just like she does every night.

She's used to the weight of this time of day, to the world being predictable. The way it's been since she came home with me 4 years ago and I finally outran the nightmares.

The quiet should calm me, but instead it makes the air suffocating. The living room lamp casts its usual warm glow, yet my shoulders stay rigid.

The day clings to me.

Smiles stretched wide, conversations barely heard, and decisions dodged with nods and half-promises.

Jason's name still flashes in my mind, and the pauses in his retelling linger in my ears.

Everything in me went still as he spoke.

I can't shake the feeling of everything unraveling thread by thread as reality crashes around my ears.

And just like all those years ago, the guilt is heavy on my shoulders. A mantle given to me at too tender an age, and inexplicably, I can't shake the need to be the perfect daughter still.

But now...

I might finally get a chance, no matter how small, to get some closure. The kind I was never brave enough to reach for before because rocking the boat wasn't a good enough reason to deal with the fallout.

Jason can't - won't - do this by himself, and my father has no one else to pick up the slack.

5

Moving my small child will be hard enough once, let alone the back-and-forth that could be required if he needs a long term caregiver. I don't have time to stop and consider other options.

Paying rent in two locations for however long this drags out is impossible.

Thoughts of my daughter summon the pitter-patter of tiny feet rushing down the hallway. Her giggles surround us as she takes a running flop onto my lap.

I laugh, though it's a little strained, and hoist her into my arms, smothering her sweet face with kisses.

"What are you doing, little monster?" She squeals as I tickle her belly and continue to kiss her cheeks.

"Savie-monster get mommy." Her laughter is contagious as her little hands tickle at my neck and shoulder.

Her fingers are useless for actual tickling, but I chuckle anyway.

She is pure joy. The chaos fueling my life. Three years of boundless energy and unconditional love.

Savannah Grace, the light of my life, came screaming into the world at six pounds, eight ounces, with a shock of dark hair that still refuses to be tamed. My eyes welled with tears, and my heart cracked wide open as they set her squalling, still-damp body on my chest.

I sobbed with hands shaking as I cradled her, wishing her deadbeat father hadn't ghosted me with the first positive pregnancy test. He hadn't bothered to answer after the second, third, or the doctor's blood test either.

I brought her into this world alone, with only the nurses and doctors by my bedside. In those moments, I had wished for the mother I couldn't rely on, because I desperately needed someone in that room. I had wished I wasn't alone with my brand-new baby... because a girl should have her mom with her when she gives birth.

I called her from that empty room. The need for a mother outweighed the need to stay away.

Desperately alone people do crazy things like that.

She answered.

Or she called me back, at least.

We have been trying to repair what we could of our relationship since. Maybe I was still a naive child at heart, but I had hope the years of silence had changed her.

Our relationship is still heavily bound in barbed wire. With boundaries and rules. Ultimatums and distance. Despite my attempts at forgiveness.

It was shocking when she put forth any effort, but she's shown up for Savie in a way she never did for me. It's like the fairy tale grandmother is an easier skin to slip into than motherhood was.

I don't understand it. But I don't fight it either. Because Savie deserves more than I got.

My chest tightens with the thought of them being so close but, I remind myself, she's been easier since Savie was born.

And if we are back in Port Arbor, she is going to be physically in Savie's life, so I can't avoid this conversation for much longer.

Savie bites my cheek, pretending to eat me, jerking me back into reality.

"Savie-monster eat mommy." I gasp dramatically, wrapping my arms around her squirming body and bending us forward. I blow raspberries onto her soft tummy as she squirms in my arms, her feet waving about.

"Mommy-monster eat Savie!" I growl against her skin, laughter spilling from her.

She wiggles in my arms. "No, Mommy! No eat Savie!"

This.

This moment right here, with Savie in my arms and my dog at my feet. I try to press every detail into my mind before we go back. Something to anchor me when everything else tilts. This impossible, overwhelming love, so fierce it almost hurts.

"Okay, sweets." I laugh, lifting us both upright and settling back into the couch cushions. She curls into my chest like she did the day she was born. Only now her limbs are longer, and her hair is a little wilder. "Does Savie want to go see Nana and Poppy?"

She lifts her curly head, eyes going wide. "Nana and Poppy? Yes! Oh, Mommy, yes!" She scans the room in confusion for a moment before she turns back to me. "Where's your 'puter?"

I smooth back her curls and smile, though it wobbles at the edges.

"We are going to move closer to Nana and Poppy. Then you can see them whenever you want, without the 'puter." My words are steady, but a rush of dread runs through me. "Poppy isn't feeling good right now, sweetheart."

"Like when I wasn't feeling good, and I had to go get poked?" She wrinkles her nose. "I didn't like it."

7

I brush the wild curls away again before rubbing gently at her back.

"Sort of, but he's really sick and staying with the doctors. And we are going to go live very, very close to them so we can go see him and give him some feel better kisses." I press my lips to her forehead, and my eyes close.

I wish I could wrap her in her happy little bubble. Keep her from the beeping machines, the tubes, the strange man in the hospital bed who used to make her laugh.

I straighten my face as I pull back to look her in the eyes again. "So, we aren't going to see them tonight, but in a week-or-so we will."

"How long is a week-or-so, Mommy?" She lays her head back onto my chest.

I hesitate.

"Well, my love, it means more than seven days, but I don't know how many more days. Mommy has to make some plans and probably see if Uncle Jason or maybe Uncle Brandon can come down and help wrangle your wiggly butt." I pray the forced levity in my voice is enough to buoy her.

She looks over at Trixi, our ever-faithful Rottweiler, who is still curled by my feet. "I thought Trixi was the wiggle butt."

I chuckle. "Welp, I think you might be spending too much time with Trixi, and you are turning into a wiggle butt."

Trixi's head lifts as we look over at her, her thick, full tail thumping against the couch before she snuggles back in. Rusty eyebrows lift, and her sleepy eyes land on Savie, full of love.

Savie giggles. The soft, sleepy sound warms the room.

"No, Mommy." A yawn cracks her mouth wide open. "I not spend too much time with Trixi."

"I agree," I whisper into her hair. "I don't think we could ever spend too much time with Trixi."

Stand with her in my arms, we head toward her bedroom. I tuck her in with kisses and Trixi hops onto the bed to curl at Savie's feet.

Her room is soft colors with pastel blue bedding on her toddler bed and toy piles upon toy piles. The fairy lights, strung up and glowing softly above her bed, highlight her walls enough to make more decorations unnecessary.

I kiss her forehead. Then Trixi's. I switch off the fairy lights and leave only the soft glow of the nightlight in case she wakes. I pause in the doorway to take in one more warm moment.

"Mommy?" her little voice is thoughtful as she snuggles into her pillows.

I hesitate before answering her. "Yes, my love?"

"Can I hug Poppy when we go see him?" She wraps her hands around her blankets and pulls them closer to her face.

I swallow the lump I find rising in my throat. "I don't know, sweetheart. He's really sick. That's why we're going. So he knows we love him. That's the most important thing, okay?"

She nods, her face pressing further into the pillows as her eyes begin to flutter. Tears well as I pull the door until it is just ajar enough Trixi's nose can bump it open if she wants.

My feet drag down the hall. I groan as I flop onto the couch and slide open my phone, thumbing through my messages again, pulling open my brother's thread.

Fuck, I have to go back.

I close the thread and call my mother.

The phone rings until it runs to voicemail.

"Hey, Mom, it's me.

Chapter 2

Chris

THE RHYTHMIC CRUNCH AND release of the rower vibrates through my hands, each pull straining my body as I row furiously. The whirring of the cables fills the humid back room of my parents' home. It's the soundtrack playing over the soft tunes drifting in from somewhere.

I'm pushing myself - too hard probably, but I do it anyway. I was finally release from my sling this week and taking full advantage of the freedom

The weary pain in my shoulder never seems to dull despite the efforts I have put into fixing. The rest of my body is tired too. Aches have popped up in places they've never been before, like trying to compensate for the weakness in my shoulder has now made everything harder.

The loud ringing of my phone cuts through the noise. I already know who it is, and I don't want to answer.

I do it anyway.

My agent, Dan Bellows, has been with me since I signed seven years ago and there is no avoiding him when he wants attention.

"Hey, man. What's up?" I try to sound steady despite the way my chest heaves as I wipe sweat from my forehead with my towel.

I toss it against the chair in the corner but make no effort to stand, ignoring the way the muscles around my shoulder protest.

"Bart," His voice is tight, irritated, and expected. "Bernadette called. She said you were working out outside of PT."

I grind my teeth and let his words wash over me. I have nothing to offer him in return.

"Chris," he chews on my name, frustrated. "We got you *special clearance* to do rehab in your hometown. That wasn't a freebie. The team's stipulation for being allowed to rehab outside the rink is that you follow the rules of the PT they found you. I had to talk your team into believing you wouldn't go rogue out there. You promised. Remember that?"

Nurse Ratched warned me again this morning, but her plan drags. And if I follow it, I'll still be benched by preseason. My body isn't recovering the way it should. Still, I can't let my team down, not when we finally have a real shot at the cup this year.

I have worked too hard for too long to let this small injury take me out. Rolling the stiffness out of my shoulders, I pull my knees to my chest and let my elbows rest on them.

"Yeah. I remember." I grumble.

Pausing, I debate the rationale of saying what I want to say.

I say it anyway.

"You and Cliff said she was going to be a competent PT, but she's not working hard enough. My shoulder isn't healing fast enough." The muscles go rigid in my shoulders when I toss my hand up, pulling a full-body wince at the strain as if proving my point.

"Kid," There's a long pause and a loud swishing in my ear at exact moment he pinches the bridge of his nose. "She's the best PT in the state of Ohio. We are paying for her to live in your podunk hometown for the summer. You need to listen to her. That shoulder's half a millimeter away from popping like a champagne cork, and you're playing Rocky? This isn't negotiable. You make a mess of this, and they yank you back to the facility. No more working out in peace. No more solo PT."

I clench my fists around the phone, jaw tight. "I'm not playing Rocky. I'm not playing at anything here."

"Look, I know you're going stir-crazy." The creak of his chair is loud before his hand slams against his desk with a low thud. "You've been benched for weeks, and your body's ready before the doc says it is. I get it. *I really do.* But if you blow this. That's it. So please, for once in your stubborn, Polish, hockey-playing life, chill."

"I'm careful," I argue.

"Careful is a vague intention you mutter before doing something dumb." Dan barks out with a humorless laugh.

If I were sitting in front of him, I could watch the fabric of his expensive suit tighten to the point of pain over his thin arms as he lifts them to mock the quotation.

He barrels on, ignoring my disgusted sound. "You want to get back on the ice without tearing that thing again? *Then get off the damn rower and sit the hell down.*"

"Get me someone better!" I thunder.

The phone groans in my fist so loud I'm afraid I'm going to break it. "I can't sit in this house and listen to my family talk about my 'bum shoulder' like I'm already out to pasture."

"Then get a hobby! Or call that sweet ex of yours – the one that won't stop calling *me* – and get laid." Another creak of his chair tells me he is leaning back, his tone laced with smug satisfaction. "Find a different pair of legs to get buried in. I don't really care what you do, but you need to slow down on the exercise before you can't do your damn job. Or you could just come back east and spend time with your team."

I blow out a breath, already regretting the outburst. I know he has me. I *could* go back and spend my downtime with my team, but they're worse than my family.

"I make no promises, Dan, but I'll try. Okay?"

"Good. Ice your damn shoulder. Hydrate. Eat a banana. I don't care. Just don't invent your own recovery plan. Seriously, kid, I appreciate the enthusiasm but slow the roll."

"Bananas?" I can't stop the smile fracturing the angry scowl on my face. "Since when do you care about bananas?"

"Since I started managing athletes with the survival instincts of golden retrievers." Dan's laugh cuts the last of the tension blistering between us. "If I hear about so much as a push-up grunt, I swear to God I'll fly out there and duct tape you to a recliner."

"Got it. No rower, no pushups, or I get the tape." I grab the towel to wipe my face again as sweat continues to prickle against my flushed body. "I'm getting off the rower. I'll go for a run instead. That better?"

"Yeah, that's better. And Bart?" His voice softens, just a little. "I give you crap because I know how badly you want back. You've got more than a jersey waiting. You guys have a real shot at the cup this year and hundreds of thousands of dollars in brand deals if you get this right."

I nod in time with the squeak of leather as his knee bounces.

He sighs. "Moving on. You have some appearances you need to make over the next 30 days and beyond. I'll send your schedule over. Should I CC your mom?"

I groan, laughing. "Nah, man. I've managed my own schedule for the last five years. I'll keep it just fine now. And I hear you. I'll take it easy on the shoulder, but I'm not going to stop exercising the rest of my body. I'll behave otherwise. I promise."

I have no intention of actually stopping. I'll just have to be smarter about when, especially since someone's been tattling.

"Thank you, Bart. I'll be in L.A. with you when you fly out. So will Pasha. The Kid's Foundation is looking forward to the two of you being there."

He goes over some other obligations we have before we exchange our goodbyes. I grab my towel and head into the kitchen, muscles cooling but nerves still hot. This injury has changed more than just the way my body feels. I'm angry and frustrated.

The kitchen greets me the way it always has. The clanging of pots and pans as Mom sways, dancing like no one is watching. Except, unlike when I was young, my father is here, enjoying his retired life.

The music is loud, coming from the brand-new speaker system I had installed for her. The sounds of dinner cooking are the driving beat of her private concert.

I pause in the doorway, my towel hanging loosely around my neck, and watch as Dad wraps his arms around her waist. He sways her side to side as she tries to laugh him off, protesting, despite the grin on her face.

Mom's sun-kissed skin crinkles around her still brilliantly blue eyes, deepening the smile lines bracketing her mouth. Dad presses a kiss to her cheek, his grey-streaked hair catching the light filtering through the windows.

These two have been grossly in love with each other from the first moment they met in high school, way back when. One of those forever-love stories you assume only happens in old books or bad Hallmark movies. It's annoyingly perfect.

It's exactly what I want someday.

Watching them like this makes me think of the girl who grew up next door. The girl I pined for as a teen. The girl others warned me away from, pushing me too far away to try anything with.

Too bad I'll probably never see her again.

13

A grin spreads over my face as I watch my dad – a man I so closely resemble – spin Mom away from the stove with all the finesse of a man half his age.

His body sways too dramatically for the music playing; the same mischievous eyes my brother Charlie inherited twinkle around the love he has for his wife.

Dad spins her into another twirl, and I sweep in before he can pull her back towards his body, plucking Mom out of his hands. She laughs, full and surprised, her fingers curling into my bicep as I dance her away from him before he can stop me.

A soft hand gently pats my cheek, beaming at Dad's playful outrage, "Son, you give me my wife back."

Mom's round face is iridescent in her joy. She studies me while we twirl.

"Not happening, old man." I grin, tossing a wink his way. "I don't want to see you get handsy with my mother. She's a classy lady, Dad. She should be felt up outside of passing eyes."

He snorts, crossing his arms. His own smile answering mine.

"Son, I'll feel my wife up, any damn place I want," he cackles.

I dip Mom low enough to make her shriek before I twirl her back toward his waiting arms.

"You should know that by now," he continues, pulling Mom in close.

"Gross," I grin.

They're ridiculous.

And I love them for it.

"Mark," she scolds, pressing a kiss on my Dad's lips before returning to the stove in the kitchen I had upgraded for her with my first bonus.

The kitchen with its quartz island and high-end appliances still smells like the one I grew up with – smells like home.

"Leave the poor boy alone. Our baby is hurt," she says, waving her spatula at him.

"Mom, I'm not hurt anymore." I shrug, rolling my shoulder despite the ache. Blanking my face to hide the wince wanting to shout with the motion. "I'm *healing*."

His big hand lands roughly on my thankfully uninjured side.

"Don't fib a fibber, son." He plops himself onto a stool and watches Mom with reverence. His eyes meet mine, worry barely concealed under their usual warmth. "It's not a bad thing to take it easy for a change. You've been working so hard for so long."

Mom gives him a sideways look, before she turns her focus on me. "Your dad's right, hon. We just worry about you."

"I'm fine, Ma." She hums a non-committal sound as she rolls her eyes. Before either one of them can argue more, I pivot. "In other news, I'm going to go for a run. I should be back in an hour before dinner is ready."

I turn and head for the door.

Hoping this tiny Port Arbor town can offer me some of the peace I wanted to find coming back here to rehab my shoulder.

The kind of quiet that can only be found at home.

Chapter 3

Tiffany

I'VE BARELY FALLEN INTO MY bed when the phone rings on the nightstand next to me. I don't check who it is before answering. Only two people would call this late without texting first, and one of them is lying in a hospital bed.

"Hello?"

"Tiff? It's Mom." Her voice is breezy; years of pretending not to be a monster help her perfect the tone. "I'm just calling you back. You said your dad is in the hospital?"

"Hey," I roll onto my back, pressing the phone tighter to my ear. "Yeah, he's in the hospital. Jason says it's some sort of stroke. He's in a coma. I just wanted to let you know that Savie and I are going to be moving home when I find a suitable place to live. Just in case he needs help when he wakes up."

The muffled laughter and the murmur of a TV in the background cover her pause.

"Well, why don't the two of you stay in my house?" She asks with an air of casual indifference.

I groan, my hand rubbing at the furrowed pinch of my eyebrows. "You know why, Mother. Boundaries."

"I don't understand why you won't just let that go," she huffs. Her tone sharp. It's always the same whenever she's pressed. "I know you think I'm a terrible mother but I did the best I could. Besides, I'm living with Frank, and we are getting married!"

My teeth grind as I bite back a sigh.

But I play along to keep the peace. "That's great, Mother. Let me think about it, okay? And if we do this - if I say yes - you can't come back to live in the house with us, *and* it won't be forever."

"Well, you *think* about it then." She talks over me, not hearing a word I'm saying. "And let us know, but either way, the house is empty. Even if it's only for a few weeks until you find something better."

"Okay, yeah," I bite my cheek. It's a familiar trap of reeling me in with things I need. "We might do that."

It *would* be easier.

"Okay! Let us know." She hangs up without a goodbye.

Pulling the phone from my ear, I stare at it for a moment.

I pull up my thread with Brandon, hoping my best friend of a million years can offer a little levity and at least he'll be happy to know that we are coming home

Tiffany

Me and Savie are going to be moving back. Dad's in the hospital. It's not good.

Brandon

I'm so sorry but YAASS we can't wait to have you home!

Brandon

When?

Tiffany

Soon

Brandon

Solid plan *Eye Roll*

The next morning, I wake up to find Savie in my bed. I lean over to wipe the hair out of Savie's face. "Hey, mamacita. Time to wake up."

She stirs with a groan.

"Momma." The whine in her voice tells me staying home is a good call. I'm not the only one who needs comfort.

I stroke her hair out of her face again. "Guess what?"

Trixi's tail begins to beat a steady rhythm against the mattress, sensing the shift. Savie groans again, this time rolling toward me. "What?"

"Today is a Mommy-Savie day." I scoop her up and sit back against the headboard with her sprawled across my chest. "Just us. Doesn't that sound good?"

She sighs into my neck, melting into me. It's a soft, sleepy agreement. I hold her there for a long moment, mooring myself in the warm weight of her little body, in the familiar scent of my little girl.

We head into the living room and get started preparing for our day.

It takes us just under thirty minutes in the warming Georgia spring air to walk to our favorite park. It's warmer here this time of year then it is back in Port Arbor - it always is in April. The heat wraps around me like a thick blanket on a cool day, pulling the reminder of why I settled here - safely away from all things Midwest - all those years ago to the forefront of my mind.

The warm people we pass are in no rush, they mosey between stores, offering smiles and waves as we pass. Some even stopping us to say hi.

Savie insists on holding Trixi's leash the whole way, her tiny voice narrating her planned adventures while I trail behind, laptop bag bouncing against my hip and heart full of these girls.

We enter the playground and Savie is off to play in the sand, Trixi standing sentinel like a furry foreman as they build sandcastles.

I settle in at a nearby table and open my laptop, opening the listings that Brandon and Shawn had been sending late into the night. Six houses deep and still no luck - pet restrictions, outrageous pricing, or questionable ads. I'm overwhelmed and questioning my ability to pull this off.

My eyes drift over to Savie time and again. She's squealing with laughter, burying Trixi under layers of sand, unaware of how close we are to not having anywhere to go.

Should we even be doing this?

Brandon's name brightens my phone next to my laptop, dragging my attention away from the girls.

"Hey girl!" He greets me. He's upbeat like normal, but there is a wariness in his tone not buried as deep as he would probably like.

"Hey, what's up?" I pretend just as hard as he does to sound cheerful. "I'm looking at some of those listings you guys sent. So far, no luck, but don't worry, I'll find something. I mean, I've got to, right?"

There is rustling on the other end of the line before he responds, his slow agreement sets me on edge. "I know you can do it."

"Yes! I can totally do this." I say, squaring my shoulders as if that alone could steady me. "But what was it that you called about? I'm sure it's not to check on me and my house hunting abilities."

He hesitates again, and my shoulders tense. "So, your brother called me. He told me about your mother's offer."

"No." I snap, my whole body winding tight at the direction he's taking us. "How does he even know? I barely talked to her before you called me last night. And why did he call *you* about it?"

"I know, I know you don't like the idea," he rushes. "But she called him, I guess, after you turned her down. He said he would have called, but he was certain you'd say no just to spite him."

"I –"

He cuts me off before any words leave my lips. "Don't even try to deny it. I know you better than that. You 100% would do that. I love you, but you do the exact opposite of what people tell you to do, which, I'm not, by the way. I just think you would be crazy to stay anywhere else. She said, 'free of charge', right?"

A bitter laugh before it falls from my lips.

"Yeah. *Free.*" He can't see the sarcastic nod of my head, but it gives me the tiniest bit of satisfaction. "Nothing is ever free with her. Look, if you knew what she was like, you wouldn't be suggesting what you're suggesting."

"But I don't." The softness in his tone hits harder than if he'd yelled. "You won't talk about it. What if she's changed? Like, really changed. You said things have been easier."

Few people in my life have been careful with me and my feelings, and I'm used to it. But at this moment, talking as if I didn't wade through hell just to get out, hurts.

"Easier doesn't mean changed." The sharp words drag a cloud of silence between us that neither of us can breach for a moment. Tears I thought were done last night begin welling, and my heart races in my chest. "Look, can we just not. I can't go back there. I cannot. I just need a little bit of time to figure this out."

"Tiff -"

"No." My voice cracks. "I just need time."

"What if ... What if your dad doesn't have time?" The words suck the air right out of my lungs. He keeps going, gentle but relentless. "It's already going to take more time than you might have. You have *years* of your life to pack and move. And that takes more than twenty-four hours. Not to mention credit and background checks, deposit and rent money, setting up utilities, driving time, and all the other things that are involved. They all take time."

"*I can't*, Bran." Every breath is ripped from my chest, and my body folds over on itself.

Savie calls my name, and I paste a wobbly smile on my face, waving at her, my fingers trembling. She waves back, her little fingers sticky with sand and probably dog drool, then happily returns to burying Trixi in the sand as the silence on the phone ends.

"Just for a little bit." Brandon's voice drops into a low, unwavering tone. "Shawn and I will help, and you could stay with us, but we only have one spare room. We'd make it work but you could have a whole house to spread out into, and everything is already turned on; she's already paying the bills. So, toss her a couple hundred to pay her something so she can't come back later."

"Bran-" My throat closes. I want to argue. I want to scream. But I can't. Because everything he's saying is *true*, and I *hate* it. "I don't trust her."

He doesn't hesitate, but his tone is gentler. "I know, but I think you need to consider it. At least until you can find a different place and a job."

Shoving my laptop out of the way, I drop my head onto the worn wood of the picnic table. I can't hold myself up anymore. For a moment, we both breathe down the line. My eyes find Savie and Trixi running around, locked in some chaotic version of tag. Trixi's leash is tight in her grasp, giggles floating in the breeze.

Brandon's voice is quiet when he starts in again. "Tiff, you'd only be moving if you thought you'd regret not doing it. Not being here. Don't let your stubbornness make you miss this. It doesn't have to be forever, even just a few weeks would be better than nothing."

"Okay," I whisper.

The word crashes over me, hitting me with a staggering force.

"Okay?" He asks, surprise edging into his voice.

"Yeah." The word scrapes out as I force it past the lump rising in my throat.

"Good. Shawn and I will be there this week to help you pack."

An overhead speaker blares in the background. The words too garbled to make sense of.

He pauses for a second before continuing. "We've sent boxes to your apartment with tape and packing material. Should be there before you get home from the park. Do what you can, but we'll be there to help soon. You'll home by the start of next week."

I'm nodding, but the words are stuck in my throat. My gaze clings to Savie, the only source of brightness in my life.

"You're nodding, aren't you?" There is a hint of laughter in his voice as I manage a choked exhale.

"Tiff," he says, his voice ringing with quiet certainty. It wraps around me like one of his warm hugs. "You are strong. You don't have to do anything if you don't want to. You are not responsible for any person but you and your daughter. No one who matters can judge you for that. Catch your breath, I can feel your anxiety through the phone. I'm going to be there soon, and I'm going to give you the biggest hug you've ever gotten."

I force myself upright, calling out to Savie and waving her over. "Okay. I'll see you in a couple of days."

Savie launches herself into my arms as she nears the table, and just like that, I find the strength to move forward. It doesn't take us long to pack and head home. Her little hand swinging in mine as she tells me all about how her and Trixi played in the sandbox as if I wasn't watching them.

She is halfway through recounting her rousing game of tag when we reach our apartment hallway. We both stall as we round the corner toward our door. My eyes widen, taking in the broad width of my best friend. His grey eyes are crinkled under his perfectly arched brows as he smiles at me. He has folded boxes and bags lying near his feet as he slouches against the wall near my door. The smooth curve of his jaw is covered in an unusual amount of stubble, but his trademark smirk is firm on his mouth.

His grin widens. "Hey."

Savie barrels into him as I stand gaping at my best friend, who is unexpectedly in front of me.

There is worry behind his eyes as he scoops the little monster, who is launching herself at him, into his arms.

"Wha- What is happening right now?" I blink at him like my brain needs a minute to reboot.

"Ta-da!" He laughs as he makes the stupid jazz hands he's been doing since we were young. "Suprise!"

A real laugh breaks free from my chest at the absurdity of him standing in front of me. "You son of a gun! You were at the airport when you called, weren't you?"

"*Maybe.*" He smirks.

I close the distance and hug both of them close, my arms wrapping around his waist. Brandon sways back and forth with us in his arms as long as Savie will allow.

It doesn't take long before she is wiggling to be put down. We pick up the boxes and bags and head inside, settling Savie and Trixi in her room to play.

He's packing the living room linens when I return. The boxes are already assembled and stacked neatly against the wall. "You'll need those for sleeping."

He tosses a wink over his shoulder. "Psht. I'll be sleeping in your bed, thank you very much!"

The familiarity of him making jokes, of him giving me space to feel, makes everything feel possible.

"What is Shawn going to think when he gets here, and you're in *another* girl's bed?" I joke; the memory of the high school party has him shooting me a stink eye. "What?"

He points a dramatic finger at me in outrage. "That happened one time in high school before we started dating. Besides, you know he'll be joining us in your bed when he gets here this weekend."

I raise my hands, letting him off the hook before I grab the packing tape. We move slowly around the house, packing what won't be needed.

"Hey, remember Chris? From the hockey team in high school?"

My eyes drift to stare out the window. In my mind, a gray sedan blurs past.

He was the hottest guy in high school. And I used to watch for him and his cheshire cat grin, in his perfectly safe life.

He'd zip into his driveway, and I would listen for the slam of his car door as he jogged into the predictably happy house.

It was everything mine wasn't.

I was glad he had it, because a boy that good deserved something like that. No matter how jealous I was of him.

But the way he always appeared when I needed him most made him the center of my childhood fantasies.

I turn to look at him as he move around the apartment with me, bouncing around in a way that wouldn't make sense to any one else but me. "The one that went pro?"

"Yep." The 'p' pops loudly in my ear.

"My neighbor growing up?"

"Girl, that's the one," he exhales dramatically. "He got hurt at the end of last season. So, he's home. Recuperating. We saw him jogging the other day, lookin' *fine*. Woo, girl!"

"What does that have to do with me, exactly?"

"Eye candy, Tiff!" He throws hands in the air, eyebrows wiggling. "Eye candy. And, maybe a *distraction*?"

My laugh is fragile but real when it escapes me. "What would Shawn say if he heard you say that?"

"Oh, he'd probably agree." We both chuckle, and I offer him a strained smile for his effort. "Might even offer to drive us past Chris's house himself."

Brandon's surprise appearance keeps me steady as everything changes. He holds my hand while I call and accept my mother's offer to stay in her house. He helps me corral Savie when I need a break, and he holds me when I can't keep the tears off my face.

On Saturday morning, the doorbell rings, and I open it to a dimple creasing Shawn's cheek. His smile wraps me in warmth, and is so much larger than I would have expected this early in the morning.

His dark brown eyes are soft under the long lashes I have been envious of since we met. He lifts a hand, waving U-Haul keys in my face.

Savie packs and re-packs her bag of toys for the road five times before she allows us to finish packing anything else in her room. Shawn and Brandon busy themselves with loading any unneeded furniture while I continue to work on boxing whatever is left.

By the time Saturday night falls, my living room is empty of everything except the TV. The bedrooms and kitchen are bare except for what we need for the night, and boxes are piled everywhere.

"Thank you both for this," I collapse into the bed next to Brandon. "I honestly don't know how I would have gotten this all done by myself."

"You never have to thank us for something like this," Shawn says, half-asleep, already tangled around Brandon.

Brandon agrees as he puts his arms around me, pulling me closer. "Just like old times, huh?"

Shawn's fingers scratch my back lightly before falling back to Brandon's chest.

"Yeah," I murmur as I close my eyes. "Just like old times.

Port Arbor, here we come.

Chapter 4

Chris

THE NEXT FEW DAYS, as the air warms around Port Arbor, I keep most of my promise. I spend more time running, and I only get on the rower when there is absolutely no one around to watch me and report my misbehavior.

But today, I can't stop my knee from bouncing. Every time I try to relax, I wind up back in the exercise room, and my parents' watchful eyes never leave me.

I'm in a fishbowl in this house. Every move scrutinized with apprehension as if they are just waiting for me to snap.

I try to keep a pleasant smile on my face, but I'm not sure I make it work.

Because Dan called again, and some of the brand deals are holding off on signing me again until they know I'm back on the ice. It's not the money I'm worried about necessarily, but the tone of it, the implications of their hesitation opens a pit in my stomach.

By the time the afternoon rolls around, I'm not able to sit still anymore. I pop into the kitchen where my parents' dinner routine is in full swing. Dad's just about to sweep Mom into his arms, and the music is loud.

"Hey, I'm going out for a run." I shake my jogging armband and headphone case in their direction.

"Okay, just be careful," she says, her eyes say more than her words do. "That Samson girl is moving back into her mother's house today, and there have been cars coming and going since just after lunchtime."

I freeze mid-step. The weight of her eyes rests on my back, watching for a reaction. "You remember her, right? You all went to high school together. Her brother is -"

"Jake's best friend? Yeah, Ma." I nod, cutting her off. "I remember her."

How could I forget the quarterback's little sister, with her honey-brown eyes? The dream girl who was off limits to me?

She was all long curls and sharp comebacks, a wild streak behind quiet eyes that held secrets I never got the chance to learn. She left our little town like it was on fire and never looked back.

Still, no matter how many years pass, I find myself looking over at her house every time I pull into my parents' driveway. As if one day, she'll come strolling out like she used to, flopping onto the grass with a notebook on her lap and no shoes on her feet, and everything will be different than it was last time around.

"I'll be careful," I say, not turning around.

The normally lazy street is filled with cars, and a U-Haul is angled across the driveway. I slow, pulse skipping, as she walks out of the house.

The pretty brunette isn't wearing braids and bows now. But the heart-shaped face still gives her an approachable beauty, and her full lips with a natural curve still make her look a little amused. The sight of her brings me back to the day we met when I was just 7 years old.

The dresses and dolls are gone, and not much has changed over the years, but she looks steadier than she used to.

She doesn't look at me, but I stare at her.

I shake the past from my shoulders as she turns. Our eyes connect for a moment, just like they did all those years ago, and my heart stumbles in my chest. Her warm honey eyes have darkened, more bitter whiskey than before.

My lungs quicken their pace as if I'm returning from my run instead of starting it.

But before I can make heads or tails of the look in her eyes, a tiny giggle drags my gaze toward the door of the Samson house again. There is a miniature version of the woman I could never quite forget standing in the open frame. The same curly hair and heart-shaped face, the grin on her mouth, all of it's familiar.

I scan the lawn, and there's Jason, her older brother, standing near the U-Haul, his eyes narrowed in my direction, which I ignore. The two guys she was inseparable from in high school linger nearby. But no other man – or woman - in sight.

The little girl comes barreling down the steps and straight into Tiffany's arms. Her little voice is high and excited as she shouts. "Mommy!"

My breath catches in my throat.

They disappear into the house, the spell her eyes cast on me gone finally, and I begin to move.

True to my word, I am back on our street within the hour. The warmth I've worked up makes the cool air of Ohio in late spring feel refreshing. My feet slap the pavement in a constant rhythm, and my eyes are firm on the concrete in front of me, trying not to think about anything but the ache in my legs.

I slow to a walk as I near my parents' house, my sweat cooling with the breeze on my overheated skin.

Then I spot them.

Mom stands outside, apron still tied at her waist, talking to someone. It takes me less than half a second to recognize Tiffany. And perched on Tiffany's hip, staring straight at me, is her little girl with clear blue eyes instead of honey.

I tug out my earbuds as I get closer, lifting my hand, waving. The kid shyly tucks her head into the hair covering Tiffany's neck despite the little grin I catch curling at the corner of her mouth.

The movement alerts the two women to my presence, and Mom turns, beaming at me.

"Chris," she calls, as I pocket my earbuds. "You remember Tiffany? Right?"

"Of course." I nod toward Tiffany, swiping at the sweat on my forehead with the back of my arm. "And who is this cutie that's hiding here?"

I shouldn't be staring, but I am. My eyes trace Tiffany's body. She's older, of course she is, but she's still somehow the girl I remember.

She's still petite, though softer than before; lean angles of youth rounded from time and childbirth and more enticing than they should be.

Her strong legs are hidden in the deliciously tight leggings, drawing my eyes as I watch the way her hips shift under the weight of her daughter, before I remember I'm not alone.

Pieces of her dark brown hair fall out of her messy half-do, framing the face I used to study. It's one more piece of the teenage girl I used to know; she's in the shadows of the beautiful woman in front of me.

My eyes catch the look my mom's giving me. Upraised eyebrows as she questions my wayward gaze without saying anything. Her eyes twinkle.

And now I'm expecting something embarrassing from her.

I turn back to Tiffany, who's still looking at me, her daughter peering over her shoulder in my direction.

"Chris," she drags my name out as she studies me. "Um, this is my daughter, Savannah. Savie."

There's the slightest southern twang that threads through her words now. It doesn't cover the subtle slur of the midwestern tone we all have. It makes me wonder if I sound different to her too.

She bounces the little girl on her shoulder, softly jarring her. "Savannah. This is Mommy's friend from when she was a little girl. His name is Chris. Can you say hi, Savie?"

"Hi, Savie," she murmurs, the hint of a smile curling her lips again.

She peeks at me, eyes wide. This tiny human, who looks so much like her mother it hurts, has grabbed every ounce of my attention.

I chuckle softly; Mom's laugh in the background mirrors mine.

"Well, hello," I say with a grin, giving her another little wave. She sets her chin on her mother's shoulder, eyes narrowed, studying me. With the same impish spark Tiffany had as a child, she wrinkles her nose and sticks out her tongue.

A loud laugh rips out from my chest, and a wicked grin pulls at my lips.

She's definitely Tiffany's daughter. The perfect mini-me.

Tiffany gasps. "Savannah!"

"No, no, it's perfect!" I say, grinning. "I guess that seals it then. You are definitely your mother's daughter. Your mommy did that the first time we met, too."

Tiffany's eyes widen in horror before she laughs, and the tension finally breaks. "Did I really?"

"You did." I wink at Tiffany before I glance back at Savie. "Don't worry, Savie, I think that means you and I will be good friends. Just like your mommy and I were when we were little."

Tiffany's face softens, her hand resting on Savie's back. My chest tightens as I watch them together.

"Chis?" Savie blinks at me, considering me.

"That's me, little one," I respond softly, gently smiling at her.

She nods, finally untucking herself from her mother's neck just before she reaches for me. I pause, surprised, and look at Tiff for permission. She hesitates, a flicker of something... uncertain tightening her jaw.

"You know what, little one?" I offer Tiffany the out she's clearly looking for. "I'm all sweaty from my run, but next time, you and me, we're on like Donkey Kong."

She wrinkles her little nose again with a sweet little giggle as her arms circle back around Tiffany's neck. "You is silly, Chis."

"Tiff," my mom says, clearing her throat. She's plotting. "Why don't you and Savie come over for dinner? That house has been empty for too long, and I know you have been moving all day. Probably haven't had a chance to grocery shop for you and that sweet little pea. I know my Mark would love to see you after so long."

"Umm." Tiffany looks at me for half a second. It's barely a glance, before she turns back to my mom, the hesitation clear in her eyes.

There's no ring on her finger as she brushes back her daughter's hair.

"That's so nice, Mrs. B, but I promised Miss Savie here that I would order us some pizza as a treat for being such a good girl the last two days while we traveled." She presses a kiss to Savie's temple. "And promises are important, aren't they, Savie?"

Savie nods, grinning like she won the lottery.

Tiffany smiles softly, and for a moment she looks... Lighter.

The warmth of it hits me weird. It's beautiful in the way it unsettles me. My hand drifts to the back of my neck.

"Well, another time then." My mom says. A sly grin splits her lips. "Maybe you and your girl can convince this one to see the benefits of settling down. Grandbabies and all that."

"Mom!" I say, horrified, before turning back to Tiff and Savie. "I'm so sorry about that, about her. None of her kids are married yet, and she's gotten baby fever, apparently."

I scrub at the back of my neck, a sheepish grin lifting my lips.

"It's okay," Tiffany says, her smile softer, but her eyes are still guarded. "Your mom's always been good at making everyone see the wisdom in her ideas. Eventually."

We say our goodbyes, and I herd my mom back inside before she can keep embarrassing me. But she's exuberant in her excitement.

Mom gushes about Tiffany and Savie all through dinner; she's fascinated. Dad's enraptured with her monologue, but to him, it doesn't really matter what the topic is as long as she's the one speaking.

And me, well, I mostly push food around my plate. Because all that's on my mind is the girl I grew up with.

By the end of the week, I find myself on the front porch more than I have probably ever been. Not that I'd admit it to anyone, not even myself.

But I keep telling myself the fresh air is good for me, good for my recovery. And that the good weather is reason enough to be outside.

That resting my body is what Bernadette and Coach would want.

It's what Dan made me promise anyway.

My eyes stray toward the house on the left, which has had visitors coming and going for the last two days.

Tiffany's brother and her two best friends have stopped by several times a day to help them settle in. And for the last two days, my butt has been planted on these uncomfortable steps just watching.

I tell myself I'm not looking for the brunette who haunts me, but no matter how much I say it, I can't keep my eyes from drifting.

For once, I follow Bernadette's orders, and I'm dutifully icing my shoulder, the confining wrap trapping the ice against my body. My mind is questioning everything laid out at physical therapy. The things Bernadette and the doctor said about the overuse of my shoulder up to this point.

The slam of a door and childish giggles catch my attention and drag me out of my musing. For the ten thousandth time, I find my gaze wandering to the neighbor's yard.

"Hello! I'm Princess Savie." Familiar wild curls flying around her face as she talks into a pink toy phone. Her little feet are dancing to some unknown rhythm as she zigzags around the yard.

Her eyes meet mine as she announces, "I fly to the moon! Ready for takeoff!"

She makes zooming noises, her flight around the grass between our houses is firing at full speed. A huge grin tugs at my lips as I try not to laugh.

I push off the porch, crossing to meet her in the middle, where I kneel as she skids to a stop.

"That sounds like a very important mission. Do you need a co-pilot for your space adventure, Princess Savie?"

Her eyes widen, and a grin brightens her face. Her little hand reaches into her wild curls to tug at a tiara I didn't see before. I reach out to help her untangle it, only for her to offer it to me.

Her voice is serious as she tells me the tiara can be mine. "You can be my space friend! We fly together."

"Space friend Chris, reporting for duty! Ready to blast off with the princess," I carefully set the tiara back on her head, tucking her unruly hair behind her ears. "But I can't take your tiara. Otherwise, how would the aliens know that you're a princess? We can't have that, can we?"

"You are so smart, space friend Chis." She tries to help me to my feet, her fingers wrapping around my much larger hand. "You ready?"

I nod, leaning in conspiratorially. "Definitely Princess Savie, but where is our rocket?"

"Umm." She looks around, tapping her chin. It makes me grin with restrained laughter. "I don't know, Chis, can you help me find it?"

"Sure can!" I scoop her into my arms, holding her out like Superman mid-flight. She squeals with delight as I pretend to start our rocket, rocking and shaking her. "Can you show me how a princess flies a rocket?"

"Go!" She giggles, and I stop swaying her.

I set off into a wild race across the grass, zoom noises vibrating both of our chests as we fly to the moon. Savie's giggles increase in volume with every dip and dive of our rocket.

I'm just about to land our rocket when I catch some movement out of the corner of my eye.

Tiffany is barefoot and breathless as she bursts out the door. We lock eyes as I gently set Savie down. I offer her a sheepish wave and a gentle smile. Her hand settles against her heaving chest, but she smiles back weakly.

Kneeling beside Savie, I nod toward the house. "You're very brave, Princess Savie. I'm lucky to be your co-pilot, but I think it's time to return to earth." My eyes dart to Tiffany, checking on her again.

She glances at Tiffany, guilty, before she turns back to me.

Her voice is serious as she leans into my chest and whispers. "You're my friend now."

There's a tug at my heart. The feeling is unfamiliar and fiercely tender. "And you're my friend too, Savie."

I rub my hand over her back before I turn her toward Tiffany and send her back with a gentle push. Her giggles take over as she races back to her mom.

Getting back to my feet, I follow. Tiffany meets her halfway, scooping her up with practiced ease as I approach.

"Hey, sorry. I didn't realize you didn't know where she was," I say. "I would've sent her right back."

"No, it's okay. I'm glad she wasn't out here by herself." Her exhale sounds like relief mixed with exasperation. She turns her sights to Savie, who looks contrite. "But Savie absolutely knows she is not supposed to go out the front door by herself."

She turns back to me, hoisting Savie more securely against her hip. "The only reason I knew she wasn't where I left her was because our dog was freaking out. She apparently snuck past both of us."

"Note to self." I deadpan. "If I see a mini-Tiffany in the front yard, return her to her maker."

Tiffany laughs, and Savie tucks herself into Tiffany's neck, much like the other night, a little smirk tugs at her lips.

"Yes, please do." Her eyes flick to the wrap on my shoulder, "I'm sorry about her, she shouldn't have asked you to play like that."

I shake my head. "No, she didn't do anything wrong asking me to play. I offered to be her rocket ship. Plus, she hardly weighs anything at all."

Tiffany's eyes linger, an indecipherable emotion flashing there before she glances at Savie.

"Thanks for keeping an eye on her," she murmurs.

"Always," I say, and I mean it more than I should.

Savie rests her head against Tiffany's shoulder, one thumb sneaking into her mouth, worn out from her space travels.

"She really likes you," Tiffany says finally, and there's a softness in her voice she hasn't had since we were young.

My throat tightens as I nod.

"Yeah. She's," I clear my throat, "easy to like."

There's a pause. A long one. The kind of pause that contains possibilities.

Her eyes flick to mine, and something hooks inside me, tugging me toward them, though I stay rooted where I am.

"You doing okay?" she asks finally, her head nodding at the wrap around my chest again.

"Getting there." I shrug with my good shoulder, shifting my feet uncomfortably. "The doctor wasn't thrilled today. Mostly with me."

Tiffany studies me. She looks like she's going to ask what I mean. But she doesn't. Which is good because I'm not sure why I told her this much in the first place.

"Well, we're around if you need anything," she says.

And then she's gone, the screen door swinging shut behind her.

I head back to my own porch, sitting back on the steps, ice long melted, the evening air thick with summer and something I won't attempt to name. My eyes are once again drawn toward the neighboring yard, but a smile tugs at my lips now.

Chapter 5

Tiffany

THE ALARM BLARES AT 5:30 a.m.

A rustle of sheets beside me makes my heart sink. I plead with God for it to be Trixi moving and not the sweet little child of chaos that I birthed.

"Mama?" The sleepy voice of my little girl filters from under the sheets next to me.

I roll over and pull her into my body, spooning her into my warmth.

"Yeah, my love?" I press a kiss to her head as she nestles closer. Her lashes flutter as she fights the pull of sleep. "You can sleep, sweetheart. We have all day together. We don't have to be up early like normal."

Her little face tilts toward mine, blinking. "But what 'bout our run, Mama?"

"We can run later. That sound good?" I brush her hair away from her forehead and press a kiss on her exposed skin. She nods, and I tuck her tighter to me, hoping I've bought us at least another thirty more minutes. Hoping the warmth from me and Trixi, who is now curled on the other side of her, will pull her back to sleep again.

Nope.

Twenty-five minutes later, I'm slipping her into the jogging stroller. I pull her sippy cup from the handle and tuck it into her side just like our normal routine before clipping Trixi into the ring on my jogging belt. "Okay, sweets, you ready?"

Her quiet agreement meets my ears as I tuck her blanket around her chest and pull my leggings a little higher.

My lightweight sweatshirt is partially zipped over my cropped work-out shirt, chasing away the lingering chill from the familiar Midwest wind on the early spring day.

I shut the garage door behind us; the boxes we still haven't touched stare at me accusingly. Stuff we still need to get working on to live semi-comfortably in the house of horrors I grew up in.

My long ponytail brushes against my shoulders as we start walking, pulling at my attention while I skip through songs. I drag my gaze away from my phone and collide with a familiar pair of hazel eyes. The same eyes that had reassured me when he returned Savie to my frantic arms.

A song about kissing pulses out of my headphones as we stare at each other.

Chris.

He still stands at least 6 or 7 inches taller than my 5-foot, 7-inch frame. He's always been tall, but now he is also broad. The sweaty T-shirt he wore on my first night back had hinted at the miles of tanned skin carved by years of playing hockey.

His sweat glistened in the fading tones of the sun in the late spring evening. Drawing my gaze places my eyes had no business lingering. He's as captivating as he was back in high school.

Time changed him, polished him in ways I didn't expect. But it hasn't dulled the way he affects me. The thrumming under my skin would call me a liar if I tried to deny it.

His eyes meet mine over the roof of the car he's about to climb into.

Some things about this man never change. Like the wide smile cautiously painted over his mouth, the crinkling of his eyes as he grins, and the Lexus he's had since we were in high school.

He captures me with his eyes, my feet slowing as our gazes hold. And like yesterday, something about the both of us here again – home again – sends a thrill through my body that covers up some of the tension that lingers in me.

"Mommy? Why we goin' so slow?" Savie's sleepy voice calls out from the stroller.

I jerk my attention away from Chris, blinking to clear the trance he has sucked me into.

"Sorry, my love. Let's go." By the time I glance back, Chris is sliding into his car.

I push off again.

If Savie doesn't nap in the stroller for at least an hour, I'm in trouble. I'll have a cranky girl on my hands before the end of the day.

She sleeps as we jog the familiar, too-quiet streets of my childhood.

The neighborhood is just as peaceful as I remember. The brick and vinyl houses still look like the picture of idyllic, happy homes. Everything here has always been quiet.

Except our house, where the shouting used to spill out into the night.

The shivers left over from the first night spent in my childhood home still wrack my body every now and again.

But I have Savie. And she is *everything*.

Her morning talent show includes three renditions of "*Let It Go*" while we wait for the internet to be installed. A freestyle dance session with Trixi mid-afternoon while we unpack her toys and movies. And a stuffed animal tea party, during which I'm demoted from guest of honor to table decoration, rounds out our day when I can't give her the princess astronaut room she wants.

I'm grateful for the distraction. And grateful she's adaptable... for now.

Brandon and Shawn are coming to help me take out the bedroom set currently occupying the room that will be Savie's and put in her child-sized furniture, while mine stays packed away in the garage with the rest of our stuff from the apartment.

Trixi trots inside just as a knock comes at the door. She runs, barking like I've trained her to guard Buckingham Palace. I shush her before I open the door, and find my besties standing on my porch, and Chris's car finally entering the neighboring driveway.

Not that I had noticed it was empty each time I looked out the windows today. Because I totally hadn't.

Brandon's eyebrows raise, tracking my eyes to the old Lexus. I shake my head to try to stop him before he says anything. He is utterly incapable of keeping his mouth shut, no matter how much I tell him no.

"Girl..." His hand fans his face dramatically before he looks back at me with a sly smile.

"Brandon," I warn, my hand already closing around his wrist.

"What?" He grins, eyes twinkling. His eyebrows wiggle with delight on his forehead. "I'm not saying anything... But he is *rude* for looking like that in broad daylight."

I yank him inside before he can wave, yell, or do anything else equally humiliating. "One of these days, you are going to embarrass me."

Brandon and Shawn look at each other before a full-body laugh overtakes them.

"Brandon, I'm serious. Don't make this a thing. I got Savie and my family to think about, and a new job to find still." I point at his face. "I don't have time for what your eyebrows are insinuating."

"My eyebrows are insinuating nothing." Brandon smirks.

I raise my own in disbelief.

"Unfair slander," Brandon whines as he turns towards Shawn, who is on the ground with Trixi.

"Sorry, Babe, Trixi and I don't believe you." Shawn's hands run over her glossy black head. "Right, Trixi?"

"She won't answer you. She loves her Uncle Bran too much." Brandon preens, joining him on the floor.

"Uncle Bran," A sassy little voice comes from the living room just beyond the kitchen. "She can't answer yous. Doggies don't talk."

We all pivot toward Savie, who's standing with her hands on her hips about a second away from tapping a foot.

Brandon draws in a loud, theatrical breath.

It's a struggle not to laugh at the two of them.

"Savie, my brilliant niece. You might be onto something there." Brandon sweeps Savie into his arms, much to her delight. "Were you a good girl for your mommy today?"

"Mhmm." She nods vigorously. "I was *such* a good girl."

He lifts an eyebrow in my direction, a question in the tilt of his perfect arch.

"She was so good. She even took Trixi out for all her potty breaks." I concede.

Savie puffs her chest as she is set on the floor, dancing her little body around the room. "All right now, mamacita. Uncle Bran and Uncle Shawn are going to help me get your room set up, and I'm going to order some food. Then beddy time for you. Okay?"

She huffs, but a big smile spreads across her lips as Shawn lifts her for a big hug.

And as we all head upstairs, the weight of the day is a little lighter. The ghosts of my past may be in the walls. But, I have my daughter, my friends, and maybe just a little bit of peace. We work swiftly, and Savie goes to bed right after dinner.

"Okay, guys, Savie is down," I say as I drift into the kitchen, cracking open the fridge. "You want some wine?"

"We would love a glass." Shawn agrees. He turns his gaze knowingly on his husband. "But only one glass. We have to work tomorrow, Babe."

Brandon steps into the kitchen, shoving his long, dirty blonde hair off his forehead, groaning. "I know, but boo. We just got our girl back."

Brandon's arms circle my shoulders as he pulls me into his wide chest.

"Whoa, watch the wine." I laugh, elbowing him off gently as the bottle sloshes in my hand, the wine almost splashing out of the glass I'm filling.

"Okay. One for you." I hand a glass to Shawn, who steps up to my other side. We both laugh at Brandon's offended cry before I hand Brandon his glass. "And one for my bestie."

"Damn right! I'm the bestie." Brandon grumbles as we all pile onto the couches in the living room at the back of the house, which means Savie won't be disturbed.

For a moment, it's like old times.

Brandon leans into Shawn, glancing at me.

He chews on the inside of his cheek, eyes darting down to his wine before he speaks. "So, have you seen your mother yet?"

I flinch a little. But enough, I can't pretend I didn't hear him.

"No. Not yet." I shift uncomfortably as they just look at me. "What? She said she was going to stop by next week to visit us. I think I'm going to suggest dinner at that new place down the road."

Neither of them says anything for a beat. They don't need to. But Brandon reaches out and wraps his fingers around mine. His touch is warm.

"It's weird being back in this house. It feels like a really shitty time capsule," Brandon says as he lets go of my hand.

"Yeah, tell me about it." I nod, sipping my wine.

I look around the house, still wearing the same colors as when we first moved in, all those years ago. The sun faded fabrics filling the house look the same as they did the last time I walked out the door.

The slightly musty smell of a house left untended for long periods lingers. It covers the smell of burnt food from inexperienced but hungry hands and a sour washing machine that used to fill the house. Though those linger underneath, too.

Everything perfectly preserved, like nothing bad ever happened here. Except I remember *everything*.

"Speaking of Chris..." Brandon nudges me again.

I cover my pause with a sip of my wine. "We weren't speaking of him." He rolls his eyes.

"Well, either way, you've got man candy living next to you for the summer." Brandon exhales dramatically as Shawn swats at his thigh. "What? It's true! That man got *fiiiinee*. You've got a full-on Sports Illustrated centerfold living next door. Those arms? That jawline? We've been watching him on screen, hoping for a hometown trade."

"You still follow hockey?" I lean over to set my empty glass on the table. "I don't know why I'm surprised; you used to drag me to every game you could afford growing up."

"Yup. Same as always." Brandon stands and reaches down to help his husband to his feet. "We should catch some this fall, but Shawn and I better get going because as much as I hate to say Shawn is right, he is right. This girl can't get wine drunk and still work well tomorrow."

I pull him into a hug, his muscular arms wrapping tightly around me.

I take the three glasses over to the sink on the way out. Trixi finally decides to make her presence known again as I open the door to let them out, only to find Chris standing there, hand halfway raised like he was about to knock.

He freezes.

"Chris?" My gaze jumps between the men beside me and the one at the door.

"Um, yeah." His eyes widen, darting to Brandon and Shawn. He finally lets his arm drop with an awkward wave of his hand. "Hey, guys."

"Hey, Chris," Brandon says with a sly grin, leaning his chin on my shoulder playfully for a moment. Pressing a brief kiss on my cheek. "We were just on our way out, but it was good to see you."

"Um, yeah, good to see you guys too." Chris shifts, scratching the back of his head as they pass.

Brandon's eyebrows waggle as he turns to look at me from behind Chris's back, and I grit my teeth in his direction, narrowing my eyes.

I turn back to Chris's handsome face, and my gaze clashes with his. The slow, intent way he looks at me trails heat across my skin and sends a shiver curling up my spine. The bump on his nose from a break in high school looks more pronounced than I remember it, like he's done it again since then. And the scar accompanying it on his eyebrow makes him look more deliciously rugged and all man.

Gone is the softness that hugged the edges in my childhood memories.

"Chris?" I question when the silence drags out.

"Oh, shit. My mom wanted me to bring these for you." He stumbles over his words in his rush to start talking. He lifts his hand to present a tin. "They are, um, chocolate chip, I think. Mom didn't know if your little girl had any allergies, but figured these would be safest."

My eyes drop to the tin still in his hands. "She doesn't have any allergies unless you count bath time."

He chuckles.

"Noted." He lifts the tin again. "You want these?"

"Shit, yeah. Yes. Sorry." I laugh, brushing my hair off my cheek. "You want to come in? The guys and I just had a glass of wine, but they had to leave, gotta work in the morning. I still don't have a job yet, so no bedtime for me."

He hesitates before he nods. I open the door wider. "Just, um, don't mind Trixi. She's usually a little standoffish-"

My words trail off as I watch my usually reserved dog start jumping at Chris's broad chest for attention. Like she just found her favorite person.

She's only like this with Savie.

He chuckles as he leans down to pet her. His hands run gently over her head before flipping her soft ears back and forth for a moment. She melts under his touch, sliding down his body to thump against the ground.

"She never warms up to people this quickly, let alone men," I mumble, blinking at the miracle in front of me. "It took her almost a full 24 hours to warm to Brandon and Shawn after I brought Savie home from the hospital."

Chris glances at me, a cheeky grin on his face. "Dogs love me."

"I guess so. She usually doesn't like men in the house with her girl." I nod toward the stairs, smiling despite myself.

"Ah, well she's doing a good job. Right?" He pats her head one more time before he stands again.

His body towers over me as he steps closer. Trixi's tail wags happily back and forth as she offers him one more lick on his hand, trotting back upstairs and likely back into bed with Savie.

I motion into the house, pausing just long enough as we walk through the kitchen to offer him a beer and grab myself another glass of wine.

"Sorry. The house is a mess." I hand over the cold beer as he sits before I sink into the sofa opposite him.

He settles deeper into the couch, his deep-set hazel eyes fix on my face, drinking me in as deeply as he does the beer in his hand.

My pulse quickens as I meet his gaze.

"Honestly, for having just moved in, it's not as bad as I would expect it to be." His words linger, slow like molasses in winter.

Slow like the way his eyes trace my body.

"Well, it's just temporary." I shrug, staring just a little too long, a little too intently at his still way too handsome face. "So, I didn't want to do too much to my mother's house, just enough to keep Savie happy until I find something permanent."

"So, did you move back, or no?" He leans forward, perching his elbows on his knees.

I dip my head. "Yeah. Technically."

He's quiet for a beat, his eyes still studying me, and a flush is probably making my cheeks bright red. "Sorry, I don't mean to pry, but Mom said you told her you were back because your father was in the hospital, but didn't offer much more than that. I also have to admit that she was going to come drop the cookies off, but I was curious. We didn't get to catch up yesterday with my nosy mother around."

"When did that ever stop you before?" I laugh, remembering all his random questions that often interrupted conversations as we were growing up and how it irritated his mother to no end.

We grin at each other as memories simmer between us.

"Well, I grew up." He holds his arms out to his sides, offering his body for inspection. It's a good view. It confirms the muscles I glimpsed the other day are as impressive as I thought. "And I got myself in trouble with Coach when I did it on air one too many times."

"And there it is," I shift forward, leaning in toward him. My laughter quiets, my smile dropping a little as I finally answer his question. "I'm here for good. Just not this house."

"Your mom moving back in eventually?" He cocks his head, staring me down when I don't offer any answers besides a shrug of my shoulders. "So, if you aren't sure that she's going to return, why move into a different place?"

"It's," I pause to throw back the last of my wine, "well, it's complicated. I'm sure you all heard our screaming matches. I can't risk exposing Savie to that."

"I get that, you guys were intense. My mom will be sad when you leave the neighborhood again." Chris stands and drains his beer. "You'll have to come around to keep her company after I leave to head back East."

I rise with him. "And when is that?"

He motions for the door, and we amble toward it. "Well, if that physical therapist they hired is any good. I'll go back before the preseason in September."

"Is that where you went today?" He nods; his face is drawn into annoyance. I press, just a little, same as he did. "That was awfully early for a physical therapy appointment, wasn't it?"

"You're one to speak." He grins in my direction, without an answer of his own. "That was an awfully early run for someone with a munchkin."

My feet shuffle through the carpet at the reminder of how much things have changed since the last time we saw each other. "That's what remains of our daily schedule from Georgia. It was warm enough year-round for me to get my exercise in before work. We've been doing it since six weeks after Savie was born. I don't know what we will do here when winter comes."

"You'll figure it out." He steps in close and wraps those ridiculous arms around me. My own hands fumble before resting softly around his waist as my body melts into his warmth.

He pulls back slightly but doesn't drop his hands. "Well, don't be a stranger. I'm home most days, except for Tuesday when I get my skate in after PT. So, if you ever need anything..."

His hands slide down my arms, grasping my own for a moment before dropping them. His eyes are intensely warm as they search my face. And just like that, I'm sixteen again in the arms of the boy who made me feel safe.

Savie's unexpected cry has us jumping apart. I nod, acknowledging his words. "Thanks."

He pulls the door open before hesitating and turning back in my direction. "Tiff?"

I hum in response.

He leans back toward me, his lips brushing softly against my cheek just at the corner of my mouth.

"You grew up *real* good."

Then he's gone.

I close the door, hand pressed to my cheek where his lips touched, heat rising under my fingers. My face is warm. My *entire body* is warm.

Savie's second cry rises to the level of slightly hysterical, and I hurry to soothe her and get us both to bed with a smile on my still-warm face.

Chapter 6

Chris

I GLANCE AT MY watch as I hurry toward the local bar and grill - the out-side of The Rust & Rail hasn't changed in the years it's been open. The same faded sign and hand-painted lettering on the door's glass welcomes guests.

Nothing's changed.

I push through the doors, tugging my hat lower on my brows as I look around for my brothers. The dim lights against the dark wood walls make it hard to scan the place without drawing attention, but it's not like my brothers are easy to miss. Every last one of us is built like a linebacker, or in my case, a hockey player.

I pull my hat lower before heading to the table where my brothers are seated. Charlie's already waving like an idiot. A grin spreads across my face. He's still got the easy charm in the sharpness of his jaw and the rugged features. Or maybe it's in our mother's softness tucked in around the edges, especially in the laugh lines that are just barely beginning to peek out.

Junior doesn't smile. Of course, he doesn't.

His grunt pulls my focus over to him.

The oldest of the Bartkowski clan is impeccably dressed, just like every other time I've seen him recently. He looks like he flew in straight from a meeting in the high-rise his office calls home. The New York financial district has settled a coldness into my brother that only seems to thaw during the weekends he makes it home.

"You're late," he says, flicking his eyes to his watch – the same one I wear. The same model our father gave us all on our 18th birthday. "What kept you so long this time? PT or Mom babying you?"

I open my mouth as I roll my eyes, but Charlie jumps in with a laugh. "Definitely, Mom. There is no way it wasn't Mom."

I find my lips twitch despite myself.

"It was open skate after PT, actually." I drop into the seat beside Jake, who gives me a nod but little else. I raise my eyebrow at Charlie, who is still laughing at his joke. "I just lost track of time, sorry."

"Just ignore Junior," Charlie says, fingers tapping on the table. His body shakes, already bouncing a leg under the table. "He's just annoyed that not everyone sticks to the time on his Google invites to the T."

Jake smirks, his blue eyes dancing with mirth. "Technically, only Chris managed not to stick to the calendar invite."

I punch his shoulder gently. "Yeah, yeah, yeah. I'm hurt, and you guys can't even give me a break?"

Jake snorts, and Junior rolls his eyes, but Charlie's grin widens as he waves over the waitress. She's quick to scamper over as she pulls the notepad out of her apron. Her weighty stare is heavy on the side of my face, eyebrows furrowing like she's trying to place me, before I turn further toward my brothers, tugging again at the rim of my cap. She snaps her gum hard enough to grab my eyes for a moment, before I dart them away just as quick.

"Hey, sweetness," Charlie croons as he pulls her attention to him. "My brothers and I would like a round of whatever's on tap here."

Junior is quick to correct him. "I would like your best bourbon, please. No beer for me."

Jake is just about ready to change his own order before something on his phone pulls his focus. It doesn't take long for Junior's attention to be pulled toward his phone as well. Charlie just keeps flirting with the waitress who is still lingering at our table.

I clear my throat, and Jake's gaze cuts toward me. A dull thud reaches my ears just before Charlie's yelp of outrage pulls eyes from all around in our direction.

45

Charlie and Jake, the second and third born in our parents' quartet of kids, have been out with me several times since I've been back in Port Arbor. And it always goes like this.

They both settled back in town and recently started their own company together. But Junior and I only make it back home sporadically when our schedules allow. So, Mom's been happier than usual lately, having us all back in town at the same time so much.

"Subtle," I mutter toward Jake, who smirks as I adjust my hat again. "I would have liked a little less attention drawn our way."

"At least it got her away from Casanova." Jake reaches back to fix the messy little bun at the back of his head.

"Hey!" Charlie grins. "I can't help it that the ladies love me."

He puckers dramatically, making kissy noises at Jake, who groans and flips him off. It makes us all laugh, even Junior, who finally sets his phone down. It doesn't take long before Charlie takes over the conversation. His larger-than-life personality is the thing that simultaneously got him in and out of trouble when we were younger.

We all laugh, loud and out of control.

For a minute, it's good.

Easy.

Charlie launches into one of his greatest hits: the night he got caught sneaking back into the house in senior year after sneaking *out* of some girl's house.

"Oh man, she was so mad at you!" I say, laughing. "She woke up the whole house checking the rest of our beds."

Charlie scratches the back of his neck, sheepish at the memory. "I forgot she did that."

Junior chuckles.

"Even I got a call from Mom," his grin widens, smug, "to make sure I was in my bed. I just didn't tell her I wasn't *alone*."

We lose it, laughter echoing off the wood-paneled walls around us. The stories flow freely until our dinners arrive, and quiet settles over the table as we begin to eat.

Junior clears his throat, changing the topic. "So, what's the deal with the physical therapist? Are they going to have you back on the ice before preseason?"

"Mom told you to ask, didn't she?" A sigh falls from my lips as he shrugs.

"Like I've told her. Technically, I can get on the ice and skate, and I have been once a week, which is all I'm currently being allowed. I just can't play." I pause, fork scraping against the plate. "According to the doctors and *Nurse Ratched*, I'm on track to be ready to play by the time preseason rolls around. Coach said that I got lucky with the timing of my injury. I only had to sit out of 2 games, so they are *optimistic* I'll get our team to the cup this year."

"It just doesn't feel like we are doing enough." I glance at Junior's furrowed brow. "They say it's minor. But they always say that, right before a guy's contract expires and nobody calls back."

I glance up. All three of them are watching me, brows furrowed and mouths tight lines across their faces. They all try and fail to find something to say. So, no one says anything at all.

"What?" I ask, voice sharper than I intend. "Were you expecting something else from me? Something I hadn't already told her? Did she think I was lying to her?"

Jake's smirk is slow but irritating. "She didn't think you were being entirely honest."

"Well, I was." I drop my eyes to my plate again. "Just like I told her yesterday after my call with Coach."

Charlie smirks playfully. "That's not the only thing she told us yesterday."

Jake stiffens beside me. My eyes shoot to him before bouncing back to Charlie, his smirk growing. There is silence at the table as all three of my brothers stare at me.

I swallow dryly, the food catching uncomfortably as I try to choke out the word. "What?"

Charlie leans back in his chair, looking far too pleased with himself. "Mom was happy to tell us that our pretty little neighbor moved back in next door to her."

Jake raises an eyebrow.

Charlie shrugs. "What? Mom might have also said that she grew up into a beautiful woman. Gorgeous, I think was the word she used. And I remember exactly how our baby brother used to look at her."

Junior joins in, voice smooth, smirking. "Mom also mentioned that she sent you over with a welcome home plate of cookies and that it took you more than a half an hour to come back."

Dropping my face into my hands, I glance at them through my fingers. "We just talked, just catching up."

Jake's lips thin as he eyes me, jaw flexing. His expression is hard to read. Closed off in the way he gets when he's deciding whether or not to believe you.

The tension between me and Jake hums beneath the table like a live wire. Same as it has ever since Jason, his best friend and Tiffany's brother, laid down that off-limits rule in high school.

Back then, Jake had stood behind Jason because they were best friends, but when Jason had walked away, Jake had dug the knife in deeper.

And maybe because I've seen Tiffany again - spent time with her and her daughter - innocent as it was, the memory resurfaces.

"I'm asking you to stop, because if you try," Jake says, looking toward Tiffany, his voice catching. "You won't survive it either. I'm doing this because I love you, Chris. And because I know you'd break yourself trying to love her."

Junior and Charlie carry the bulk of the conversation as we work our way into our third round. But I'm only half listening.

I'm about to make my escape as Charlie waves the waitress down again when Jake's phone buzzes against the wood of the table and his frown stops me. He glances down and mutters to himself. "Well, look who's finally responding to my text."

Charlie's voice is teasing as he reaches for Jake's phone. "Is it your boyfriend?"

Jake snorts, snatching the phone away.

A playful note enters his tone. "No. Just my emotionally repressed soulmate - slash - business partner."

"Jason?" I shake the tension in my shoulder, fighting the way they want to creep up when he hums his confirmation.

It's confirmation I don't need as the large, muscular frame of Tiffany's older brother enters the bar, headed straight toward our table.

Jason Samson.

He's just as massive as I remember. His blue eyes and blonde hair are a contrast to his sister's dark features. Where Tiffany has soft curves and expressive features filled with her warmth, Jason is all square lines and stone-faced silence, masking an underlying rage.

He gives a curt nod to Junior and Charlie, his hand landing softly on Jake's shoulder as he moves around him, lingering as he glances everywhere but at me.

Finally, he looks at me. We both pause, his eyes measuring me again, like he always has, and I still come up short. After all these years, I'm still not enough for him.

His jaw tightens, and his eyes narrow.

Even with a professional hockey career under my belt, I'll never be good enough for his little sister.

Not that I'm trying to be enough for her.

I'm not.

His nose wrinkles, like his sister's, when he's displeased. It's one of the few things that they share.

And clearly, I've displeased him. Like, just because his sister is back in town, I've become a problem... again.

He slides into the seat beside Jake. "Been a while."

He's not talking to any of my brothers. His tone makes it clear he's talking to me with his roughened voice, like he barely uses it.

"Yeah. It has." I say. I clear my throat to try again. "Sorry to hear about your dad."

Jason nods.

It's all I get.

Jake pats him on the back, but Jason's eyes have already moved on.

His voice cuts through the noise, though he doesn't look at me. "You back for long?"

I shake my head, "Just long enough to heal."

"Good." His response is cold and dismissive.

There it is.

The warning.

The line in the sand without saying her name. And I'm dragged back to sixteen years old, and Jason's in my face.

"Don't do the puppy-eyes thing with her. Don't get cute. Don't go looking for reasons to sit next to her. She's getting out of here. Full ride or not, she's gone the second she graduates. She has to go. If she gets attached to anything that keeps her here..."

He had meant me back then and Jason's decade-old warning is loud in my ears as I scrape back my chair, because nothing has truly changed from his perspective. "Well, guys, I'm going to head out. I've got PT pretty early in the morning."

My brothers throw some half-hearted jabs at me as I stand, but I don't really hear them.

I don't look back.

49

I don't have to.

I don't need to see the watchful eyes on me because it doesn't matter. I'm not back for long. I'm out of here in just a few months. He did his job of reminding me, without words I'm not to go near his sister. Making sure I remember who she belongs to.

Chapter 7

Tiffany

I SIT IN THE driver's seat of my car for a moment after killing the engine. In the rearview mirror, Savie bops along to some kids' tune coming out of her iPad. Her distraction allows me a moment to catch my breath as I look toward the hospital looming in front of me. She's blissfully unaware of the weight pressing on my chest.

It's taken me two weeks to build up the courage to bring Savie with me to the hospital where my father is. Thankfully, Brandon and Shawn watched her for me for a few times since we got into town, so I could come and figure out what was going on. But May is finally here and there hasn't been any change, he's still just in a coma for no explainable reason.

I glance back at Savie again; her usually unruly hair is corralled into curly pigtails, and she's wearing her 'fancy tights' just for her Poppy. Shaking myself, I pull my keys from the ignition and drop them into my purse. I twist around in my seat and catch her eye. "Hey, sugar plum, you ready to go see Poppy?"

She nods and drops her tablet onto the floor in front of her. Her tablet joins my keys in my purse as I help her out of the car. I wipe my sweaty palms on the fabric of my leggings before grabbing her hand and starting the walk into the hospital.

The hospital hums with quiet urgency as we make our way toward the elevators and to the ICU. It doesn't take long until we are in the silent hall where my father's room is located.

I stop at the threshold to the room holding my father and squat down in front of my little girl, smoothing my hands over her hair.

"My love, Poppy is in the room right there." I point to the door we are about to enter. "Poppy, might look a little scary at first, but he's still your Poppy, okay?"

She nods, but her thumb slips into her mouth, and she lifts her other arm in a silent ask to be held. She's truly nervous, but she keeps a brave face on. She tucks herself into my chest and holds her thumb between her teeth. I stand, and we step inside his room.

The machines hiss and beep in a slow, steady rhythm. Her voice is muffled around her thumb. "Poppy has a space mask."

I press my forehead against her curls, giving myself a moment to collect myself before I answer. "That space mask is called a ventilator. It helps him breathe, just like astronaut helmets do. Remember I told you that Poppy got sick, and his body needed some extra help?"

She nods, finally pulling her thumb free. There are little red indents where her teeth were.

"But he doesn't talk to me. Poppy always talks to me." Her voice is thin with worry.

I pull back just enough to study her face. "Poppy still loves you very much, sugar plum, but sometimes when we're hurt or sick, our bodies take a long time to feel better. Like how turtles hide in their shells. He's kind of like that, hiding while his body works hard to heal."

"Will he come out of his shell?" She squirms in my arms, but when I set her down, she presses herself tightly against my leg.

I glance at the ceiling tiles, breathing through the crack in my chest.

I have to work hard to stop the shake in my voice before I answer. "I hope so. The doctors are trying to help him, but he's sleeping right now."

We move around the bed to the chair next to my father, and I settle her in my lap.

He looks like a shell of the man I knew growing up.

My father was the picture of charismatic failure. His dark, straight hair is peppered with gray. The hair he has always kept neatly trimmed is softening around the edges. Hazel eyes that flicker between green and gold like faded whiskey – the eyes that I inherited - covered by his pale eyelids.

The once charismatic man is still as the machines beep around us. He was never outright cruel, just absent, a man who smiled for school events and disappeared when things got hard.

Until Savie came along. I don't know what happened, but he started making time.

I never understood why he could love her so easily when I had to beg for time.

Savie is quiet as she sits in my lap, resting against my chest again, and for a few moments she studies him, in that quiet, uncanny way only toddlers can manage. "Is he dreaming?"

"Kind of." I kiss the top of her head. "I think that maybe he's dreaming about rocket ships and stars and you."

"Can I draw him a picture?" She pulls away, scooting off my lap, and digs through my purse to look for the crayons and coloring book I had shoved in there earlier.

"I think he would like that very much." I smile, nodding toward the bench by the window. "Why don't you go sit over there and color, and Mommy is going to talk to Poppy until Uncle Jason gets here, okay?"

She hums in agreement as she heads over to the bench to begin coloring. She colors so long she falls asleep right there, slumped over the page, one crayon still in her fist as morning rolls into nap time. When she's finally fully asleep, I rest my elbows against my father's bed.

"You know," My voice is quiet, but I don't hold back. "I used to sit in my room at night and pretend you were coming to get me. Every time I heard cars passing by. Every time, she would scream or call me names. Every time she laid her hands on me. I waited for you."

Tears slip down my face, warm and heavy with shame and years of unspoken hurt. Filled with words I was never brave enough to say.

"But you never came." I pause a moment, wiping angrily at my cheeks.

"Maybe we didn't tell you everything that was going on," I concede. "But if you'd been paying attention, if you'd looked a little closer, you would've seen it."

I look at Savie again to make sure she's still sleeping. She is so peaceful, unconcerned with the chaos around her.

"You missed everything. You're still loved, somehow. Me. Savie. Jason." I laugh under my breath, the sound cracking under the weight of the room, and the bitter swirl of hurt in my chest.

My voice cracks as I lean closer to the bed, eyes stinging. "Seems unfair, doesn't it? I got blamed just for looking like you, and I still love you. You two trained me well, I guess."

I reach for his hand. It's cold, limp.

There is no life in him.

"But here I am. And maybe it's time to stop waiting to tell you things." My breath hitches in my chest. "I hate you. I hate that I love you."

A quiet throat-clearing startles me. I look over at the bright blue eyes, so similar to my mother's, only softer on my brother's face. Jason stands in the doorway, hunched like gravity is hitting him harder than usual. The man who normally towers over everyone is stooped and shamefaced. His fingers rake through the short side of his blond hair as his gaze shifts to Savie, asleep beside her coloring book.

"She looks peaceful," he murmurs. "He does too."

I scoff. Anger, or maybe grief, fills my body. "Yeah. Peaceful. Guess all it took was a massive stroke and a ventilator."

Jason doesn't respond right away. His eyes linger on our father before sliding back to me, unable to meet my gaze. "You hate him?"

"I don't know." I shrug before wiping at my face again, sniffing back the tears threatening to keep trailing down my cheeks. "He was never around long enough for me to figure it out properly."

He peels away from the doorway and rests a hand on my shoulder. His attempt at comfort. "Did the doctors talk to you about what's going on?"

I nod. "Yeah, when I came by the other day. They said he didn't have any sort of directive, so we have some choices to make."

"Well, what do you think?" he asks, voice low as his hand squeezes my shoulder before he moves toward the other chair in the room.

"There isn't much to think about right now." I remind him as he drops into the chair opposite mine. "They don't think it's time for big decisions yet."

"Yeah, but what if we have to make that choice?" His voice is careful, but the tension beneath it is impossible to miss.

I pause to consider the question for a moment as I look at my brother. His face is broad and strong jawed, with a calm, steady expression rarely giving away the storm beneath. His skin is lightly tanned, so similar to my own. "I think we pull the plug when it's time. *If* it comes to that."

He bristles. His eyes flick briefly to Savie, reminding himself to keep his voice down. "You just want this over. It's like you need to erase him before he even dies."

"You don't get to say that." I hiss. "You don't get to be the golden son. And the moral compass. Not when I was the one who protected you when you couldn't protect yourself."

He flinches. I said the one thing we never talk about, but I'm too tired, and the memories from our house are too close to the surface to stop me.

His words are intended to shock me, but they don't. "You think I was the lucky one?"

"You were." I laugh, bitter and hollow.

Savie stirs, but the words keep spilling anyway. "You didn't get bruises. You didn't have to carry them into school and pretend you were just clumsy. And you didn't have to uproot your life and move back into the house that traumatized you, because I can't make decisions by myself."

"Tiff, I tried." He swallows hard like he's just come up for air after years underwater. "I swear, I tried, but -"

My angry hum cuts him off. He opens his mouth again to argue, but he stops when Savie finally stirs enough to call out to him. "Uncle Jason?"

He turns to her and opens his ridiculously muscular arms as she toddles over to him. "Hey chickadee."

Her coloring book clutched in her hands, against her chest. It takes Jason just a moment to notice it. When he asks what she has in her hands, she starts flipping to the pages she had been coloring.

"Poppy can have this," she says seriously. She holds out a purple turtle for him to inspect, the colors spilling outside the lines. "For his dreams."

Jason swallows visibly as their blue eyes lock together. Her's are so much lighter than his troubled ones. "Can I tell him I miss him?"

He hesitates, but I step in before the silence swallows the moment.

"Yes, sweet girl." My throat tightens, and I clench my jaw against the emotion that threatens to overwhelm me. "That's exactly what he needs to hear."

Jason lifts her carefully so she can lean over the bed. She whispers to my father how much she misses him. After that, there isn't much left to say between us. There never really is. I gather our things. Jason nods once, eyes back on the bed.

He stays, and we leave.

We're halfway home when Savie breaks the silence from the back seat. "Will he wake up tomorrow?"

I glance at her in the rearview mirror; her eyes are sad, and her hair is slipping free from its pigtails. So much hope in one little voice

"I don't know, sweetheart." Honesty is all I can answer with. "But we'll be here. Because we love him."

Chapter 8

Tiffany

THE REST OF THE week passes smoothly, almost deceptively so, as Savie and I settle into the house that once hid all my worst moments. Summer has warmed the cold edges of spring, and every window in the house is open as I try to air out the history in the house.

There was no way I was meeting her in the house, if for no other reason than I'm not sure I can see the changes she's made if we were both in the same house where everything happened. Which is how I find myself heading for breakfast at the local diner before we go check out some of the daycare centers, the ones she insisted on visiting.

"Savannah Grace!" I call out to my runaway daughter as she giggles somewhere above me. A grin pulls at my lips as I work to keep my tone from encouraging her to fumble around longer. "You already packed six toys. Nana is waiting for us!"

Her little feet run toward the stairs with a cry of 'Nana!' like she has done the five other times I had reminded her of our breakfast date, but she keeps going back to look for all the toys she wants to show my mother. She appears with the urgency only a three-year-old can conjure, clutching a stuffed bear like it's treasure.

I unzip my bag so she can tuck it in, and I guide her out the door before she remembers a seventh must-see item.

Chris's mother is outside and shouts a greeting at us as we hurry toward my SUV.

Savie lights up. "Hey Granny B! We go see Nana!"

She tries to sprint toward her, and I grab the back of her shirt just in time. "Savannah," I mutter, trying really hard not to grit my teeth.

"That's wonderful, sweet girl!" Mrs. Bartkowski shouts back with a wide, mischievous grin.

The one that reminds me so much of Chris.

She walks back toward her house, mail clutched in her hand, waving. "Have fun!"

"All right then, little girl, up you go." I hoist my mini-me into her car seat and strap her in. "Ready to go see Nana?"

"Oh yes, yes, yes!" She sings, clapping her hands, her feet drumming against the seat. "Nana!"

I close the door, rubbing at the tightness in my chest. The weight of meeting my mother sits just below my lungs.

We pull into the diner near the water, just in time to spot my mother getting out of her car. She's polished in ways she didn't used to be. The messy buns and angry eyes are gone, her clothes are crisp, and her curly hair is swept back into a neat chignon.

And for my daughter's sake, I hope they are gone for good.

Savie's practically vibrating with delight when she spots her. A familiar ache pulses as I watch her joy. Her happiness is so simple. So easy. So freely given.

I can't remember ever feeling that way when my mother is around.

I try to roll my shoulders, to force out the stiffness ingrained in my muscles. It's beginning to feel like it'll never fade as long as we are in Port Arbor.

The tension lingers, unaffected by my attempts to breathe it away.

Savie waves wildly at my mother, who walks toward us with a disquieting grin. It's not the same cruel smile from my childhood, but it's too bright to be completely genuine either.

My hands shake as I try to wrangle the bouncing bean that doubles as my daughter.

"Okay, monke—" Savie interrupts me as I pull her from her seat, screaming out for my mother again.

I freeze when my mother's deep chuckle rakes across my spine like sharp nails. She crouches just in time to catch Savie as she launches into her arms.

"Nana! I missed you!" Savie shrieks, wrapping her tiny arms around her neck.

My mother hugs her back, smiling like this is the best day ever.

"Hey, Mom." My voice is flat, and I can tell she catches it by the way her lips pucker. "Savie is hungry, so let's head in."

I gesture them forward, trying to hurry this day along. Savie chatters all the way into the restaurant and until we are tucked into our breakfast. She tells my mother all about the move, her new room, the backyard adventures she has had with Trixi, and her new neighbors.

She listens - really listens

She nods, smiles, and responds in a tone so full of affection that my stomach turns from how sweet it is.

My mother dotes on her in a way I never got. I don't know what to do with the way it guts me.

Because this version of her, the soft one, where was she for me?

Why now?

Why weren't we enough?

I sip my coffee and try not to flinch when her hand brushes Savie's curls with the tenderness I used to dream about. I'm grateful for it, for Savie, but that doesn't keep the sting away.

With Savie distracted and trying to corral her eggs onto her spoon, I turn to my mother, hands twining together.

I'm not sure I really want to ask. I'm not sure it's the safe thing to do, but she's been so good with her...

"Mom, I have an interview next week. Is there any way you can watch Savie if I can't get her into a daycare today?"

"Um. Yeah. I think I can do that." She hums, her eyes never leaving Savie. "What day?"

My mother's gaze runs over Savie, who is dancing in her seat, humming to herself as she shovels eggs into her mouth.

I run a hand through my hair, biting at my cheek. "Um, Wednesday? Let me confirm, and I'll text you. Do you need me to bring her to you?"

"No, I'll come by the house." She finally looks at me. "You look well, sweetheart. The move suits you. Have you been to see your father?"

I nod, but drop my eyes to my plate, unable to keep eye contact with her. Her gaze makes me feel small despite the way she's been trying to be better since Savie was born. And my body follows its trained response, slinking down into my seat, knee bouncing. My fingers tap a staccato rhythm on the vinyl booth seat, just out of my mother's view.

"Yeah, a couple of times. He's on a ventilator still. The doctor said they've seen some improvement, but it's still touch-and-go. Once I find a daycare for her, I'll get to see him more often. At least until I find a job."

"Well, I'm sure you will be just fine. Your father, too," she scoffs. "That bastard never did stay down long."

The venom in her voice slices through the calm. My eyes race up to her face; her expression is sour and familiar. My whole body tenses, ready to sweep Savie up into my arms and haul both of us out of this restaurant.

It takes me back to the days of phone calls to my father as she stood over me, prompting me to remind him he owed his child support or whatever other demand she wanted me to pass along. To the days of me parroting her words to a man she resented but still depended on.

"Mom!" My voice is a warning, quiet but firm. I glance toward Savie, who's still humming and dancing in her seat, blissfully unaware. "You can't talk like that. My daughter is sitting right there."

I lower my voice and lean in before continuing. "I know you never cared how your words affected your children, but I won't let you do the same to my child. If you can't manage to keep things civil, then I'll have to find someone else to watch her."

My mother's back straightens, indignation flaring in her eyes.

"I did what I could with what I had," she snaps, baring her teeth in my direction. "Don't threaten to take my access to her away from me."

My jaw tightens. I press my hands flat on the table, grounding myself before I speak. I remind myself that the sharp tone I want to use on her will definitely draw Savie's attention.

"Mother," I say, more patient than she deserves. "It is not a threat. It's a boundary. She deserves that. I *deserved* that growing up."

Narrowing my eyes, I continue, "I won't have the past repeated for her."

"Mommy?" She looks between us, assessing. "Are you mad at Nana?"

I manage to smile, though it's strained. "Oh, sweet pea, sometimes adults just disagree, and they have to talk through it. That's all. I'm not mad at Nana."

She nods her head as if considering my words and returns to her plate. I'm so glad she is easy to please. All it takes is a simple explanation to satisfy her curiosity, and she is happy to move on to the next thing her little mind wanders to.

Her world is still safe.

Still simple.

We make our rounds to the daycare facilities in the area, three of which have put us on the waiting list. The other two are out of the question. On the drive home, Savie chatters about all the new friends she's going to make. She lists names from her old daycare and invents ones for the kids she hasn't met yet.

Her innocent chatter washes away some of the residue my mother left behind.

The kind my mother doles out without realizing the impact she has on people. The words are different and yet somehow the same. She undercuts with silk now, the knives stowed under softness.

Savie's joy is loud, unfiltered, and free. And in the wake of my mother's shadow, it fills the space with a levity it's never held before.

For now, I can breathe again.

Chapter 9

Tiffany

DAYS LATER, I PACE in front of the window like a caged animal, muttering under my breath, my eyes darting between the door and the windows.

My mother said she'd come. She promised, but here I am, once again, praying she doesn't let me down again.

I should have known better than to ask her without a backup plan!

Savie comes hopping down the stairs as I'm making a tenth circuit.

"Mommy?" Her voice cuts through my spiral. I glance over to find her at the bottom of the stairs, blinking sleep from her eyes, dressed in her mismatched pajamas.

Despite my worry, I smile fondly.

"You work today?" She asks, eyeing my slacks and blouse.

I scoop her into my arms, burying my face into her curls. "No, mamacita. Not really. Mommy is trying to get a job."

She crinkles her button nose before a giant smile pulls across her face. "You stay with Savie. No more works!"

"You want Mommy to stay home with you all the time?" Her giggle bubbles out as I snort playfully against her skin, and Trixi bounces at my feet, barking with enthusiasm.

She nods furiously, unable to catch her breath from laughing. "Oh, sweet one, I wish I could, but you and Trixi eat too much."

"Not me, Mommy." She leans over to reach for Trixi, almost launching herself out of my arms with a giggle. "Trixi eat too much."

"Whoa there, careful." I smile, pressing a kiss to her cheek as I glance at the clock.

We are running out of time before I'll be late, and my mother still hasn't called me back from any of the voicemails I've left her this morning.

I shift Savie around in my arms, hiking her up to rest more comfortably on my hip.

"What do you say we go see if you can hang out with Granny B while Mommy goes to her interview? It won't be long, and then we can grab some lunch."

Savie brightens. "No, Nana?"

There's a flicker of relief in her voice that catches me off guard, but I don't have the luxury of digging into it now.

I open the front door, ready to leave. "Apparently not, sweet one."

Setting Savie on her feet when we reach their house, I knock on the front door, foot tapping in time with my heartbeat.

Please be home. Please, Brenda.

When no answer comes, I knock a little louder, praying someone is home. I'm screwed otherwise. I lift my hand to knock again as the heavy thud of footsteps jogging toward the door begins. I hope it's Mark, since the sound definitely isn't coming from Brenda.

The door opens, and my eyes land on an unmistakably male chest.

It's not Brenda.

And it's definitely not Mark.

"Tiff?" I freeze at the out-of-breath question.

His warm eyes meet mine and flare with a fire that darkens the color. My breath catches in my throat as my gaze drags over his sweaty skin.

God help me. He's shirtless.

Of course he's shirtless.

His defined abs and sun-tanned skin are lightly peppered with hair leading to his low-slung shorts. I jerk my eyes away with a flush I have no hope of stopping, not before he notices.

I suppress a shudder as the heat of his attention licks at my skin.

"Need something?" A smirk tugs at his lips.

His voice is husky, and it sounds suspiciously like he's making an inappropriate suggestion. I scramble to get my brain working again and to keep my eyes away from where they want to trail across his tempting body.

"Um, I was – uh –" I blink wildly, desperate to clear my thoughts.

Savie interrupts brightly. "Chis, no Nana today."

"That so munchkin?" He crouches, still towering over her.

His fingers brush her curls from her eyes with surprising gentleness. The softness in him relaxes me.

It reminds me so much of the boy who sat with me in the soft glow of a porch light. The one who knew he would be in trouble for being late, but did it anyway because I was sad.

I huff out a breath, forcing myself to forget about that boy – *man* – in front of me and focus on getting Savie taken care of so I can leave.

"Yeah, I'm so sorry to bother you. I was hoping your mom was around and that she'd be willing to watch Savie here while I go to an interview."

My hand reaches down to swipe Savie's wild curls out of her face, a habit I can't quite kick, and my fingers accidentally brush his on their path.

"My mother is..." I clear my throat, searching for the least traumatizing word for Savie's sake. "Unreachable."

He shakes his head. "No can do, darling. Mom's not home."

My shoulders sag, and I tip my head back, willing the angry tears not to spill as they begin to well in my eyes. The roof over the porch matches my dark mood as I stare at it, trying not to break down, when thick fingers cup the back of my neck, forcing me to look at him.

"Tiff?" His voice is low and steady.

Warm fingers against my skin tighten gently before relaxing. He studies my face, his eyebrows furrowing the longer he looks.

I swipe roughly at the hair tickling my neck, and our fingers meet again.

"Is your dad home? Would he be willing?" The words tremble out of me as I struggle not to scream at the world.

He shakes his head again, his thumb brushing against my cheek, and I lean into his warmth without thinking. "Sorry, they went out to run errands together. I'm sure they would if they were home."

Shit, balls, son of a bitch. I should have asked them before this. I know better than to count on that woman.

"Tiff, um, I don't know much about kids," he chews on his lip. "But if you are desperate, I can hang out with her for a little bit, and if my mom gets home before you do, she'll be happy to help."

My eyebrows dart up as he pulls his hand off my neck to rub at his own.

"You don't seem comfortable with that idea." I begin to decline the offer, cringing at the thought of how much it will hurt my chances for this job. "I'll just have to reschedule my interview."

He shrugs. "She's basically your twin. How hard can it be?"

A laugh tries to rise in me, but the weight of the moment sits too heavy on my chest. I open my mouth to try and decline again, as Savie's hand tugs mine, her little feet jumping.

"Chis?" She squeals with excitement. "You play with me?"

He swallows but hefts a grin for her, squatting again. "If your mom is okay with that."

Make a choice, Tiffany. You are out of time and out of options. This is stupid. I barely know him anymore. But I've got no one else. God, what am I doing?

"You sure you're okay with this? It should only be about an hour and a half."

"Yeah," he enthuses, holding out a hand for a high five. She jumps to tap her little hand against his with a giggle. "It will be great!"

I let out a deep breath and dip my chin, accepting I am out of options. "Okay. If you don't mind, you can stay with her at my place. All the things she might need will be there anyway."

"Yeah, that's just fine. I'll just grab my phone and lock up here. Give me just a moment." He moves back too quickly for me to hesitate any longer.

Scooping Savie into my arms, I turn, heading home. Her eyes focused on the house behind us.

A hand lands on my lower back, startling me. The heat radiating from his palm sends shivers up my spine, and I have to force myself not to lean back into it.

"I told you to wait." He grins as he meets my eyes again.

"Sorry. I just can't be late. I really need this job. It'll be literally perfect." I keep my eyes focused on the door we are nearing instead of his handsome face. "It's only 10 minutes from the house and near two of the three daycare centers I have her on the waitlist for."

When I peek over at him, thankfully, his chest is covered with a shirt.

"Okay, munchkin." He claps his hands together before he scoops her out of my arms. "Let's get this party started."

Savie wiggles out of his arms and takes off toward the back room with Trixi, giggles on her lips. I watch her go with a hesitation I don't quite understand before I turn back to him. "Thank you again, Chris. I owe you so much for this."

"Nope." He meets my eyes, soft and unwavering. "You don't owe me anything. I'm happy to help, and I get to hang out with your mini-me. What could be better?"

"Okay, then," I say, studying the sharp angles of his handsome face for a long moment. "You might regret that statement."

I appreciate that he's attempting to keep an easy smile on his face despite the reluctance growing in his eyes. "Everything else she could need is in there with her. She is great at entertaining herself, so don't feel like you need to do everything she asks of you. Snacks are in the same place as when we were kids."

He tucks a strand of hair behind my ear, fingers brushing my cheek. Warmth lingering on my skin.

"It'll be okay." The gentleness in his touch rattles me as he turns me around and guides me toward the door. "Scoot, we will be fine."

"Okay, well, text me if you need me. My number is on the fridge. I'll keep my phone on me." I try to turn back toward him to ask if he's okay one last time, but his hands grasp my shoulders tighter, keeping me pointed toward the door.

"Nope, we will be okay," he says with a grin, hands firm. "Scoot."

He shoves me gently before his palm taps my ass, playful and unmistakable. I spin to look at him, eyes wide, heart stuttering, and mouth gaping.

My words are stuck in my throat as I stare at him. He just winks and shoos me again as I nod my head woodenly.

He laughs, and Savie screams his name.

I barely remember getting into my car.

He just smacked my ass.

I don't get far before a ping comes from my phone. I don't look at it until I'm safely in a parking space for my interview. When I open it to an unknown number, a wide grin stretches across my face without my permission. Sure enough, it's two messages from Chris.

Chris

This is Chris, rock that interview.

Chris

Me and Savie got this.

I check the time on my car radio as I pull into my driveway. I'm later than I planned. My stomach twists with guilt. I really hope Chris isn't mad at me, or at least his mother has returned to take over for him. The interview went really well, and I'm crossing my fingers that this works out for me.

My keys jingle as I slide them into the handle, relieved to find the door locked.

The house is quiet when I enter, which is not what I anticipated.

I was expecting giggles or tears from one or both of them. Not silence.

The stillness draws me forward. I spot them and freeze.

My eyes widen at the sight in front of me. I try to hold back my laughter, not wanting to alert the two of them that I'm here until I can take this in.

Chris has barrettes in the longer hair on top of his head.

Bright, sparkly barrettes.

And I think there is glitter on the trimmed sides.

Chris is slouched on the couch, sinking into the cushions, his head tilted back, eyes closed. His chin hides Savie's head, and she is curled into his neck with one arm flung across his broad chest as if he belongs to her.

The laugh bubbles up before I can stop it. I clap a hand over my mouth, not wanting to break the spell. My heart, the traitor that it is, pounds harder than it should.

Savie *trusts* him. I've never seen her so comfortable with someone so soon after meeting them.

I pull my phone out of my purse and snap a picture of the two of them.

"If that photo gets out," Chris murmurs without opening his eyes. "I'll know it was you."

I laugh. "How much money do you think I could sell this for? Enough that I don't have to work for a while?"

He cracks one eye open as I cross the room toward them. A cheeky smile pulls at his lips.

"Tempting, isn't it?"

I gently lift Savie into my arms. Her little hand grips his shirt tighter before letting go with a sleepy sigh. I run my eyes along his body before I can stop myself. The bulk of him is less imposing now that he's softened with sleep.

He sits up, rubs his hands through his hair until they snag on the barrettes, and shrugs sheepishly.

"Sorry for the mess." His words prompt me to finally look around, only to see it's still mostly contained in the living room. "We had a princess astronaut tea party. I'm not entirely sure what that is still, to be honest. She said I had to be more princess-y."

"I'm actually impressed at how contained it is." I run a hand over her back softly. "The first time Brandon and Shawn watched her for me once she was mobile, there was kids' crap everywhere. And I mean everywhere. My underwear drawer. The fridge. Everywhere."

He chuckles, but when our eyes meet, the moment shifts. It slows, and his laughter dies.

I hold his stare as Savie starts to stir in my arms, bouncing her familiar weight. He stands, and his eyes follow her with an unreadable intensity. His hand reaches out, running gently down her back, brushing mine as it continues its path.

I freeze.

The heat of it lingers, and I can't breathe for a second.

"Chis?" Savie stirs against me.

"Yeah, I'm still here, little one," he says softly, stepping into her view. "But I think it's time for me to head home. Your mama is here."

"Mama?" Her sleepy voice melts me. "You home?"

"Yeah, sweetheart," I whisper, swiping her hair from her face. "Did you have fun with Chris?"

She tucks her head into my neck as she nods. I bounce my shoulder, nudging her to stay awake.

"You've got to stay awake, sweetheart." I coo into her hair

"Come on, little one." Chris's voice rumbles beside me, soft and low.

My body goes rigid when Chris's hand lands on my lower back. Unconsciously cocooning us in his arms, his gaze still on Savie.

Her head lifts. She reaches for him. He pulls her from me gently, holding her like he's done it a hundred times.

I drag in a ragged breath when his hand leaves my back.

Her hands frame his face, squishing his cheeks.

"Time for me to go back home, but I'll come play again sometime. How does that sound?" His voice is muffled around the press of his cheeks.

"Okay." She slides down and scrambles out of the room. "I go potty!"

Trixi follows her, nails clicking on the floor.

We both watch her go.

He reaches to unsnap one of the barrettes, his fingers fumbling. I step closer to help him remove the rest, his hair soft beneath my fingertips.

We both pause, hands tangled for a moment too long. I flush but don't look away from the way his eyes lock on my face.

Swallowing hard, I step back.

I gesture toward the door. "Let me walk you out."

"Sure." His heavy steps follow me toward the front of the house.

Savie is loud as she talks to Trixi in the bathroom, her voice like a thread tethering me to reality—a reminder of how complicated my life is. No matter how good this man looks at my door, this is more than he bargained for, despite how my belly swoops in his presence.

"Chris," I try to steady the shake in my voice. "Thank you. For everything."

His eyes hold mine, warm and unreadable as we stand in the doorway. I suck in a deep, steady breath before lifting on my toes to gently press my lips to his cheek.

He smiles and nods.

He steps out without a word.

And I watch the door close behind him with my heart caught somewhere between my ribs and my throat.

Chapter 10

Chris

I RUB MY HAND against my cheek where Tiffany's soft, pouty lips had landed. A goofy grin on my face, but I've got no say in the smile splitting my lips. It's ridiculous, really. I've been walking around like some idiot.

And to think, I almost missed out on it because I was busy trying to out-row my stubbornly sore shoulder since no one was around to tell me I couldn't, or rather, I shouldn't.

My shoulder still twinges in a way I don't like. No matter what *Nurse Ratched* says, I know it needs extra work.

I open the door to my parents' house, and my older brother, Charlie, is there chatting with them. His loud, obnoxious laugh is as familiar as the smell of dinner on the stove.

When I step into the kitchen, I catch sight of my brother sitting on the island. His feet kicking back and forth, heels banging against the wood of the cabinets like he did when we were kids.

Their conversation pauses as he and Mom look in my direction. Dad is absently flipping through the paper in his hands.

Charlie studies me for a moment, his eyes widening, and then he loses it, howling with laughter.

He points a finger at my head. "Something you want to tell us, little bro?"

"What do you mean?" I lift a hand to brush at my cheeks. "Do I have something on my face?"

Mom steps forward, a soft smile playing on her lips.

"Sweetheart, you have glitter in your hair." She brushes her fingers along the side of my head.

They come away sparkling.

"Oh," I chuckle, that goofy grin back on my face. "That."

Charlie's laughter muddies his words. "Yes, that. You nincompoop. Did you stop at a strip club before coming home?"

"No. Tiff's mom didn't show to watch her kid." I turn towards my mom. Her frown deepens as I continue. "She came over to ask you or Dad if you could watch her while she went to her interview. Obviously, you couldn't do that because you weren't here. So, I offered."

"You ... offered?" She sounds as confused as I was when I first made the suggestion. "That doesn't seem like something you would like."

I shrug. "It actually wasn't that bad. She's a good kid."

I have no better explanation for my behavior either.

Mom smiles and opens her mouth, but Charlie cuts her off, jumping off the island.

He crosses his arms over his chest. "Tiff, who? Next door, Tiff?"

"Yeah." I nod.

"She has a little girl?" Charlie's confusion is loud on his face, which makes me feel better. I'm not the only Bartkowski who didn't know she had a kid. Jake and Jason have been keeping secrets from all of us. "Uh, since when?"

"She's three, so I guess since then." I shoot him a pointed look. Mom's face softens as I press a gentle kiss on her cheek. I clap Charlie and Dad on the shoulder and head toward the stairs. "I'm going to shower. I'll be down after my call with Dan."

I barely make it to my bedroom before my phone pings with a message. Tiffany's name flashes across the screen, and there goes a stupid smile pulling at my lips again.

I have never been happier exchanging numbers with someone.

Tiffany

> Here you go. Now, if I sell this, I'm not the only one with a copy, and you can't confirm it was me. ;)

Half a second later, the photo comes through.

Everything in me goes still. My breath caught in my throat.

It's me and Savie.

I'm asleep against the arm of the couch with the curly-headed little girl tucked under my chin, head tilted into my neck. Her tiny fingers are clutching my shirt. My arm rests protectively around her back, holding her just as tightly to me.

My heart clenches at the sight of Savie on my chest. I break, wide open, with raw and unfamiliar feelings. There's a longing in my heart for something – someone – that I barely know.

It shouldn't feel like this.

But it does.

Something fierce flooded into my chest when that little girl crawled into my lap and laid her trust on me.

That little girl has me wrapped around her finger already.

And Tiff? The echo of her lips on my cheek. The warmth of her laugh. The look in her eyes when she handed her daughter over to me, scared, out of options, but with a kernel of trust.

She is definitely not what I should be thinking about when I lie in bed at night or when I wake up early in the morning, just like I have every day since she showed back up in my life.

My fingers hover over the phone.

I should let it go.

Focus on training. Preseason. My shoulder. My future.

I have to get my head on straight, or I won't be ready for the start of preseason.

I look back at my phone, at the picture.

But I don't let it go.

Instead, I type out the only thing that feels right.

Chris

> I'm pretty sure, I'd still know it was you, darling. Thanks for letting me spend time with Savie. She's a special little girl.

I stare at the screen, thumb hovering.

Then I send it.

Flipping the phone over, I toss it onto the bed. No waiting for a reply. No overthinking.

Get your head on straight, Chris.

Yeah. Right after I figure out how the hell I'm supposed to forget the way that little girl feels tucked into my arms.

And the way her mother still makes my world tilt.

Before I can consider not doing it, I grab my phone. Opening it to look at the photo one more time.

The next morning, I step out into a morning still wrapped in the night's leftover hush. My flight to L.A. doesn't leave until mid-morning, but I need to run off the restless energy twisting in my chest.

I'm barely out the door when excited barking splits the silence. Tiffany is trying to settle Savie in her stroller, and Trixi is dancing at the end of her leash, which is wrapped around Tiffany's trim waist.

Tiffany struggles with Savie while trying to shush Trixi. She braces her hands on her bare waist, head tilted back, breathing deep like she's bargaining with a higher power for the strength to deal with her uncooperative child.

The stretch of tan skin between her shirt and running pants glows under the porch light, catching my eye.

My feet move before I can reconsider. "Hey, stranger. Need some help?"

"Chis!" Savie brightens at my voice. She is way more awake this morning than she was the last time they were out this early for a run.

"Hey, little one!" I grin and unclip the leash from Tiffany's belt. My fingers graze her waist, the heat of her soft skin playing over my fingers. Her breath hitches, eyes flick to mine, but she doesn't stop me.

"I no want to run today." Savie folds her arms in full mutiny, her feet kicking irritably.

Tiffany stomps a foot, just out of sight of the stroller.

It's adorable.

It draws my attention away from Savie, and I find my eyes drifting to the exposed abs under her cropped shirt before I pop them back to her face.

Tiff exhales like she's been holding her breath all morning. "Savie, Mommy wants to run. Mommy *needs* to run, and I can't leave you home alone."

"As much as I'd love to right now," she murmurs under her breath.

Their matching scowls would be hilarious if Tiffany didn't look ready to cry. Angry red flares on both of their cheeks. I crouch down to Savie's height, hoping to stop both of them from going to pieces.

I try but fail to dodge the kisses Trixi plants on my cheek. Savie giggles, reaching out for me.

"How about this?" I catch her little fingers in mine and look up into Tiffany's eyes. "You let me push you while Mommy takes Trixi. I was just about to go on my own run, and I'd be happy to join you and your pretty mama."

Tiffany flushes.

Her voice is still thick with frustration. "Chris, you don't hav-"

I cut her off with a lifted hand. She freezes. We both do, suspended in each other's eyes for a moment.

My gaze drops to look at Savie, who is mulling over my suggestion. Her face is so much like her mother's, pinched in contemplation. Tiffany's toe taps in my peripheral vision as time ticks on by, waiting for Savie to decide. I know if I look over, her arms will be wrapped across her chest, propping her already perky breasts up higher. It's a sight I don't need to witness if I plan to keep my eyeballs in my head.

My training. Preseason. My shoulder. My future.

It's the mantra in my head as I try to keep my eyes from straying.

Savie's eyes bounce between me and Tiffany for a moment.

"I guess," she drawls.

"That's a yes! Great!" I stand before she can change her mind.

"Mommy can take Trixi," I hand the leash back to Tiffany, who is in fact crossing her arms. A stupid grin on my face as my eyes rove over her, her whiskey eyes burning on my skin. "And I'll push Savie. Let's roll out!"

I grab the stroller's handles and start pushing it out of the garage. It's a weird but decidedly not unwelcome feeling, having something in my hands as I step out to run.

I'm halfway down the drive, but Tiffany hasn't followed us. When I turn to look at her, she's distracted by something in my direction. I can only hope it's my ass. A smirk tips up my lips as I clear my throat.

She jumps, the flush on her cheeks darkening, and she avoids my eyes as she jogs over.

I don't say anything, but I do raise my eyebrow in her direction. It's my turn to stare as she approaches me and the stroller. A whisper of heat reaches out from her body as it nears mine.

I grin like an idiot – I just can't seem to stop.

I keep sneaking glances as we run. Her curls bouncing with every effortless stride, sweat trailing down her back. My eyes linger too long on the sway of her body. Her clothing clings to places I probably shouldn't be staring at.

But I do anyway.

We stop at a crosswalk about 30 minutes in. "How far do you usually run, darling?"

I grab my ankle to stretch as I turn to look at her, keeping one hand on the handles of the stroller. The sudden worry about what could happen at the crosswalk has my hands clenching tighter around the handlebars' neoprene.

"However far I think I can get in about an hour, it's usually a couple miles." She grins as she crouches to re-tie her laces.

I nod, watching her.

"I really do appreciate you helping me this morning. She was fussy yesterday after you left, so she went to bed early. And she woke up cranky. I suppose I could have just not gone running, but I was feeling antsy," she sighs, her whole body tensing. "Sorry. You don't need to know any of that."

"No, it's fine," I say, reaching for her hand without thinking. My thumb swipes over her knuckles. "I'm sorry if I made her cranky for you last night."

"No. No." She shakes her head, pulling her hand away to flutter at the loose hair around her face. "It wasn't your fault. We've just been on such a schedule since the day she was born, and I don't have a job, so our schedule is all wonky. She will be fine once we get back on it."

I nod and start to move again when the light changes.

She glances over. "Why were you out for a run so early in the morning?"

I look down, Savie's arm is hanging out the side of the stroller, waving at Trixi for the tenth time, and dragging a smile up my face. "I've got a flight to catch, midday. I'm headed out to L.A. for a couple of days."

"L.A.?" Her voice lifts with curiosity, gathering a little speed as we start the trek down the small hill. "What for?"

"Me and a teammate are expected at a charity event. Then we have a couple of sponsorship ads to film." I catch her eyes just as the sun edges up behind her, haloing her in morning light. She looks familiar and completely different all at once.

"Wow, what a life you live." She smirks as she meets my eyes for a moment. "So why are you still single?"

I shrug. "I don't know. I just haven't found the right person yet. It's easy to find the right nows, but not so easy for the forevers."

Her smile drops. Her eyes linger for a second before she turns away. "Yeah. I know what you mean."

We run in silence the rest of the way. It's not awkward exactly, but full. Savie hums and sings. The stroller wheels roll smoothly over the sidewalk. Our breathing falls in sync.

I take a peek at the woman next to me, who looks lost in thought. I startle when she grabs the handle and maneuvers the stroller in front of her as we slow to a walk near our homes.

I let go reluctantly.

My hands are bereft, and the urge to reach out and take the stroller back hits me. I *want* to reach for it... or to reach for something else.

We pause in front of her house, neither of us moving. She looks at me, her eyes full of... consideration. I think it might be interest or maybe it's just what I'm telling myself. "Thanks for this. You saved me ... again."

"Anytime," I say.

She smiles, pushing Savie toward her open garage. Boxes still line the walls. The mess of a life mid-rebuild.

I should go.

But I stand there, watching her disappear inside.

Chapter 11

Chris

A PING DRAWS ME from the endless blue stretching beyond the plane window.

Tiffany

> **aklllllllllllshcnkel ladkenkw**

A grin spreads across my face.

Either Savie's gotten hold of Tiffany's phone, or I'm getting my first butt text. I scroll to the picture of Savie curled into my chest. My thumb lingers over the screen as my heartbeat thunders beneath my ribs.

"What's that look on your face?" Pasha rumbles in his too-tired, Russian-thick accent. His weary tone drags me away from my phone as he drops into the seat across from me.

I scroll back to the most recent message and tilt my screen toward him. His eyebrows furrow for a moment as he looks at the screen before raising his eyes back to me.

"Who is Tiffany, and why did that nonsense make you smile like that?" My best friend asks.

I laugh as I set my phone down and focus on his angular face. "She's a girl I grew up with. She moved back home, next to my parents. And I think her little girl is the one who sent the nonsense, not her."

Several pings come in rapid succession from my phone. It's Tiffany apologizing for Savie. I chuckle at her clearly frazzled reply.

It looks like her day hasn't improved from the struggle she was having this morning, and I can't stop my fingers from dancing across the screen to check in on them. "I was right."

Pasha swirls the ice in his glass, watching me closely.

A grin pulls at his thin lips. "That's a good look on you, man. I don't think I've seen you this happy in a while. You happy to be home?"

"It's not like that," I shake my head, but my eyes dip back to my phone. "But yeah. It's been good. My family is just as pushy as ever, but I've missed them."

Another ping, and this time, when I peek at it, it's a voice memo.

I click play, and Savie's voice comes through. "Chis. Where you? I want a princess astronaut tea party 'gain."

Tiffany's voice comes across at the end of the memo, distant but still clear. "Savie, Chris is working, my love. He can't talk to you, and how do you keep getting my phone?"

That little voice and my name on Tiffany's tongue wraps around my chest, digging in deep. I lean back, warmth pulsing through me like sunlight. I've got that stupid grin on my face again, and I just can't find it in myself to care.

Pasha whistles low.

"It's not like that, huh?" He leans forward, grinning. "You got any pictures?"

"I think she has some on her socials. Hold on." I open the app and navigate to her profile.

A picture of them from what must have been a park in Georgia is the most recent one. They're both dressed in summer clothes; grass is stuck in their hair, and they have the biggest smiles pasted on their faces.

I study the girls for a moment before sliding it over to my friend.

Another low whistle hits my ears. He flips back and forth through them, something I've found myself doing with increasing frequency over the last few weeks.

He stops, his eyebrows raising. When he passes my phone back, it's a picture of Tiffany in a tiny black bikini with a chubby-cheeked Savie propped on her hip. Sunlight kisses their skin. My eyes trace the length of her smooth back, noting a small tattoo just under her perfect ass that looks like it wraps around to the front of her thigh.

They stand in the shallow water of the ocean. Waves caressing her ankles, and Savie's hand is outstretched toward the water.

I open the messages from the girls.

Pressing record, I softly say, "Hey, little one. I'm on a plane, but I'll call you when I land if you behave for your Mama."

"Oh, it's so like that." Pasha raises an eyebrow and watches me with pointed silence before saying, "You sure this is a good idea, man? Your shoulder is going to be healed in no time, and you'll be back on the East Coast ice with the rest of the team."

My hand clenches at my side. "I promise, man. It's really not. We aren't even really friends anymore. I can't say we ever really were. Her brother was friends with my older brother, Jake, and it was clear she was off-limits in high school. So, I stayed away as much as possible. She's only been back for a little while, and I've helped her out a couple of times."

"Once," I correct myself after a beat, "I've helped her out just once."

My hands run through my hair and over my face. The thought of her situation sends a painful twist to my gut. I blow out a breath and consider my best friend. I debate telling him all about her in high school. All the little things I noticed back then haven't changed with age. I want to tell him all about how I used to watch her draw in her yard for hours, the backyard visible from my bedroom window.

We might not have been friends, but I couldn't keep my eyes off her then, and I can't seem to do it now.

He doesn't say anything, just watches me struggle to find the words. The silence isn't doing me any favors. And even though he looks like he wants me to tell him all the things inside my head, I turn back to what's actually happening.

"She's all by herself, man, and her dad is in a coma on a vent. And if that wasn't hard enough, she left her job to move home to help her brother take care of him. So, she has no job, a little girl, and a sick father."

I look into his green eyes for a moment before they drop back to the drink on the table in front of me. "Her mom bailed on watching Savie, so Tiffany could go to a job interview. She came over looking for my parents, but they were out running errands. I offered to watch her for Tiffany. It got me off the rower for a couple of hours, if nothing else. That's all, Pash. I swear."

"I hear you. But you don't grin like that for someone you helped 'just once'." He's quiet for a moment.

I have nothing to offer him. No excuse. No explanation that would make sense because the way I feel around them doesn't make sense.

He leans forward, voice low. "It's a shitty hand she got dealt for sure. But that grin on your face when you got their messages says it all. I want to see you happy, but just make sure you aren't the only one who ends up happy with how it all does, or doesn't, turn out."

I nod, but my feet shift restlessly.

"I hear you, man. I promise I'm not trying to make any moves on her." I say, but I don't fully believe myself either. "I've got to get back on the ice. That's the focus."

Pasha nods, but not without a trace of concern. "It's only been two months. You have to give it time and not overwork it."

I shift uncomfortably but refocus on his face, there's a kind smile as he continues. "Dan's been tattling on you to Coach. And Coach asked me to talk to you. You'll get there, and I'll have my brother back on the ice with me for all the fun this year."

Despite the fact that everything inside me disagrees, I find myself nodding. It's not the time off that feels wrong. It's everything else.

"I know... just something feels different this time."

I grab my phone off the table as a new message pings through from Tiffany. I head to the couch at the back of the jet, my legs hang off the end, before I open the thread again.

Tiffany

You don't have to do that, but we'll be home all day.

Chris

I want to. We have about 4+ hours until we land.

Chris

I'll text you beforehand so you know when I'll call.

80

Tiffany

I stare at the screen a moment longer than I should. I'm only going to be in L.A. for three days.

But it already feels like it's too long.

Chapter 12

Tiffany

DID I PLAY CHRIS'S voice note over and over after Savie stopped asking me to? The world may never know.

The rough rasp of his voice, low and gentle in that way men don't realize is hot, sends chills down my spine every time. No matter how innocent the words.

Did my phone stay glued to me as we waited for Chris to text us?

Absolutely not.

That would be pathetic.

And did my heart skip when the message came through that he'd checked into the hotel and was about to call?

I will neither confirm nor deny how fast I unlocked my screen.

Savie squeals when Chris's face illuminates the phone. He is so patient as he talks with her for over an hour. She walks around the house showing him her toys and Trixi.

She chatters nonsensically, and he never gets annoyed or bored when, I'm sure, ninety percent of the time, all he sees is her side or the shifting of her body instead of her face or things she is trying to show him.

The whole time they are on the phone, I keep expecting her precious little heart to break when he loses his mind and can't handle it anymore, but it never happens. The worry kicks in again as she hangs up because she's hardly spent any time with him, and she's attached already.

All I can think is, please don't let him break her heart. I remember the feeling from the first time I met him as a child. Safety radiates off of him in waves, but the world can be unkind to people who rely too much on others.

I busy myself with chores, trying not to worry, and by the time it's mid-morning, I find myself standing in Savie's room, holding a half-folded dress in one hand as I put away the laundry. I glance up, and my eyes land on a tote on the highest shelf in the room that used to be Jason's.

Tucked high on the top shelf. The smarter part of me says to walk away, but my body moves before I can stop it.

My hands tremble as I lower it to the floor. The plastic lid resists for a second, like it knows what's inside and wants to keep me out.

Then it pops open.

Photos spill out, faded with the passing years. Image after image of happy moments that I've all but forgotten. Memories eclipsed by the steady, suffocating rhythm of trauma that defined this house. I look. Then again. And again.

Every childish smile feels heavier than the last. The cake smeared faces, Halloween costumes, times that should have been happy, that should find me nostalgic.

But then, I find glimpses of my reality peeking out from the edges. My own face, young, tired, hollow-eyed. Back then, I didn't think anyone could tell; maybe they couldn't, but I can see it. The shadows peeking out of my clothing, or dark crescents beneath my eyes.

Things that show 'an active child who doesn't sleep well.' A lie my mother used regularly.

There's tension in the photos, the clenching of my jaw, in the way I angled away from the person holding the camera.

From her.

My mother.

Some of the photos still smell like her perfume. That floral powdery stench that clung to everything. Strangling the fragile calm, I have been struggling with.

A dry sob claws its way out of my throat as my fingers twitch over the glossy surface of another photo I don't want to see. It's a picture of me at maybe eight years old, holding a stuffed bear with a crooked smile. A dull shine in our eyes. I look just as absent as the toy in my arms.

"Mommy?" Savie's voice slices through the silence, yanking me back. Panicking, I shove the photos back in, slam the lid shut, and push the tote back on the shelf. I shove it out of sight, out of reach, hidden beneath an old scarf like a secret I'm not ready to face. As if a thin layer of fabric can bury the years I just unboxed.

I find her in the hallway, rubbing her eyes, yawning wide.

"You look tired, baby," I say, sweeping her into my arms.

"I not tired," she lies, her head already dropping to my shoulder.

By the time I tuck her in, her eyes are barely open. I smooth her hair, press a kiss to her temple, and step out before the weight behind my ribs cracks me open again.

It takes me the whole of her nap to get my breathing back under control and do the only thing I can to keep from falling apart. I close the door on the memories and lock it, hoping the rattling isn't an omen and it holds.

That evening, when the doorbell rings and our normal finally feels steady, little feet go running to the door. "Mommy! Uncle Bran here!"

I smile indulgently and toss a dishtowel over my shoulder and open the door to Brandon's grinning face. He scoops her into his arms, and they're already whispering conspiratorially before they've cleared the entryway.

She tells him all about her week and goes on and on about Chris. How they played together and about the drama that apparently unfolded at their tea party. She tells him about their phone call, and I catch the look he throws my way.

He mouths, 'We'll talk about this later,' at me, and I shake my head, sticking my tongue out.

When later arrives, I settle onto the couch beside him. My head lands on his shoulder like muscle memory, his cheek resting against my hair.

He slaps a hand on my thigh. Hard.

"Ouch. Ass." I pinch the back of his hand in retaliation.

He laughs. "So. Chris, huh?"

I groan, and Brandon pulls me tighter into his body, his arm resting around my shoulders.

I shake my head, and my hair twists under his cheek. "Nope. No. Absolutely not."

"Oh girl, we are so talking about it." He leans forward, grabs the two wine glasses on the coffee table, and hands one to me before circling my shoulders again.

I drink half of the sweet wine Brandon prefers in one go. "There is nothing to talk about. I've seen him like... twice. He watched Savie for me during my interview when my mom bailed on me. Then he came on a run with us this morning before he left for his plane because he saw me struggling with Savie, who was in a monster mood this morning."

"She stole my phone this afternoon and texted him, don't ask me how she knew it was him, but she figured it out without me, so he video called her when he landed." I shrug, pretending to be nonchalant. Pretending I'm not remembering all the ways my body heats under his intense eyes. "So, that's it. See, nothing to tell."

"Girl, that blush on your face tells me that is not all."

He pulls away to face me, crossing his legs and leaning over them. His wine glass is clutched in both hands.

I groan again, this time flopping dramatically onto the couch; one arm tossed over my eyes.

"HemayhavesmackedmyasswhenIleft," I mumble.

"What was that?" He cups a hand to his ear. "Say that again for the class?"

"Shut *up*." I bury my face in a pillow.

His big, dumb face is stretched into a grin telling me he knows *exactly* what I said. When he tips his head back and laughs, heat rushes up my neck so fast I'm sure I'm glowing.

I shush him. "He might have said some things that I can't stop thinking about. And maybe he might have smacked my ass when I was walking out the door for my interview."

"He what?" Brandon shimmies his whole body. "Girl!"

My face gets hotter as I try to explain it away. "I think the smack was just like a locker room 'atta boy.' Maybe?"

Brandon leans closer to inspect my face. "Honey, that man hasn't been in a locker room with *you*. That was not a platonic pat on the patooty."

My eyes drifting toward my phone on the table. "I can't. Even if I, *if we*, wanted to, I can't. This is all too much. *We* are too much for that man."

He scoots closer, knees brushing my thigh. "There's nothing wrong with having a little fun sometimes."

"I can't be like her. I won't. She ruined me." I finish my wine in one breath and set the glass down.

My elbows drop to my knees, and I tangle my hands in my hair. There's another clink of glass on the coffee table before his strong arms wrap around my back, pulling me into his body.

"You're nothing like her." His voice is low and certain, his hands rubbing my back. I shudder. "You haven't thought of yourself first since the day you found out you were pregnant. You have been a fierce momma, and Shawn and I are in awe of you. That little girl is so, *so* lucky that you are her mom."

We sit, pressed together in the silence for a moment as I try to gather myself.

Finally, I shift back into the couch, wrapping the throw around my shoulders, closing myself off to whatever else he might say. His fingers reach out to rub the blanket between two fingers.

He's always been so good with his silent support, to me and everyone one else, but the thing I appreciate the most is that he knows when not to push.

Like now, when every inch of my body is screaming at him that I'm uncomfortable with the direction this conversation has taken. Thankfully, he doesn't say anything more about it.

"Thanks. I don't know what we would do without you." I turn to study his face and suck in a steadying breath, shutting down the past that wants to drown me in it.

"And you'll never have to find out." He leans forward to brush my hair away from my face and pulls me into him as he turns my TV on to our favorite movie. "Now, shut up and watch *Clueless* with me, or I'm telling Shawn about the ass slap."

Chapter 13

Tiffany

Jason and I sit at the table doing homework when my mother's giggle floats down the stairs. The sound that follows makes me freeze. There's a thudding, rhythmic knocking against the wall, and she starts making those weird noises again, like she's in pain, but we both know better than to check on her.

Last time I did, she backhanded me across the face and sent me to bed without dinner. My cheek stayed red until morning.

Jason's face creases like when he yells at me, but there's no sound. He doesn't yell when Mommy is around.

"Jason, I'm hungry," I whisper, barely loud enough for him to hear as I shift toward him.

He grabs his eraser and chucks it at me. It hits my forehead and bounces into the kitchen with a soft plunk.

"Shut up," he snaps. "I'm not getting in trouble because of you."

I blink fast to keep from crying and stare back at the math worksheet I don't understand. The numbers blur. My stomach growls again, louder this time. I know I shouldn't whine, but I'm hungry, and I don't want to keep working on my homework.

"Jason," I whisper again, but his eyes flash toward me, sharp and cold. I bite my lip when mommy cries out.

It isn't long before two sets of footsteps come down the stairs, and I stiffen in my chair. When my mommy rounds the kitchen wall, her messy bun is off-center, and her face is flushed and shiny.

Her eyes drop to the eraser Jason threw, and a shiver runs across my shoulders when her smile disappears.

Once the door closes behind her boyfriend, she rounds on us.

"You guys are so embarrassing," she hisses.

Her hand snakes out and grabs my arm, yanking me to the floor. Pain flares in my wrist. "Why are you throwing shit around my house!"

"I didn't, Mommy, I promise." The tears come too fast to stop. I scramble to sit up, but her shadow looms over me.

Her hand draws back, and I know what's going to happen. I flinch away from her as her hand starts to swing.

I jolt awake, my heart thundering so hard I feel it in my throat. The room is dark, but I'm searching the shadows for ghosts. My chest heaves and my hands are clammy, like I'm still ten years old and bracing for the next hit.

The soft thump of paws on ancient carpet as Trixi jumps from Savie's bed draws my eyes toward the hallway.

She pads into the room and pushes the door open with her big, fuzzy head. I flinch when the door bounces off the wall. She leaps onto the bed, and I grab her like a life raft. Her warm weight settles against me, and I bury my face into her fur, breathing deep. Her steady heartbeat calms mine.

It's over.

It's not real.

It's just a dream.

I remind myself, over and over again. I lie to myself because the door didn't hold, and it wasn't a dream.

It's a memory.

A buzz from the nightstand grabs my attention. My screen glows with a message.

I reach for it with a still trembling hand and swipe open the message from Chris that's waiting for me.

Chris

Tell Savie that I got the pièce de résistance for future tea parties

Just above the message, there's a photo. A sparkly pink astronaut helmet. A glittering, and absolutely ridiculous in the best way, helmet. A tiny tiara set just above the open eye space. My heart, still pounding from the nightmare, stutters again, but this time for an entirely different reason.

I smile, despite the way my fingers still tremble.

Tiffany

Chris you didn't have to do that.

Tiffany

She will love it though.

His reply comes fast.

Chris

What are you doing up?

I hesitate for half a second.

Tiffany

Nightmare.

I don't know why I tell him, but just like when we were kids, he has this quiet way of slipping past my defenses.

Ten seconds after the delivered status appears under my message, my phone begins to ring. The photo of Savie and him on the couch pops up on my screen.

I hesitate, then swipe to answer, pressing the phone to my ear and drawing in a shaky breath.

"Hello?" My voice is raspier than it should be, which means I was probably talking in my sleep. Again.

There's a soft rustle on the other end before his voice breaks through. It's low and concerned. "Darling? You okay?"

That pet name. *Darling*. It sets butterflies winging their way around my stomach.

"Yeah." I turn onto my side and close my eyes. "No. I don't know. It was a weird night, and I think Brandon and I had too much wine."

He chuckles, and the sound is warm, like being wrapped in a hoodie that still smells like home. "I'm glad you got to spend some time with your friend. You want to talk about the nightmare? Or do you want a distraction?"

The dream still clings to me like sweat. It's heavy, sticky, and shameful. But his voice cuts through the fog like an ember glowing in the darkness.

"Distraction, please." I feel terrible about asking, but I whisper the words anyway. "But if you're busy or heading to bed, it's okay—."

"Don't even worry about it," he cuts me off. "I just got back from dinner with Pasha. I'm in bed, feet up, regretting eating too much pasta. I've got time."

I smile into my pillow. There's those damn butterflies again.

The sheets rustle as he shifts on the other end of the line. "Want to hear about the charity stuff we are doing tomorrow?"

"Yeah," I breathe. "I'd like that."

And so, he talks. About how he and Pasha will be visiting sick kids in the morning, and about attending the formal foundation dinner. He talks about who he's excited to meet. He talks about the other famous people who are supposed to be there.

He talks for so long he runs out of charity topics. And then he turns to stories about how nervous Pasha gets around celebrities, about the inside jokes between them. He teases stories out of memory like he knows I need the noise to push back the dark.

His voice is steady and warm, like a lullaby I didn't know I needed. He keeps talking.

And I start to fall.

Bit by bit, I drift off, wrapped in the warmth of his words. Wrapped in the way he fills the space, taking away the edge of fear.

By the time sleep finally claims me, it's not the nightmare I carry with me into my dreams.

It's his voice.

The next few days are filled with sparkly tea parties, sticky fingers at the park, and lunch with Mrs. B, but I'm staring at a reality I've been hoping to avoid.

My bank account is dwindling, and we'll be broke in just a few short weeks.

My fingers are flying over the keyboard, working through yet another job application, when there's a knock at the door.

Little feet race toward the door before I heft myself out of my seat.

"Chis!" She squeals.

My heart beats wildly as the door creaks open. *She has got to stop doing this.* I rush through the house behind her.

"Savannah Grace, you had better not have opened that door without me!"

There's a quiet 'uh oh' from her just before I round the corner in time to see her frozen beside an amused Chris, who's crouched at her level. She looks up at me, wide-eyed and guilty.

Chris's eyebrow cocks, and his soft smile curves into a brilliant grin. He leans in close and stage whispers, "Savie, did you just get us in trouble with your momma?"

I shake my head, trying to control my grin. "Come on in. Why do we have the pleasure of your company tonight?"

"Yeah, Chis. Come in and see me." Savie grabs his hand as he stands and drags him in behind her.

He gathers her up and blows loud raspberries into her cheek. She squeals with delight and leans forward to blow her own raspberries on his cheek. By the expression on his face, I can tell he got one of the wet ones that she is well known for. His grimace is priceless. Against my best defense, I snicker at the two of them as we stand in the hallway leading to the kitchen.

"I came by to invite-" My ringing phone interrupts him with an unknown local number.

My heart lodges in my throat, my breath catching.

"Hold on. I need to take this." I murmur, already walking into the kitchen. I'm hopefully just far enough that if it is someone from the hospital with more bad news, Savie won't hear.

I clear my throat, then answer. "Hello?"

"Ms. Samson? This is Clarissa; we met the other day for your interview?"

My hand grips the edge of the counter as she gives me the details.

The warm kitchen holds me for just moments, but when I leave, I've got a job.

His gaze lingers on me as I walk back into the family room in a daze, like my thoughts are written all over my face. Chris steps closer, hands gently lifting my chin. "Everything okay?"

"Yeah," I smile brightly, but it slips before it can land. My mind spins back to childcare concerns. "I got the job."

Without hesitation, he pulls me into his firm chest and lifts me off the ground, spinning me in circles. "Congrats, darling! I'm so proud of you!"

He sets me on my feet and picks Savie up, repeating his wild circles. She dissolves into delighted giggles.

"Thank you," I whisper, but all I can focus on is the logistics.

"You're happy, right?" He pulls me back into his body with the arm not holding Savie.

I suck in a breath as the heat of him surrounds me, his hand lingering on my waist. My body slows with the heat of him surrounding me and I rest a languid hand against his stomach. There is a hum everywhere my body touches his.

I nod, but my shoulders fall under the weight still pressing in on me.

"Yeah. I just still have a lot to figure out for Savie." I let my head drop to his chest for a moment before I pull back enough to look at him. "She's still on waitlists for daycare, so I'm going to have to call around and try to find something. I might have to look at neighboring towns, but-"

"I'll watch her!" His words cut me off and shock me all at once.

He's smiling like it's the most obvious thing in the world. Like, he didn't just offer me this huge thing.

"Well, I'll watch her when I don't have PT or free skates. But I can totally move those around to when you aren't at work. At least until I have to go back. But by then, you should have heard back from the daycares, right?"

Gently, I pull Savie into my arms, needing space and something to hold onto as I step away from his warmth.

"I can't ask you to do that, and I definitely can't afford your time." My voice is sharp, too sharp for someone offering me the thing I desperately need, and Savie buries her face into my neck, sensing the shift in my tone.

There it is again. His impossible kindness and too-easy solutions. His hand reaching in to lift a weight I've been carrying alone for so long, that it's a part of me.

I want to say yes.

God, I want to say yes.

But needing someone has never ended well for me. It's a dangerous desire.

Chris steps closer to me as I try to step away.

"You didn't ask. I offered," he pauses, his voice gentling. "Well, I suppose I should also talk to my mom so there is a backup just in case, but if I know her, and I do, she will love spending time with Savie. Free of charge. For both of us."

He's thought of everything, offering a solution and a backup to make me more comfortable. My chest tightens, and every part of me wants to lean in. And I can't believe this isn't too good to be true. But I've been burned before. And it's not just me on the line here.

So, I nod, just barely. Not a yes. Not a no.

Just... Just maybe.

Chapter 14

Chris

THE NIGHT I OFFER to watch Savie, I start figuring out how to rearrange my schedule — just in case I need to. If I can't get my mom to agree to take over watching her while I'm at PT in the middle of the day, I need a solid backup plan.

I don't say anything to anyone until I'm certain I have everything figured out, every piece in order. Turns out I have so little going on in my life that it only takes me until just before family dinner on Sunday.

In some ways, it's depressing how easy it is to shift everything around because there's not much to shift. Just empty time, rehab, and thinking too much. But the space could finally be used for something good.

The front door slams, and I know my brothers have started arriving. The slam is all Charlie, in his loud, chaotic, and impossible-to-miss exuberance. Mom's been cooking all day, and if I didn't know any better, I would say she was expecting an army.

I hit the last stair and leap onto Charlie's back like I'm twelve again. My arm snakes around his neck in a mock chokehold. Charlie belly laughs as I lurch us backwards enough he has to bend to keep the pressure off his neck.

"Still trying to take me on with only one good shoulder?" He says, twisting his body around until he grabs me and flips me over his shoulder like a sack of potatoes.

"Oof, Charlie!" I groan as my shoulder protests.

I release my grip before I tweak the shoulder I've spent all this time healing.

He awkwardly carries me into the kitchen like a human trophy while I hang on, laughing. Mom waves her spatula at us, trying, and failing, not to smile. Charlie drops me to my feet and swings his arm around me; his grin is just a touch too wide to be truly innocent.

"Hey, Mama!" he says, all innocent charm, before he turns to me with a wicked grin. "Just wanted to make sure my injured baby brother could make it to dinner on time."

Mom snorts but turns back to finishing dinner without a word.

"I had my rotator cuff repaired, not a damn leg amputation," I mutter.

"Why were you late for dinner the other night if nothing's wrong with your legs?" I whip my head around to a grinning Junior who is leaning against the door frame. *Smartass.*

"Now, now, son," Dad says with a wink at me and Charlie, squeezing Junior's shoulder as he passes. A laugh is barely contained as he continues to give me a hard time. "Your brother has been busy healing."

He nods his head at the food waiting to be moved. It's a silent command to help our mother. The three of us start transferring everything to the table.

These are the rhythms of home.

The teasing, the loud entrances, the never-ending food. The things I miss every time I'm out East and away from them.

The last dish is set when the telltale sound of the front door opening echoes through the house. It's Jake.

He walks in, blue eyes scanning our grinning faces before he groans. "Well, get on with it. What is it this time?"

It's our tradition, the last one to dinner gets assigned chores first.

Laughter breaks out around the table as Mom assigns him clean-up duty, and we all sit down. Once plates are passed and the room settles into the familiar family hum, I lean toward Mom, pulse ticking up a notch.

"So," I pause to clear my throat, gathering courage, or something like it. "Tiff got a job. Did she tell you?"

Mom brightens. "Oh, honey, that's great news! Now she won't have to worry so much. I'm so happy for her, but no, she hadn't told me that yet."

"Yeah, I was dropping off the present I got for Savie in L.A. when she got the call." I start to push the food on my plate around, so I don't have to meet my mom's pale blue eyes. "I, uh, I told Tiff that I would watch Savie for her until a daycare spot opens up."

The sudden silence around the table is deafening. It stretches, thick and heavy, like everyone's afraid to break it.

The next sound is Mom's chair scraping gently across the wood floor as she turns to face me.

"Chris, sweetheart," her voice is soft and steady. She rests her hand on my arm, squeezing gently, forcing me to look at her.

"That's very kind, but are you sure you're really ready for this? Watching a three-year-old every day is not like watching her for a couple hours during an interview."

"No, I know." I nod. "That's why I figured everything out before saying anything. I was hoping you could be my backup. After what happened with Tiff's mom..."

Jake's eyes snap to mine. There's an impassiveness in them; it looks like concern, but he looks away before I can confirm it.

The look has me recalling something he said - hinted at - a long time ago.

It makes me reevaluate the way Jason acted at the bar the other night. The tension in his voice. The things he didn't say.

"What are you going to do about physical therapy? And those free skates?" Mom's brow furrows as she grabs my attention again.

"Well, I was hoping that you would watch her, so I don't have to move anything around," I shrug. "But if you can't or won't, Bernadette is here for me. I'm the only person she's working with, so she'll have to work on my schedule. So, if that means I go after Tiffany gets home from work, then so be it."

I take a bite of my dinner, and everyone else follows suit. But they keep looking at me.

"As for free skates, I called the rink, and they have time on the weekend if I need to change days. It'll just be really early in the morning, like back in high school. Not ideal, but it's doable."

Jake cuts in. "You really trust yourself with that much responsibility every day? What happens when you need to ramp up your training? Or if Tiffany needs more than just a couple weeks?"

"I guess we will cross that bridge if we come to it." I snap at my brother as old frustration rears its head.

The air gets tight around us. The tension creeps in like smoke, familiar and bitter. The old warnings fan the flames of my irritation. Jake's the one who could never quite separate the way he sees me from Jason's exacting requirements for being around Tiffany.

He holds my gaze for a second too long, but, for once, doesn't push. I know it won't be long before he is running off to tell Jason all about my agreement to watch his niece. I'm sure he will want me to answer to Jason as well, but I'm not a teenager anymore, and I know exactly what my expectations are in this situation.

I won't be intimidated or persuaded away.

Not again.

Not from being the friend she needs.

It's quiet for a moment before Charlie chimes in with a laugh.

"You? In charge of snack time and nap schedules?" He laughs again before he settles. "You're gonna get dunked on by a three-year-old with pigtails and glitter in her arsenal."

I nod in agreement, as laughter erupts around the table. "100%. She already got me with the glitter last time, remember? She talked me into playing dress up with her."

Junior chokes on his drink as he raises his eyebrows at me. "I'm not surprised - look at who her mother is."

"Yeah, she's definitely Tiffany's mini me. No doubt." I agree, smiling.

"I think it's a nice thing to offer," Mom's voice is warm and full of affection. She rests a hand on my forearm. "I admire it. Truly. And of course, you don't have to change your schedule. Your father and I have no problem helping out when needed."

"Your mom is right, son." Dad finally speaks. "You're doing the right thing, helping those girls out. You're doing a thing that matters, not something easy. That's how you know it's the right thing to do."

Everyone around the table agrees, and there's a quiet vote of confidence in it. I turn to Jake, silently asking him not to make this harder than it already is.

Words slip out before I can reconsider them. "This isn't about anything other than helping them out of a tough spot. And even though it's only temporary. It felt worth it to offer."

Jake's eyes soften, just for a moment.

He nods.

He won't keep it from Jason.

I know that.

He isn't capable of keeping this to himself, but he understands where I'm coming from now.

"Okay," Mom claps her hands together. "What do we need to do then?"

She turns on planning mode, and I know I have the support I'll need. That we can really make this work for Tiffany.

Helping Tiffany and Savie doesn't just feel like the right thing — it's the beginning of something that matters.

Over the next week and a half, my mom and I wear Tiffany down. She's reluctant, but she eventually gives in. Mom is thrilled, already stockpiling juice boxes and child-appropriate coloring books like she's preparing for battle. Savie's more excited every time we stop by.

The plan is simple: I'll head over every morning just before 7:30, hang with Savie until ten minutes before my PT session, and then Mom will tag in. Tiffany's one condition? I don't reschedule therapy under any circumstances.

I promised her. Swore on my life, in fact.

Looking at my watch, I only have a couple more minutes before I'm supposed to meet Tiffany. I take the stairs two at a time and find my mom at the stove, flipping eggs with casual precision. "Hey, Ma."

I drop onto the stool at the island, tapping my foot against the bottom rung. My knee starts bouncing before I can stop it.

She turns a wry grin in my direction. "Impatient?"

"No." I pause, laughing as I shake my head. "Is it weird to say I'm nervous?"

"No, sweet one. It's not." She plates her food, sliding onto the stool next to me, and resting her hand on my bicep. My eyes meet hers, and her voice softens. "Those girls are special, and they've had a tough go of it. But son, are you *sure* you want to do this?"

I pause a moment to let the question settle because I know it's what she expects. She wouldn't accept a quick answer anyway.

"Yeah, Mom. I do."

She dips her head, like she's bracing herself.

"I know you had feelings for that girl growing up," she cuts me off before I can disagree. "Don't try to deny it. I'm your mother. I always knew."

"Mom, we're just friends. That's all." I say it too fast.

She cocks an eyebrow and finishes her breakfast. When she stands, she walks to the sink with a small smirk that makes my stomach twist. "You're both adults and can make your own decisions. Whatever they may be. But I, not so secretly, hope you pursue things with her."

I blush and hurry out the door.

It's Tiffany's first day.

Seven-twenty on the dot, I'm at Tiffany's door, knocking quietly, hoping Savie has stuck to her normal pattern and is sleeping soundly. I rock back on my heels, trying not to overthink the day ahead, or the fact I've never done this before. Not like this.

The door opens with a soft creak, and Tiffany appears like a dream. Her normally wild curls are tamed into sleek, loose waves that fall just below her perky breast, and the navy blue blazer that hugs her waist over a yellow dress that shouldn't be allowed to look this good this early in the morning.

"Hey," she whispers as she ushers me into the house. "Thank you again for watching her. Hopefully, this will only be a couple of days, and I'll get her into daycare."

She's talking fast, like she's still trying to convince herself this isn't a mistake. Before she can get any further, I place a hand gently on her shoulder to stop her.

"Tiff," I say, my hand guiding her chin up. Forcing her to look at me because I want to make sure she really hears me. "Don't worry about it, darling. If you had heard my agent on the phone the week you showed up, well, let's just put it this way: he's ecstatic I found a better way to occupy my time other than on the rower."

Her laugh is warm and low. The throaty sound does something to me that I wasn't expecting. I never knew a laugh could be something I found sexy. I clear my throat and step back, suddenly hyper-aware of every inch of space between us.

Praying to God, my dick behaves himself. I don't need to give her any reason to question if I can handle this. Runaway hormones would definitely do it.

"Okay then," she says, grabbing her purse and adjusting the strap. "I'll be on my way. I should be home by 5:30 at the latest."

"Don't worry, darling. Take whatever time you need. Savie and I got this. If not," I pause with a laugh. "I'll call my mom."

Her hand lands on my chest, and my muscles flex under her tiny fingers. Tingles rippling out from where we touch, warmth rushing quickly behind. Her hand on me is exhilarating.

She leans in a little closer. "You *can* call me. If she needs me."

"I know, but we will be okay. You'll see." I turn her around, promising her everything will be okay.

She looks at me like she's searching for something, and maybe she finds it, because she finally nods, exhales, and walks out the door.

The day starts great. I hand Savie off to my mom around ten for nap time and PT. I'm back in just over an hour.

We help Mom out the door, and by one, we're back in the living room surrounded by stuffed animals.

We're halfway through the newest game of stuffy hospital when my phone vibrates, and I open it to a couple of unread texts in the group chat with my brothers.

Junior is asking how it's going, and Charlie wants to know if I've been glittered again.

Chris

We are currently performing surgery on The Giraffe.

Chris

The Giraffe is a dog stuffy.

Chris

No glitter.

Chris

Yet

Junior

This is the most detailed training you've ever had.

Jake

You volunteered. This is on you.

Jake

Accept your fate.

Charlie

Pics or it didn't happen.

I snap a photo of Savie with a toy stethoscope around her neck, hovering over the patient with intense focus, and the dog stuffy being held down by my hand. I also take a quick video as her fake tools fly wildly around, and she tells me about what is wrong with The Giraffe and how she's going to fix it. I send it over to them. Charlie sends a string of laughing cry emojis.

Junior

Doctor in the making?

Charlie's eye-rolling emoji covers everyone's reaction to his really lame joke.

Jake

...is that a turkey baster?

> It's her "puffy fixer machine." I'm not asking questions anymore.

I slide my phone back into my pocket and glance over just in time to watch Savie twist her mouth in concentration, tongue sticking out, as she presses the baster to the stuffed dog's side.

Being here has changed everything.

These amazing girls have changed something so critical to who I am, and I don't know what to do about it. Because suddenly I'm the one she looks at when she wants to show off her glitter wand or play stuffy hospital.

And the terrifying thing?

I don't want to be anywhere else.

Chapter 15

Tiffany

AFTER HANGING UP WITH Chris at the end of lunch, I head back in, my heels clicking softly on the laminate. The hum of fluorescent lights and distant phone chatter wraps around me in the quiet of post-lunch office space.

I settle into the high-backed chair and begin to tidy the mess my boss and I left behind during our earlier whirlwind training session. While waiting for her to return, I can't stop myself from looking at the pictures Chris sent me this morning.

The first one I open is the photo he sent me just before he left for physical therapy. It's Savie, curled up tight on the couch, her favorite stuffed bunny tucked under one arm.

Her hair's been gently smoothed back. I can tell it's Chris's handiwork. The curls are more tamed, but still defiant. My chest clenches as I zoom in slightly.

Her face is relaxed in the I'm completely safe kind of way.

This feeling. It's like an ache and a balm all at once as I look into her peaceful face.

I scroll to the next photo. It's Chris and Savie's selfie. She's wearing that absurd pink astronaut helmet with the glued-on tiara again, smiling so big her dimples practically leap off the screen. The helmet will probably be too big on her head when she's grown, but the giant smile tells me letting him do this is worth it.

Every ounce of struggle and every bit of exhaustion is worth it for that smile.

My eyes drift to Chris, lingering. His light brown hair is tousled and no longer the neat style from this morning. It stands out in disheveled waves, clearly at the mercy of toddler hands.

His eyes are what hold me the longest, though. They are tired but warm. The type of tiredness I've seen in the mirror. The kind that comes from loving someone so much it rewires your body.

He's handsome. He's *always* been handsome. Unfairly so. And now? With a child – my child - on his hip?

It threatens my stability.

It's not just the stubble or the eyes or even the athletic build that turns heads wherever he goes. It's the way he shows up. He's kind. I don't know anyone else, especially someone with the fame and resources he's achieved, who would volunteer to watch a 3-year-old.

My perfect, rambunctious, wildly imaginative, 3-year-old.

And he's happy to do it.

"Your husband?" My boss's voice startles me so much I fumble my phone. She's standing at the side of my desk, one eyebrow raised, an amused look on her face.

"He's, um, just a friend." I drop my phone on my desk. "He's actually watching my daughter until a daycare spot opens up."

She leans against the wall behind her, arms crossed. "Well, *friend* or not, I can definitely tell that little one's yours. That smile? All you."

I let out a breathy laugh and nod. "Yeah. She's my mini-me in every way."

"Mmm." My boss smiles, but it's a *knowing* smile. Like she's already writing our love story in her head. "Well. Some friends make life a whole lot easier."

She winks at me but turns back to training. I stare at my phone for a beat longer, her words still echoing as I try to shake off the weird feeling of almost painful loneliness at the reminder that Chris is just a friend.

The end of the day is approaching when my phone buzzes again; thankfully, my boss has left me to my own devices for a while.

I grab the phone as Chris's name flashes across the screen.

Chris

I was told I'm not exempt from becoming a princess even though I'm a boy

A laugh escapes before I can stop it. It's loud enough to draw a glance from someone two desks over. I cover my mouth as another message rolls in.

It's another photo — another selfie.

Chris is wearing a tiara that's minuscule in the mess of his hair. His smile is wide and unbothered. Savie's perched on his lap, her pigtails slightly uneven but adorable, her own shiny blue tiara slipping sideways like a crown mid-battle.

My chest fills again. The strange warmth, the softness that's almost painful rises again. It's an echo of the feelings he inspired while we were growing up, and I don't know what to do with it.

Tiffany

How exciting for you! ;)

Tiffany

Doesn't every man wish they could be a princess?

Chris

Well I'm not nearly as pretty as a princess but I do feel bonita.

Tiffany

Maybe not a pretty princess but definitely handsome enough to be someone's prince.

I stare at the screen a moment longer than I should after hitting send. Because why am I flirting with a man I have no interest in?

Because I *don't* have an interest in him.

He's just the man who's taking considerable time out of his life to help me out of a tough spot.

The unfairly handsome man, who's unerringly kind and smart. Generous in a way that no normal human being could possibly be.

And did I mention, handsome?

Chris

Not really prince material here

Chris

But keep the compliments coming

Tiffany

You are definitely prince material

Tiffany

you swooped in and saved our behinds.

Tiffany

I'm not sure where we'd be without you.

Chris

You'd be more than fine.

Chris

But I'm glad I could help

Tiffany

This is more than just help

Tiffany

I don't think you understand just how much your help means to us.

Chris

I think I'm starting to get it.

I read the last message three times. Replaying it over and over in my head. It's short and simple, but it feels like things are shifting. Like we're standing on the same side of the window instead of me looking out at him like I did our whole childhood

I want to reply.

I almost do.

My fingers hover over the keyboard. But instead, I lock my phone and set it face down on the desk again.

I'm not even sure what I would say back.

Not because I'm unsure of him.

Because I'm unsure of *me*.

Chapter 16

Chris

BY THE TIME FRIDAY of the first week rolls around, the routine is starting to feel familiar.

After years of being a professional athlete, I'm used to the daily structure.

But this?

This isn't a schedule dictated by a whistle or a stopwatch. It's pancakes, morning cartoons, and tiaras glued to astronaut helmets. It's chaos wrapped in pink glitter and syrup stains.

And, it's exactly what I didn't know I needed. If the phone call from Dan the night before is anything to go by, Bernadette and Coach are happy with the change this week. Probably because I've been too busy playing pretend hospital and tea party host to obsess over my shoulder 24/7.

Tiffany's touch lingers on my arm again this morning. Just before she leaves, her hand slides across my shoulder, fingers grazing me a second too long.

A shudder runs through me at the heat her touch inspires. She smiles soft and weary, and slips out the door. It's all starting to feel domestic.

And it should terrify me. But it doesn't.

It's a slow start, peaceful even. The house is quiet. It takes about another hour and a half before Savie stirs. A sleepy yawn from the baby monitor has me headed toward her room. Trixi's feet softly thudding to the floor above confirms they are both awake.

I open the bedroom door to find a little tousled head barely poking out from under a nest of blankets. Savie's hair is a chaotic halo around her head, her eyes puffy with sleep. Her lashes stick together as she sits sleepily in her bed.

It takes no time at all to tuck her against my chest, her small body heavy with trust. She rests her cheek on my shoulder, and her breath is soft and slow against my collarbone. My eyes clench against the swell in my chest as I press my lips against the curly mess of hair and breathe her in.

Her little voice saying my name fills my body with an emotion I've never experienced before. It's warm and tight, a mix of comfort and anxiety I don't quite know what to do with. I'm not sure if I like it or hate it. I rest my hand gently on her back. Holding her tight to me.

"Chis, you stay with us today?" She mumbles, her voice tired and whiny.

"Yeah, little one. I'm with you today." I say, my voice catching. "Mommy had to work. Granny B will be by for a little bit so I can go to the doctor. Is that okay with you?"

Trixi shoots down the stairs before us, and Savie nods sleepily, pressing her face back into my neck. Her little fingers curl into the collar of my t-shirt, wedging herself deeper into my chest.

There's a tender ache under where she settles, one I can't describe, but I know she's the cause of it.

I don't feel entirely worthy of it either.

And by the time I'm done cooking, she's more alert and chattering. One bite into breakfast and she's keen to go, spinning in circles to the movie's soundtrack with syrup on her face and sticky fingers waving in the air. Her joy is infectious. She burns so bright in the space around her, I can't help but laugh.

When she finishes her breakfast, she starts rip-roaring around the house, bopping to the tunes in the movie. It's fascinating to watch her change from the sleepy girl I carried down the stairs to the rambunctious firefly flitting around the house.

Three invented games in, and I've lost track of time.

I'm caught completely off guard when my mom's voice floats through the front door.

Savie beams. "Granny B!"

The pink astronaut helmet covering her curly head wobbles precariously as she tows my mom over.

"Time for me to go, little one," I say gently.

Her knowing eyes are watching me as my mom lowers herself to the floor, where we've set up the tiny purple tea set. Savie doesn't want me to leave. Her bottom lip starts to tremble, and her eyes flick to mine, pleading.

I don't want to leave either.

But I force a smile, kiss the top of her head, and let my mom shoo me out the door as she does her best to distract Savie with promises of Trixi makeovers.

Physical therapy drags. My body is going through the motions, but my mind is somewhere else. Somewhere pink and plastic and filled with syrup and tiny hands tugging on mine.

I'm faster, more focused. And it's not the shoulder that's pushing me to move harder, as much as it should be. It's a deeper feeling. A pull I can't shake.

Bernadette, my least favorite PT and unofficial drill sergeant, catches me as I grab my bag to leave.

"What's up, Bernadette? I've got to get back to my house. I'm kind of in a hurry here." My knee bounces, restless. I can't sit still. "Really. I have people waiting on me."

She just watches me for a beat. With her too-patient stare that means she's noticed something about me. "Your shoulder seems better today. Not as fatigued. I thought I'd noticed earlier in the week, but now I'm sure of it. Would these people waiting on you have anything to do with it?"

"I don't know... probably. I've been watching my friend's daughter while I'm in town until a daycare spot opens for her," I say a little defensively. "So it's keeping me busy, but I'm still working on all the exercises you want me to do at home, and you can tell Coach that I'm still keeping the rest of me in shape as well."

"Mmm."

I *hate* that sound.

"Babysitting?" she asks, finally.

"Yeah, I just said that," I remind her. "A friend's daughter. Just until she can get into daycare."

"Well, it's working. And not just physically." She leans forward, her elbows on her knees, and lets out a weary sigh. "Chris, most top-tier athletes are hard to work with. Most of you are obsessed with control. Pushing yourselves to get back to the game. But you might be the worst."

I frown.

"What do you mean?" Irritation layers over the anxiety. My eyes dart over to the clock on the wall as the minutes continue to wither away. "I work my ass off."

"Well, yes, you do. But what I mean is you don't look like a man drowning in pressure for the first time since we met. She's forcing you to slow down. And frankly, you needed that."

She runs her hand across the wrinkled skin around her eyes. "But you were working too hard. You were going to set yourself back if you had kept this up. I told you that already. Your injury needs rehabbing, yes. But it also needs rest. So, I'm glad you are babysitting this little girl. That's all I'm saying. It is not a judgment, which is what I can tell by your face that you think this is."

I bristle. But not because she's wrong. And that's what worries me.

The churning of my stomach starts to ease the closer I get to home, finally disappearing when I walk back into Tiffany's house. By the time I'm through the door, Savie's already running toward me.

And I drop my bag right there in the entryway and catch her, lifting her high above my head. Her laughter spills out of her like sunshine spills over the horizon at daybreak. It's a wild joy that overtakes everything that it touches.

"Missed you, Chis!" she exclaims, wrapping her arms around my neck.

I press my face into her mess of curls and breathe in her sweet scent still tinged with syrup. I don't even realize how tightly I'm holding her until my mom gently clears her throat and gives me a soft smile.

After Mom leaves, it's just the two of us — Savie and me. We eat the lunch Savie made with my mom and spend the rest of the afternoon playing, drawing, and just letting our imaginations run wild.

And somewhere in the middle of coloring outside the lines and naming her favorite stuffies, a fullness settles in my chest. I don't know what to call it. This feeling. But I know I don't want it to end.

I have to accept I'm falling for both of them. For a life, I never thought I could want.

It's barely been a week, and I can't imagine my life without this.

Shortly after five, I settle Savie in front of the TV and head to the kitchen to cook dinner. Stirring the pot on the stove, I let the scent of garlic and tomato fill the kitchen. It's peaceful in that quiet, contented way that sneaks up on you.

I'm startled when Tiffany's voice comes from behind me.

"Mmm," Tiffany hums, her voice like velvet. "Smells good."

I turn just as she brushes past me with an absent-minded hand trailing across my lower back. It's nothing intentional, nothing bold. But it sends a surge of heat straight through me, sharp and warm. She crosses to peek into the living room at Savie, but I'm stuck standing there like an idiot, rooted in place by the ghost of her fingers on my spine.

All week, she keeps touching me like it's nothing, but every time she does, it wrecks me. It pulls at the core of me.

And some very inconvenient parts of me take notice.

I clear my throat, trying to sound casual, even though I've been burned, set on fire by her presence. "Should be done any minute, and I'll be out of your hair."

But instead of moving away. Instead of checking in with Savie or Trixi, who are lying in the other room. Instead of doing anything else, she leans over my arm to smell the food I'm cooking. Her breast presses softly against my skin as she rolls onto her toes to peek at the food.

She lets out a quiet sound of approval. It's barely more than a breath, and I swear my knees go weak and my cock twitches in my pants. The throaty sound sends desire prowling through me. I can't remember the last time someone's presence made a kitchen this hot.

"You don't have to leave," she whispers. Not quite teasing, not quite serious, but it's enough to make me forget how to breathe. "You've taken such good care of us this week."

She's close when I glance at her. Her eyes lift to mine, and there is a softness to them. They pull me in, and there's something there I haven't let myself hope for.

An invitation.

God, she's so beautiful.

Even more so like this. Worn out from the week, hair falling loosely over her shoulders, makeup faint and faded.

Her presence pulls at something in me that isn't just lust. It deepens the space she's carved in my life without even trying.

My heart stumbles into a faster rhythm. My hands flex at my sides. I lean in, just a little. Not enough to cross the line, but enough to blur it.

She doesn't move away.

Her voice is softer this time. It's a secret meant only for me. "Stay."

The air between us hums. Her lips part slightly, and my name is a whisper off them. My fingers twitch, ready to close the distance. I'm about to answer. About to do something I'll either regret or remember forever, when the timer blares behind us, and we both flinch back like teenagers caught doing something they shouldn't.

Savie barrels into the room at full speed. "Dinner?"

"Yeah," I say, forcing a strained smile. "Why don't you and your mommy go wash your hands? I'll have it on the table by the time you're done."

Tiffany lifts Savie into her arms, casting one last lingering glance at me over her shoulder. I don't know what's written on my face, but the look she gives me in return sends heat teetering through me.

I have to adjust myself before I can move away from the stove. My mind plays every disgusting image I can conjure to convince my cock to settle down.

Tension buzzes under my skin as I plate the food in silence, grabbing every ounce of my attention away from the task I'm trying to perform.

I'm just putting away leftovers for the girls when they come back down the stairs.

Tiffany has changed.

The dress she wore to work is nowhere to be seen, but this dressed-down version is my new favorite. The sway of her chest against the soft, threadbare blue t-shirt that hangs off her shoulder catches my eye. And flowy linen pants that barely hide the shape of her figure have my fingers itching to wrap around her waist and pull her into my body. To feel her warmth against my own.

It's not flashy. It's not intentional. But it's devastating.

My throat tightens. I swallow hard and turn toward the sink, trying to look busy, trying to hide the way my cock begins to press against the zipper of my jeans again. All my effort before they went upstairs is straight out the window.

"Okay, ladies, enjoy your dinner, and I will see you both on Monday," I say too fast, my voice mimicking a 12-year-old boy going through puberty, high and cracking, as I stumble over the words.

Tiffany tilts her head at me. She doesn't say anything, but the smirk on her lips tells me she sees more than I'd like to.

"I'll let myself out," I add. "Just lock the door when you're done."

I make it out the door with a muttered goodbye and a strained smile. My steps are uneven as I cross the lawn, every nerve in my body still tuned to her voice, her scent, the ghost of her on my arm.

By the time I reach my parents' house, I'm breathing like I've run a marathon, and I have to adjust myself in my jeans before I make an inappropriate entrance.

I bolt upstairs, close the bathroom door behind me, and turn the shower on.

I look in the mirror, bracing both hands on the edge of the sink.

I am untethered and also more grounded than I've ever been before.

Steam fogs the mirror, but my reflection already told me the truth.

I'm in trouble.

I step away from my steamy reflection, my hand reaching out to palm my throbbing cock behind my jeans as my mind flashes back to the way Tiffany's eyes looked as she was pressed against me.

I try to quiet my groan as my head tips back. I undress as I let my mind play back the many versions of Tiffany I've seen this week. By the time I step into the shower, my dick is swollen with desire for the curly-headed brunette.

The water runs over my sensitized skin as I lean my forehead against the cool tile with an arm braced over my head. My other hand wraps tightly around the base that's throbbing with need, squeezing. My eyelids crash together.

I replay Tiffany walking toward me in just her threadbare t-shirt, but in my mind, her hard nipples are peaked against the thin fabric, and a pair of pale pink panties are the only thing hiding her from my view.

I grip myself tighter, my hand slides over my cock as the Tiffany in my mind lifts her shirt over her head, and her petal pink nipples tighten under my gaze.

"Tiffany." I groan lowly into the steam around me as she drops to her knees, her panties exposing her arousal as it pools against the fabric between her toned thighs.

I don't try to fight it. I let myself fall fully into the fantasy of her body as I work myself closer to release.

"Chris, please," she begs so beautifully, her fingers gripping my legs as she shuffles closer. *"Please, please, can I?"*

Her hands glide gently up toward my hips before her nails drag back down with the touch of pain. I hiss out a breath.

"Can you what, baby girl?" I grip her chin and tilt her eyes to mine, my thumb resting against her pink champagne lips. She's everything I could ever want.

Her tongue darts out to taste my thumb. *"Can I put my lips on you? Suck you deep into the warm, wet heat of my mouth and let you fuck it? Can I taste your cock until your come pours down my throat?"*

I groan, something like agreement falling from lips that are unable to form any words. My hand slips to the back of her head, gently gathering her hair into my fist. Her tongue darts out to lick at the bead of precum resting on the tip.

One of her hands grips the base of me while her other hand reaches out to squeeze my ass, drawing me closer to her.

I'm close, and she's barely touching me. It takes everything in me to hold off my release when she sucks me into her mouth, so deep I feel the back of her throat while she gags around me.

Another groan falls from me. I'm overwhelmed with the sight of her on her knees, my cock buried so deep within her mouth. With the feeling of her tongue as it runs along the underside of me every time I pull back enough for her to breathe.

"Play with yourself, baby girl," I grunt as the vibrations of her moans hit me, making my knees quake. *"Touch that sweet pussy, and don't stop until I tell you to."*

Her hand leaves my ass to drop into her panties. The outline of her fingers is barely visible as they glide over her clit, and she sucks harder. *"Oh, baby girl, that's right."*

Her moans have my hips starting to move in time with her mouth, and my fist pulls harder on her hair.

"Faster, please. Faster." I let my head hang so I can look at where her fingers are dancing. Around and around before her hand dips farther into her panties. Fingers pressing into her perfect pussy.

A long moan flies from my throat as I watch her come on her own hand. My release is ripped from my cock by her greedy mouth.

My eyes clench closed, fighting the stars dancing in my vision.

I drop down to my knees and lift my hands toward her face, cupping her cheeks before I open my eyes.

The steam of my shower greets me when my eyes flash open. I look around, disoriented for a moment before I look down at my cock, still jerking against my thigh.

"Shit," I murmur. I push back to my feet, and satisfied lethargy settles over me.

A knock on the door makes me jump. "If you're done beating your meat," Jake calls through the door, his voice is way too cheerful. "Mom is about to serve dinner, and I don't want a cold meal because her baby boy is showering."

I stare at the water still running over my chest, his voice dragging me back to earth like a slap. I'd just been standing here, lost in a fantasy I shouldn't be having. Not about just some nameless face.

Definitely not about *Tiffany* and the woman she's grown into who keeps looking at me like she's not sure if she wants me to stay or leave.

I should feel guilty.

I should be ashamed of myself.

But I'm not.

Because nothing about this feels wrong. Not the way she touched me earlier. Not the way her voice went soft when she asked me to stay. Not the way she keeps letting me in. Into her home, her life, her daughter's world.

If all I get are these brief quiet moments, fragments of what we could be. I'll keep them - keep her - safe in my mind.

I let out a short, bitter laugh and finally start washing myself off, scrubbing away the evidence of my release.

"Yeah, yeah." I call back through the door. "I'll be out in a minute."

Chapter 17

Tiffany

THE FIRST COUPLE OF weeks at work pass far faster than I expect them to, the heat of summer fully taking over Port Arbor. Every day except Tuesdays, I come home to a clean house, dinner warm on the stove, and Chris and Savie dancing in the kitchen or curled under blankets watching a movie. On the rare days he stays to eat, he hurries out afterward like he's afraid of what might happen if he lingers too long.

Tuesdays are Brenda and Mark's days. Their warmth and laughter fill the house, along with toys I didn't buy and food I didn't cook, despite my assurances that they don't need to spend their money on us.

I know they mean well, but it makes me nervous how natural all this is. How easily Savie has fit into their world. How much I *want* to fit too.

Three weeks into this unconventional arrangement, before they leave for the day, Savie and I are invited to a barbecue with their family on the weekend as if it's already assumed we'll be there. Part of the family. All four of their boys are in town again, and she wants us to join.

I had said yes, but standing in front of the mirror with my hair half-straightened and my heart pounding, I wonder if this is a mistake. What if this makes it harder? What if Savie doesn't want to leave?

What if *I* don't?

I stare at my reflection, brushing concealer under tired eyes. The nightmares have gotten worse the longer we are here. They're relentless, digging up buried trauma like it's owed something from me.

I'm exhausted.

But I can't talk about it. I *won't* talk about it.

Some truths are best left locked away, far from where they can hurt anyone else.

The scars I've hidden under clothes tell enough stories.

And I don't need pity.

I just need to survive.

"We go see Granny B and Pawpaw now?" Savie asks from around the bathroom corner, giggling just before the little whirlwind crashes into my legs.

"Almost. You ready?" I look down at where she's plastered to my leg. She nods, hopping on her little toes.

My arms open wide to catch her as she launches herself at me. I hold her tight, breathing her in and swaying for a moment. She smells like childhood and syrup, and she radiates joy.

Once she's dressed, we stop in the bathroom, and I pull the side of her hair out of her face with a barrette. The same one that had been in Chris's hair the first time I had let him watch her. And the memory brings a smile to my face.

I'm sitting near the door, about to slide on my sandals, when a knock sounds.

"Chis!" Savie cries out as she darts towards the door.

"Wait, wait—" I laugh, catching her before she can body-slam the cold metal.

I open it, and he's standing right there.

Despite myself, my body's reaction to him is immediate. My thighs clench, and heat settles low in my belly.

It puts me a little off kilter.

His hair is wet and curling slightly at the ends of the un-styled length on top of his head. A grin pulls at his full lips, and his eyes are filled with laughter as he greets us.

"Hey, ladies." He's wearing a T-shirt that does criminal things to my ability to speak. It clings in all the right places, and I suddenly forget how to breathe, much less respond. "You ready?"

Savie's clapping hands are loud near my ears, snapping me out of my stupor. "Oh, um, yeah. I just need to put our shoes on, and we're ready to go."

"I'll help my little one so you can do yours," he offers.

Savie leaps into his arms like she was waiting for the invitation.

She chatters away as he kneels in front of her and helps her into her shoes.

It's so easy to picture this happening every day. With the way he cares for her - for us - he could slot himself into this role and neither one of us would be worse off for it.

It terrifies me how naturally he takes to it.

I force myself to break the moment, shooing her out of the room to go grab the two toys we'd agreed she could bring.

He stands, muscles stretching under his shirt as he rises. He steps toward me and lifts a hand to brush hair from my face. I flinch, but his fingers are gentle.

My breath catches, and my heart thuds in my chest when he takes another step closer. Any closer and his body would brush against mine.

"Chris?" My eyes dart back and forth between his. My voice unsteady.

"Shh, darling," he whispers, the heat of his breath washes over my cheek. "Just let me look at you."

His thumb rests lightly on my lower lip, and I can't stop the way my tongue flicks out in reflex. His thumb drags my lip down as he groans, low and thrilling.

His fingers trail down my throat, barely grazing my skin, leaving goosebumps in their wake.

"Beautiful Mama," he whispers.

My reply is embarrassingly breathy. "You don't look so bad yourself, Chris."

The look in his eyes stops me cold. It's hot, intense, and far too knowing. It steals the words from my tongue.

My breath hitches, and my heart races, and all I want to do is step back. But before I can decide what to say, I'm cut off by Savie crashing into my legs again.

The spell breaks, and I reach out, smoothing her hair, swallowing hard. "Ready, Savie?"

"Yeah!" She hands me her toys and lifts her arms toward Chris. "Chis, up!"

His laugh is warm and easy as he lifts her again. "Okay, little one. Let's roll out."

He places a guiding hand on my lower back. Not possessive. But not casual either. It's a touch meant to leave an imprint. It's a whisper of promise, of possibility, of things neither of us have spoken out loud.

His thumb draws lazy circles into the fabric of my dress as we walk, each one sending a new wave of goosebumps across my skin. He moves us toward the gate to the yard, and the voices of familiar men, most likely a brother or two, rumble in the backyard.

My name is shouted as we round the corner into the yard, and I look up into the blue eyes of Chris's oldest brother, Marcus Jr.

"Junior!" I slip away from Chris's heat and into the open arms of the broad man in front of me. Junior, the most polished of the Bartkowski brothers, inherited their father's thick, dark brown hair, which he wears in a textured taper cut with not a strand out of place. His blue eyes are sharp, calculating, but not unkind, just observant. He's tall and broad, like all the Bartkowski men. He's leaner than Chris but still muscular.

He's just as gorgeous as all of his brothers.

He wraps me in a firm hug. "I'm sorry to hear about your dad. If there is anything we can do."

"I'm sure you'll know before I can ask." I grin, and he winks, handing me off to Chris, who's just reached us. "This is my daughter, Savannah. Savie, this is Chris's brother, Junior. Just like how Uncle Jason is Mommy's brother."

Savie tucks herself tighter to Chris's chest, thumb hovering at her mouth as her eyes sweep the backyard.

I'm about to try and coax her out when a wall of muscle slams into my back and wraps around my waist.

"Oof!" Savie's eyes pop open wide. Chris's grin confirms it. Charlie Bartkowski, the wild one. "Charlie!"

The tallest of the Bartkowski clan spins me into his chest, rocking us with a laugh. He pulls back to look me over. His kind eyes are amused.

"Tiffany, look at you! All growed up." His gaze cuts over to his brother, who still stands beside us with my wide-eyed daughter. "And with a baby."

"Yeah." My eyes flick to Savie, still tucked into Chris's neck. "She's the best thing that ever happened to me."

Charlie grins and scoops me back up into those brawny arms, spinning me in a circle. "Charlie!"

He laughs into my hair. The second born of the Bartkoski clan has his mother's coloring, dirty blond hair shaved short from his years in the military, but with his father's hazel eyes.

He lifts his hand to razz my hair, and I duck out of his grasp. "Oh no, Charlie! Absolutely not my hair!"

Laughing, he pulls me in for one more hug before finally letting me go.

When I finally settle back into Chris's side, I turn to scan the yard and freeze.

Quiet blue eyes meet mine.

It's Jake.

My brother's best friend. He doesn't rise from his seat across the yard, which is no surprise. He's the quietest and most serious of the bunch. He never really liked me much.

How he and Jason became friends is beyond me.

"Hey, Jake." I wave and smile.

He lifts a hand in return, lips twitching into a faint smile before he glances back at his phone, long blond hair slipping from his bun and into his face.

The sliding door opens, and the whole crowd turns to look. Brenda stands in the doorway. The woman who had birthed these four gorgeous men, all of whom tower over her petite frame. She can't be much taller than I am, and she's aged beautifully.

Her once-bright blonde hair has faded to a soft, silvery gold. Her blue eyes are still vivid, but now they are framed by smile lines earned through years of laughter.

She's a little sun-kissed, with soft hands, a round face, and an easy, open expression, which she turns on us.

The quiet is broken as Savie squirms out of Chris's arms, determined. He reluctantly sets her on her feet so she can run across the yard and launch into Brenda's arms.

I catch the concern etched into Chris's face and instinctively move closer. Close enough for his hand to find the small of my back, and I shiver with the light pressure.

The way Chris holds me is too easy. Too natural. Like it means something and nothing all at once. And the worst part about it is I want it to keep happening.

But it must be a habit, a reflex, something learned by watching his parents and done without a thought. It has to be nothing, even if it's a glimpse at something I don't want to move away from.

We all settle into the folding tables that are at the end of the picnic table in the yard, and Charlie sinks into a chair across from Chris and me, his smirk already forming.

"So, Tiff," he says, mischief in his eyes. "Has the hockey hunk told you about his new career ambitions?"

"Oh?" I raise a brow, playing along. Charlie is the most fun in the group. "Let me guess... baking? Or wait, painting?"

Charlie shakes his head. "Nope."

"Nannying!" He howls with laughter. "That's right! Christopher Bartkowski—future Hockey Hall of Famer, resident tough guy. He volunteered as tribute to babysit a four-year-old like it was a casual weekend hike. Full-on Mr. Mom situation."

Chris groans in good humor before correcting him. "Charlie, she's actually three years old."

"Straight-up told the whole family over a Sunday dinner." Charlie barrels on, ignoring Chris. Pausing every few words to try to contain his laughter that's threatening to spill out. "Mom went full protective grandma. And Junior? You'd think Chris announced he was opening a yoga studio in Bali. Dad? Shockingly chill."

From down the table, Brenda calls out. "It's not that I didn't support it." Her embarrassed flush is bright. "I just wanted him to have a plan. A child isn't a post-game interview that you can breeze on past if you don't feel like talking!"

Tiny fingers grab my arm. When I turn to look at Savie, her sticky fingers aren't just gripping me; they are also holding on to Chris.

"Chis, can we play?"

Charlie gasps dramatically, but there's a longing in his eyes. "Oh, it's official. I'm printing business cards: Christopher Bartkowski—Defender of Pucks, Pourer of Apple Juice, Wielder of Baby Wipes."

Everyone laughs.

It takes some time, but eventually, Savie warms to Chris's brothers. I sit and watch as she wraps all of the Bartkowski clan around her little fingers. Charlie even gets on his hands and knees to play pony for her after dinner is over.

All night, every time Chris is near, his hands find their way onto my body. The touches aren't intimate or inappropriate, but the reaction is the same as if they were. Lighting me on fire, the heat of his fingers trailing outside of prying eyes.

Every touch sparks memories of the casual touches between us over the last few weeks. The heat, the lingering warmth, the way my body reacts before my mind can catch up.

As the barbecue starts to wind down and the evening follows the sunset, the heat we've been banking all week turns to a simmer as Chris presses into my back. I try to ignore it as Savie yawns in my arms, whining softly for him to hold her.

He looks around, catching what I've already seen. The rest of his family is giving me, well, us, a bit of privacy to deal with my whiny child.

Chris shifts closer until his thighs loosely bracket mine as he sits straddling the bench of the picnic table. He reaches out and lifts Savie into his strong arms, tucking her against his broad chest. The way they both sigh says everything.

They are content with each other.

I lift my phone to capture the moment from over my shoulder, hoping to catch them unaware.

But before I can take the picture, his hand snakes out, sliding around my waist and pulling me against the free side of his chest. Savie pats my head before drooping back against Chris.

My heart begins to hammer, skipping erratically.

He leans closer.

"Want you in that picture too, darling," he murmurs into my neck, breath hot against my skin.

I raise my phone again, angling for the shot. My eyes are fixed on the camera as I try to find an angle that gets us all in. Just as I press the button, Chris's hand slithers lower, resting above my pelvis, fingers close enough to brush over my pussy if they inched down slightly. His eyes meet mine, honey gold and emerald green, flecked with darker brown.

The world slows around us.

His eyes drop to my lips before meeting mine again. "I think you got it, baby girl. Time to get our little one to bed."

There's a strange quiet in me, like the storm that's been raging has finally lost strength, if only for a moment, if only because of this man. I nod, speechless. And for the first time, I don't worry about what this means for the future. Because he cradles Savie like she's his whole world and holds me like he's trying to be a part of mine.

I pull away from his arms and look at the photo on my phone. The heat in his eyes as they stare at me has wetness pooling in my panties.

The casual competence in his hand, resting on Savie's back as her body goes slack with sleep, has me longing for something I can't let happen.

I pull away, slipping out from between his thighs.

I'm thankful no one witnessed our little moment.

But it still slithers all the way down my body.

When I finish saying my goodbyes, Chris is by the gate, Savie curled sleepily against his chest.

I reach for her, but he turns slightly, blocking me with his broad frame and nodding toward the gate in silence.

His hand drops to the small of my back and ushers me forward. "Chris?"

"I got her. I'm not going to let you walk home alone in the dark." His voice is quiet but firm. The hand on Savie moves higher, fully covering her back. "It's not safe."

I raise a brow, half smiling as I lean into him. "It's literally next door, Chris. We'd be fine."

"Doesn't matter." He leans to growl in my ear. The low rasp in his words sends a pulse of heat down my spine, drawing shivers across my skin as we approach the front door. "Open the door, baby girl. Let's get her in bed."

I do as I'm told.

The door swings open, and I've barely greeted Trixi, before Chris is up the stairs.

He's sweet.

Too sweet.

And I'm pliant and helpless against it tonight.

By the time I enter Savie's room, he has her in her jammies and is tucking her stuffy under her arm. He presses a kiss to her forehead before he turns toward me, expression unreadable.

I move closer and press a kiss to the crown of her head. My body brushes against Chris, who is still perched on the edge of her bed. Warmth skirts across my body from where we touch.

I nod to the door, grabbing his hand and towing him behind me, my fingers lacing through his. There's a tremble between our hands as he follows me. Maybe it's just me, or maybe both of us are nervous. His hand swallows mine, and his thumb runs over my skin.

When we reach the kitchen, I back away to give myself some space to think.

He exhales sharply, raking a hand through his hair, and pins me with a look that strips me bare. "I don't know how you do this."

I blink. "Do what?"

"Ever let her go." He leans back against the counter and crosses his arms over his wide, muscular chest. His voice is rough and low. "It feels wrong. More wrong every time I leave her."

My breath hitches.

I glance toward the stairs. "That's how being a parent feels. Like your heart lives outside your body."

He moves without a sound. One moment he's across the room, the next he's pulling me tightly to his chest and tucking my head against him as he wraps his arms around my body.

"Chris?"

"Shh." His hand cups the back of my head, gentle at first, before he grips the hair at the nape of my neck, tugging.

He pulls softly until my eyes meet his, leaning closer, resting his forehead against mine. His other hand lands low on my back, fingers clutching the fabric of my dress just above my ass.

We begin to sway.

Now I'm sure the trembling is coming from me as I shiver each time his hand flexes against me.

His voice is barely above a whisper. "Just don't say anything. Just be here with me. For just a minute."

I can't breathe. Or maybe I'm breathing too much. Our noses brush together, and still he doesn't move.

He just stares at me in a way that should make me uncomfortable. In a way that would make me uncomfortable if it were anyone else.

The heat in his eyes turns molten. Like embers drifting from a burning tree in a forest fire, reaching out to pull other trees into the flame. A slow burn finally catches flame, licking at the edges of my restraint.

"You are the strongest woman I've ever known," he murmurs, voice like gravel and smoke as it rakes down my spine.

I try to shake my head as he breathes the words into my skin, but his hand tightens in my hair.

"No, you are," he growls. "You don't get to argue with me on this. You've raised this wonderful child all on your own. I'm in awe."

His hand shifts to cradle my cheek.

"I'm going to kiss you," he says.

He's not asking. He's telling. Even as he waits for me to consent.

The way he watches me, the heat simmering behind those gold-and-green eyes. It's not just desire. It's worship. Need rages within him, and a shiver of answering desire rolls through me as I lean closer.

My lips part as I tilt my head toward him.

"Okay," I whisper, the word ghosting against his lips.

His kiss is gentle at first, just a tease of his mouth against mine.

He pulls back just enough to look at me, and something snaps.

He sweeps back in, devouring me, claiming me, deep and demanding. His tongue strokes the seam of my lips to beg for entrance.

I open for him, tasting him, wrapping my arms around him to grab the shirt at his waist because he's the only thing keeping me upright.

He walks me backwards until the edge of the counter presses into my back, his body fitting against mine like we were made for this.

And in this moment, with his hands cradling my face, his mouth claiming mine, I forget to be afraid of wanting more.

I curl my body deeper into his. There's no space between us.

He runs his hand up my side to gently brush against my hardened nipples. The fabric under his fingers is grating against my skin, sending tingles straight to my core.

He breaks our kiss to trace his lips down my neck, the hand still at my jaw tips my head to the side, making more room for him to lick and nip at my skin.

"Chris, please," I beg.

Beg him to stop. Beg him to keep going. Beg him to tell me what I need because I'm not sure anymore.

He groans, and the vibration ignites heat low in my belly. My thighs clench tight, arousal flooding my already wet panties. He presses his forehead to mine for a moment, his chest heaving as he drags air into his lungs.

"Baby girl, you don't know what you are begging for." He grips my waist, stopping me from grinding against him, before his fingers dance my dress up my legs.

"Please. Chris, more." The weight of his cock presses into the softness of my stomach. He's thick and long and hard as he flexes into me a second time.

I run my hands under his shirt and rake my nails across his back.

He hisses with the bite of pain.

His hands slide down my legs, lifting me just enough to set my bare thighs on the cold counter. I squeak as my head drops back against the cabinets, my thighs widening to make more room for him to settle against me.

Tugging at him, I wrap my legs around his hips before I pull his lips back to mine.

I ache for him as I rock into his body, his mouth capturing my moans. His hands settle on my hips, clenching, stopping my movement before his kiss turns gentle.

Heartbreakingly tender.

He pulls back slightly despite my protest, our chests rising and falling in sync. His hips are still pressed firmly against me. My own held in check only by the strength of his hands.

His eyes search mine, raw and conflicted. But he presses one more fleeting kiss to my lips before he rests his head against mine. "Every time I see you I'm in awe of you. I crave you in a way I shouldn't, but still can't seem to stop. I know we shouldn't. Everyone agrees we shouldn't."

"What about me? What about what I want?" I whisper, brushing a kiss across his lips, my words melting into his mouth.

The anxiety that's gripped me since he started watching Savie slips away.

"And what do you want, baby girl?" His lips graze mine as he speaks.

"I, um, what if we jus– " I pause, letting my eyes dart between his. "Just do this, for the next however many months we have left? No pressure. Just...casual."

He exhales roughly, his breath ghosting over my heated skin. "I don't know, darling. I don't know if I can do casual with you. You're my forever type of girl."

I cradle his cheek, pulling back just enough to take him in. His lips are kiss-swollen, scruff shadowing his jaw – and his eyes. God, his eyes burn with something overwhelming.

They're brilliant under the heat of our desire.

I kiss him again. Slower this time. "Just think about it."

He nods, brushing one last kiss to my lips before helping me off the counter. He grabs my hand, walking us to the door.

"Send me that picture from tonight," he murmurs, fingers lingering before letting go.

He caresses my cheek before he leaves, and our gazes hold for a moment. The door closes behind him. I lock it, pressing my back to the cool steel. My thighs clench against the ache he left behind, but I'm oddly grateful he stopped. The weight of reality returns, heavy and familiar.

What was I thinking? Offering that to him?

My phone pings. I grab it, flicking off lights as I head upstairs. I finally open my messages as I enter my room.

It's a photo of us from another angle. My arm outstretched to take our selfie, his arm curled around me protectively. Savie's head is barely peeking out from his shoulder.

But what freezes me is the way I'm looking at him. Because it's already more than casual.

And I just don't know what to do with that.

I attach the picture and find myself smiling. We look like a family.

My heart kicks into a sprint, caught somewhere between the heat of wanting him and the icy bite of panic slipping around the edges. I have no idea what I'm doing with him.

My gut tells me to chase the feelings, but my brain? She's telling me to run as hard and as fast in the other direction unless I want to become my mother. Unless I want to be a mom who thinks only of herself first.

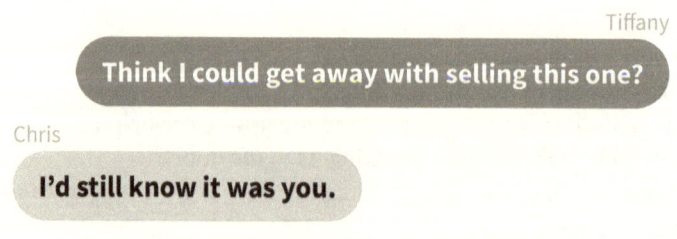

Chris

You're beautiful.

Tiffany

You make me feel that way.

Chapter 18

Chris

MONDAY, FOLLOWING THE BARBECUE, I knock on Tiffany's door, expecting the usual, Tiffany looking powerful in her pant suit and pumps or a dress that cuts strong lines, but the sight that greets me nearly knocks me off my feet.

She opens the door in a pale green dress that hugs every curve of her body and leaves little to the imagination.

It's a dress meant to convince a man to sin. She looks shy, eyes flicking to mine before darting away, her cheeks warm with a soft pink.

Her thick curly hair has been straightened but not tamed. The silky strands I had my hands buried in last night tumble haphazardly over her shoulders and down her back. When she turns away to let me in, the ends sway along her lower back.

She is so beautiful, my fingers ache to reach out and touch her. To kiss her senseless and make her mine.

She turns to look at me when the quiet stretches out for too long. "Chris?"

"Yes. Sorry." I scrub my hand over my face. Her lips quirk in the ghost of a smile, but it's gone as fast as it came. "Everything okay, darling?"

She tosses a jacket over that sin of a dress, and I huff out a breath in relief.

I have no right to the possessiveness that I feel. But I still want to rip the dress off her so no one else can see her in it. No one but me. At least the jacket is shapeless enough to conceal some of her generous curves.

"Mhmm," she hums as she hurries into a pair of pale brown pumps that flex her toned legs like she's trying to escape me. Escape a conversation that hangs unspoken between us. "I'm fine."

Her movements are jerky as she collects the rest of her things.

"I'll call the daycares again and see if there has been any movement. Hopefully, we will be out of your hair before long." Her eyes look lost when she finally turns them back on me.

"Hey," I say, reaching out, catching her hand, and pulling her into my chest. "You're not in my hair. Don't worry about us. Savie and I are having so much fun. Promise."

"Right." Her fingers clench my shirt, and she stares blankly at my chest.

I lift her chin and press a gentle kiss to her lips.

Her eyes dance over my face as she pulls away, a hand lingering, tracing down my arm. Her breath hitches, and she turns and walks out the door.

The house is quiet as I look around, taking in the space. The gently rising sun cascades across the walls as I walk into the living room, illuminating all the memories hanging up. There's something eerie about them when I look closely enough, so I try not to do that.

Savie is asleep in a mountain of blankets and pillows, curled up like a kitten as the TV plays in the background.

Trixi, who lies protectively beside her, raises her head, her chocolate stare judging me before she lays her head back on Savie's leg.

"Yeah, girl. I'm just as gone for them as you are. But keep that between us, okay?" The slight wag of her tail softens her judgment.

I watch the gentle rise and fall of Savie's chest as she dreams on, studying her little face, so much like my memories of Tiffany as a child. They look so similar, and yet something about them is different. Not in the curve of her nose or shape of her jaw—something beneath her appearance. And the difference sends a quiet chill through me, one I can't name.

I reach down to pat Trixi on the head before moving to make breakfast for Savie.

The first pancake is barely off the pan when a quiet voice calls out to me. "Hey, little one! Good morning!" I greet her cheerfully.

"Chis. Where mommy?" I turn at the quiver in her voice. She's standing at the edge of the room, rubbing her eyes.

Tears begin to pool in her lashes, and her hand rests on Trixi's back, clutching at her fur. "Need Mommy."

"Oh, sweet girl. Mommy went to work." I say gently, peeking at the new pancake to make sure it isn't burning before refocusing on her. "You get to hang out with me today, and I'm making pancakes!"

She shuffles over and wraps her arms around my leg, burying her face in my jeans.

"Want mommy," she whimpers, and the sound breaks my heart.

I gather her into my arms only to find myself at a disadvantage with the stove and a pancake almost burning.

I take hold of the skillet, pull out my best impression of someone who can actually cook, and try to flip the pancake one-handed, but it lands halfway off the pan, splattering. The mess finally earns me a giggle from the little girl in my arms, who's resting her cheek on my shoulder.

"Well, okay, not my finest moment." I bounce her gently as I press my lips to her forehead. "Why don't I put you in your seat and finish these for you. Hmm?"

She sniffles again as I set her in her chair.

We move through the motions of the morning, a few moments away from tears at any given time. We make it through breakfast, but she barely eats. A quick game of tag ends with her arms wrapped around my neck again and tears threatening to fall. Coloring only lasts minutes before she finally crumples into tears.

She's not angry, there are no tantrums, no screaming. Her sadness is quiet and unrelenting. She's unable to articulate what's bothering her. Feelings that are too big for her tiny body spill over her eyes when she's frustrated with them.

Nothing keeps the tears at bay except cuddling as we watch a movie. I hold her through most of the morning until she finally falls asleep against me, exhausted.

Just as her breathing evens out, a knock comes from the door. I move fast, heart pounding, not wanting the sound to wake her.

Mom's bright smile meets me as I swing the door open and immediately press a finger to my lips before she can voice her greeting.

"I just got her down for a nap," I whisper, stepping aside to let Mom in. "What are you doing here so early? I don't have to leave for PT for another hour or so."

Her smile softens as she slips past me, already toeing off her shoes. "Something told me you might need some reinforcements today."

I sigh, rubbing the back of my neck. "We've had a very sad morning. She's been crying on and off since she woke up. I couldn't distract her with anything. She just wants Tiffany, and I can't seem to cheer her up. She cried herself to sleep maybe ten minutes ago."

Mom's soft hands find my cheeks, warm and grounding. A quiet chuckle leaves her lips, but her eyes are full of understanding. "Oh, son, some days are just like that with little kids. I'm sure you are doing everything right, even if it doesn't feel that way."

"All she wanted to do was cuddle, which is okay, but I promised Tiffany that we would have fun and I'm failing at that spectacularly." My voice cracks a little, and I lean into her hand.

She wraps her arms around me, like she used to when I came home from school after a bad day, despite the fact I tower over her.

"Chris," she murmurs into my chest, "if I learned anything from raising you four hellions, it's the quiet days, the days they only want to cuddle, those are the days you miss the most when they are grown. So, enjoy the quiet. Let her need you."

I nod and let myself breathe in the comfort of her arms as I settle my head on her shoulder, bending almost in half just to fit. I let the silence stretch.

"I'm sure she will feel better after her nap and be back to the bright sunny girl she normally is. She is probably just cranky because she's tired. You and Charlie used to cry for me like that, and there was nothing your father could do to change your minds." Her hands run over my back for a second, holding me softly.

"I don't remember any of that," I say, standing upright again.

"Well, of course you don't." A gentle amusement lines her face. "You were just a small fry. Now look at you, all grown into a fully baked potato."

That earns a real laugh out of me.

She wanders into the kitchen like she owns the place, opening cabinets and pulling out plates, ingredients, and measuring by instinct.

"What are you doing, Ma?" I lean against the counter, watching her work.

"I'm making you two some lunch. It's tough caring for children, and this is your first time with a cranky kid." She shoos me out. "I figured I'd make it a little easier on you."

I barely register Mom moving around the kitchen, the soft clatter of pans and dishes mixing with the cartoon soundtrack.

True to Mom's prediction, it is like a light switch has been flipped, and the wild ball of energy I am used to is back.

She bounces into the kitchen like a tiny whirlwind, humming to herself, grabbing for a chicken tender before even sitting.

"Did you have good dreams, sunshine?" my mom asks, handing her a plate.

Savie nods and starts telling us about a castle made of pancakes and a dragon that talked like a cat. She talks around a mouthful of food, which should, arguably, be gross, but I find it endearing. I watch her, captivated, as she dances in her seat, swaying to a beat only she can hear.

I rush through the door less than an hour and a half later, catching Savie when she launches herself into my arms. I swing her around with a laugh, her squeals filling the room.

"Okay, munchkin," my mom says, scooping her from my arms and peppering kisses across her chubby cheeks. I'm going to head back home. You and Chris have fun the rest of the day, and it'll be you and me for a little while longer tomorrow. Sound good?"

Savie nods so hard she almost tips herself out of Mom's arms, curls bouncing wildly. "Sound good, Granny B!"

She squirms to get let down and runs back toward the living room, and I usher my mom out the door with a quick goodbye.

I follow the sounds of giggles and find her yanking her toys out of the bin while Trixi tries to lick every inch of her face. Trixi's tail wags wildly as Savie pushes her away between laughs. The toys clatter to the ancient, dingy carpet below her feet as she looks for her toy.

"What are you looking for, little one?" I ask.

She pauses, analyzing me, before turning back to the toy bin. "My make cup."

"Oh?" I grin. "Are you going to let me do your makeup this time?"

Her head snaps around, scandalized.

"No!" Her adorably chunky pointer finger is forcefully tossed in my direction. "Yous a boy! You no know make cup. Momma taughted me right."

I lift her, ignoring her squeals of protest as I tickle her belly. "Oh, she did, did she?"

Her giggles roar out, contagious and wild, laughter making her breathless. "Stop! Stop it, Chis!"

"I don't think I will." I tease, laughing as I slow my dancing fingers. "Boys can do makeup too."

"Chis," she sighs dramatically as I pull her against my chest, cuddling her to me. "I's do you make cup. You be so pretty."

"Okay, little one." I hold her tighter for a moment. "How can I say no to that?"

I sway gently, her warm weight tucked into me, curly head nodding against my neck. It feels natural, as if this is the only thing my body can do with her tucked into me.

After a minute, she squirms out of my arms and dives back into the toy chest.

By the time we are done with our makeup routines, I have four barrettes jammed in the waves of my hair and blue eyeshadow trailing over the side of my face. There is enough bright red blush over my cheeks and my left ear to make a clown jealous.

I pin her wild hair out of her eyes with her favorite-colored bows when I finally talk her into letting me try. I paint her face as lightly as I can with the vibrant playset.

Turning her around, I gather her into my arms. "Trixi, come here!"

Trixi, who has been pouting since Savie clipped a bow on her head, refuses to come to my call. "Savie, call Trixi over and give her a smooch so I can show Mommy how much fun we are having today."

"Trixi, Mere!" She calls.

The bow hangs on by mere strands of Trixi's fur when she looks over at Savie. There is heavy judgment in her glare. She reluctantly comes to us.

She can't deny Savie anything either.

I stretch my arm out and snap a picture of the three of us as I try to keep Savie from diving out of my arms. She winds herself around Trixi, clinging to her neck. I look at my phone and chuckle at the sight of my face.

My heart stutters. It's just a silly picture. But something about it. The makeup, the mess, the little girl beaming in my arms. It hits too hard and too fast, the way she has wormed her way into my heart. This little chaos gremlin has become an integral part of my day, and I no longer know how I'm going to walk away from this unscathed.

"Okay, Savie," I say, placing her on the ground before scooting backwards and pointing the phone at the two of them. "One more, just you and Trixi." She nods eagerly.

I snap the shot, immediately setting it as my phone background.

"Let me see, Chis!" I show her, and she squeals with delight, pressing the phone back into my hand. "Now, me and you!"

"Alright," I say, pulling her into my lap. She throws her arms around my neck. A big, cheeky grin plastered on her face. "Say cheese!"

"Cheese!" Her shout is loud in my ear, but I don't care. I snap the photo, and one more just as she squeezes my neck tightly, giggling uncontrollably. My heart thuds, ripping the air right out of my lungs and settling me in an unexplainable way.

"Okay, little one," I plop her on her feet and point her toward our mess. "Let's clean up the makeup and pick a different game."

She races off to toss things back into the bin, in that chaotic way only toddlers can manage. I open the best photo of her and Trixi and text it to Tiffany.

Chris

We did "Make Cup".

I tuck my phone back into my jeans and turn back to help Savie clean. But instead, her tea set is being pulled out of the rest of her toys that sit haphazardly in the chest in a way that suggests one strong breeze could topple the whole thing.

"Princess tea party?" I ask.

She turns, and it's clear she thinks I'm crazy. "Princess ASTRO-NAUT tea party."

I let out a low chuckle and bow with exaggerated flair. "My deepest apologies, Princess." I settle on the ground next to the child-sized teapot. "Are you ready for teatime?"

"Yes!" She dumps the rest of the tea set in my lap with zero ceremony before running back to grab her crowned, pink astronaut helmet.

It's smudged with fingerprints, and the plastic is dulled from use. The hours I spent hunting it down across L.A. are worth it when her joy lights up the room.

We dive in. A full tea service is turned out, complete with imaginary scones and finger sandwiches, while she gives me all the gossip. The drama between her stuffed animals and *Barbies*. It just so happens the alligator that her Uncle Jason got her when she moved home has had trouble making friends with the rest of her stuffies and she had to mediate a serious meeting between them.

I get so drawn into the stories she is making up I don't notice how late it has gotten until the door clicks shut, and the click-clack of Tiffany's heels announces her as she enters the living room.

"Oh gosh!" She laughs. I twist around and grins spreads across both our faces. "She got you again, huh?"

I nod, lips twitching as Savie sprints into her mother's arms. "Momma!"

Tiffany bends to grab Savie, her hand brushing across the untamable curls on Savie's head. She presses her nose into Savie's temple and breathes her in, her eyes closing gently for a moment. It's something I've caught myself doing too, every time she's in my arms.

"Okay, sweet girl," Tiffany murmurs. "Let's start cleaning the living room and let Chris clean his face up before he goes home."

She glances back at me, giggling as she holds out a hand. "Come on. I'll get you a makeup wipe."

I take it, thumb tracing the soft skin on the back of her hand, and follow her into the bathroom. One look at my face in the mirror and, yeah, I'm a goddamn rainbow.

"She was good today," I say, grinning as I turn my head to take in the full scope of what Savie did to my face. "She had a pretty weepy morning, though. She just wanted her Momma."

Tiffany exhales, bending over to search the drawer. The breathy sound drags my eyes to her. Her hips shift her perfect ass under the gorgeous green dress. It has my body reacting before I can stop it. My cock stirs behind my jeans, and I shift to try to hide the evidence.

"She gets that way sometimes. I'm sorry."

I must not respond fast enough because she straightens and looks at me. "Chris?"

"Yeah. Sorry." I step closer, my voice turning husky. Need pulsing through me. "I guess I got distracted."

She holds out the wipe with a knowing smirk, her body tipping toward mine. "Well, Casanova. I can't take you seriously with that makeup on your face."

I don't take it. My hands capture her waist, gently pulling her hips into mine. "Want to help me with that?"

I run my nose softly along the column of her neck. Her eyes drop closed, tilting her head slightly, a sharp breath escaping her mouth.

I let my lips gently press against her pulse, whispering. "I'd like to kiss you."

Her fingers tremble as she gently rubs the damp cloth over my face, trailing across my skin. There's wonder in her eyes as mine begin to droop. I drown in the intimacy. My hands squeeze her hips as her thumb drags over my lips.

Her fingers move to the tangles in my hair, tugging out the tiny clips Savie had decorated me with hard enough to pop my eyes open. "Ow."

"Sorry," she giggles, but continues to thread her fingers through my hair. "I figured you didn't want to leave with these."

"You'd be right. Charlie is coming over for dinner tonight. I'd never hear the end of it." I laugh.

My face is clear of the bright makeup the next time I look in the mirror. My hair is disheveled but free of the barrettes.

Her eyes are gentle on my face, and her smile soft. I pull her fully into me, fitting her body against mine, perfectly aligning.

I trap her between me and the counter behind her. "Now about that kiss."

My hands slip down her body, gently caressing as I lean into her. I draw my nose along her neck again, peppering kisses, savoring the taste of her skin. Her breath catches, and her fingers dig into my shoulders.

"Yeah," she whispers. "You definitely deserve it."

I keep going, torturously slow, until I'm gently kissing the corner of her mouth. Her arms wrap around my neck as she rolls onto her toes, aligning her body more comfortably into mine. Our lips barely brushing, suspended in the heat of almost as we breathe each other in.

Trying not to get more invested is a joke at this point – I'm already there – but I beg myself to pull away. Her offer still lingers in my mind, reminding me I'm not alone in this attraction.

"I'll see you both tomorrow." I breathe the words directly into her mouth.

I'm helpless against the way she looks tucked into me.

Diving in after the words meant to pull us apart, I kiss her. I plunder her mouth, devouring her. My kiss promises her things we're definitely not ready for.

I kiss her long enough to have her moaning softly as she gently rocks into me. Long enough, I know if I were to reach between us, I would find her wet and wanting.

When I pull away, I press one last kiss to her forehead, then head for the door with goodbyes and promises to see them tomorrow.

Charlie's grinning face greets me as he steps out of his car. Propping his elbows on the open door, laughing like a man who's going to tease me for the next decade. "Just helping a friend out, huh?"

"Yeah," I try to keep my blush in check, but I know I'm failing. My reluctance to meet his eyes is a dead giveaway. "That's all it is."

He shakes his head as he slams the door to his car, his arm swinging around my shoulder. "Might want to fix your hair, Romeo. And maybe wipe the lipstick off your face."

Chapter 19

Chris

We make it to the middle of June in a similar fashion. Savie and Tiffany, and our routine becomes something I didn't know I needed. Sometimes I'm lucky enough to coax her into a goodnight kiss at the end of the long day. Just a peck on the cheek, but it still sends me reeling.

I thought long and hard about her proposition over the weekend while she was with her friends, and I still haven't decided what I want to do.

And if what I want is the right thing to do.

The door creaks open after a quiet day with Savie, just before heels clicking on the hardwood floor at the entrance of the house rise over the movie on the TV.

When Savie catches the sound, she runs.

I stand slowly, brushing invisible lint off my jeans.

"Hey," I wave awkwardly.

Her smile is soft and tired as she cradles Savie to her chest, like she's had the most impossible day and is still somehow able to set it aside for her daughter.

In this moment, I decide. I want her.

I can do this with Tiffany.

Even if I have to lie to myself, and even if it breaks my own heart.

"Hey," she says gently.

"Um, dinner is in the oven," I nod toward the kitchen. "Should be done in about 15 minutes."

"I'll just, uh, be on my way." Glancing down, Savie is cuddled into Tiffany's chest, happy but quiet, like she had been all day.

My hand reaches out to smooth the curls at the back of Savie's head. I can't help it.

And that's when I feel it.

Tiffany's hand on my wrist freezes me.

Her teeth catch her bottom lip, pulling my eyes to them. The pink champagne color, darkened with lip stain before she left for work, makes her pouty lips look fuller than usual.

I want to kiss them.

"Stay," she breathes out. "For dinner, I mean."

"Chis has dinner with us?" Savie looks at Tiffany before turning to me.

Then both girls turn their questioning eyes on me.

I cave before I can even think better about it. "Yeah, little one. I'll stay for dinner."

Savie brightens with both of us at the table. She talks a mile a minute, telling us about her dreams, her new toy, her plans for tomorrow, her unkind thoughts on broccoli.

When dinner is finally, mercifully over, Savie's yawning. I push back my chair. "I'll clean up. You two head up."

Tiffany nods and scoops her daughter into her arms. I watch them go. Warmth and ache tangle in my chest. The low hum of voices upstairs as she tries to settle the little hellion is my background music to clean to.

It takes less than ten minutes to clear the table and wash the dishes. I'm rinsing the last plate when little feet go running to the top of the stairs and Savie calls my name.

I put the dish in the dish rack and walk over to look at her from the bottom of the stairs. "What's the matter, little one?"

"Chis read me a bedtime story? Pretty please?" She clutches a book to her chest, her feet tapping impatiently.

I can't refuse her. I take the stairs two at a time, lifting and tossing her over my shoulder like a sack of giggling potatoes. Her laughter bounces off the narrow walls of the hallway.

"Chris, don't be winding her up," Tiffany's teasing cuts through the moment.

She steps out of her room, dressed in the tiniest shorts I'd ever seen and a massive off-the-shoulder sweater that slides down one arm, exposing the soft slope of her collarbone.

I nearly groan aloud.

"Who? Me?" I swing Savie into the cradle of my arms, both of us grinning. "I'd never wind up the little monkey."

I plop Savie on the bed and tuck her in. Tiffany's eyes settle on me from where she is leaning against the door jam, arms crossed and watching. By the time I finish reading the book, little eyes are fluttering closed. I press a kiss to her forehead.

My heartbreaks again as I remind myself that I'm going to have to give this up eventually.

I force myself to my feet and turn to look at Tiffany. Her smile is gentle as she lets her arms drop to her sides.

Tiffany motions to the hallway with a tilt of her head, and I would follow the two of them anywhere at this point.

The silence thickens and hums between us as we walk down the stairs. At the front door, she turns, looking at me.

Before I can even take a breath, she is on her toes pressing a soft, lingering kiss to my cheek.

My hands fall to her waist to steady her. She's so small there. *So* right. Time stands still as she settles back on her feet. Looking uncertain in a way she hasn't since the week I started watching Savie.

Something is different today.

"Tiff?" I murmur.

Her eyes lift to mine. There's a storm behind them, quiet but dangerous.

"I don't know, Chris." Her voice trembles, and she shakes her head. "Just... Thank you. For everything."

Her eyes search mine for a moment, indecisive, before she presses up on her toes again. This time her lips meet mine. Just a brush.

A soft, gentle, and trembling touch of her lips.

Like she's waiting for me to make the next move. To decide how much farther to take this.

And I'm helpless with her in my arms.

"Tiff..." I hesitate, words slipping out, low and full of hope. "You really want to try to do this... Friends-with-benefits thing?"

I brush the hair off her face and cup her cheek, bringing her eyes back to mine.

They twinkle with some hesitant humor. "Thinking my offer?"

"Fuck, yeah." I surge forward, my hand sliding to the back of her neck.

My lips descend on hers. I kiss her like I've wanted to since the moment she let me into her world. It's messy, and hungry, and dangerous. This isn't the chaste stolen moments we've shared so far. This is claiming.

When her arms circle my neck, I take the chance to dive deeper into her, my tongue running along the seam of her lips, begging for her to open to me. Sighing in relief when she does.

I kiss her roughly, but press her gently into the wall behind her.

I groan into her mouth as her hands pull at my hair. A wildfire rolls over my body, licking up my spine. My hands run down to her legs and lift them, wrapping them around my waist. Her hips start to roll as I settle into the cradle of her thighs, grinding against my rapidly rising cock.

I've imagined this moment a thousand times, but this is better. Giving into this thing between us... It's everything.

I want to remember this forever. Every look. Every touch. I palm her ass, pulling us away from the wall and walking toward the living room.

I lower her gently onto the couch, pulling my lips away from hers with a reluctant gasp.

Our eyes meet, chests rising in tandem, raw, wild need pulses between us. The overwhelming craving should be scary, but it's just right in this moment.

If only she knew what she did to me.

What she's always done to me.

I press slow kisses down the line of her neck, over the exposed skin on her shoulder, tasting her warmth. My hands slip beneath the fabric of her sweater, finding her waist, her ribs. Anything I can reach with my wandering hands. Each touch is an attempt to etch the fire inside me into her skin.

Her head falls into the cushions, chest arching toward me, and the soft sound that leaves her lips tears through me. Her moans drown out everything else. There's only her.

I trail kisses lower, chasing each new inch of exposed skin with my mouth and hands. Her stomach shifts, muscles trembling under my lips. My hands pause at the edge of her shorts, fingers dipping just beneath the waistband.

She's not just beautiful like this. She's the girl I've always wanted, the one I should have fought for when we were younger. The one I lost because I let others' voices drown out my own.

But not this time.

This time, I'm going to be brave enough to keep going. To take as much as she will give me.

I'm going to love her until she loves me back.

I'm not sure where the thought comes from, but it feels right. It feels like that is where this is headed.

I prop my chin on her thigh, pausing, needing to look at her. Her lust-drunk eyes are heavy and golden with desire. She's stunning, her cheeks flushed, lips parted. I want her like this, with her eyes filled with desire for the rest of our days.

"Tiffany," I growl, waiting. Her eyes flutter open and meet mine. I snap the band of her shorts just enough to tease. "Can I?"

She hesitates, drawing her bottom lip between her teeth.

I press a kiss to her thigh. "We can stop this at any time. I promise."

She nods.

Gently, I ease her shorts and panties down her legs, kissing along her skin as I go, fingers sliding with lingering touches. My breath catches when I see them, the pale white lines at the tops of her thighs. Faint with age, but impossible to miss.

Scars.

My hands slow, but don't stop. Because I'm not pulling away from her. Never again. But I need a second. I need her to know I see them. That I see her.

I don't ask. I just trace a reverent line up her leg, fingertips raising goosebumps in my wake.

"Chris." My name breaks the silence like a prayer. I lift my eyes to hers, and there it is. Desire, yes, but layered beneath it is fear.

I don't say anything. I just press my lips to the scars. She shifts beneath me, her hands clenching at her sides, then slipping under the hem of her sweater like she's trying to distract me from what's in front of me.

I lean forward, pressing a tender kiss to one thigh, then the other.

Then one last one on the edge of the tattoo that peeks at me. The edge is barely noticeable from where I sit between her legs, but I see it.

She hisses from between her gritted teeth.

"Chris, please," her voice is tight and desperate.

Not just from lust, but from the weight of everything she's letting go of to be here with me.

This isn't just a moment.

It's a choice.

It's trust.

"What do you want, baby girl?" I ask, lifting her thighs to drape over my shoulder, wedging myself in closer to drag my tongue through her dripping pussy. "Do you want me to devour you? Lick you until you can't help but fall over the edge? Do you want me to press my fingers into your pretty, pink pussy so you can feel me between your thighs whenever you sit down tomorrow?"

This is no longer just about wanting her.

It's about earning her because in the span of minutes, it's become essential to me.

"Yes! Oh God." A moan tears from her throat as I run my tongue over her clit, and through her pussy. The taste of her explodes on my tongue. The musky heat driving me toward madness.

I lift my hand to cover her mouth, picking her hips off the couch and bending her so I can reach.

I back away only far enough she can hear my words without them being muffled by her arousal. "Shh, baby girl. We don't want to wake Savie before you come in my mouth."

I move back in, pressing a single finger into her as I lash at her clit. Her hips rocking against my face as she moans into my palm, her hands threading into my hair, pulling at the strands.

"Chris, faster. Please, please, please." Her words are garbled by my fingers pressing tightly against her lips.

She's the most intoxicating thing I've ever tasted. Her thighs part wider as we both work to get closer to each other. I have no free hands to steady her trembling legs as I draw slow, deliberate strokes through her swollen pussy.

She's drenched.

"Shh, baby girl. I got you." I push in a second finger and then a third quickly after, her hips rolling with desperation. Her breath hitches, and her heels dig into my back as I suck her clit into my mouth, tongue flicking along the bud.

She's so close. I can feel it in the way she clenches, her muscles straining to control her body as she jerks against me.

She whimpers helplessly against my palm as I thrust my fingers faster, my tongue matching the rhythm against her clit.

"Come for me, baby girl," I growl against her.

Her teeth bite into my hand as her pussy clamps down on my fingers. Basking in her as she comes, hips twitching with every swipe of my tongue against her heated flesh.

Reluctance presses on my chest like a weight, but I force myself to shift, my fingers slipping from the cocoon of her warmth to sit on the couch. The distance makes me ache in a way that's is becoming more familiar the longer I spend with these two.

I open my arms, and she crawls into them without hesitation, tucking her head against my chest like we've done this a hundred times.

When she shivers, I reach for the blanket draped over the back of the couch and pull it around us both, wrapping her tighter to me.

I try to ignore my cock still straining against the jeans I'm wearing, throbbing with every brush of her body, but I can't stop the way my hips flex under her when she sinks her weight fully on top of me.

We sit in the silence for a moment, letting what happened settle between us. With the sound of our harsh breathing wrapping around us.

"Chris, that was..." Her lips find the curve of my neck, the words trailing off into skin and silence.

"Baby girl, you have the most beautiful pussy I've ever seen. I'd live the rest of my days with my tongue buried inside your cunt if I could, savoring the taste of you on my lips." My breath hitches as her mouth moves again.

I catch her chin gently, pressing my lips to hers one more time, letting her taste herself on my lips.

When I pull back, she looks undone, not just from the release I gave her.

"Tiff?"

She doesn't pull away, but her voice is smaller when it comes. "Chris, my life's a mess, and your life is public in a way I don't even think I understand yet. We're insulated here. We grew up here, on this street, and everyone knew you before you got famous. Us here, we might make sense, but out there..."

Her forehead drops to my shoulder, and my hands trace over her spine, comforting her.

Or maybe myself.

"But," her voice cracks. "With you here, I feel a little less lost. Like I found my feet underwater, and I'm not going to drown."

"Darling," I murmur, pressing a kiss to her hair, holding her a little closer. "You really want to do this whole..."

I hesitate to finish the sentence.

This won't be what I want. Not with the way things stand and not with the way I feel.

Because I'll never be the same after this, and that was exactly what I had been worried about.

But if it gives me her, at least for now, it'll be worth the agony.

When I don't continue, she finishes for me, whispering. "Friends-with-benefits."

We both laugh, but the sound trails off. The words landing like stones on my chest.

She pulls back a little, dragging the blanket to shield just her lower half, bracing herself for rejection.

As if that's something I could do after this. After she fell apart on my tongue.

I rake a hand through my hair as I force myself to look at her.

"If that's what you want. But know I'll put Savie first too. She doesn't have to know anything's changed with us. I'll be gone in two months. And she'll probably have a daycare spot before I go." I close my eyes and drop my head to the back of the couch. "But I need to say this. Even if I'm not sure how you'll take it."

She freezes, listening. Tense like the words I'm about to say will change everything.

And they might.

"If we do this, I don't want this to ruin our friendship. I want to stay in touch, and now that you're back in my life and I know Savie, I don't know if I can go back to the way it was before. I'm not sure I'll have the strength to walk away from both of you." I open my eyes, staring at the ceiling.

Two months isn't enough time.

Not for this.

Not for her.

Not for us.

Chapter 20

Tiffany

I SUCK IN A sharp breath, and his head snaps up from the couch. His words tear at me, raw and disarming. My heart is racing just like it had been when his head was buried between my thighs just moments ago.

This shouldn't feel this good. But I desperately want to believe him. For the first time in a long time, I want to trust.

His light brown hair is a mess, tousled from my fingers gripping the wavy strands.

I search his handsome face. There's no sign of wavering.

He's serious. Serious about wanting to stay in Savie's life.

As friends.

I lean forward, determined not to question the disappointment mounting in my chest, kissing him. My hips drag over his still-hard cock, pulling a groan from him.

I giggle into his mouth before I sit back slightly, rolling my hips just enough to tease him.

His hands grip my hips to stop them from moving. "Baby girl, you are killing me."

He leans in and presses a lingering kiss to my lips. It's slow, achingly tender, and full of restraint.

His gentle hands shift me off his lap.

My body protests the distance, still humming from his touch.

"Time for me to go, darling. You've got work tomorrow."

He gathers my panties and shorts and hands them back to me. He winks as I take them and I tug them back on, cheeks burning.

We mosey toward the door, hands laced together.

Before I can say goodbye, he has me pressed up against the same wall as before. Like he can't help himself. His mouth crashes into mine, hands gripping my ass and pulling me flush against him. I melt into the kiss.

He dominates it, his lips, his tongue. The way his fingers roam beneath my clothes, on my ass, up my back. I clutch at his shoulders, breathless and dazed. I'm not kissing him back. I'm holding on for dear life. He is the only thing keeping me standing as I swoon.

He breaks away, resting his forehead against mine, breath ragged. "See you in the morning?"

I can only nod, too stunned to speak. He smirks, that maddening, confident smirk, and walks out, adjusting himself in his jeans as he disappears into the night.

The door clicks shut.

I slide down the wall, my legs weak, heart thundering. My fingers press to my kiss-swollen lips, and a breathless laugh escapes, wild and giddy as I kick my feet excitedly against the floor.

I'm undone by him.

The next morning passes in a blur of routines and responsibilities, but not the awkward tension I had braced for. I'm almost disappointed until Chris pulls me into him and presses a gentle kiss to my lips before I leave for work. Just like that, I'm smiling the rest of the day.

By the time I step back into the house in the evening, a strange, unexpected peace has settled in. The air is cool, the quiet hum of home life is soothing, and for the first time ever, coming home feels safe.

Savie's laughter echoes from the living room, and something smells amazing from the kitchen.

But there's no sign of Chris.

I round the corner and find Mrs. B at the stove. I do my best to hide the disappointment tugging at my chest, because I knew he wouldn't be here and I shouldn't be disappointed.

"You know..." I say, trying to sound casual, but I let a grin pull at my lips. "I know I've told both you and your son that I don't expect dinner on the table when I get home. Savie is used to waiting for me to cook dinner after we get home for the day."

Her smile is warm, but tight around the edges. "I know, dear."

I lean on the counter beside her and study her face. "Is everything okay?"

"Yes. It'll be fine." She stirs the food in the pan. "Chris's coach is flying in next week to check on his progress. His surgeon will be here too. I'm sure everything will be okay. They'll evaluate everything and see where he really stands. His agent, too - he'll be here to talk about the state of his brand deals too, I suppose. "

She looks over at me, eyes soft and tired. "He's been better since you've been home."

I blush, blinking innocently. "What do you mean?"

"Before you and Savie showed up, that boy was working so hard he was getting in trouble left, right, and center. We could keep him off the ice, but that damn rower, in the house, not so much. Everyone was worried he would make it worse, ruin the surgery. But you two?" She smiles. "You and your little girl, well, you've given him something else to focus on, and for that I can't thank you enough."

"Mrs. B —"

"Brenda," she says gently, cutting me off. "Please."

I smile, surprised by how real it is. "Brenda, you and Chris have done more for me than I can explain. I should be the one thanking you."

I glance over at Savie, who's sprawled on the rug with a book, leaning against Trixi. She's wearing that ridiculous pink astronaut helmet Chris bought her. She's happy as she tells a story to go along with the pictures in her book.

"I *am* thanking you. She's so happy every day when I get home," I say softly. "And I know she's safe with you guys. That means everything. I really am looking for other options so we can get out of your hair, sooner than later. We don't want to overstay our welcome."

The spatula clatters onto the stovetop, and before I can react, Brenda's strong hands are on my shoulders, turning me to face her.

"You and Savie are not burdens to us," she says firmly. "There is no need to keep looking. Even after Chris goes back East, I'll watch her. Mark and I will. We love her."

I am speechless, both by the strength in her fingers and the conviction in her voice. It makes my chest ache.

I stare at her, words sticking in my throat. "Brenda. I can't ask that of you guys. That's too much."

"It's not too much, and you aren't asking," she says simply, shaking her head. "We're offering."

"You're... offering?" I question, laughing despite myself. "Does your husband know you are offering his services?"

Her grin is a little crooked, just like Chris's. "He wouldn't say no, even if I had asked him."

"Is he going to be joining us for dinner?" I ask, still a little dazed. "We'd love it if he did. Maybe ask him about the plans you've just given him."

We both laugh, and she turns back to the stove.

"Is there anything I can do to help?" I look around, but she's got everything covered.

She nods over to Savie.

"Go spend time with your little girl, they don't stay little for long." She turns her kind eyes back to me. "I'll call Mark and have him join us."

I watch her for a moment, tender love pulling at my heart. There's a distant look in her eyes, but her smile is soft. I can't imagine how I'll feel when Savie is Chris's age. What I will miss after years of raising her.

I look at Savie, who's looking back at me. The pink astronaut helmet is slightly askew. A new sparkly crown has been applied to the top.

I cross the room and sink down beside her, pulling her into my lap to actually read the book she's holding. She snuggles into my arms, and her laughter is enough to make me smile. We read until a knock sounds at my door.

I smooth my expression, but my pulse betrays me the moment I open it. Chris stands just behind his father. Savie, however, makes no effort to hide her excitement. She launches herself straight into his arms.

The deep timber of his voice as he murmurs to her sends a shiver racing down my spine, I am unable to control. I know he noticed it. His sly grin says as much. He finds it amusing.

Mark steals Savie from his arms with a chuckle, and Chris protests half-heartedly. But as they round the corner, Chris leans in, his lips brushing my ear.

"I missed you girls today." His breath is warm against my skin.

My fingers, fist in the fabric of his shirt at his waist.

"Let me take you out," he murmurs. "Just for drinks. We can invite friends. Make it casual, if you'd rather it not be a date."

He leans back, and when I study him, all I find is a soft, steady smile that disarms me. I nod, hesitant but excited. Because spending more time with him sounds like something I want to try.

He glances toward the kitchen, then he reaches for me. His hand curving around the back of my neck, thumb brushing the line of my jaw.

The same brilliant smile flickers across his face before he leans in for a gentle kiss. Brief but full of promise.

We walk into the kitchen together, and Mark raises an eyebrow, amused. Heat creeps up my neck, my face flushing.

"Hey, Mom, Dad," Chris says, turning to his parents. "Would you mind watching Savie on Friday night? Derek invited me out for some drinks with some other friends from school, and when I told him Tiff was back in town, he asked me to invite her, Brandon, and Shawn. I told him, I'd ask, but she can't go unless she has a sitter."

He moves to serve Savie dinner and sits down next to her. Helping her eat without any prompting, like he's been doing this every day of her life. His parents stare in stunned silence. Watching him with a quiet disbelief, as if this is a version of their son they hadn't realized existed.

Chris looks up when the silence stretches too long. "So, what do you think? Could you?"

Before they can answer, I chime in. "I'll come home from work and get her ready for bed. You don't even have to do that much."

"No, dear," Brenda starts, and a resigned sigh builds in my chest. Her voice is firm, but kind as she continues. "Savie can sleep over at our place. It'll be a little adventure for her. You two enjoy yourselves."

The rest of the night is full of warmth and noise. Savie steals the show with her stories, keeping everyone laughing. Chris's hand brushes my thigh more than once during dinner, his thumb lingering over the seam of my slacks before retreating. Each touch sends heat skittering under my skin, a low pulse awakening deep in my core.

When they finally leave, Savie passes out before we even get to story time, her little arms curled around Trixi's warm body.

I shower, slip into bed, and barely have time to settle before my phone buzzes with a message from Chris.

My phone rings softly within seconds of my reply.

"Hey," he says, voice low and velvety through the line. "What are you wearing?"

I laugh, pressing my face into my pillow to muffle the sound. "What are you doing?"

"Calling you to ask what you're wearing." His chuckle rumbles in my ear, lazy and warm.

"Um," I glance down at myself. The ratty, threadbare t-shirt I'd stolen from an ex hangs off my shoulder, and the black leggings I wear most evenings when Chris isn't here wrap around my legs. "That would be pajamas."

"Mmm," he hums, as if I just described the most delicate lingerie possible. "So, you are telling me you are wearing those sexy little shorts again?"

I roll onto my back, heart thudding. "Nope. Not tonight."

He laughs again, deeper this time. "Are you wearing that comfy off-the-shoulder sweatshirt or that almost see-through t-shirt that had me so hard the first time I saw it, I had to rush home to hide in the shower and jack off."

I gasp, delighted, "You did not!"

There's a pause.

I realize I *am* wearing one of those T-shirts, and suddenly I'm warmer, and his presence is more immediate.

He chuckles, low and smug, entirely too pleased with himself. "Oh, I did."

"Is that why you have been rushing out of here?" I close my eyes, letting his voice wash over me like a tide I don't want to resist, lifting a hand to cover my grin.

"What can I say?" His voice drops into the rough, hungry register he used last night between my thighs. "You walk around with that tight little body, and I'm supposed to just sit there? Besides, I didn't think you or your daughter would appreciate me hanging around... *visibly affected.*"

His words drag over my skin like silk and smoke, leaving heat in their wake. My pulse stumbles and my breath hitches.

His tone sharpens, quieter but no less commanding. "Baby girl, I've asked you a question twice now. I'll be very upset if I have to ask a third time."

A flush blooms across my cheeks, sinking lower, deeper. My thighs clench, helpless to stop the throb. The sound he pressed the heat deeper into my skin.

"Yeah," I whisper, voice thick with desire. "I'm wearing leggings and an old t-shirt. It's not the one you saw, but it's just as thin. Just as soft."

He groans, low and ragged, right against my ear. "Good girl."

The words slice through me. I can't stop the soft, needy whimper that slips out.

"I'm dying for another taste of that pretty pussy," he breathes into the phone, but it feels like he's right next to me with the way I'm overheating. "This Friday I'm going to worship that body of yours."

"Yeah?" I ask, my voice breathy.

"Oh, baby girl," he rumbles. "The things I'm going to do to you."

There's more rustling on his end, and a dark groan rumbles through the phone. "Okay. Time to change the subject."

I laugh at his frustrated groan and settle in deeper under my covers, pressing the phone a little closer to my ear, as if it could bring him closer. My fingers curl into the sheets, holding on to the warmth he doesn't realize he gives me.

And for the next hour, we just talk. About everything. And nothing.

Chapter 21

Chris

"I REALLY DID MISS you girls today. I'm glad I got to see you both at dinner." I hesitate, then add. "I know you said yes to drinks, but I didn't actually ask if Friday works for you. I know you have other stuff going on with your dad and other friends. I don't want to assume."

There's a pause. Then she exhales softly down the line.

"It's okay," she says, her voice softer, like she's actually going to let me in. Like she's giving me a piece of her that she keeps locked away. "I've actually got it worked out so I can see him during my lunch time. He's still in a coma, so he doesn't know I'm there, but I get to see him every day."

She keeps talking—about the doctors, the treatments, all the things they've tried that haven't worked. Her voice drifts, sometimes strong.

Sometimes breaking a little.

I don't say anything. I just let her talk, soaking in every word because it matters to her. She slows her cadence and picks each syllable with care, giving me something she didn't plan on sharing. I hold it tight to my chest because it's the most precious thing she could offer me.

Pieces of her heart.

Her voice gets sleepier, yawns slipping in between thoughts, as she circles back around to Friday. "Is it really going to be a bunch of people from school?"

"Well, yeah. Derek invited me, and you can definitely invite Brandon and Shawn," I pause, hoping she'll take the out I'm offering. If she says yes, I'd have her all to myself for the night. "Or we can go someplace else just the two of us."

"Friends first, right?" She sounds like she's not entirely convinced of the choice herself. "Let's go out with the group."

I clench my eyes shut, swallowing the disappointment.

"Okay. Call Brandon and Shawn, see if they want in." I try to keep my tone light. "But *you*, darling, need sleep. I'll see you in the morning for our run."

"Oh, you're going to be joining us now, are you?" She teases.

I laugh softly, pulling my blankets tighter around me. "I'll take any time I can get with you, darling."

Time seems to fly by as I anxiously await Friday.

Dinners with the girls. Tucking Savie in. Fooling around with Tiffany before I slip out of the house. Late-night phone calls until one of us falls asleep.

Mornings are for sneaking in kisses during our pre-dawn runs and cuddles before she walks out the door for work.

It's a life I could get used to.

Savie keeps my days full. She helps keep my mind off the looming visit from my coach, doctor, and agent.

The real world is knocking on the door, and for the first time, I don't want to answer.

I already miss it, this version of life.

This version of us. My little one. Tiffany.

And it isn't even over yet.

Every time I picture my cold, quiet penthouse in Boston, my chest sinks, a weight that gets harder to move the longer I'm here with them.

I miss the ice, yeah.

The freedom.

The rush.

But lately, I'm starting to wonder if it's worth what I'd be walking away from here.

Still, I know what I have to do. I have responsibilities. A career. My people to take care of – my family and my team. How could I look at myself if I stopped? I'm not even sure I could legally walk away from it now, even if I wanted to.

I'll be fine. Right?

I stare at myself in the mirror as I'm toweling off after my shower on Friday night. The scar on my shoulder from surgery is still a sharp burgundy color, but it is no longer tender.

It hasn't been in weeks.

Not since the girls got home.

I run a thumb over the raised line, before turning away and heading to the bedroom. I tell myself not to overdo it. It's just beers at the Tavern. But even as I choose the navy henley and clean jeans after cycling through my whole damn closet, I know who I'm dressing for.

The desire to impress Tiffany is the driving force behind everything lately.

I'm about to look through my closet one last time when a knock comes from downstairs, and I rush down as my mom opens the door for my girls.

No. Not mine. I remind myself. *Not my girls.*

Savie looks a little nervous stepping inside, but my brother is in the living room, and he'll keep her and Trixi entertained while we're gone – he's nothing but a big kid anyway.

I lift Savie into my arms, my eyes drifting to her pretty momma. She's standing in the doorway in a summer dress that hugs her in all the wrong ways for a man trying to be respectful. The way it clings to her curves and the soft sway of her chest sends heat blooming low and fast through my body.

For a second, I forget what I'm doing.

I struggle to pull my gaze off her, but I finally manage to focus back on the little girl in my arms.

"Hey, little one. You going to be good for Granny B and Paw-paw?" She nods, curling closer to me. Trixi licks the back of my hand as I press a kiss to the top of Savie's head. "If you need me or Mama, you tell Granny B to call, and we'll come right back."

She reaches for my mom, who takes her by the hand with a reassuring smile and shoos us toward the door. We both kiss Savie goodbye, whispering promises to come back if she needs us.

Outside, we pause. Tiffany fidgets with a strand of hair, nerves all over her face. I want to say something to make it easier, to cut the tension, but all I can do is reach out and tuck the hair behind her ear.

"You ready?"

She nods. "Yeah."

Leading her to the car, I open the door for her, pressing a gentle, careful kiss to her lips as she settles before walking around to the driver's side.

I glance over at her from my seat. "You look beautiful, darling."

My hand finds the soft skin of her thigh, and I grip it just enough to show her how desperate I am for her. She sucks in a quiet breath, her fingers tightening over mine where they rest.

"I don't know how I'm going to keep my hands off you all night."

"What if I don't want you to?" She murmurs, sliding my hand higher up her thigh. "Just maybe keep it cool where others can see?"

I groan, thumping my head back against the headrest.

"Fine," I mutter, caving, even though keeping it cool around her is getting damn near impossible.

She laughs, bright and free.

The Tavern is more packed than I expected, and my nerves spike.

Now, I'm hoping I have a hat in the backseat. I know Tiffany is uncomfortable with the fame that comes with my job, and I don't want to make it worse. Despite being in our hometown and most people being kind enough to leave me be, it just feels wrong to draw more attention to us than necessary.

"Give me a second," I reach back to dig through the backseat until I find a hat. I settle it on my head as I step out and hurry around the car.

When I open her door, she's laughing.

She flicks the brim. "What's with the hat?"

I lean down to kiss her. It's supposed to be quick, but she tastes like lip gloss and something sweet that makes it impossible to stop. My tongue sweeps across her bottom lip, and when she moans softly into my mouth, I'm done for.

I have to force myself to stop. I could spend a lifetime just tasting her.

"I don't want to get recognized and ruin our night." I press my forehead to hers, and my hat slips sideways, threatening to fall off

Her eyes soften as she swipes at the lip gloss she left on my lips.

I kiss her again, chastely this time.

"Come on, darling." I lace our hands together and haul her toward the door.

We spot our friends right away and make our way over. I wedge myself into the corner and pull Tiffany in close beside me. My hand lands on her thigh when she's close enough to touch.

Brandon drops onto her other side, and Shawn takes the head of the table. Across from me, my oldest friend Derek grins, his arm slung casually around Jenna.

And then there's Sarah.

Jenna's friend.

The last one on their side. Her lip gloss is shiny, cleavage spilling out, and clearly not here just for the fries. She leans onto the table, almost falling out of her shirt as she offers me her hand.

"Heya, Chris," she purrs, her sultry tone just on the edge of inappropriate.

When I shake her hand politely and introduce the rest of my group, her eyes flick from me to Jenna, and then to Tiffany.

One glance is enough. I already know what this is. Derek brought her for me. And, I might have taken the bait not long ago, before I knew Tiffany was an option.

Tiffany goes still beside me. Her eyes bounce between Sarah and me like she's bracing for impact. Like she's waiting for me to move on.

But I'm not sure that will ever happen. I squeeze her thigh where my hand rests, and she relaxes slightly.

"So, Chris," Sarah says, voice suddenly bright, "how long are you in town for? I heard training preseason's starting in a few months."

I offer a polite smile. "Not sure. Coach and my doc are coming in to check me out next week."

She laughs. "Oh, I bet they are."

Tiffany shifts beside me; her posture tighter.

I laugh uncomfortably. "Yeah. It's been a few months since I've seen them in person, and even though I see PT every day and the doctor here every week, the team wants their eyes on me."

"I don't blame them. It's a good sight." She licks her lips, and I cringe into Tiffany.

Brandon leans toward her. "It *is* a good sight, but I'm afraid you're missing the mark. If your genders were reversed, he could claim harassment. Best to back off while you can."

Tiffany, Shawn, and Derek laugh at him, and the conversation drifts away from me.

For a while.

It doesn't stop Sarah from continuing to make flirty attempts to drag me into conversation. I answer Sarah's questions as politely as possible before turning back to the others.

But the tension lingers until Tiffany's hand drops to my thigh as she finishes her second margarita. Her fingers tracing idle lines, slow and lazy but intentional.

I lean close, letting the music cover our voices. "Are you trying to kill me, baby girl?"

I catch her hand and guide it higher, just for a second, to show her how hard she's made my cock. Her breath catches, but the mischief in her eyes tells me everything I need to know.

She's happy with herself.

I groan softly into her ear, placing her hand back on her lap. "Now, keep your hands to yourself, or I'm going to embarrass us both when we stand up."

She takes my breath away as I watch the blush steal over her cheeks.

Across the table, Derek raises a brow at me, clocking our closeness. I shake my head. It's not the time to discuss what's going on between us.

"So, Chris," he says loud enough to grab everyone's attention, and turns the conversation back to me. Like everyone else in my life lately, they all want to know about my arm. "You ready for the new season? I've got some money riding on you."

"Yeah?" I laugh, forcing a casual tone.

Tiffany tenses beside me, even though she's turned back to her conversation with her friends, something about some fashion show they are all excited about, but there's effort in her voice.

"Well, I'll know more next week." I continue, my eyes darting over to Tiffany, both of us bracing. "I'm ready to get back on the ice, though. I'm only getting one day of skating right now, and it's not enough. I'm also not allowed to do any stick work, so hopefully I get cleared soon."

I reach under the table and squeeze Tiffany's hand, just for a second. A reminder I'm still here with her.

"Well, the whole town's rooting for you," Derek says. Thankfully, he pivots the conversation to high school memories.

When the waitress swings by to drop off another round, I lean back into Tiffany's ear, the warm air between us still charged.

"Don't drink that one, baby girl, I want you sober when I drive my cock into your warm, wet pussy." I whisper

She shifts in her seat, her breath hitching, and her head snaps toward me, eyes wide.

"Chris!" She gasps, trying to sound stern, but her voice is too breathy to hold any weight.

Still, she asks for water, pushing her margarita aside. The others keep drinking. Their laughter gets louder, and they slur the jokes they tell.

It isn't long before they spill out of the booth and onto the dance floor, Brandon tugging Tiffany behind him.

I can't take my eyes off her – the way her body moves to the beat, her dress hugging her just right. Her smile is soft and a little hazy from the drinks. She rocks into Brandon's body, and I have to remind myself to breathe.

It's not like that for them.

"Dude, what's going on with you and Tiff?" Derek asks.

I force my gaze away from her. "Nothing, man. Really, we are just friends."

Both Derek and Shawn laugh at me.

Shawn snorts. "*Mhmm*, okay. I don't look at *my* friends like that."

I run my hands through my hair as Derek agrees.

"Guys, it can't be more than friends." I rub my hands together, wiping the condensation from my palms. "If I get cleared next week, I'm back in Boston by the end of the month. She's got a little girl to think of. Her dad's still in the ICU."

Derek just raises his eyebrows. "You might want to stop looking at her like she belongs to you, then."

I try.

I swear I do.

But my eyes are drawn back as some wiry jackass moves in on her, pressing too close and ignoring the shake of her head. My chest tightens, and my fists follow. He just keeps pressing in on her.

I'm out of the booth and stalking across the floor before I've even thought it through. I grab his arm and pull him back, stepping between them on instinct.

"My girl said no," I growl, eyes locked on his. "Kindly walk the fuck away."

His eyes go wide. "Y-yo-your Chris Bartkowski!"

Tiffany flinches at the volume of his voice. People start turning. Heads swivel and phones come out.

Others turn toward the commotion, but I don't stop.

"Yeah, man, I am," I say, keeping my voice low but firm. "But my friends here are trying to have a good time. She said no. Respect that."

He stammers, stumbling back. "Yeah, man. No problem. I didn't realize she was your girl! I'm a huge fan!"

He turns to his buddies at the bar and shouts again. "Guys! It's Chris Bartkowski!"

I cinch my eyes shut because just like that, the rest of the night is ruined.

This is the part where Tiffany pulls away from me again.

The buzz of recognition rolls through the bar. People twist in their seats. More phones come out.

I close my eyes and work my tight jaw as I try to not explode.

Derek and Shawn are suddenly at my back, a wall of support, but it's too late.

Tiffany's wide-eyed, scanning the crowd. I catch her gaze and motion toward the door. She agrees with a nod and grabs Brandon and Jenna's hands and pulls them out of the crush.

I turn to the guys and mutter, "Go. I'll be right behind you."

Wading through the sea of fans is like moving through wet cement. I nod and smile, thanking people I don't have the energy for. I make it to the door, finally, and spot her already waiting at the car, arms wrapped around herself.

I'm frustrated we were interrupted on what had, up until that point, been a fun night.

The night is quieter now than it was before as we buckle. The tension in the car is sharp enough to cut with a blade.

I glance at her, cringing. "I'm sorry."

Chapter 22

Tiffany

My heart is still thundering in my chest, and my wide eyes stay focused on Chris, who hasn't said a word since we got in the car. His grip on the steering wheel is tight, and his knuckles are pale. His jaw ticks under the weight of my stare.

When he finally glances at me, there's regret in his eyes. Not just for the scene, but for dragging me into his world at all. I can't deny the swift change to the bar air was beautifully terrifying and delightfully overwhelming.

Watching people recognize the most deserving man was nice, but it clearly spoiled his evening of anonymity. I know how it feels to have your safety ripped out from under you. I just can't imagine it happening so publicly.

"I'm sorry," he says again, softer this time, like he's sinking deeper into self-blame for things that are not his fault. "I'd understand if this became too much for you. It's too much for me sometimes."

I reach out, brushing my fingers along the stubble on his cheek. He leans into my touch as if it surprises him, like maybe he doesn't deserve it.

"It's not your fault," I whisper. "He didn't listen when I said no. You stepped in. You did what *any* good man would have done."

His jaw softens under my fingers. I trail them down, cupping his face, making him look at me as we pause at a stoplight.

"You *are* a good man, Chris. And you still gave those fans your time. Even when you didn't owe them a damn thing."

A rough sound exhales from his throat, and his fingers begin to dance on the steering wheel.

"I'm just... lucky," he mutters. "Lucky, I get to play a game for money. Lucky, I can use the money to take care of my family. I'm grateful for them most of the time."

"But it's not just luck, Chris." I let my hand drop, reaching for his, and our fingers tangle. "You put in the work. You *sacrificed* for it. You earned everything you've got."

He squeezes my hand, saying nothing. Just stares at the road, his shoulders still too tight, like he's carrying something he can't shake.

We ride the rest of the way in silence. It's not uncomfortable. It's just heavy.

Our fingers stay tangled. And the way his thumb keeps brushing over my skin has tingles rippling out from where he touches me.

By the time we pull into his driveway, the quiet has built into a roaring fire of tension. We sit for a second, not moving, not speaking.

We crash together, like we've been holding our breath all night, and we've finally come up for air. Lips and teeth and need. There's something devastating in the way his hands grip me.

His mouth claims mine, tongue sweeping the seam of my lips until I open with a breathless gasp. He groans softly into the kiss, threading his hands into my hair, gripping my jaw, and guiding me exactly where he wants me.

Where I already want to be.

He dominates me. Overwhelms me, and I give in to it completely, melting beneath the force of him.

I let him take control. Let him lead me.

I let myself give in, completely undone by how badly I want him.

"I need you." I breathe into his mouth.

His lips claim mine again before he tears his mouth away with a rough exhale. "Need you too."

He's out of the car and around my side in seconds. The door flies open, and he hauls me straight into his chest. I barely have time to blink before he's backing me into the side of the car, kissing me like it's the only way to stay standing. He ravishes my mouth again, grinding his painfully hard cock into me.

"Tiffany," he murmurs.

My name is a reverent breath against my lips, like a prayer and a warning all at once.

I push against his chest just enough to slip from under him, my breath catching with the thrill already curling through me.

"Chase me." His eyes flare, and I bolt.

Laughter bursts from my lungs as I sprint for my front door, but I only make it to the steps before his foot falls are close behind me, low and fast like a storm rolling in.

His body slams into mine, his arms catching me as we crash into the cold steel of the door.

I gasp, the chill seizes the breath from my chest, but I don't have time to catch it before his mouth is on my neck. He drags fire down my spine, leaving goosebumps in his wake.

My knees buckle. I'm molten in his arms, clinging to him, lost in the heat. I moan as I rock back into him.

"You're trouble." He grins, just before plucking the keys from my trembling hand.

And I melt.

Right there.

A breathless mess against the door, barely able to stand from the way his touch unravels me. Undone by his voice and the way he touches me like he already owns every inch.

The door swings open, and I press a kiss to his lips over my shoulder, and take off again, heart racing, feet flying over the stairs.

This time, it's not from fear. This time, it's exactly what I want.

I don't get far.

I shriek with laughter as he lifts me, slinging me over his shoulder like I weigh nothing. A sharp smack lands on my ass, and I gasp, breathless, as he carries me up the stairs.

Up towards my room.

His teeth bite lightly into the newly exposed skin of my thigh. A tremor passes through me, raising the hair on my body. A moan rips through my gritted teeth as his possessive touch lands on me. Fingers clenching into the back of my thighs before dancing a trail along my damp panties.

I run my hands over his ass, squeezing hard enough to pull a groan from his lips.

When we reach my room, he lowers me to my feet, dragging my body along every sculpted inch of his. The heat of his muscles scorches me through his clothes as my toes brush the floor, barely taking my weight before his mouth finds my neck.

His hands slide up my back, purposeful as they find the zipper of my dress and pull it down in one smooth motion. The material grazes over my pebbled nipples as it slips to the floor, my head falling back on a moan.

He groans, his eyes dragging over every inch of me, like he's memorizing my body. I should feel exposed, naked beneath the weight of his gaze. This man is a perfect specimen, all sculpted muscles, effortless fame, and eyes so kind they make me ache.

And me? I'm just a normal woman. I'm soft in places I didn't use to be. A woman who's carried life and bears the marks of it. The roundness of my hips, the craters that are my stretch marks, and the way my breasts sag from feeding my child.

But the way he looks at me. It's more than just a desire for a naked, willing body.

It's nothing like I expected.

It's awe.

As if I'm the most beautiful thing he's ever seen.

"Oh, baby girl, did you do this for me?" His hand roams my body, gently caressing my breasts, rolling my nipples between his fingers, pulling at the tightened buds. "Did you leave the house without a bra on so I could get my hands on you as soon as I got you home?"

"No," I whisper, meeting his eyes. "But it did come with some nice perks."

My arms wrap around him as he leans down and lifts me. The brush of his shirt over my sensitive skin sends tingles rushing through my body and settling into a low throb between my thighs. My legs wrap loosely around his waist as he sits me on the bed.

"You're beautiful, baby girl." He pulls back to memorize me with his gaze again. "I could stare at you for hours."

He dips his head to mine, running his nose along the skin of my cheek, inhaling me. His heated breath fans my skin, flames licking at me with every exhale.

His lips travel down my body, nipping and licking. They shower me with hot kisses as I squirm underneath his attention. He lingers over my breasts, biting and licking, kneading at them, learning everything that makes me writhe and moan.

I'm set on fire under his focus.

I'm drenched with the sensations he's pulling from my body. Every jolt, every sweep of flames, every tingle of electricity. He worships me. His mouth on my skin is rewriting everything I thought I knew about desire.

I dig my hands into his hair, pulling, pushing. I'm not sure if I want him to kiss me again or if I want to shove him toward where he's headed. He presses his mouth into the softness of my belly as he chuckles. His teeth nip at my skin before he grabs the elastic of my panties, allowing them to snap against me.

"Baby girl. Are you wet for me?" He growls. "When I take these panties off you, are you going to be dripping?"

I nod frantically, arching my back. Groaning, I try to get closer to him, pulling at him. "Yes, Chris. So wet. Please. Just put your mouth on me."

My eyes squeeze tight as my head grinds back into the mattress. I'm not above begging him at this point to get the relief he can provide. His fingers grip my panties, pausing to run his nose down the line of my belly. His hands slide down my legs. I bite down on my lip, moaning softly.

"Baby girl," Chris's voice is a warning as he nips the skin of my thigh. "I want to hear you tonight. I want to hear you scream my name when you come on my tongue and then on my cock. I want you to scream so loud that everyone knows you're mine."

He yanks my ass to the edge of the bed and shifts my legs over his shoulders. His arms loop over my hips, locking my body into place. I can't move my lower half as he lowers his head.

I push up to my elbows to look at him between my thighs, and our eyes lock.

For a moment, I'm terrified at how much I want this. Not just this moment, but this man. The way he steadies me without asking.

My head drops between my shoulders the moment his mouth meets my pussy. He drags his tongue over me, licking slowly through me, like he's making up for lost time.

He explores my cunt as thoroughly as he did my breasts.

He's in no hurry tonight.

I squirm with every swipe of his tongue against me.

Moans and pleas falling from my lips.

Pleas to keep going, and pleas to stop torturing me.

I beg him to let me come as my orgasm starts to crawl its way up my spine, my fingers and toes curling. My pussy throbs with the pressure of it.

The sounds from between my thighs are obscene as he continues to feast. I'm so wet it drips down me to the cleft of my ass.

"God, you are so wet for me." He pulls his mouth just far enough that he has room to press two fingers into my empty core. "You going to come for me, baby girl?"

A small shriek pulls from my lips at the intrusion; my thighs widen. "Yes, Chris. Please. So close."

"I got you." His fingers turn over inside me, sweeping through me before pressing back inside me.

They alternate between curling and thrusting, sending me so high it feels impossible to fall off the cliff. I'm stalled so high I might never come down.

I grasp the sheets by my hips as I grind onto his hand, his mouth. "Chris, please."

"Come, baby girl. Just let go. Come for me." He latches on to my clit with a desperate pull, his teeth nibbling, and I detonate.

I scream his name, sobbing as my body stiffens, back arching and toes curling. My pussy clenches around his fingers, the world becoming silent as the waves of my release take me under.

Stars dance behind lids that are clenched so tightly the light is gone.

My body jerks with every touch. Chris's mouth dances over me as he works his way back up. He kisses my lips, and I can taste the slight muskiness of my cunt on his tongue.

"Open those beautiful whiskey eyes for me, baby girl." He presses his lips to mine again, like he can't stand to part from me. "Come on, darling. Open those eyes."

I force my eyes open, locking onto his gaze, dark and heavy with hunger, pupils blown wide. Desire twists low in me, and my breath stutters.

"You're wearing too many clothes," I murmur, the words slipping out on a shaky exhale, every inch of me aching for more.

His dark laugh rumbles against my skin before he pulls back. One hand lifts to the back of his neck, pulling his shirt off in one fluid motion, tossed aside like he's done this a thousand times.

And maybe he has.

The years have been good to him.

Too good.

Muscles ripple across his chest, his stomach a roadmap of strength and control. I swallow hard. My eyes drag over every inch of him, and the hard line pressing against his jeans makes my breath hitch.

"Move up the bed, baby girl. Put your head on the pillows."

I scramble back, heart pounding as he strips off his jeans and briefs in one smooth, practiced motion.

He's not just beautiful.

He's devastating.

And he has the most perfect cock, thick and long, in a way that tells me I'll feel him for days. My eyes trace the veins up his length to the slightly darker head.

I don't know how this thing with him will last. I don't even know who I'll be tomorrow.

But tonight, I'm his.

I reach for him as he starts to crawl over my body, my arms wrapping around his shoulders. I run my tongue along the curve of his ear, biting gently on his earlobe. "I want you to come in me."

He groans, forehead dropping to my chest like he needs the moment to breathe me in. When he lifts his head, a wicked smile curves his lips. He leans back, his gaze burns over me, lighting every nerve on fire.

He tilts my hips before he drapes his body back over mine. His skin whispers his wicked intentions into me, shifting against me, and dragging his cock through my pussy. A whimper falls from my throat as he moves.

"Eyes on me, baby girl."

He slots himself at my entrance before pressing in, stretching me, and dragging a hiss from between my teeth. My eyes struggle to stay open against the bite of pain that threatens to overwhelm the pleasure of him inside me.

"Good girl. You're so good for me," he hisses.

"Chris, you're so big," I whine, scrambling back against the pillows, nerves buzzing and heat coiling tighter inside me. "Too big."

"You can take it," he promises, pressing his lips to mine as he stops moving against me, giving me a second to adjust.

"You're such a good girl. Taking me in this sweet pussy of yours." He breathes the words into the curve of my neck, his voice sinking beneath my skin. His fingers slip down to my clit, rubbing fire into my body. "Just relax, baby girl. Let me in."

A long breath slips past my lips as I focus on his fingers. Each stroke setting my skin alight, each pause a silent promise. When my hips start to jerk, he presses further into me. Both of us groan once he's fully seated inside me.

"Chris," My arms wind around him, nails digging into his back. "So full."

"Yes, you are." He shifts his hips back before driving into me, a cry falling from my lips. "You are taking me so well."

His words set him on a brutal pace, dragging me higher with every breath, every thrust. He's rough, reverent, and unrelenting. We've just started, and I'm already shaking, heading toward a release I might not survive. My nails rake down the skin of his back as he kisses me, overwhelming me from both ends.

He pulls back, taking my wrists in his hands, and lifts them above my head. He pins them with one hand before dragging his mouth across my skin, hot and deliberate.

"Chris, I'm so close," I whine.

He groans against my throat before pulling out of me.

"Not yet." He flips me onto my stomach, stuffing a pillow under my hips. "I have so many plans for you."

He places my hands flat against the headboard.

"These stay here, baby girl." His voice is wrecked as he lifts my hips and presses back into me. "Cross your ankles."

He taps my hip, encouraging me, and I groan with the fullness of him inside me when I do as he asks. He settles over me, warm and solid. His hand finds my hair, brushing it gently aside, and his teeth trail down my neck, slow and careful, before pressing his lips against the curve of my shoulder.

His hand winds into my hair, wrenching it to the side so he can kiss my lips. I groan against the bite of pain in my scalp.

The rhythm he finds is slower, less forceful, but every moment feels fuller, more intentional. Like he's trying to brand himself into me.

Even with the slower pace, it doesn't take long before I'm squirming again as his cock drags against the sensitive walls inside me. Heat licks over me, everywhere our bodies touch, and I am hurtling toward my second orgasm.

"Chris!" I cry.

"Hold on, baby girl," he murmurs into my skin. "Not yet."

He drives in harder, the sounds of our skin slapping marks his rhythm. His touch traces fire along my body, his fingers settling at my throat.

He grips my neck gently, tilting my head back against his shoulder. His other hand finds the bed near my waist, anchoring us both. As if he needs something to hold on to.

I'm stretched out beneath him, arms against the headboard, hips locked between him and the pillow. He has my breath shallow under his hand.

I feel everything all at once.

And it's too much.

It blurs my eyes with tears I can't stop.

I try desperately to stop myself from coming, to be a good girl for him. Every muscle tightens, my body begging me to give in. Screaming to let go.

I want to beg him, but I have no extra breath to let the words fall from my lips.

His voice, low and relentless, plays like a mantra against my skin, grounding me, until his hand slips from my throat, and I gasp, shuddering on the edge.

"Oh, God, Chris. I can't hold it anymore. I have to come." I beg, writhing under him, trying to move, to do anything with the parts he hasn't pinned in place. Desperate to let go. "Please, please, please let me come."

"Okay, baby girl," he pants, his hand closes on my throat again, and his thrusts speed up. "Come for me. Now."

I break with a sharp cry. The pressure shattering. A helpless shout tears from my throat as I fall, weightless and wrecked, over the edge he's kept me dancing on.

I fall into the most explosive orgasm I've ever had. It rolls through me in waves, and I can barely feel Chris continuing to pound into me as he chases his own release.

The aftershocks have me so sensitized another orgasm sweeps me up. Chris grunts heavily in my ear as he comes inside me. He coats my insides as my third release rolls through my core, more subdued but still curling my toes. My hands grasp for leverage against the smooth headboard.

"Oh shit, shit, shit," he chants against my sweat-soaked skin as his hand loosens but doesn't let go. His words curl into my pores like smoke, each syllable branding me. "That's it. Good girl. You come so pretty for me."

"Chris," I whine. "Too much."

"I know." His grip softens further before releasing my neck, like he's reluctant to let me go.

He exhales and rolls to the side. His fingers find my forehead, damp with sweat, and gently push the hair back, like he's trying to memorize the shape of me with a tenderness that threatens to undo me.

"You are so beautiful," he whispers.

I roll to my side, breathless as I meet his eyes. "I'm covered in sweat and come. I can't be looking that good."

"Oh no, baby girl," he murmurs, voice low and raw. His breath catches in his throat.

"You are the most beautiful you've ever been. Covered in me. In us." He pulls me closer until the length of his body presses against mine, our lips barely brushing. "I could die a happy man. I don't think it's ever been this good before."

I lean in for another kiss, soft and sweet, before pulling back to smile at him. My fingers reach for his face, trembling slightly as they brush his sweat-damp hair away from his forehead.

"It was the best I'd ever had, too." My voice drops, lazy and thick with satisfaction. "I think you wore me out."

He rises, helping me out of bed.

"Come on, darling," he says, steady and warm. "Up you go. Let's get you cleaned up before we lay you down to sleep."

I rest my head against his chest, feeling the steady beat of his heart as the shower starts to warm.

"You'll stay?" I ask, hesitating, not wanting to break the quiet.

"Yeah." His kiss lands softly on the crown of my head. "I'm not done with you yet, and even if all we do is lie here and cuddle the rest of the night, I'll be happy."

Chapter 23

Tiffany

I WAKE UP WITH a full body stretch, every muscle groaning in protest, and a strong, muscular arm tightens around my bare stomach. Chris's warmth as shifts slightly, his skin pressing hotter against my back. His breath tickles the nape of my neck, sending shivers racing down my spine, and a soft groan slips from my throat.

I roll over, searching for his eyes. They are still closed, his hazel eyes hidden, drowsy with leftover sleep.

Pressing a soft kiss to his lips before draping a leg over him, feeling the steady rise and fall of his chest beneath me.

"Morning," I whisper.

"A man could get used to this," he murmurs, threading his arms tighter around me, pulling me closer like I'm the only place he wants to be. He settles me over his morning erection, pressing against my rapidly dampening pussy. My *well-used* pussy. "Oh, baby girl, are you getting wet for me?"

"Very reluctantly," I tease, laughing as he cracks one eye open and squints at me. "I think you broke it."

He groans, pressing his forehead to my shoulder as laughter rumbles through him. The sound vibrates against my skin, and I can't help but join in, wrapping my arms around his head, fingers twisting in his hair.

We shake with laughter, tangled up in each other, until the moment softens. His lips find my collarbone with soft, lingering kisses that he trails up the side of my neck.

His hands start to wander over my body, and I feel his hips thrust against me slightly. "Can you give me one more? Then we can go get our little one and maybe take her to the park down by the water?"

"Yeah," I sigh, soft and involuntary, tilting my head back to offer him more of my neck. The gesture, a silent invitation. His mouth finds the exposed skin like he's been waiting for it, and heat pulses through me with every slow kiss he plants there. "Yeah, that sounds great."

It's almost nine by the time we finally roll out of bed. The scent of sex still lingers in the room, clinging to the sheets, the air, and my skin.

If my body weren't aching in the best way, I would probably be filled with anxiety at how good this feels.

I shake the thought away and slip into my favorite sundress and sandals while Chris disappears into the bathroom.

When I follow him in to refresh my curls, I look closely in the mirror. My hair is screaming what we got up to.

I'm separating the worst of my curls when he steps behind me and presses a kiss to my bare shoulder.

"Darling," he murmurs into my skin. "You are beautiful."

"You're not so bad yourself, big man." I bump him with my hip, smiling. "Now, I need a minute to fix my hair, or everyone will know exactly what we've been doing all night."

He leans back against the door jam, arms crossed, smug grin in place. "And this morning."

I shoot him a look in the mirror, lifting a brow as I press my lips together, fighting a smile.

"What? Just being accurate," he says innocently, before he wisely changes the subject. "My mom just texted me. She said Savie's still sleeping. So, you have a minute. Knowing her, she had Savie up way past her bedtime."

I pull half my hair up, spritz the rest, and swipe on a bit of makeup. Just some light foundation to dull the evidence of his stubble and teeth on my neck. Chris watches from the doorway like I'm a show he's unwilling to miss.

Every time our eyes meet in the mirror, I raise a questioning brow.

He chuckles and flashes that damn cocky smile.

Other than the light dusting of stubble, he looks nearly flawless. Like we hadn't spent the last eight hours wrapped up in each other. Like he had when we left his house last night.

When I finally turn to face him, ready to go, he reaches out and laces our fingers together.

Just before we reach the front door to his parents' house, I drop his hand. He gives me a questioning look, but I just shrug, cheeks warming.

The house is still quiet when we walk in. I glance around and spot his brother passed out on the couch, one arm flung dramatically over his face, drool pooling on his pillow.

I step closer to Chris, whispering into his shoulder. "Chris, where is everyone?"

"Well." He looks at his watch. "Nine-thirty and Charlie is passed out on the couch, for reasons unknown. If I had to guess, Mom's either in the den or the kitchen. And it's a Saturday, so my dad will be at the diner with friends."

We move further into the house, and sure enough, we find Brenda in the kitchen, humming as she flips something on the stove.

"Morning, Mom," Chris calls out.

Brenda turns to us with a wide, knowing smile. "Morning, son. Tiffany."

She looks at the two of us with raised brows, and I flush low on my chest but it spreads all the way up my face. There's no way she doesn't know.

Thankfully, she doesn't comment on it. "Savie and Trixi are upstairs in Charlie and Junior's room. Breakfast should be done shortly. Chris, why don't you show Tiff where she is?"

"Sure thing, Mom."

"And wake your brother on your way down, please," she calls over her shoulder. "He was a huge help with Savie last night, other than the fact that he kept us all up past our bedtimes."

She shoos us out with a wave, not bothering to glance back.

Chris squeezes my thigh before he stands, and on his way past, lightly pats my ass. I clench my teeth to lock down the gasp that tries to escape me and follow him.

Once we are on the second floor, I swat his ass in retaliation. He chuckles, pulling me under his arm as we walk to the last door in the hall. He eases it open.

Savie is still asleep, cuddling a brand-new teddy under her little arm. Trixi is lying beside her, protecting her.

Chris's arm tightens over my shoulder. I look at him and my heart stumbles.

He looks absolutely gone for her. Like she hung every star in his sky.

Tears prick the back of my eyes. She *deserves* this. I press a kiss to his chest where my head rests. I don't know how long we'll have him, but I plan to enjoy every moment.

He slips away, and I watch from the doorway as he kneels by the bed. He wakes her gently, voice soft as he runs his hand over her back. She stirs, arms lifting to wrap around his neck.

Her bedhead is wild, which tells me it had been messy when she fell asleep the night before. She had a good night.

When he picks her up, she melts into every curve of his body like he was made to hold her. He rocks her gently around the room, coaxing her into wakefulness.

I can't look away.

His eyes meet mine, and a soft smile crosses his face. "What?"

"Just admiring the view." I move in closer and press a kiss to her little cheek. "Morning, my love. Did you have fun with Granny B and Pawpaw?"

"Mommy," she mumbles, still sleepy, and she turns her body toward mine, arms outstretched.

I lift her from his arms and settle her against my chest. "Why don't you wake your brother. I'll change her and bring her down for breakfast."

He nods, pressing a kiss to Savie's forehead, to my temple, and heads out with Trixi at his heels.

Even my damn dog likes him.

I tuck my face into her hair. "You okay, sweetheart?"

She sighs, but it sounds happy.

I set her down to pull her jammies off, and she flops back on the bed. We giggle as I pull her back to sitting, helping her into some leggings and a tank top. "Want to go to the park after breakfast?"

"Chis take me?" She asks, brightening.

I laugh, hoisting her into my arms. "Can I come too?"

"Yes!" She grabs my cheeks. "Mommy and Chis go park with Savie!"

Her joy is infectious, bubbling out of her tiny frame and seeping into my chest like sunlight. She vibrates with excitement as I carry her downstairs, and something warm and aching shackles me, like hope wrapped in fear.

Breakfast is a blur of noise and laughter. Charlie and Chris dote on Savie, hanging on every word. Even when they don't make sense. Even when she loses the thread halfway through her sentences. They don't care. They just smile and nod, letting her light the whole room.

Before long, we've dropped Trixi off and are seated in Chris's car. It has a top-of-the-line car seat in the back for Savie, I somehow missed last night.

"You got that for her?" I ask, my voice a little too soft.

He shrugs, like it's no big deal. "Did some research. She deserves the best."

I can't speak, so I just reach over and squeeze his hand.

She babbles on in the back seat, recounting dreams and Charlie's crimes from the night before. I try to stay engaged, but Chris keeps catching me staring.

I'm in awe of him. Every time he flashes me one of those boyish grins, I fall a little further. He threads his fingers through mine, careful to keep them hidden from our nosy gossip in the back.

When we get to the park, even though it's Saturday, it's fairly empty. I do a quick scan, thankfully there's only a handful of moms with their kids.

But unease still tugs at my chest. I just hope Chris doesn't get bothered here. I don't want to disappoint Savie, but now that we are parked, all I want to do is leave.

Chris notices my hesitation.

"Tiff?" He asks gently, giving my hand a squeeze. "Everything okay?"

"Yeah," I force a smile, but my voice comes out in a whisper, hoping Savie is sufficiently distracted in the back seat. "I'm fine. I was just checking out the layout. Trying to see the likelihood that we would get interrupted, and you get recognized."

He chuckles through clenched teeth, eyes scanning the park with narrowed, assessing eyes. "And, what's your assessment?"

"Seems more likely that they'll try to flirt with you than recognize you." My jaw tightens. I try to relax it, but the knowing softness in his eyes says I'm failing miserably.

"Darling," he says, brushing his thumb across my knuckles, "even if they did. I'm more of a one-woman-at-a-time man."

He peeks back at Savie, who is still looking at all the stuff outside the car. When he turns back to me, he lifts my hand to press a kiss to it. "Besides, I think you've ruined me. I'm not sure anyone else would even register."

He looks at me earnestly. "I'm going to wear my hat, darling. I'd never risk exposing Savie to something like last night."

I pull my hand from his reluctantly and turn to Savie. "Ready to play, mamacita?"

"Yes! Chis, get me!" She squeals, clapping her hands as Chris and I climb out of the car.

Chris grins and tugs his hat lower before hiking her onto his hip. "As my princess commands."

I grab my purse and round the car. Without thinking, I reach for his free hand, and he squeezes it back. He's patient even when Savie starts grabbing and slapping his cheeks with unbridled joy. He just laughs, bouncing her in his arms, listening intently as she rambles.

As we near the play structure, he gently sets her down. "Go on, little one. I'll be right behind you."

We both watch as she bolts straight for the stairs to the slide.

"I've got her, darling," he says, pressing a soft kiss to my forehead. My eyes close as I lean into him, gripping his shirt at his sides.

His lips stay gently resting on my forehead as he whispers into my skin. "Go. Sit. Rest that gorgeous behind. I'd like to get a repeat of last night and this morning, and I don't want you too sore to keep up."

A shocked laugh bursts out of me as I pull away. "You are incorrigible! Who says I'll give you a repeat?"

He smirks. "I've got it on good authority that it was the best you've ever had."

He turns me gently, swatting my ass, and he sends me stumbling toward the park benches. "Go. Bench. Now. We will join you when the boss needs a break."

I bite my lip as I turn back to him, but continue to walk toward the closest bench. He groans, and I catch the wink he flashes before running after Savie.

The rest of the morning, I sit and watch the two of them play. Both are covered in sand more than once when they race over to me for the water bottles I have tucked in my purse. Despite the hungry stares from nearby moms who look like they'd eat Chris alive, we're left alone.

The park finally begins to fill just as I'm about to call the two of them back for lunch. I've barely lifted my arm to get Chris's attention when a flash of grey catches my eye.

"Your husband reminds me of my Edward."

I blink and turn. An older woman sits next to me, her cardigan soft with faded flowers, eyes lined with the weight of years.

"Ma'am?" I'm certain she's confused. She smiles and pats my hand, her fingers paper-thin and warm. She nods toward Chris, who's swinging Savie in circles, and I finally catch what she means.

"He's not my husband. He's just an old friend." I say.

She hums. "You should think about changing that."

I glance over at Chris again, and he's holding Savie in his arms, she clings to him. My heart aches with something too big to name.

"My Edward was a lot like him." The woman says. "Attentive to our kids. He doted on me, much like your man has all day. He looked at me like I was the only woman on Earth. We were married for 55 years. 55 years of laughter, love." She turns towards me, eyes twinkling. "Passion."

She laughs softly, her voice weathered by years. Yet it carries a joy laced with grief, both quiet and profound.

"It sounds like you and Edward lived a charmed life, ma'am."

"We did." She looks at me carefully. "But I wouldn't have had it if I'd let fear win."

I turn to face her, gently resting my hand over the one that still warms mine. "Really, he's only home for the summer, and he's been helping with my daughter while we wait for an opening at the daycare center in town."

"Sweet girl, that man looks at you like you're his whole future. He'd stay forever if you let him." Her smile lifts, holding the years of love inside the curve. "You'd keep him, too, if you could, wouldn't you?"

I swallow hard. She's not wrong, but I'm not ready to admit it.

She nods her head sagely, even though I don't respond. "You don't have to answer that. It's written all over your face. Sweet girl, you don't meet many men who would gladly take on another man's child, but that man looks at your little girl like she was made to be his. Don't let him go, you'll regret it."

Before I can respond, Chris and Savie appear at my side. He's grinning, eyes crinkling, rubbing her back as she clings to him.

"Who's your new friend, darling?"

The old woman lifts her eyebrow in my direction and laughs at the flush blooming on my cheeks. "Just a nosy old woman who thought to bother your beautiful girlfriend while she watched her beau playing with her child."

"We're just friends, ma'am," Chris says, gently setting Savie in my lap. He offers the woman his hand. "Can we help you get somewhere? The little boss is calling for lunch, so we've gotta head out."

"Oh no, son. My daughter will be here shortly with the great grand-kids, and I'll be leaving with them." She smiles at me.

"Well, it was lovely meeting you." He nods, helping me to my feet with Savie in my arms. "Thanks for keeping my girl company."

"It was nice to have a good conversation." She winks. "Keep in mind what I said, sweet girl."

"Bye, old lady!" Savie chirps.

"Savannah!" I gasp, ready to apologize, but the woman waves it off with a warm laugh.

I set Savie on her feet, and Chris takes her other hand. We walk back to the car, swinging her between us. She's giggling wildly. He's smiling like the world's exactly as it should be.

But my chest is full of knots I can't untangle.

Her words echo in my head for the rest of the day. I don't believe her. I *can't* believe her because there was no way.

But every time I see him hold Savie, I start to want more.

And that scares the hell out of me.

Chapter 24

Chris

By the time the bill for lunch is paid, Savie's eyes are drooping, and yawns erupt from her mouth more than words. She had talked all through lunch, but Tiffany hadn't said much at all. Not just quiet. I wouldn't have worried except she missed several of Savie's questions.

We rush home, settle Savie and Trixi into bed for nap time, and I lead Tiffany downstairs, our fingers laced. Sitting, I gently guide her onto my lap.

My fingers raise to brush her wild curls away from her face. "Okay, darling. What's going on with you? What did that lady say that's got you so quiet?"

Tiffany looks away.

"Nothing really," she murmurs. "She was just telling me about her husband. He's passed away."

A deep flush blooms across her cheeks. "She thought you were my husband at first. Said you reminded her of him. It just made me sad, that's all."

Her chin dips, and I lift it with a finger. "Tiff? What about that made you this sad?"

"She seemed so happy but also so lost. And I tried to picture myself in her shoes," her voice wavers. "She was with him for 55 years. Can you imagine that kind of love? That kind of loss?"

Her eyes brim with tears that don't quite fall, and my hand cradles her cheek.

"Shit, I've never been able to make anything work for more than a year," she says softly, like it's a confession.

Her shoulders droop, and she leans into me, pressing her lips against my neck. Her words are whispered into my skin, and carved heavy into my chest. "Just makes you think, you know? How it would feel to have that."

I wrap my arms around her, hands gliding over her back. "Yeah. I can imagine."

And I can.

I can imagine Tiffany in my arms for the rest of my life. Waking up beside her. I can see Savie in a cap and gown, myself walking her down the aisle to the love of her life. More kids. Maybe another dog or two. Laughter and love.

A dozen moments stitched together until they become a lifetime.

But the road between here and there is fogged with things I can't change. Not now. Not with two more years on my contract in Boston. Not with her life rooted here. Not with the stability they both need.

Stability I can't give.

We stay wrapped in silence while Savie naps upstairs. Unspoken words press into the space between us. My mind races, wondering if she sees the same things I do. Because everything about this – *her, Savie, the three of us* – feels right. Feels like forever.

And I love them.

The confession, even in my mind, has my breath hitching in my chest. I'm not just falling. I'm already there. So irrevocably in love with her.

My thoughts drive through every neighborhood of a picture-perfect life I never could have dreamed of before them.

When footsteps hit the stairs, she pulls away like a tide retreating from shore. Distance floods in. I trace her unreadable face with my eyes. My hands catch her hips to keep her close a moment longer.

Her eyes shutter before she moves my hands and stands.

"You should probably go," she whispers. "I'm sure your parents are wondering where you are."

I'm on my feet in a heartbeat, catching her wrist, turning her to face me. "Tiff. You can talk to me. About anything."

She nods, but her eyes won't meet mine.

I can't let this be the last time I hold her like this because it *feels* a little too much like goodbye.

"Can I see you later?"

"Yeah." She nods softly, voice quiet. "After Savie's in bed for the night. I'll text you."

I nod, but everything in me rebels. I don't want to miss bedtime. This was supposed to be casual, but it stopped being that a long time ago.

I go through the motions the rest of the day – smiles, nods, half-heard stories – but the second my phone rings and Dan's name lights the screen, I bolt for my room.

Any excuse to get away from my parents' prying eyes.

"Chris?" His voice is sharp. No hello. No pleasantries. "Tell me why your PR team is asking about a woman and a little girl you were seen with today."

"What are you talking about?" My heart stutters and kicks into over-drive. My chest tightens with a fierce, immediate protectiveness. "Dan?"

He huffs into the receiver.

"Jesus, Chris." His fingers fly across the keyboard in the background. "Check your email. I sent you the photos they're asking us to comment on."

I grab my iPad and open them.

And my stomach drops.

Photo after photo. Me and Savie at the playground. She's hugging me while I spin her in circles. Tiffany hands us water as we rest from playing. Her hand rubs my back as I sit on the ground near her, watching Savie dance. Tiffany's arms looped around my shoulders as I press her into the car. Talking. Kissing.

Moments that were private, sacred. Turned into fodder for the world.

They didn't sign up for this. My breath shudders out of me.

Dan's voice fades away. Just static, a low roaring in my ears. There's no privacy – not in my hometown, not anywhere.

"Shut it down, Dan." I choke out.

My chest heaves.

I can't breathe.

I'm drowning in this tunnel of noise. Dan's shouts are muffled in my ear, panic making me deaf. "Please, please, Dan. Shut it down."

"Breathe, Chris," he says, voice low and urgent. "You need to breathe. Right now. With me, okay? In and out. That's right. In two, three, four. Out..."

I mimic him, fists clenched around my phone like it's a lifeline. Inhale. Exhale.

Again.

And again.

Minutes pass.

I don't know how many it takes for the darkness behind my eyes to fade. My knees buckle, and I sink to the floor, the iPad clutched to my chest, as if I can somehow hold everything together. Like, I can hide them forever.

"Calm down, Chris. Talk to me." Dan's fingers click back to life on the keyboard.

She's going to leave me.

The thought runs through my mind unbidden, the root of my panic shocking me enough to finally speak.

"They can't post those." I rasp. "Tiffany and Savie don't deserve to have their privacy invaded just for being my friends and spending time with me. I want it pulled entirely. Not just blurred. Gone."

A shudder rolls through me as I move to lean against my bed.

He blows out a harsh breath. "Okay, here's what's going to happen. You are going to answer Natalie's phone call when she reaches out, understood?" He pauses. "You need to go talk to Tiffany and let her know what happened and what we are going to try to do."

"She's going to be upset," I admit. "She's going to hate me for this."

"Maybe," he concedes. "You never know until you talk to her."

Dan gives me a few more instructions before hanging up, and I sit in silence, staring at the ceiling, phone still in hand.

Chapter 25

Tiffany

I NEVER THOUGHT A big, brave, used-to-the-public-eye, pro-athlete would shake like this at the thought of the public knowing about his private life. But his fingers are trembling where they grip mine in my lap, and his words come out uneven, telling me what happened.

I can't tell if he's scared for us or for how his reputation will look if he's with a single mom and her daughter. I have no right to ask, but the wondering lodges in my throat anyway.

I'm not happy – of course I'm not – but this man, he's downright terrified. This isn't what I wanted for my daughter, but we can't change the past. And Chris is beating himself up more than I ever could.

Savie and Trixi eventually join us on the couch. We huddle together and let a movie fill the room. When the credits roll, I rise and lift Savie from where she lies on his chest, passed out.

Chris's big hand finds mine, and together we tuck her into bed. We slip into my room without a word. He lowers his head into my lap, and I lean against the headboard, combing my fingers through his hair.

"Chris. I'm not mad." I whisper as I gently roll my fingertips over the scar on his brow and down the crooked slope of his nose, tracing the shape of his lips before slipping them back into his hair. "I'm worried about what this will mean for us. But I'm not mad."

"Why?"

"I'm good in an emergency, I guess." I shrug. "And, to be honest, this doesn't feel like an emergency. It's not good, but also not an emergency."

Silence stretches for a beat, then a sharp, breathless giggle escapes me. The sound is too loud in the dim room.

I bury my face into my hands, stifling my laughter, so I don't wake Savie.

"You think it's funny, do you, darling?" His voice is a low rumble, playful but warm. There's a smile in his voice as he pulls my hands away and presses me gently back into the mattress.

"It's just funny that after the show you put on last night in the bar, you got caught playing with a three-year-old." Another laugh bubbles up, quieter this time, but no less shaky. Everything about tonight feels surreal. "And that's what is going to get you splashed across headlines."

His weight above me is familiar and comforting. For a moment, his grin mirrors mine – it fades, replaced by something softer, heavier.

His eyes hold mine. "I'm so sorry again, darling."

"It's okay." I shake my head. "I mean, it's not, but it's not your fault."

He lowers his forehead to mine, closing the small space between us until our breaths mingle. His voice drops to a whisper, rough at the edges. "You deserve so much better."

His nose brushes mine tenderly.

The air between us hums.

"You do too, you know," I whisper back, eyes fluttering shut to block out the intensity of his gaze. "Deserve better. You deserve to walk out your door without people taking photos of you."

For a heartbeat, we just breathe, foreheads pressed together. His thumb strokes a slow line across my jaw.

He kisses me. Softly at first, a question more than a claim. But when I slide my arms around his neck, it becomes a demand.

Heat rolls through the kiss, setting me ablaze as his tongue teases the seam of my lips, begging for entrance. I open for him without hesitation, drawing his warmth inside.

His hands glide to my waist, fingers curling into my shirt, pushing the fabric away until his fingertips find bare skin. Heat sparks wherever he touches, chasing away the world outside.

Chris drops his head to my shoulder, his lips brushing softly against the curve of my neck. His breath is hot as his mouth trails open over my skin. His hands slide beneath the thin fabric of my shirt, fingers splaying wide against the bare skin of my back – a touch that's both reverent and hungry.

My head tips back into the pillows, a gasp escaping before I can catch it. He unravels me, thread by thread.

My fingers slip from his hair, tracing the strong line of his neck, the stubble along his jaw.

I guide him up, needing his mouth on mine again.

Our lips meet.

And in the silence, between heartbeats and breath, we say everything we haven't dared to speak out loud.

I reach down and pull my shirt over my head, the fabric whispering against my skin as it slips away. For a breathless moment, everything goes still, his hands finding me again.

Chris draws in a sharp breath, his palms trailing over my sides. His fingertips barely skimming my skin, igniting a fire in their wake. There's nothing rushed in his reverent touch.

Like I'm something fragile he doesn't want to break.

My heart hammers in my chest, not from nerves, but from the weight of the moment. The way he's looking at me like I matter. Like I'm his. Like he's mine.

"Jesus," he murmurs, voice rough as his eyes roam my face, my body. "You're so damn beautiful."

The words wrap around me tighter than his arms ever could, and I can't stop the small sound that escapes my throat. Half-laugh, half-sob.

I pull him back to me, kissing him deeply, slowly. Letting him feel what I don't know how to say yet.

His fingers brush lightly over the tight peaks of my breasts, breath catching with every pass, hands needing my flesh into pure sensation. I can't stop the way my hips tilt, rocking into him. My body moves on instinct. They're drawn to him like a tide to the shore. I couldn't fight it if I tried.

But his hands still my movement.

I freeze, breath catching in my throat, body burning, every nerve ending alive. His eyes search mine not just with heat, but something deeper.

I want to turn away so I can't see it, but his words hold me captive.

"It's not just casual," he murmurs, voice thick, rough around the edges as if the words cost him something. "You. Us. We aren't casual."

I gasp when his mouth lowers, when his lips find my breast. Heat surges, delicious and overwhelming, pooling low in my belly. But it's his words that crack me open.

Because he's right. It hasn't been casual. Not since he held Savie's hand like it was the most natural thing in the world. Not since he kissed me like I mattered. Not for a long time.

Not since I realized that I haven't had any nightmares since we started whatever this is that we are doing.

My hands curl around his shoulders, fingernails dragging lightly across his back as he shifts, worshiping me with his mouth, memorizing every inch. My chest arches, mouth parting in a quiet plea I can't voice.

"It's not," I whisper in agreement. "Not now."

His eyes dart to mine, and the way he looks at me in this moment, like I gave him air when he was drowning, steals the breath from my lungs. My fingers tangle into his hair, pulling his lips back to mine. Like we have all the time in the world.

I reach down, sliding his shirt over his head, baring skin that's already flushed with heat. My hands roam across him, over scorching skin and hard lines of muscle. A shiver rippling down his spine. I wrap my legs around the backs of his thighs, anchoring him to me as my fingers trace the grooves of his back, the breadth of his shoulders, the ridges of his abs.

When I've touched all that I can reach. When there is no more new skin to trace. I cradle his face in my hands, holding him.

Chris leans back just enough to look at me, his hands resting on my thighs where they're still wrapped around his hips. His thumbs trace slow, lazy circles against my skin.

One hand slides up my leg, his fingers light but sure, skimming over the softness of my stomach, the rise of my ribs, the curve of my breast.

"You don't even know what you do to me," he whispers.

Goosebumps rise along my skin, following the path of his fingers like a trail of sparks. His palms trail down my sides, meeting at the waistband of my leggings. He hesitates for a breath, his eyes flicking to mine, asking without words. I nod, and his fingers slip beneath the soft fabric, the warmth of his skin against mine.

I toss my head back and arch my back as his fingers dip into me, smoothing the slick arousal on my skin. His thumb flicking against my clit, enough to jolt my body before pulling back out of my pants, a heady groan falling from me.

Chris gently unwinds my legs from his waist. He holds my gaze for a heartbeat before his fingers curl around the waistband of my leggings. He eases them down my hips, his touch dragging fire in its wake. My underwear slips away with them, soft fabric trailing down my thighs until I'm bare beneath him.

A soft moan slips from my chest, unbidden, as my head presses into the pillow. The sensation is too much and not enough all at once – heat blooming beneath my skin, tension coiling low in my belly. He's everywhere, even in places he hasn't touched yet.

Chris grazes his lips over the soft skin of my thighs, the nip of his teeth following each press against me.

"You deserve to be worshiped," he whispers into my skin, his voice wrecked, like the words have been waiting on the edge of his tongue for far too long.

He presses forward, lips trailing up the inside of my thigh, stopping just shy of where I ache for him most. The denial is deliberate and maddening. It's a silent promise whispered against my skin.

He shifts, repeating the same slow, reverent path on the other side, building the tension like it's a language only we speak.

I rise over my elbows to watch as he spreads me open, his warm eyes are blown black with desire. He leans towards the warmth in front of him, his lips wrapping around my clit as he slips his fingers into me, one at first, then two more.

He works me higher, and my arms give way. I collapse onto the mattress below, the rush of heat and need crashing over me, my hips dancing and swaying in time with his rhythm.

I squeeze my eyes shut, fingers digging into the soft waves at the crown of his head, pulling him in like my whole world depends on it.

I need him closer. I need to drown in him.

"Please." My voice cracks with hunger and desperation. "More."

He answers without hesitation, his touch growing fiercer, more urgent.

Every movement drives me deeper into the storm of sensation as I writhe beneath him, losing myself completely. My orgasm slams into me, and my whole body tightens around a silent scream, my hands grasping roughly at the strands still clutched in my fingers.

My hips twitch uncontrollably in the aftermath, still trembling with need, as Chris drags himself away from my pussy to settle against my side. I reach over to wipe away the arousal still coating his chin as he grins at me.

"You like that, baby girl?"

Giggling softly, I press my lips to his, tasting myself in the warmth of his mouth. "Yeah. I really do."

I push him onto his back, settling over his lean waist, my heart pounding with every breath. I roll my hips over the rise of his erection. Intertwining our hands, I slide his palms up from my waist, drawing slow, deliberate circles that make my skin tingle under his touch, settling them on my breasts.

"Take me out of my jeans, baby girl." Chris's eyes trail over my body as I release his hands that linger with a mix of hunger and tenderness.

I pull away briefly, reaching down to help him out of his jeans as he lifts his hips to help me.

He pulls me forward as I settle my soaking cunt against him. Rocking over his cock, drenching him in my arousal, jerking with every motion of my hips.

"Put my cock inside your pussy. I want to be so far inside you, you'll never forget me."

I grasp him, and we both groan as I sink onto him.

My hands brace on his chest as he reaches deep within me. "Ride me. I want to watch you take what you need and fall apart all over me."

I pause as the fullness overwhelms me before I drive my hips forward slowly, my clit dragging over his pelvis with each pulse of my body. Nails digging into his skin as I throw my head back.

"You take me so good, baby girl," he groans, his hands clenching on my hips.

I snap forward with more tempo as I race toward the cliff of release again.

"So good," I whisper, my voice rough with need as I lean down to kiss him.

His arms wrap around my waist, pulling me tighter against his chest, every heartbeat syncing with mine in a fierce, urgent rhythm. He plants his feet, lifting his hips off the bed to pound into me, and a loud cry escapes me.

"Just like that," he groans. "You're so perfect."

He pauses to readjust, his arms shifting toward my shoulders. I wrap my arms around his head, pressing his face deep into the warmth of my neck.

I round my back to rock against him again. Faster, harder, and with desperation as I drag my body along his. The heat between us intensifies with every deliberate motion.

"Come for me," he begs.

And my body starts to shake against him as my orgasm rises from deep within me.

"Come for me, baby girl." He's not begging anymore.

He's demanding it.

The powerful thrum pulses deeper than anything I've ever known, stealing my breath and freezing me for a heartbeat.

I'm swept away again, carried on another silent, desperate cry.

"Ah, fuck." Chris thrusts into my shaking body a few more times before a groan tears from his lips, and he spills into me. "Shit, shit, shit. Baby girl, you ruin me."

He presses his mouth to my neck, his lips whispering over my sweaty skin.

"I'm yours, baby girl," he whispers into me, his words consuming my ability to think. "Yours, yours, yours."

I collapse onto his hard chest, our sweat-soaked skin melding together, every heartbeat pounding in sync beneath me. I can't even muster up a proper response to the words murmured at me. A panic I should be feeling is nowhere to be found.

Because the words he just etched in my skin are more real than this was ever supposed to be.

We lay together long enough for him to soften, a moan falling from my lips as he slips from my body. Eventually, he rolls us over, tugging the blankets from where they'd bunched below us to drape over our cooling skin.

Chris wraps me tightly in his arms, and I'm left feeling not just satisfied but deeply settled. I've finally found a place to rest, grounded in the safety of him.

"I thought you'd never want to see me again," he murmurs, voice low against my hair. "I was terrified... terrified you'd hate me. That I'd never get to hold you like this again. Never see Savie playing astronaut princess. That I would miss out on..."

"On?" I press gently, nudging closer, desperate to fill the silence he leaves hanging.

"On this. On us," he breathes out, his shoulders tightening, trying to play it off like it's no big deal. But his eyes betray him. There's fear there. A quiet vulnerability.

I shake my head, swallowing the lump rising in my throat. "You never have to worry about that, Chris. We're friends and friends don't turn on each other for things outside their control."

The desire to keep him floods me, a wave I can't fight, so I close my eyes, hiding the storm inside. My lips press softly to the steady beat of his chest.

No more words, just his heartbeat and the slow lull of sleep pulling me under.

Chapter 26

Chris

THE NEXT COUPLE DAYS are some of the best of my life. Tiffany and I spend every spare moment we can wrapped around each other. Even just the thought of her naked in the soft glow of the lamp has my cock twitching.

But it isn't just the sex.

God, it's so much more than that.

It's the way she laughs until she cries, and how easy it is to be with her. When we aren't falling into bed, we're falling over laughing. And somewhere along the way, I've stopped noticing where helping ends and *wanting* begins.

I'm wrapped around both of their little fingers, and honestly, there's no place I'd rather be.

But I'm not in the bed I want to be in tonight as I roll over, with my phone in my hand. There's Ohio restate website tabs that I thumbed through still open in the internet browser app, minimized but ruminating in my mind. Several houses favorited as if there is any possibility of staying. I've spent the last two hours scrolling and dreaming of what it might be like.

I force myself away from something that I can't make happen and open the thread between me and Tiffany and stare at her last message. I've stared at it seven times in the past hour.

The reason I'm not with her?

Brandon and Shawn are over for girls' night.

I had joked that I have the same parts as Brandon and Shawn, but that got shot down fast. Technically true, sure. But I'm definitely *not* 'one of the girls.' I text her again anyway.

I don't even care if I sound needy.

I am.

Chris

I miss you.

Chris

Tell Savie I miss her too.

My phone pings immediately, and my pulse jumps, mouth curling before I can stop it.

Tiffany

You just saw us three hours ago.

Tiffany

But Savie can't stop talking about you. Safe to say she misses you too.

Chris

Just Savie?

Tiffany

I'm currently mad at you.

Chris

What? Why?

Tiffany

> **I definitely think you broke it this morning.**

Chris

> **If you let me come over. I'll apologize directly to her.**

Tiffany

> **I'll think about it.**

The kissy face emoji pulls a laugh from me just as my bedroom door flies open and all three of my brothers pour in.

I lock my phone screen when Charlie dives onto my bed, trying to snatch it from me.

"Hey! What are you doing?" I stretch my arms above my head, keeping the phone out of his reach.

"Trying to see what you and Tiffany are chatting about." His tone is all faux-innocence, but the cheeky smirk gives him away. "You have been neglecting us, baby brother."

"How have I been neglecting you? Junior spends most of his time in New York, and you two are busy with your super-secret new business venture." I roll my eyes, fighting a smile. "Besides, I've been helping Tiff with Savie and rehabbing my shoulder. Not a lot of time outside of that."

"Mom says you've been staying over there later and later. Missing dinner." Jake chimes in from where he's leaning against my dresser, arms crossed, eyes sharp. There's something in his voice that grates at me, a flicker of annoyance. "You aren't just doing those two things, are you?"

"What's it to you?" My phone disappears under my thigh as I shove Charlie off me, glaring at Jake. "You sound almost... jealous?"

Charlie props himself on one elbow from the floor, grinning. "Yeah, you *do* sound jealous."

Junior drops onto the edge of the bed near my feet, leaning back on his hands, quiet but watchful. "Why do you care, Jake?"

"I don't!" Jake snaps, but he crosses his arms tighter, eyes darting. He's half the reason I stayed away from Tiffany all those years ago. Half the reason I missed out on this, on *her*, for so long.

"I just don't see the point," he mutters.

195

"Have you seen that woman?" Charlie waggles his eyebrows. Reaching forward, I smack the back of his head. The idiot laughs as he ducks away. "What? She's turned into a fine woman."

"Charlie!" Jake and I bark at the same time, but he just laughs harder. Heat creeps up my neck, and I press my tongue to the back of my teeth, biting back a sharp response I want to hurl at Jake.

"What?" Charlie asks as he falls back onto his elbows again. Junior shakes his head, but his chest shakes with laughter. "She has!"

"Look," Jake exhales hard, scrubbing at his thighs, jaw tight with something he's not saying. "Jason's my best friend. You know how he is. And she's got a little girl now. Jason's even weirder about his niece. I just don't want to deal with him when this ends. That's all."

I push back against the headboard, my pulse drumming in my ears. "There is nothing to end, Jake. We're just friends."

All three of them turn their heads and give me the same skeptical look. *Liar.*

I am a liar. In the worst way, because I want nothing more than to keep them. And both Tiffany and I agree this is more than casual. Even if she isn't ready to label it.

There is something important between us, and my heart is already shattered on the floor around me, knowing our time is running out.

"What?" I snap, grinding my teeth together. "We *are* just friends."

"Friends with benefits, maybe." Charlie teases, and I smack the back of his head a third time. He raises an eyebrow as he ducks away from me again.

"Look," I exhale, my voice dropping. "I'm not going to lie and say I don't like her. She's beautiful, and she's funny, and she's raised an amazing little girl. I think she might be one of my best friends, but that's all it's ever going to be. I don't live here. She's got too much going on to move there."

I raise my voice before Jake can cut me off. "Even if - *even if* – a relationship was something the two of us wanted to attempt. It would be none of your or Jason's business. But it isn't, okay?"

Jake rolls his eyes, but his hands relax before he crosses them over his chest. "Doesn't sound like you don't want a relationship."

I don't answer. I can't.

Because he's right.

I hate the way the lie tastes every time it leaves my mouth. I'm so far underwater with the two of them, I'll never recover.

They've become my home, and leaving is going to hurt.

But what choice do I have? I could try to make a clean break. Let Mom help Tiffany instead, leave a little early. But I already know I'm not strong enough to walk away.

So, I'm staying until I have no other choice.

I'm going to risk the pain, risk falling deeper in love. I'll make more memories I won't forget. Hope we can hold on to *something* after all this.

Because what I want doesn't matter. What matters is protecting them.

"Hellooo. Earth to Chris." Charlie waves a hand in front of my face, dragging me back to them. "Man, you've got it *bad*, baby bro."

I shake him off. "Nah, man, it's not like that. I told you already. What are all of you guys here for anyway?"

"We came to get your mind off tomorrow." Junior kicks his feet up on my bed. "Thought you'd be wallowing. Prepping for the big talk with Coach and the doc."

"But you *weren't* wallowing," Charlie snorts. "Not about your shoulder anyway."

"My shoulder feels good," I say with a shrug. "Dan hasn't yelled at me in weeks, and *Nurse Ratched* gave me a gold star on my last visit. I figure it's just a formality, and Coach will give me the rundown on when I can get back on the ice with the team."

My phone buzzes beneath me, and my heartbeat stumbles before kicking into overdrive.

Junior stands, offering Charlie a hand. "Well, I guess we'll just leave you to it then. Mom said you've been running with Tiff and Savie at 6 am, so I'm sure you want to get some shut eye since you aren't wallowing."

The wink he throws at me is too smug to be innocent and uninformed. I snort. Of course he knows. He always knows everything somehow.

But they are still here for me. Junior even flew in just in case I needed him. And that's support you can't pay for. I'm grateful for them. Even Jake, annoying as he is.

"Thanks for checking on me, guys." I'm also extremely grateful for the out Junior just gave me.

Because while I *have* been going to Tiff's at 6 a.m., we're definitely not running. No, that cardio's got a whole different rhythm.

"If tomorrow doesn't go well, I might need you for copious amounts of alcohol." I offer them the consolation I don't want to give, but somehow, I doubt Tiffany will want to console me about not leaving her.

Charlie's eyes twinkle like I've handed him a winning lottery ticket, hefting himself back to his feet. "I'm *so* down for a drunken brothers night. Night, bro."

He slaps the doorframe as he follows Jake out, but Junior hangs back. Our eyes lock, and there's seriousness swimming in his expression.

"If she makes you happy, don't you think you should fight for that?" He asks.

I blink, startled by the softness in his voice.

"She needs help, yeah," he goes on, "but I think *you* need her too. And if what Mom says is true, that little girl needs a daddy. Because her sperm donor sure as hell isn't coming back."

"Mom's a gossip," I mumble under my breath.

He smiles but otherwise ignores me.

"I know I wasn't around much when you were in high school, and now I'm out in New York, but you've always looked at her differently. Even before you knew what it meant. Before Jake and Jason got in your head and told you it wasn't your place. Before you had some idealized notion you were doing the right thing, and that's why you had to stay away." He shrugs, but his eyes are steady, sure of himself. "But maybe it wasn't."

A beat of silence settles between us.

"If she's what you want. If she makes you happy, don't you deserve that? You don't have to carry the whole damn family on your back, Chris. We've got it. You get to want things too," he pauses. "Just keep that in mind."

And just like that, he turns and walks out. I sit there, stunned. I *know* what he said, but things aren't that easy. And if he *is* right, I don't know what to do with that.

My phone pings again.

I finally fish it out from under me.

Tiffany

The boys are gone and Savie is in bed.

Tiffany

Are you coming?

Chris

Yeah. Give me a little bit to make sure my brothers are gone. I think my parents are in bed already.

Tiffany

I feel like we are in high school all over again. Sneaking around.

I laugh as I tug on a hoodie, slipping my phone into my pocket. She's not wrong. I creep into my brother's old room – the one Savie slept in last weekend – and peek through the blinds. The driveway's empty except for my car.

I head down the stairs, and I'm glad I had the whole house redone for my parents.

The creaky stair from childhood?

Fixed.

But as soon as I hit the bottom stair, I nearly barrel straight into my dad.

We both jolt, but he recovers first, eyeing me with a wicked smirk. I cringe.

"Um, I was just, um." I flounder, glancing toward the kitchen like it might save me from the awkwardness. "Just getting water?"

He chuckles. "Mmhmm, sure. Except the kitchen's that way," he says, pointing in the opposite direction I was headed. "Unless that water's next door."

"Dad!" I sputter, heat flushing my cheeks. He's right, of course. "I jus-"

"No, don't bother, son. Go see your girl," he says, waving me off. "Just lock up behind you and don't let your mother know I knew. She's feeling decidedly protective of those girls lately."

He shuffles off in his slippers, leaving me standing there, stunned.

I'm still laughing when I reach Tiffany's porch. She opens the door, radiant in the soft hallway light.

That smile—God, that smile—undoes me every time.

"What's so funny?" She asks, arms looping around my neck as she kisses my jaw.

I sweep her into my arms, and she giggles, legs wrapping around me, my lips finding hers for a gentle kiss.

"My dad caught me sneaking out," I say, grinning as I carry her up the stairs. "Apparently, it really *is* like high school again."

She buries her face in my neck, muffling her laughter, and I don't even try to stop the way my heart soars.

My cock grows harder with each swaying step that rocks her body over my groin. I pause at the top of the stairs, my grip tightening as she grinds against me on purpose, a sultry smile on her lips. I clench my jaw, eyes slipping shut as a groan builds in my throat.

"Baby girl," I rasp, barely holding on, "if you keep that up, we aren't going to make it to your room, and the little one is just down the hall. We don't want to risk that."

"Hurry, Chris. Please," her voice is a whisper against my skin, breathless and aching. Her arms tighten around my neck like she can't get close enough, like she's trying to fuse us together.

She leans in, lips brushing the shell of my ear before she nips gently at the lobe. "I need you in me."

The words are barely spoken, exhaled in a whimper.

And God help me, in this moment, I'd burn the world down just to give her what she needs.

I quicken my pace, feet falling soft but swift over the ancient carpet.

When we reach the master, I ease the door shut behind us, careful not to let it click. We still for a moment, listening for Trixi. The traitorous little fluffball has almost blown our cover twice, and neither of us trusts her not to come barreling in with her full-body, tail-wagging with joy at my arrival.

We wait another beat.

Nothing.

I turn to Tiffany, and the look in her eyes tells me we've cleared the final hurdle.

Her smile is all mine.

I press her gently into the mattress, the room lit only by the hush of our urgency. Our hands find each other, fumbling, frantic, like we're trying to memorize skin before the moment slips away. Each touch says what neither of us has dared to voice aloud.

It doesn't take long before we are falling apart in each other's arms.

Her lips find my chest, slow and soft, and I wrap my arms tighter around her, the warmth of affection swelling in my gut like a flood I can't contain. My eyes squeeze shut just for a heartbeat before I gather the nerve to look at her, dazed and satisfied, bathed in the afterglow.

"Baby girl?" I murmur, brushing damp strands from her flushed face. "You good?"

She nods, wordless, her fingertips drifting across my stomach in lazy, aimless patterns. Each touch makes my muscles jump beneath her, too raw. I flinch away from her delicate fingers as my cock jumps to her thoughtless demand.

She tilts her head, eyes wide and unsure, the confusion on her face is sweet.

Reaching for me, she whispers, "Chris?"

"If you keep doing that, we are going to be going again before your sweet pussy has a chance to recover. You just stay right there, baby girl. I'll be right back." I press a kiss to her forehead.

I pull my basketball shorts over my hips and slip out of the room, heading toward the bathroom.

I've only just turned back toward Tiffany's room when there's a soft padding of little feet coming my way.

"Chis?" The sleepy-headed little girl is rubbing her eyes with tiny fists, hair tousled, sleep clinging to her like a second skin. Her voice is barely more than a whisper. "Where you shirt?"

I laugh softly and kneel to gather her to my chest, her small body melting against mine. "Why are you up, little one?"

She lays her head on my shoulder, warm and heavy with sleep. Around the corner, I catch sight of a big, shadowy shape – Trixi peeking around, alert and protective. I wave her gently back toward Savie's room and follow the swish of her wagging tail.

"I heard a noise," she whispers, "It waked me up."

I press a kiss to her messy curls as I peel back the covers on her bed. I guess Tiff and I weren't as quiet as we thought.

"It was just me and your mommy talking," I say softly, shifting her higher on my hip. "Let's get you back to bed."

Settling her onto the mattress, I pull the covers over her small frame and pat the bed to invite Trixi to lie beside her. She's half-asleep before I even finish tucking her in. "Sleep now, little one. I'll be here when you wake."

At the door, I pause. My hand on the frame, I take it all in. Memorizing the sight of Savie curled around her dog. Save the image of my girl in our bed, *her* bed, before this. And it hits me harder than I expected.

This moment.

This life.

It might be over before I know it, and I'll never get a chance to see this again.

I ache with the weight of it.

What if this slips through my fingers before I ever figure out how to hold it?

I close my eyes for a beat, then turn and head back to Tiffany.

She's already on her feet, tugging her threadbare shirt over her still naked body.

Her head snaps toward me as I walk in. "Chris? Did you get lost?"

"No, but we woke Savie. I put her back down." I chuckle, holding up the damp towel. "It might be a little cold, but get back in bed. I'm not done with you."

"She saw you?" Her voice comes out strained, making my chest tighten.

I step forward, wrapping my arms around her. She's still warm, still half-naked, and still mine for now.

"It's fine, darling. She was barely awake," I promise. "I doubt she will remember it in the morning. And me being here when she wakes up isn't unusual for her. This won't be shocking enough for her to remember."

Her brain's spinning, running the worst-case scenarios. My chest constricts, mirroring the panic behind her eyes.

Her dread falters as I slide the towel across her pussy, deliberate and unhurried as I coax her gently back to me. She gasps, and I watch the tension drain from her shoulders, her breathing evening out as her body finally begins to settle.

When she softens beneath my touch, I let the towel fall and ease her shirt back over her head, baring her to me once more.

Somehow, in the last ten weeks, she's shown me something that I didn't know I needed.

I can't do anything about the future. I can't stop what's coming. The doctor, Coach, they'll all be here tomorrow. By the end of the week, I could be on a flight back to Boston. Settled into my immaculate penthouse apartment, but all alone.

But tonight?

Right now, I can love my girl.

I let the rest fall away—the questions, the fear, the ticking clock. All I have is now.

And her.

Chapter 27

Tiffany

THE FIRST FRIDAY IN July, I take the day off since Chris is at the doctor's and Mrs. B is with him. Mark offers to watch Savie for me, but I decline. I know he wants to be there for his family.

My fingers itch to text Chris.

Just to check in.

But he's surrounded by people focused on his career – on his future. He doesn't need me to yank at his attention.

I tell myself not to be selfish, because he doesn't need the distraction of something he'll be walking away from soon.

Savie drifts from room to room, trailing chaos like a comet, and I follow behind, cleaning bits of toys and crumbs.

And I worry.

Every step, I wonder what's going to change.

What if he gets cleared to play again?

Part of me hopes he isn't. Because if he can't go back, then maybe he stays.

Savie's going to be heartbroken when he leaves. And me? I'll miss the friendship, sure. And yeah, the sex.

God, the sex.

THE HOME WE MAKE

But we're adults. And I've done long-distance friendships before. I also know how to file people away, keep them in the 'past' folder.

My chest squeezes tighter every time I imagine him gone.

I distract myself all day. Take Savie to visit my father again. We play, eat dinner, and manage a bath. I finally get her into pajamas and bed as the quiet part of the evening enters.

I press a kiss to her forehead and another to Trixi's, like always.

But tonight, instead of her curling up with Trixi, her tiny voice cuts through the quiet. "Mommy, where Chis?"

"He's with the doctor, remember?" I slide into bed beside her, running my hand through her tangled curls. Trixi's head rests heavy on my calf.

Her face tightens with concern as she stares at me from under her thick lashes. "Chis sick like Poppy?"

My heart cracks.

"No, sweetheart. Chris is okay. He'll be here tomorrow to play with you while Mommy is at work."

"Good." She nods her tiny head against my chest, snuggling into her pillow. "I miss Chis."

"I know, sweet girl." I press another kiss to her forehead before I slip out of bed. "Sleep. He'll be here when you wake."

As I step into the hallway, I glance out the window and spot his car in the neighboring driveway with three unfamiliar ones beside it.

My stomach flips with concern.

He could've at least sent a text.

I shake the thought away.

That's not fair.

He's had a long day. I don't have a claim on his time. No matter how close we've gotten, I'm not his, and he's definitely not mine.

My phone rings from inside my room.

I rush to my bedroom, expecting Chris's number, but it's the hospital. Something inside me splits, like broken glass dragging across skin.

I answer hesitantly. "Hello?"

"Hi, yes. Is this Tiffany Samson?" The voice on the other end is clipped and harried.

"Um, yes. It is." I swallow the lump in my throat before I can continue. "Can I ask what this is about?"

"Ma'am, I'm afraid something happened with your father." The quiet sounds of the hospital behind her are deafening. "And we need you to come to the hospital as soon as you can."

My knees buckle, and I collapse onto the bed. "Is – is everything okay?"

"I'm afraid I can't discuss it over the phone. Just... please get to the hospital as quickly as you safely can," her voice softens, but I already know.

I can feel it in my bones.

My dad is dead.

"Of course," I whisper. I look around the room without really seeing anything. "I just, um, I need to call my brother and find a babysitter for my daughter."

"Okay. We will see you when you get here." She hesitates, like she knows I already understand. Like she wishes she didn't have to be the one to say it. "Just be safe, ma'am."

I nod, but no words come.

My hands shake as I rush out the door.

I'm halfway across the lawn before I realize I didn't grab the baby monitor. I stop, frozen in the dark, stuck looking back at the house on unstable knees.

What do I do?

I won't be long, and Trixi would die before letting anything happen to Savie. But how can I leave her alone at a time like this?

Before I can decide whether to go back or keep moving forward, chaos erupts next door, dragging my eyes to the halo of light on the porch.

Three unfamiliar men pour out of Chris's house, and he's right behind them. His eyes meet mine, and the tears start falling before I have any hope of catching them.

He calls my name, but my own ragged breathing is loud in my ears. I'm frozen in the riot of emotions rushing through me. Anger and disbelief war for the top spot.

I stand immobile as he rushes toward me.

"Darling, what's wrong?" Chris's hands are on my face before I even realize he's reached me.

I grab his shirt like it's the only thing holding me upright.

"My father." My voice cracks. "S – something happened. I, um, have to go to the hospital."

"Not alone, you're not." He pulls me against him.

His chest rising and falling steadies me. It presses strength into my wobbly knees.

He's the anchor in the storm of my emotions.

He opens his mouth to say more when one of the unfamiliar men calls out to him. "Is everything okay over here?"

Chris doesn't look back; his eyes never leave mine. "Yes, Coach."

His body shields me from view, and I'm reminded I'm only wearing sleep shorts and the threadbare shirt he loves so much. I just don't have it in me to be embarrassed as I fall apart in his arms.

Gentle fingertips brush away my tears, but more replace them.

"Darling, go change," he says softly, brushing my hair behind my ear. "I'll ask Mom if she can sit with Savie, and I'll take you to the hospital."

I nod and hurry back to my house. His deep voice steadies me enough to start moving again, but not enough to stop the tears.

Not enough to stop the shaking.

I come back down the stairs and fall into Brenda's arms. Chris wraps around us both like a shield.

"Oh, sweet girl," Brenda whispers, cupping my face when Chris's arms fall away.

"Go take care of your father, I've got Savie," she promises, turning to her son. "Chris, drive safe and let me know when you know."

"We will, Mom. Come on, Tiff, let's go." He gently pulls me from Brenda—I can't do myself—and leads me to the car. We pull out of the driveway in silence.

"I'm so sorry, Ms. Samson. Mr. Samson." The doctor's voice filters in, from far away. "It was very quick. We don't believe he felt any pain. At this point, we suspect a blood clot, but we'll need an autopsy to confirm. If that's something the family would like?"

She's kind. Maybe even sincere. I register it, but it doesn't touch me. It's just noise.

There's nothing.

Just ... numbness.

Chris's hands dig into my shoulders. They bind me to a world that doesn't seem real. Jason's fingers curl around my hand like he's afraid I'll disappear from his side if he lets go. Like he's desperate to hold on to a time before this loss.

I look at him. Hoping he will answer her.

But he doesn't.

"Okay, then, um, I guess we want the autopsy. Just to know for sure." I say, the words barely forming, clawing their way out of my mouth. "How long until we can. Until we can plan the funeral?"

"It's generally a couple of days, sometimes weeks. You'll need to get in touch with the funeral home of your choice, and they'll direct you on the timeline from their end and arrange a pickup for your father. I'm afraid I can't give you anything more concrete than that."

The doctor runs through what we need to do, and leaves. The soft click of the door latch echos in the quiet room. The sound barely feels real, but it makes both Jason and me flinch.

I turn to him, but the first tear is already falling from his eyes. "Jason, you're the oldest. You should sign these."

"No," He shakes his head, a tremble rising from his feet to settle in his voice. "I- I can't. You have to."

"Jason –" His name catches in my throat. It echos off the walls closing in around me.

"It's okay," Chris murmurs, his hands settling more firmly on my shoulders, steadying the tremor that finds its way into my body. "Jake's waiting for you in the hall. Charlie's going to follow you home so your car doesn't get left here."

A hand moves from my shoulder to the nape of my neck, rubbing at the knot of muscle that's forming. "I'll stay with Tiffany and help her get through the paperwork. We'll meet for lunch tomorrow, okay?"

Jason nods and slips out, his eyes never meeting mine. The door clicks shut again, this time more muted under the rush of my rapid heartbeat in my ears.

Chris wraps me in his arms, pulling me close. His lips graze my temple, his hand tracing my back in slow, steady circles.

I sign everything.

One X after another.

My hand shakes, and by the time I set the pen down, when I've signed away the last piece of him.

I still don't know if I hate him or love him. I only know that he's gone. And I'll never have time to figure it out.

Chris doesn't say anything. He just sweeps me into his arms and ushers me out of the hospital.

Everything after is a blur.

We get home, and Brenda is waiting for us. She wraps me in her arms like a mother should and rocks me.

Holds me like I wish my own mother would.

Strokes my hair while I cry into her shoulder and whispers soft, comforting nonsense in my ear.

This must be what a mother's love feels like.

God, I hope Savie feels this when I hold her.

I pull back and kiss Brenda's cheek. "Thank you, Mrs. B."

"You don't have to thank me for this. Just let us know what we can do for you." She kisses my cheek in return.

The world falls out of focus as they talk over me. I don't hear what they say, but their concerned gazes are on me as they talk.

Brenda's voice catches my attention again when she turns her focus away from me. "Chris, maybe you should stay here tonight, just in case."

"I was planning on it, Ma." He ushers her out, kisses her cheek, and locks the door behind her.

I don't move as jealousy burns in my chest. It's so easy with his parents. He never has to second-guess how they feel about him. If they love him.

It isn't fair.

"Okay, darling. It's time for bed," he says, turning back to me.

I'm angry.

Flushed with a fire that isn't anyone's fault, and it's aimed right at him. I bite my tongue because it's not rational. This blaze of anger.

I shrug him off as he tries to help me up the stairs. "You don't have to stay, Chris. I'm fine. I'm just going to sleep, and I'll deal with this crap tomorrow."

"Oh no, baby girl. I'm not going anywhere." He follows me anyway. "But you're going to talk to me about whatever this is."

I roll my eyes and scoff, but don't push anymore. It's useless anyway; the stubborn set to his jaw tells me he's following me whether I want him to or not.

"Chris, just go home. I appreciate you," I snap, before I can think better of it. "But I'm not in the mood tonight."

"Tiffany, I'm not here for sex. Just talk to me, darling." He closes the door behind us softly. Stalking toward me. "What's going on in that pretty little head of yours?"

"What do you want me to talk about? Hm?" The anger has taken the reins, and the words start to barrel out of me.

I turn to face him.

It isn't fair he had two parents he could count on. And it isn't fair to blame him for that, but somehow, I do.

"That my dad died?" The laugh that spills from my lips is bitter and hollow. "That it's not fair because he was getting better? That I'm mad you have parents who actually care about you? Because that's insane. You can't control that."

He reaches for me.

My hands shove him before I can consider the consequences or about who this makes me.

He says nothing, just comes closer again.

I whimper despite my clamped lips, and he slows, frowning, not touching me. Just following me until I back into the wall. Until I crumble into the warmth of his arms. He holds me as I shove and shake; my rage and horror bleeding out until only sorrow is left.

The shock of what I've done hits me like ice. "I'm so sorry, Chris. I didn't mean –"

The tears flood my cheeks as I bite back the scream building in me. The one line I won't cross is waking up Savie.

He lifts me onto the bed, tucking us both beneath the covers when the tears finally slow. "You ready to talk now, darling?"

"I don't know what to say," I confess as I curl into his chest. "I'm sad, obviously. And I'm mad he's gone. The doctors said he was getting better. I just saw him this morning, and he looked *better*. They'd turned down the vent settings. They thought they'd get him back to breathing on his own by the weekend."

He kisses my forehead, his hands running up and down my back. "And? Why were you mad at me? Because I have good parents?"

"I – I, yes?" My throat tightens as we stare at each other. "I know it's not fair, but look at you. You're this amazing man with an amazing job and two of the kindest people in the world for parents, who love you. And I'm me, with my shitty mother and a dead, absentee father."

"You're an amazing mother and woman –" He starts to protest, but I cut him off with a sharp exhale.

"I know I'm a good person, and I try really hard to be anything other than what my parents were for Savie's sake. I don't need you to tell me that, but I've worked *so* hard."

I curl my fingers into his shirt. The anger rises again, building a tremor in my hands. "I've put in the time in therapy, at work, with boundaries and ultimatums and, and, and..."

My breath hitches as I turn away, tucking my head into a pillow. "I'm tired, Chris. It's exhausting. And still I uprooted my life for a family whose only ever leeched my time and energy."

Chris shuffles closer, dragging my body back against his chest. "Darling," he pauses, searching for words. "I can't even imagine."

This man though? The only thing he leeches from me is stress. He leaves me comforted when I shouldn't be. And warm in an embrace I'm not sure I deserve.

"My mother," my voice trembles as I recount things from my past.

The things these walls kept hidden. The invisible wounds he somehow manages to soothe.

"The things she did... it was abuse, at least that's what my therapist calls it. I just didn't know anything else and... my father," I laugh bitterly again. "So busy playing the good dad he never actually was one."

"He took time off work to be there for my brother's football games and graduations. For me? Half days... Late arrivals... Early exits." Tears I thought were gone begin to trickle again. "He always said I could come over whenever I wanted, and sometimes I did, but there was nothing there for me. No space for me to be, just a twin bed in between some exercise equipment. And I had friends and activities here I'd be away from. Things I'd miss out on - if I left my mom's house. So, I stayed here."

Chris's arms tense around me. I know it hurts to hear. It's why I've never told anyone.

But in this moment, I want someone else to hurt besides me.

"And Mom made sure to remind me, every time I thought about leaving. She made sure I knew my father didn't have the money she did." The words keep falling from my lips now that I've started. "And then when she had me cornered... she reminded me how much she hated me, how much of a burden I was to her."

"Anytime she put her hands on me. Afterward, it was lavish gifts or money – things I wanted or needed – so I would come back." I pause, every breath ripping its way out of my chest as I shake the words free from the years of chains I've kept them under. "And God help me, I did. Every time. And now they've dragged me back into this house. This house, I still have nightmares about."

A shiver runs through him, but I keep going.

I *can't* stop.

"You can't possibly understand what it was like. This house, my parents, it's why I got out as quickly as I could. I know you worked hard for what you've got," I laugh, low and cynical, "but I worked harder. And now, he's gone."

His forehead drops to my hair as he tries and fails to speak. He pulls me closer, holding me too tightly.

He exhales shakily against me, swallowing hard before he finally whispers. "Oh, darling."

"There is nothing you could have done. And there is nothing you *can* do." My voice sounds distant in my ears, the overwhelming sorrow pulling me into the black depths I always retreat into. "I'll be fine. I always, *always* am."

"You don't have to be fine." His arms tighten around me, warmth finally blooming through my chest. "I'm here either way."

"Yeah, I do." I snuggle back into him. "For Savie, I have to be."

Chapter 28

Chris

Tiffany finally drifts into a fitful sleep. But I can't. Not after what she confessed.

I stare at the ceiling, fire simmering just beneath my skin. Rage fed the fire with every slight that she recounted. At the things that kept us apart - Jake and Jason warning me away from her, myself listening to them.

I thought they were being overprotective. Turns out, they were isolating her to protect a secret that shouldn't have been a secret.

And I let them.

I could've made a difference. She could've had someone in her corner. I could've been that person.

Maybe she wouldn't have had to climb out alone. Maybe I could've gotten her out *with me*.

Tears sting my eyes, but I blink them away.

Reaching into the pocket of my jeans, I pull out my phone.

Chris

You and I have to talk. Tomorrow.

Jake

What about?

Chris

Tiffany. High School.

I shove my phone back into my pocket. It vibrates almost immediately, but I ignore it. Jake can wait. Tiffany can't.

Little feet hit the floor in the room down the hall, followed by the soft thump of paws against the dingy carpet. Tiffany's bedroom door creaks open. I sit up and turn toward the little girl who's stolen my heart.

"What are you doing up, little one?" I whisper, holding a finger to my lips.

She rubs her eyes with tiny fists, curls wild around her face. "Chis? Where's Mommy?"

I open my arms, and she climbs into them without hesitation.

"She's sleeping, sweet one." I point to Tiffany, who's restless. "She had a hard day. So, I stayed to snuggle her, just like I do with you when you have a bad day. Is that okay?"

She nods, her cheek pressed to my chest. "You give good snuggles."

My heart is cracked wide open with her words. My arms tighten around her, pressing my cheek to her hair as a fierce need to protect them takes root in me.

"Is Mommy okay?" she asks.

"Yeah, she's okay. Just sad." I tell her. Lying us both down and rolling toward Tiffany so Savie is nestled between us. "You know what I think she would really like?"

"No, what?" Savie yawns and snuggles deeper.

"A snuggle party. You, me, Mommy, and Trixi." I pat my thigh after pulling the blankets over us, encouraging Trixi to hop onto the bed. I run my hand over Savie's back before draping my arm across both of my girls.

Tiffany shifts in her sleep, releasing a sigh like her body finally believes it's allowed to rest.

I let my fingers trail over her back as my eyes keep watching the way Savie's eyes flutter, trying to stay open to soak up as much of this moment as she can. Cocooned in this space we've carved out over the weeks – months – I've been a part of their lives.

In the quiet room, I study them. Tiffany's face is slack with exhaustion, but for the first time in hours, peaceful. My gaze lingers on her, and suddenly she's someone else again: younger, sad, crying under the porch light, a memory surfacing unbidden, one I didn't even know I still carried.

The evening settles all over town as I hurry home, late from Derek's place next to the baseball field where we had been hanging out. I'm walking up to my house when I see Tiffany curled into herself at the edge of her porch, swallowed by a sweatshirt that must be her brother's. Her arms are cinched tight across her chest, head bowed, hair sliding forward. The porch light spills over her in a soft amber glow, but she looks cold, the way a bird looks cold when it tucks its wings in.

I slow, and her head lifts just enough for our eyes to meet. She's still, unnaturally still. In the ten years I've known her, she's never been still; always moving, always smiling, like something alive in mid-flight. Tonight, she looks like she's been caught midair.

My gaze flicks toward my house. I'm already late, there's trouble waiting inside, but my feet carry me to her anyway.

I ease down onto the stairs beside her.

"You know," I say with a soft smile, "the view isn't much out here. Feels like punishment staring at it."

"Maybe it is." Her voice is quiet, arms loosening just a little. She doesn't laugh, but the heat of her feels closer than before. "Maybe I like it."

Up close, I can see the rims of her eyes are red. She's been crying. I want to reach out, pull her toward me, but I don't.

"That doesn't sound like you," I say. "You don't strike me as someone who likes punishment."

"It's called masochism, dumb dumb." She huffs out a brittle laugh that dies in her throat. She finally looks at me as a tear drips from the corner of her eye. "Do you ever feel like you'd do anything to get out of this place. Like the whole town is trying to smother you until you're too tired to fight?"

I place my hand on the concrete near hers, not quite touching but close enough that a twitch of a finger would bridge the gap. Her eyes catch mine. The tears trailing down her face keep me captive. I can't look away.

"Yeah," I breathe the words, almost afraid to say them too loud. "But maybe that's because you're thinking of the town as a house with no doors. If you look closely enough, maybe you'll find one."

She frowns a little.

"You've got plans, right? College out of state?"

She nods, stiffly, wiping at her face.

I hesitate before continuing. "Well, that's your door. You just got to turn around and stop looking out the window at the town."

She doesn't say anything; she just looks back out to the street. She tips her head onto my shoulder, the weight of her is warm and trembling. I hold still, every nerve aware of her leaning into me. It takes everything in me not to react to her body against mine.

"Why did you stop?" She whispers so quietly I almost don't hear her.

"You looked like you needed someone."

She's silent for a heartbeat.

"I did," she whispers. "I just didn't know I would need you."

We sit like that until she finally pulls away, wincing as she stands. She starts for the door.

Pressing a kiss against her forehead, I let the weight of the day pull me under, too. And when I wake, I'm warmer than I've ever been before.

I stretch, fingers brushing against soft skin. Against Tiffany. The woman I love. I love her, and there's no going back for me now.

It's been true for weeks, months...maybe years.

Probably since the first time she stuck her tongue out at me at the tender age of six.

A little body shifts against me, burrowing in, and I swear I feel my heart burst clean in two.

These two, Tiffany and Savie... they're everything. I press a kiss to Savie's forehead, lifting my gaze to the sleepy eyes of my lover.

Her grief-filled eyes.

I lean over Savie and kiss her softly, trying to convey all the things she's not ready to hear.

"Stay here, cuddle your girls. I'm going to go start breakfast," I whisper. "And if I know my mom, she will be here before I even get the stove warm."

Tiffany nods, tears welling in her bloodshot eyes, still puffy from last night.

I stroke her cheek, catching the first one before it falls. "Feel whatever you need to feel, darling. I've got you."

I kiss her again before I can stop myself, quick like it's a habit. I take one last look at the pair of them under the blankets and rise.

I head downstairs, and Trixi follows, her tags clinking gently in the quiet of the morning.

Sure enough, Mom arrives before the skillet's even hot, a plate in her hands and worry on her face.

"How are your girls?" She asks as she breezes in. "I worried all night long. What can we do?"

"Slow down, Ma." I grab the plate and move toward the kitchen. "I don't think there is anything you can do right now. She's still got to tell Savie and pick a funeral home, so until those two things happen, there is nothing we can do."

"You could do something for me, though. I need to talk to Jake. Could you stay with them while I do that?" I turn back toward her after dropping the food on the counter. "I wouldn't leave if it wasn't important."

A voice cuts in behind me. "I don't need a babysitter, Chris."

Tiffany.

She stands in the doorway, Savie in her arms. She looks exhausted but steady. Though there's a tremor in her hand against Savie's back.

"Thank you for the breakfast, Mrs. B," she says. "I know that's from you. Chris hasn't had time to cook."

I cross the space and wrap them both in my arms. "I know you don't need a babysitter, but even still, I don't want you to be alone today."

I press a kiss to Tiffany's forehead, then one to the back of Savie's messy curls. I rock them gently for a moment, savoring them in my arms, before I lift Savie's weight from hers.

"Come on, little one. It's time to eat, and Granny B brought us breakfast." I buckle Savie into her booster, slide a plate in front of her, and watch her small fingers toy with the fork.

Tiffany drifts to the table in slow motion like she's moving underwater. I set a plate before her, too, but she doesn't reach for it.

"I'm going to go talk to Jake," I press another kiss to her head. "And I'll be back and help you make some calls to homes this afternoon. Okay?"

She nods once, but I can't tell if she really hears me.

Mom squeezes my shoulder, taking the chair beside Tiffany. My chest aches at the sight of them at the table, everything in me wanting to stay.

I turn away from the only place I want to be, pulling my phone from my pocket.

I walk out reading his message from last night.

Jake

What about it?

He knows something, and he's going to tell me.

Chris

Where are you?

Jake

Home, for now. I'm going to check on Jason soon.

Chris

Stay there. I'm coming.

I plug my phone into my car charger and pull out of my driveway as fast as I can.

I pull into Jake's driveway on the outskirts of town within twenty minutes. The house looks like it was pulled out of a magazine. Secluded, serene, and way too expensive looking for someone who still exclusively wears hoodies. He's on the porch, arms crossed, eyes wary. With his hood up like armor.

He watches me approach without moving, his face even more unreadable than normal.

I don't slow down.

My fist connects with his jaw before I've even thought it through. Hard enough for him to stumble backward.

"You *knew!*" My voice cracks.

I crumple onto the steps, digging my hands into my hair, the heat behind my eyes spilling over. "Why didn't you tell me what was going on with them, Jake?"

He rubs his cheek, still infuriatingly calm.

"What do you mean?" His tone is as closed off as his body posture.

"You know what I mean!" I snarl, fist clenching again. "Tell me how awful that house was! Tell me what they did to her. How she was suffering! I could have done something!"

"Like what? What could you have done?" He scoffs, the sound sharp and angry. My head twists around to look at him as he drops onto the step beside me, shoulder knocking mine. "There was nothing we could have done, and they were so broken it was safer for you to stay away. Jason agreed. Her own brother. It's why we told you to stay away. You wouldn't be where you are if she had dragged you down. And she would have."

"No, she wouldn't have!" I insist, but when I lean into him, my hands are shaking. "And that's rich coming from you."

His hand ruffles my hair the way he used to when we were little. "What's that supposed to mean?"

"You could be friends with Jason," I choke out, "but I couldn't be friends with Tiffany?"

"You didn't just want friendship, though. Did you?" He exhales heavily. "She was the target eight times out of ten. And from what I could glean over the years, the times she wasn't, she made herself the target. I can tell it was bad, just not how bad. But they weren't willing to talk about it. She wouldn't have been able to get out if you were holding her back, and the same goes for you. We did this for you both, as hard as it is to believe that."

"You could have told me, let me make the choice," I mutter, standing to pace, my fists opening and closing at my sides. "Did you even bother telling anyone? Give them the chance to get out?"

"I tried." It's the first crack in his armor.

He stares at me from the steps, his eyes endless pools of sadness. "I told the counselor in school once; Jason wouldn't talk to me for weeks afterward. He told the counselor I lied because we were in a fight. I had no details. Shit, man, I could never confirm it was going on. There was no evidence on Jason, ever, and if there was on Tiffany, I didn't know."

He drops his head into his hands, voice breaking on the edges. "Jason chose to stay and forget, but he keeps his distance from their mother.

Tiff, well, she ran and cut everyone off. I don't think she would be who she is if she hadn't had that option. Why do you think Jason was so protective of her? He didn't know how else to help her, and he wanted to make sure that she got out. He told me everytime the screaming started he just zoned out, like his body couldn't keep going."

I sink down beside him again.

"Yeah, well, not anymore. Not ever again, you understand me? Even if this is all I ever get with her and Savie. Even if..." I brace my elbows on my knees as my words jam in my throat. I can't finish the sentence, but the need to *stay*, to *be here,* swells inside me like a tide I can't fight, fierce and unstoppable.

"Yeah, I hear ya." Jake claps my shoulder as he pushes to his feet. "We'll keep an eye on them. I promise. Besides, Mom is ready to adopt them, so I don't think we have any choice anymore."

A breath of laughter escapes me, brief and brittle, but it cracks the tension between us. I stand and brush my palms on my jeans.

"We're not done talking about this," I tell him, voice firm. "I'm still pissed at you. And Jason. He should have protected her. Not the other way around. She shouldn't have had to do it alone. But I have to get back to the house and make sure she's ready to meet with Jason to discuss funeral homes."

Jake's eyes narrow, his jaw works, but he lets me go with a nod. I wave over my shoulder, and I head back to my car, but before I'm even two miles down the road, my phone rings.

Dan's name brightens the screen.

I answer with a sigh. "Hey, man."

"Chris, is everything okay?" He asks, distracted. "Your coach wants to meet with you again to firm up dates for return and whatnot."

I shift in my seat, pressing harder on the gas. The traffic thickens as the lunch rush hits the pavement, but the need to move, the need to get back, presses against me.

"It's, um," I clear my throat. "It's not actually okay. Tiff's dad passed away last night."

I pause, considering how far I can push this off, push *them* off. I glance around my car for a moment before turning back to the road in front of me.

"Chris, I thought you said this wasn't that serious. This sounds -" Dan exhales, and the edge in his voice dulls. He's being careful with me. "Bigger than that. It's not a problem as long as it doesn't interfere with your job. You have responsibilities."

My hands tighten on the steering wheel.

"Dan," I bite back the frustration in my voice, but it slips out anyway. "I know that you mean well, but kindly fuck off. My friend just lost her father and, as I'm still not required to be back on the ice yet. I'm *not* walking away from her. Not now. She's burying her father."

My eyes go a little unfocused, and my fingers tap a quick rhythm on the steering wheel. "Make no mistake, I know my job, and I'll prioritize it, but not at the cost of *them*. Not the day after she lost her dad."

"I can meet up for dinner tonight, if you all are willing to come back to my parents' house."

Dan exhales. "Got it. I'll talk to the coach and let Pasha know. Assuming that works for him, which it should because he has the company jet, we will be there around 5:30."

"Okay," I exhale. "Dan, sounds good."

I hang up. For a second, I let myself just sit with the silence. The engine hums beneath me. The road stretches forward. And somewhere on the other side of town, Tiffany and Savie are waiting.

Waiting for me.

I turn my focus to the road ahead—on getting back to *my* girls.

Chapter 29

Chris

THE REST OF THE day, I stay as close to Tiffany as I can, helping her and Jason make calls. Savie plays with my mom in the other room, her giggles a faint, ghostly echo against the low murmur of funeral-home hold music.

Tiffany hasn't been able to bring herself to tell Savie yet. She wants a plan first. Who knew there'd be this much to organize? Picking a funeral home is the first relief. A grim milestone that smooths the process but not the ache. Three weeks, they said. Three weeks to get him back. Three weeks for answers.

I'm the last to leave as five-thirty approaches. Dinner with Dan and Coach. Dread sits heavy in my chest, thickening with every passing minute. When I have no choice but to leave, I wrap my arms around both girls, *my* girls, and sway them slowly, memorizing their warmth.

When I pull away, my throat burns. Tiffany looks close to tears herself. I brush a thumb over her cheek, force myself out the door.

The walk is quick, of course it is, but it eats at me, every step heavier than the last. Leaving them, even for dinner, might be the beginning of the end.

My parents are in full host mode when I step through the door, voices pitched just a little too bright, glasses clinking in the background. Pasha's eyebrows shoot up as his gaze drifts over me, taking in the damage. I don't even have to look in a mirror to know I'm wrecked. I'm scooped out from the inside, left hollow, a shell walking in on their cheerful little scene.

Everyone's laughing. Passing plates. But my fork just scrapes across the same patch of chicken, and my charm, the smile that never fails, is gone. I do my best to contribute, but Dan and Coach are reviewing dates and logistics as if it's already settled. Like, there is no choice here.

Three weeks, if I get cleared by Bernadette. That's what I have left with the two people who have become integral to my wellbeing.

Twenty-one days; five hundred and four hours and I have to give up the one thing I desperately want to hold onto.

My eyes cinch tight as I remind myself.

It's my job, of course, there is no choice here - the contract says so.

Mom's hand finds my arm. "Are you okay?"

My jaw aches from holding back all the things I want to say that would ruin my career as nod. Because leaving them might just be the end of me.

"So Chris, it's been 11 weeks since you got out of the sling, you've got a couple weeks left of physical therapy and you're feeling good." I tune back in to listen just as Dan finally acknowledges I might have thoughts. "Does all of this work for you?"

"Ultimately, yes, but not quite so quick. I -" I hesitate, catching Dad's eyes. He's encouraging me, but I can't tell in which direction. "I just have a couple of things to finish up here first. Tiff has to bury her dad, and Savie still doesn't have full-time childcare yet."

Dan claps his hands, ignoring my caveats with clenched teeth. "Well, let's get you back East."

And just like that, the decision is made, not by me, but by everyone else, as if forward is the only direction and I'm not already cleaved in two. The rest of the meal drags under a strained silence, thick and uneven. Mom lobs gentle questions into the void. Pasha tries, too. A joke, a glance, but nothing lands.

It all falls flat.

I'm out the door the second it's polite. I don't say goodbye. My feet fly across the grass between houses until I'm knocking hard at Tiffany's door.

She opens it, red-eyed, fingers white around the frame like it's the only thing holding her upright. "I told Savie."

She sags into me, her bones gone slack. I gather her against, kicking the door shut. I lock it as her arms wrap around my neck; tears dampening the skin on my neck.

When we enter the back room, Savie is curled on the floor with Trixi, her eyes red-rimmed too. Her cheeks, still wet with grief.

The couch groans beneath us as I lower myself down, and Tiffany curls into my lap. We barely have a moment before Savie hurls herself at us, all knees and elbows and heartbreak. Her small arms clamp around my neck as she buries her face in my shoulder, her sobs hot and muffled against my skin. Tiffany reaches out, gently stroking her back, but Savie shoves her hand away.

I tilt back, trying to meet her eyes. "Savie, why don't you want Mommy to rub your back? You love that."

"She won't let me see Poppy no more." Her words are muffled against me, still unwilling to look at me. "Mommy said no more Poppy. She's mean."

When I turn to Tiffany, the tears are already spilling down her cheeks, catching in the corners of her mouth. I freeze, caught in the rawness of her expression. Her eyes are wide, devastated, like she's barely holding herself together.

Savie finally lifts her gaze when I turn back to her. Her face is blotchy, her lips trembling, but she meets my eyes at last.

"Savie," I say gently, hoping the words won't make things worse. "If your mommy could, she'd let you see Poppy. I know she would."

"Then why won't she?" Savie's little shout breaks, and she stuffs her thumb into her mouth.

"Because she can't," I whisper, brushing back the wild curls clinging to Savie's damp cheeks. My other arm tightens instinctively around Tiffany, pulling her closer. "Poppy isn't here anymore."

Savie's voice is barely more than a breath, muffled and broken. "Where did he go?"

I falter, but Tiffany doesn't. Her voice is soft, trembling, but steady enough.

"Savie, sweetheart," she says, stroking her daughter's hair, "remember how I told you Poppy went to heaven? He's watching over us now, but... he can't be here with us the way he used to."

Savie nods, and fresh tears spill over her cheeks.

"Why?" she whispers.

Tiffany folds her small body into her arms, leaning into my chest as if I'm the only solid thing left in the room.

"Sometimes people just get too sick," I say softly. "No matter how much you try, no matter how much you love them, they don't get better."

That's all it takes. Both of them dissolve. Sobs catching, shoulders trembling against me.

"You're the only person I'd want here with us," Tiffany breathes, her voice so small it barely reaches me. "I don't know why this helps."

"Sometimes people don't need questions," I murmur, brushing a thumb along her damp cheek. I kiss her gently, a promise without words. "They don't need plans or action. Sometimes they just need someone who stays."

Pulling them both close, I wrap my arms around their grief until their breathing evens out and they drift into sleep. Trixi curls at my feet, her head a warm weight on my toes.

My head tips against her hair, the scent of her pulling me through years. I kiss Tiffany's forehead, whispering into her skin. "I should've taken you with me. Away from here. Or I should have stayed."

I spend hours contemplating how to do just that.

Chapter 30

Tiffany

THE NEXT TWO DAYS unfold in slow motion, but time keeps slipping past. I don't know if it's grief or anger that keeps jerking the world forward in fits and starts, but either way, it refuses to stop.

My mother has tried on and off to contact, but I don't have the wherewithal to placate her today or deal with whatever fight, real or imagined, that her and Frank have gotten in today.

Savie melts down at fairly regular intervals, and Chris, somehow, unbelievably, is the only one who can calm her. And she refuses me more than not when I try.

He's been so great. Incredibly present. But his phone doesn't stop buzzing, and every time it does, his shoulders go stiff. His smile slips.

We haven't talked about the night my father died. I'm not ready to pop the bubble of whatever it is we're still inside. Because once I name what I'm starting to suspect—this is the end—I can't undo it. And I can't take any more loss.

This morning, we stay in bed longer than usual. Savie curled between us, her cheek against Chris's bare chest. Our fingers rest on her back, laced together. His eyes are still closed, but I watch him. The stress is there, even in sleep. Written in the tight line of his mouth.

I shift gently, reach for my phone with the hand not tucked under his, and lift it to take a photo. First of the two of them. Then I roll back into place, raise the phone above us, and take another of all three of us.

"Darling?" Chris murmurs, fingers tightening around mine.

I squeeze back. "I'm just trying to get another picture to sell to the press. This one'll fetch a lot. I mean, you're not even wearing clothes."

The joke barely lands, but his quiet chuckle eventually makes it to me.

"I'll definitely know it was you," he says.

He untangles his hand from mine and gathers me closer, wrapping us both around Savie.

His fingers find the back of my neck, tangling into my hair, tugging my head to him. He kisses me, claims me with his lips, then pulls away and reaches down to stir Savie awake.

There are words in his eyes when I meet them. Words I don't want to hear. I turn away before they find a voice.

I don't stay in bed for the now-familiar morning routine since my dad died. I can feel it already. This thing between us is fraying at the edges. I rush out of the room.

I run away.

Because this is going to end. Well before I'm ready for it.

But then again, this was always going to end.

My phone rings right as I start pulling breakfast. Jason's name flashes on the screen.

I swipe to answer.

"Jason?" My voice is flat.

We've both run out of energy for pleasantries anyway.

"I'm going to head your way in a little bit," he says.

I tuck the phone between my ear and shoulder and brace myself against the counter.

"We need to talk about the funeral." My eyebrows furrow at the topic he wants to discuss because we've already talked through everything. "I want to finalize everything before the M.E. releases him to the funeral home."

My head drops forward, my phone threatens to fall. "Fine. I'll see you soon."

He hangs up without a goodbye.

Chris and Savie are just reaching the bottom of the stairs when Jason walks through the front door. He doesn't say anything, but the suspicion in his eyes as they land on Chris is impossible to miss.

Breakfast is quiet. Tense in a way that has become expected with Jason and Chris. I didn't understand it before, but now I know why. And, there's the slightest knot of anger under all the grief that's trying to drown me.

Jason answers Savie's questions dutifully but refuses to acknowledge anything Chris says. The silence between them crackles.

I don't intervene. I don't have it in me to play peacemaker between the two men.

Eventually, the weight of it all sends Savie into tears again. Chris rises without a word and carries her out of the room. Trixi pads after them, tail low.

Jason's gaze cuts toward me, but I don't meet it. I just keep eating, eyes fixed on my plate.

Chris gets Savie settled in front of the TV, the soft sounds drift in from the background, before returns. Sinking into the chair beside me. His hand finds my lap, squeezing gently. I meet his eyes only briefly before turning back to Jason.

"Well," I say, coolly. "You wanted to finalize the arrangements. What else is there to discuss?"

Jason crosses his arms and leans back in his chair. "I don't think we need speeches or flowers or any of that. Let's keep it simple. Revisit the idea of just a graveside service. Quick, in and out."

"No," I grind out. "We already decided what we were doing. If you want to talk about what suit he should wear or where to host the wake, fine. But I've already put down a deposit, and I'm not changing a thing."

Jason's jaw clenches. "He would have hated it."

His eyes flick to Chris, who stays silent, his hand still steady on my thigh.

It's comforting.

"I don't really care," I sag into my chair, empty and exhausted. "Because maybe it's not about what he wanted. Maybe it's about what I need. And I need to let him go on my terms. For once."

"I don't get it." Jason snaps, arms unfolding. Trixi appears in the doorway, body angled protectively, hackles raised like she can feel the heat building. "I don't get *you*. You wanted it quick when it was about pulling the plug. Why give him something he doesn't deserve? Not after the way he ignored the things we went through."

"That *we* went through?" My voice cracks, and I shove my chair back, wood screeching against tile. Remembering Savie in the other room, I

228

lower my voice, but the hiss still shakes. "You mean what *I* went through! The bruises and the concussions and broken things and the anger. The things I took, so you didn't have to. That you were unable to. I never got to hash it out with him, Jason. So, I'm doing what I can to get some very small piece of closure."

I don't wait for an answer. I push past both men and stumble out to the porch, gulping for air like I'm drowning. Air I so desperately need to keep from falling any further apart. Because if I fall apart, if I do what I want to do, I might never pull it back together again.

The door snaps shut behind me. Somehow, I know it's Chris before he even touches me. He turns me wordlessly and pulls me against his chest.

"Darling," he murmurs, voice rough.

I lean back just enough to catch his eyes. They're wet, shimmering. My own tears rise fast. I tilt my head back, a silent plea for a kiss, for a reprieve from the ache. He obliges me, his lips pressing tenderly against my own. He kisses me through the mess of a sob that crawls out of me. Through the mess of tears and grief clawing its way out of my chest.

"He's leaving you." Jason's voice cracks across the porch like a whip. I pull away from Chris, heart hammering.

"You don't think I know that?" My voice is a rasp.

"Then why?" Thunder rolls in Jason's eyes. "You're acting like he isn't leaving. Like he'll stick around."

A cruel, bitter laugh escapes from my chest. A flicker of regret flashes across his face, but it's too late to stop my next words. "You don't get a say in my life anymore, Jason. Not in this. Do you *want* me to be alone? Do you hate me too?"

"I - I, Tiffanny... No." He stares, shocked, at what I'm not sure. "Never."

But I find I'm just done with this conversation. I open my mouth to kick him out of my house, or to lob more accusations at him.

Chris beats me to it. "It's time for you to go, Jason."

"Excuse me?" Jason rears back, eyes wide.

My words hang between us for a moment before his face shutters closed.

"You heard me." Chris's voice is calm but hard. "I think you've done enough damage. I get you're angry, and maybe that's your grief talking, but your sister doesn't deserve it. She deserved better back then, and she definitely deserves better now. I might've been too dumb to question things when we were kids, letting you isolate her. But I'm all grown up now."

He takes a deep breath before continuing. "I might be leaving, yeah, but she will never be alone. I will always want her, and if she ever calls me because someone isn't treating her right... Even if she called me in the middle of game 7 in the playoffs, I'd be on the first plane back here. And you had better believe, brother or not, I'll gladly kick your ass. I'll be here for her. Forever."

Silence stretches. No one moves.

"I think I agree, Jason." I fold myself back into Chris's arms. "Cool off. I need it too. We can meet at Dad's at the end of the week to start packing."

Jason stalks off without a word. He doesn't need to speak; I can read it in the stiffness of his back. Like because he hadn't been there for me, he wasn't sure how to let anyone else. He's been so busy protecting our secret he never learned how to ask for help.

Jason's gone, and part of me goes with him. But it's not the same part that used to reach for him. That part learned a long time ago how to stay quiet, because no one is coming to save me. I have to save myself.

Chris tips my chin up, his eyes scanning my face. "You okay?"

"Yeah."

And I am.

Or, at least, as okay as I could possibly be given the circumstances.

I rise onto my toes, arms looping around his neck. "Thank you. For standing up for me."

He leans into me, forehead brushing mine. A small smile pulls at his mouth. "Always, darling."

Our lips meet softly. He lingers just long enough to make my knees go soft, before pulling back with a quiet sigh. "Let's go check on Savie."

I nod, slipping my fingers through his, and tug him with me into the house. Trixi, still posted near Savie like a sentinel, finally relaxes when we step into the living room. She stretches out beside her little girl, letting out a soft huff as if releasing the tension of the morning.

For a little while, we have peace as the four of us relax together. We sink into the couch and let the quiet hold us. Savie and Trixi curl up on the floor with some pillows, the soft murmur of the TV filling the silence with just enough sound. I lean my head on Chris's shoulder, and he rests his cheek lightly against my hair.

Eventually, it's time for him to leave for physical therapy. He squeezes my hand before heading out, his eyes lingering on me like he wants to stay. I don't say anything. Just smile softly and nod.

The door clicks shut behind him.

Savie crawls into my lap without a word, and I wrap my arms around her, guiding us both down onto the couch. She settles easily, cheek pressed to my chest, and I hold her until her breathing evens out and her body goes limp with sleep.

I don't mean to fall asleep. But I must.

Because the next thing I feel is a hand. It's not small and sleepy like Savie's, but larger and warmer.

Chris's.

His fingers comb gently through my hair. My lashes flutter, and I start to stir, but his fingertips brush against my lips.

"Shh," he whispers, voice low, barely there.

He helps me untangle from Savie's limbs with practiced care, lifting her with one arm and settling her back onto the couch without waking her.

I blink at him, still caught in the haze between sleep and dream. "I thought you had PT."

"I did," he says softly, smiling down at me, before his eyes dart away and his teeth find his cheek. "But I'm done. So, I hurried back."

He pulls me into the kitchen, his grip firmer than usual, his pace just shy of frantic. Before I can ask what's wrong, he presses into me, backing me until the counter digs into my spine. His hands frame my face, holding me like I might slip away if he lets go.

He kisses me.

Once on the forehead, soft and reverent. Then each cheek, slow and shaky. Then finally, our lips meet.

His kiss lingers.

Longer than usual. Longer than it should. It tastes like longing and goodbye. Something in the way he kisses me makes my heart rate jump not just from want, but fear. He's trying to memorize this. Me. Like this is all he'll have.

Like this is the end.

I let him hold me, harder than usual, tighter than he ever has. Because suddenly I'm desperate too. I let him take everything he can from this moment, and I take just as much.

My hands slip under his t-shirt, palms skimming the smooth line of his back. His breath hitches as I pull him closer. My teeth catch his lower lip, gentle but needy, and he groans softly against my mouth.

There's a question sitting in the space between us.

Chris hesitates only a fraction of a second before his hands slide down to my thighs. With effortless strength, he lifts me. I wrap my legs around his waist, my fingers tugging his shirt over his head as we move.

He carries me to the front room, each step deliberate but gentle, like we're both trying to hold on to something slipping through our fingers. When he sinks down onto the couch, he eases me into his lap, the soft weight of my body pressing against his hard lines.

My hands explore his shoulders and back, tracing familiar paths as his fingers dig in lightly at my hips, anchoring me there. Our breath moves faster between us. Every touch is a wordless confession, every heartbeat, a promise and a plea all at once.

I rock forward, breaking the kiss just enough to trail slow, soft kisses down the curve of his neck. His hand tangles in my hair, fingers weaving through the strands, gently guiding me closer, deeper into his hold.

"Baby girl, I need you." His voice is rough, a low groan as his head falls back against the couch. "We've got to be quick and quiet before Savie wakes."

My voice slips out as a husky breath. "Yeah."

Desperate hands fumble with his sweatpants and briefs, urgency making my fingers clumsy as I push them just low enough to bare him. My breath hitches, heart pounding, as I lift myself, sliding my own soft sleep shorts aside, and sink onto him. Every inch electric, drawing us together in a hush of need and longing.

The world narrows to just this. The heat of his skin, the tremor in my limbs, and the way we fit, perfectly, as if this is where we are suppose to be.

"So perfect, baby girl," he breathes the words into my mouth.

His lips find mine again, as we give ourselves over to the quiet rhythm of shared pleasure. His fingers dig into my waist, possessive and urgent, guiding my hips in a frenzied rhythm. Each movement is a desperate plea for more.

For closeness.

For release.

Pressure builds swiftly, cresting like a tide beneath every fevered movement, until pleasure threatens to spill over, raw and unstoppable.

No words are spoken between us. Only the urgent language of hands exploring familiar curves, lips tracing silent promises.

Every touch burns with unspoken longing.

Every breath shared a quiet confession.

The room shrinks. The world outside fading until there is nothing but the heat between us and the steady rhythm of our bodies.

My whole body tenses, caught in the electric rush as waves of release crash through me, leaving me trembling in their wake.

Chris grunts into my skin as my muscles squeeze around him. His fingers weave urgently through my hair, gripping tight as if anchoring himself in the moment, while his other hand remains steadfast at my hip, guiding my trembling body with a possessive, desperate intensity.

Every thrust is a wordless plea, my body shuddering against him, caught between the pull of his hands and the ache of longing that coils between us. It wraps us in a fevered embrace.

When he finally loses himself, I feel him claim me. The warmth he paints deep within is a silent mark of everything we are in this moment and everything we are about to lose.

I settle against his chest, both of us struggling to catch our breath. His lips press softly into my hair, murmuring words I don't quite catch, but the ones that slip through are enough to break my heart and confirm my fears.

Bernadette cleared him. He can go back. A cold knot tightens my stomach, and I fight not to tense, not to let him know I heard.

Because somehow, I don't think I'm supposed to know.

"I don't want to leave," he murmurs, the words slipping into my hair. It's fragile, honest, and full of weight.

It's the last thing I let him murmur before I pull away, trying to fold a soft smile onto my face.

I press a gentle kiss to his lips.

"Not that I mind." A soft laugh escapes me, and we both groan. Every subtle shift sparks a fresh wave of sensation between our still joined bodies. "But why did you jump me like that?"

"I did kind of jump you, didn't I?" He says with a breathy laugh.

I expect him to tease me back or offer a distraction or maybe even brush it off. I expect him to make up a lie or change the subject. I expect him not to tell me all the secrets he whispered into my hair.

I expect so many things, except what he does.

His fingers tighten in my hair, like he's afraid I'll disappear right in front of him.

"I got home, and I saw you," he says softly, "and I saw the kind of forever I want. You, a home, and kids. And I just needed you. I know everything sucks right now, but—"

He stops, his eyes tracing over my face, searching my expression. I don't know what's there, but it makes his voice roughen, thick with emotion.

"I love you." His words land like thunder in a quiet room. My breath catches in my throat as he talks. "I think I might have always loved you."

His voice is gravel and truth, and every part of me wants to believe him—but I'm frozen, stunned by the weight of it all. I can't speak. Can't breathe.

But words keep spilling out of his mouth. "You're always in my head. You and Savie. I love you. I love your daughter. I want you both. Forever. I don't know how we make it happen, but I want it. Want everything you. I want to figure this out... with you."

Before I can gather my thoughts, Trixi stirs from the living room, and that means Savie won't be far behind. We hastily straighten ourselves, like nothing just changed. Like the air between us isn't heavy with something too big to name. With words, I didn't reciprocate.

But just before we step into the living room, I stop him with a hand to his chest.

The warmth of his chest and his confession about his feelings takes me back to 16 and being drunk at our house party, looking at the boy of my dreams, begging him to kiss me.

But this time, instead of being refused, he does.

He presses his lips to mine.

And even though I want to scream the I-love-yous back at him. From the rooftop and to anyone who would listen. I keep them locked against my chest.

I might love him too, but that doesn't change anything.

Chapter 31

Chris

I SEE IT IN Tiff's eyes when I turn back after lifting Savie into my arms. The flicker. She loves me too, but she's afraid.

And maybe I don't have all the answers. But I know that love like this. It can be enough. If we let it be.

Savie mumbles, half-asleep against my shoulder, asking for an astronaut princess tea party. Her voice is soft, sticky with dreams as I smooth my hand over her tiny back and tell her yes, of course.

I turn to Tiff.

She's watching us—watching *me*. Love rising in her chest, spilling out across the space between us. Quiet, hesitant, but there. And I think this is enough.

It has to be enough.

Tiff finally stirs, blinking herself out of whatever memory or fear she was caught in, her fingers tapping a rhythm against her thigh that I've seen her create before. She steps forward and places her hand on Savie's back, right over mine. I open my free arm, and she walks into it like she's settling into the idea of forever. Her body loose in my arms.

I know this is my home. Not the building we're in, not the street we're on. But these two girls. *My girls.* My heart knew before my head caught up. I've been claiming them in quiet ways since the day they arrived.

We spend the day playing with Savie, building castles, staging tea parties on distant moons. We keep her busy. We keep Tiff busy, too, and maybe that's the point. My parents come for dinner. They linger longer than they need to, none of us wanting to leave them to their grief.

My mom holds me a little tighter when she leaves.

"Take care of them," she whispers, her hand ghosting over my cheek. "I'm proud of you."

I nod, lock the door behind them, and stand there for a beat, hand still on the knob. I already know I will, no matter what I need to change to make it happen.

Over the next two days, Tiffany unravels and gathers herself again in a thousand quiet ways. Every laugh she offers Savie, every dish she rinses, every time she zones out mid-thought.

Loss carves new spaces inside her, and she's still learning how to live with the echo.

But at night, when the house finally stills, and Savie is tucked in soft and dreaming, Tiffany lets herself collapse into the quiet. She crawls into bed beside me, and curls into my side like she's done it forever. And in those few precious minutes, she stops holding it all together. Just for me. Just long enough.

This is when I get to hold her through it. Through grief, through the weight she won't name in daylight. I don't fix it. I don't try. I just stay. And she lets me.

I get to be her refuge. I get to love her, fully, wholly, in the hush that settles at night. In those sacred hours, when her guard drops and she reaches for me, I feel her choosing me. Choosing us. Choosing, if only for a moment, to surrender the ache and let tenderness fill the emptiness grief carved out.

The first Monday following his death, Tiffany goes back to work.

Both girls are a bit weepy at the separation, but Tiff leaves anyway. The house settles into a quieter kind of cozy. No tea parties, no trips to the park. Just soft music, books, and the gentle lull of a day moving slowly.

When my mom stops by to watch Savie so I can get to what's hopefully one of my last PT sessions, Savie has a meltdown of epic proportions. Big tears, small fists. The works and I cave.

In the car, I open my thread with Tiffany and type out a message.

Chris

Hey, Savie is coming with me to PT today.

Chris

She refuses to stay with my mom.

Chris

But don't worry its not a problem.

Tiffany

I'm so sorry Chris.

Tiffany

I can take my lunch early and come get her.

Chris

Absolutely not. I've got her. I've got this.

Chris

I just wanted to let you know.

Tiffany

Okay. If you are sure.

Chris

I am. 100%

Chris

I promise it's fine.

My fingers pause over what I want to say, before I figure she already knows. I've already said it. Several times in fact.

Chris

I love you.

The bubbles pop up and disappear several times before they stop altogether.

She isn't going to respond.

I tell myself it's okay. Because it has to be. She just needs a little bit of time. We'll get there.

Savie has a great time at physical therapy. She charms everyone. She keeps everyone smiling as she makes new friends with the other PTs and their patients. It keeps me distracted as Bernadette stretches and tests my shoulder, which thankfully is pain-free.

She cleared me yesterday for work. Which means the clock is ticking.

Preseason is right around the corner. Summer's fading fast. And I'm still not ready to go. Not ready to leave them.

If I want to keep them, I have to figure it out.

Fast.

We're on the way home, Savie humming along to the radio in the backseat, swinging her feet against the car seat.

Then my phone rings.

I look at the phone, Dan's name brightens the screen. My eyes snap to the rearview mirror. Savie's gone quiet. Her eyes are on me. Like she knows this is something important.

I lower the radio volume, swipe open the phone, switch it to speaker, and set it in the cup holder. "Hey Dan, I'm in the car with Savie, so make it quick, please. And please watch your language."

"We need to talk, kid." His voice carries a familiar sigh, and I remind him about the little ears in the backseat.

"Right. Okay. PG version. Boston's getting itchy. They want your ass back in the lineup by the first day of preseason training, which means you've got about two weeks? Max. You got cleared by PT, right?"

I hesitate because I know he already knows, so there is no point in trying to hide it.

I have to work to unclench my jaw. "Yeah, I'm cleared."

"Then it's go time, Bart." His tone softens. "I can stall a little, but not much longer. The shoe deal you wanted is about to fall apart too so you gotta get your skates back on. Literally. I need to book flights, media runs, the whole shebang."

I glance at Savie in the rearview mirror. Her thumb is tucked into her mouth as she watches me, those wide eyes soaking everything in. My chest tightens. She's so sensitive to my moods, because she loves me too.

"I understand."

"No. You *hear me*, but you're not listening," he huffs. I'm frustrating him, but I can't find a way through this without breaking everything apart. "Look, I don't know what's going on with you and the girls. But this is the part where you gotta decide: Are you still in the game, or are you trying to build a picket-fence life with juice boxes and bedtime stories? 'Cause I gotta tell you, the league, and the perks that come with it, doesn't wait for guys who need more time."

I swallow the lump in my throat. He's right. Of course he's right. But there *has* to be a way to have both.

Silence stretches.

He presses in, right on the weak spot. "You're a damn good player, Chris. Don't waste what you worked for. That's all I'm saying."

I nod. "I get it. I'll call you later. I just need a little more time to make a plan."

"What else is there to plan?" His voice sounds resigned. "I already told Boston you were packing."

I nearly slam the brakes right there. My grip on the steering wheel tightens. My pulse spikes, and panic claws its way up my chest.

It takes all of my ability to keep from shouting. "You told them *what?*"

"Look, just give me a call before the end of the week," he says, ending the call.

No chance for me to say anything more.

I draw a slow, steadying breath and glance at Savie again. Her small face is tight, her brow furrowed like she's trying to piece together something bigger than she can really understand. "Savie, are you okay?"

She doesn't answer, but her eyes meet mine in the rearview mirror. "Is Boston far?"

"Yeah, sweetheart. It is." My chest aches as she turns away, gazing out the window. Silent tears trace soft paths down her cheeks. So much like her mother's.

When we get home, Savie is quieter, more withdrawn than usual. She clings to me as I cook dinner, her head tucked into the hollow of my neck. Tiffany watches from the kitchen doorway, eyes sharp with questions as Savie refuses to eat anywhere but my lap.

The door slams hard against the frame just as we're finishing dinner. A low growl rumbles from Trixi's throat as she bolts to the door. Tiffany and I rush after her. Relief floods me when I recognize her mom.

But Tiffany is quicker than me. She's quick in the way that only people who've suffered at the hands of someone who is supposed to love you unconditionally can be. She stiffens, her body tightening like a drawn bow. My eyes flick to the bags resting on the floor.

"Tiffany," Dawn says, her voice a grating nasally sound. "Frank and I broke up. I'm moving back in. It's my house anyway."

My heart drops as I recall every awful thing she told me.

They can't stay here.

Chapter 32

Tiffany

"MOTHER." MY VOICE CRACKS JUST slightly, trying to keep the panic from spilling out. "We talked about this before I moved home. You promised me."

"Well, things change." She breezes past and scoops Savie into her arms as she lets herself into the living room.

I turn to Chris, eyes wide with disbelief.

His arms fold around my shoulders, steadying me. "Don't panic, Tiff. Come to my parents' house. You and Savie both. It'll be fine."

"I can't do that!" I snap. "There is no way your parents want me, my child, and my dog in their house. Not when you are leaving."

Chris freezes. We both knew this moment was coming, but my words still hit both of us hard.

I press my lips against his. Soft at first, but desperation takes over, and I cling to him like he's the only thing keeping me from unraveling. I linger in his arms, against his lips, as long as possible. But when we part, reality presses back in.

She's here.

In this house.

With Savie.

My head sinks against his chest. "You should go home tonight. We will be okay. I'll just have to find another place. Or hopefully, like every other relationship she's ever had, they will be back together before the week's out."

He turns my face, gripping my hair, desperately careful. "I don't like the idea of leaving you here alone. Come home with me."

"I can't. Savie can't." I sigh, pressing my lips to his again. "I—" The words catch in my throat.

I want to say I love you, but everything is too fragile. If nothing else in my life were falling apart... maybe I could. But this is my reality. "I appreciate you. But we'll be okay."

I pull away from him to call out to Savie. "Sav, come say bye to Chris. He's going to go home so we can spend some time with Nana."

"I can stay. Tiff." His voice trembles, almost as panicked as I am. "Please don't make me leave you here alone."

"I'm not alone. Not this time," I promise. "Trixi would never let anything happen to Savie."

"It's not Savie I'm worried about." His fingers tighten in my hair, but he releases me when Savie rounds the corner. Bending low, he lifts her, kissing her cheek. "I gotta go, little one."

"To Boston?" Her whisper breaks my heart.

Chris closes his eyes, tilting his face like he's bracing for a hit.

He turns back to Savie, voice soft. "Not yet, little one."

He kisses my forehead, then Savie's, and ruffles Trixi's fur, before he walks out the door. There are tears in his eyes when he does. And the loss of him this time feels final.

"That boy is too good for you. He's a star." My mother is leaning against the threshold, arms crossed.

I tuck Savie tighter against my chest, covering her other ear. "Mother, not now. Not in front of Savie."

She rolls her eyes. Savie jerks at her voice, like even her tiny body knows when something isn't right. "She's going to have to grow up eventually. Real life's not a fairy tale."

"She's only three!" I snap. "You spent my whole childhood reminding me I wasn't enough. I got the message."

I turn away, heading back into the living room. I busy myself keeping Savie distracted. My phone buzzes incessantly in my pocket. When it's finally time for bedtime, I am quick to scoop Savie up and take her upstairs. I grab extra pillows and blankets, building a little fort on the floor.

Lock the door, pulling Savie and Trixi into our cocoon.

Lying down next to Savie, I pull my phone out. Brandon and Shawn have texted a few times, but most of them come from Chris. I open the thread and snap a picture of us cozy in the makeshift fort. Savie's got a giant smile. My smile looks like it is faltering, but it's there.

I send it.

The phone rings, and I answer it. Chris is frantic.

"We are fine." I look at Savie, who's practically vibrating. "Someone wants to talk to you."

I pull the phone away from my ear and switch over to speaker-phone. "Savie, why don't you tell Chris what we are doing tonight?"

She takes the phone, lying back on Trixi's belly. "Chis. Mommy and Trixi are sleeping in my room. We have a fort."

"That sounds like so much fun, little one." Chris's voice soften as Savie tosses her feet onto my hip. "I wish I could see your fort. I bet it's so cool."

"There's room next to Mommy. You can come to our fort." Her eyes flutter as sleep edges in.

He sucks in a breath, like he'd be here if he could. If I'd let him.

The desire to be here is thick in his voice as he speaks. "Maybe another day, little one. Can you give the phone back to Mommy?"

She hands me the phone and rolls over onto her side. All she needs for her world to be right is to hear his voice.

I miss his arms as we settle in.

My mom getting settled into the bed I've been using since I got home is loud enough to jar me into moving. I turn off the speakerphone and press the phone to my ear, listening to Chris breathe while keeping my ear on the commotion in the next room.

"Darling?" he whispers eventually. "Are you actually okay?"

I look at Savie. Sleeping. Finally, I let the tears come, quiet sobs breaking loose. "I don't know. Everything is such a mess."

"Let me fix it, Tiff." His voice cracks, and my heart breaks. "Let me get you both out of there. Please."

"You can't." I cover my mouth, sucking in a shaky breath. "There is absolutely nothing that you can do. You're leaving. What happens when you're gone?"

"I'll never leave you." I roll away from Savie and bury my face in a pillow, shoulders shaking.

When I finally collect myself, I whisper. "Chris, you can't promise that. You have a full life in Boston. Me and Savie, we'll be okay."

"I love you, Tiff." I clamp my hand over my mouth to hold back another sob. "I would do anything for you."

"I can't ask you to do anything, Chris, I -" I breathe out, the words sticking in my throat. "I care about you, too. We will be fine. It's just a little hiccup. Maybe it won't be so bad. Maybe... she's better than before."

It's a lie, of course it's a lie. Because breakups are the thing that makes her the most unpredictable.

"Let me come over," desperation leaks through his voice. Or maybe fear. "Or come here. I want to hold you. Please?"

"I think I need to stay here tonight." As much as I hate this. "I think it would make it harder on Savie if I didn't."

He tries a couple more times to beg me to come to him, but I need to be here. Not because he won't take care of us, but because I'm afraid he would. That's what terrifies me. There's no future where he doesn't leave. I have to learn to stand on my own again.

When we finally hang up, the silence in the room is heavier than before. I risk unlocking the door and slip downstairs for a glass of water.

The footsteps following in my wake send lightning spikes of fear down my spine, quick and hot. But just like when I was younger, I steady my trembling hands by gripping the counter edge until my knuckles ache, leaning forward, hair curtaining my face.

Tears streak down my cheeks, and my sniffling betrays me.

She circles me like a shark but I say nothing. It won't matter what I say anyway.

The bite in her voice is so familiar it makes my stomach clench. "Do you honestly think you deserve a man like that?"

I lift my head, eyes red and raw, searching her face for some flicker of softness, some remnant of a mother. Hoping she has a shred of maternal affection left in her. Once again, she disappoints me. There's nothing but the same bitter anger she held onto throughout my childhood.

"You'll end up alone, just like me," she whispers, close enough for her breath to graze my skin. The quietness of it hits harder than any slap, any punch she'd given me. "Bitter. Just like me. You'll hate her, just like me. Just like I hated you."

"Never." I bite out, realizing my mistake in answering her as her grim smile spreads, devouring any hint of warmth. "I'd never blame her for something she has no control over."

"You will," she says simply. "You're more like me than you're comfortable admitting. Becuase the sacrifice of being a single parent with no help... it changes you. And when that person who's supposed to support you through it all leaves for something shinier, it takes something from you. Your father's shiny object was a younger pair of legs to get buried in. That boy, well I'm sure he'll find those eventually, but the shine of fame? It's definitely more than you can offer."

I go silent, because silence is safer. It's the only possible way to protect Savie. Because that's my greatest fear. Becoming like her. All the screaming and shouting I grew up with would be so easy to slip back into. I think I might understand Jason's silence just a bit better now.

Exhaustion drags at me as I turn away and climb the stairs. No goodbye. No words.

I'm thankful she doesn't follow.

In Savie's room, I lock the door behind me and sink to the floor beside her. I watch her small chest rise and fall and wonder how much longer I can keep the truth from her.

Monday comes too fast, like the crash after a fall. We haven't seen much of Chris since my mother barged back into our lives on Friday. I'm running on fumes and caffeine, playing pretend for Savie's sake, like everything's fine when it's not.

Savie and I have been making ourselves scarce. We spent Saturday night at Brandon's, where Savie curled into Shawn's lap and lost herself in Disney movies. She was laughing, but the separation from Chris has been wearing her thin. I don't have it in my heart to break it to her this is what we need to expect from now on.

No Chris in sight.

All of our normal has been infiltrated by him, and I don't know how we will go back to what we were before.

Chris texted a few times over the weekend. Most of which I left unanswered. Not because I didn't want to reply. I just didn't know how to answer his desperate pleas. Not with my heart intact.

We've arranged for Savie to spend the day with him at Mark and Brenda's while I work. But when she wakes, and he isn't the one to rouse her from bed, she falls apart. She loses whatever cool her sleepy little body could have found.

She clings to me like she's drowning as I try to get us both ready for the day. Her small arms wrapped tight around my neck, her tears soaking into my shirt. I try to wrangle shoes onto both of us while holding her, but every time I set her down, she screams like I'm breaking her in half.

I'm already fraying when my mother's footsteps on the stairs grow louder. Savie goes rigid in my arms, crying harder.

"Come on, Savie." I plead, trying to keep my voice steady. It takes all of my energy to try to keep from snapping at her. "Help Mommy out, sweetheart. Please."

She sobs against my shoulder, and I know I'm losing this battle.

"I can't believe you let her act like this, Tiffany." My mother watches me lift Savie and try to step into my shoes. Her arms are crossed over her petite frame, judging. "She's going to be a spoiled brat if you don't give her some boundaries."

I don't answer. I can't. I just glance around the chaos of the entryway, desperate for my keys. I look everywhere while Savie clings to me. I'm sure I look like a mess, but trying to get ready with a three-year-old attached to my hip is especially difficult.

"Savie-baby, did you take Mommy's keys again?" I ask softly, bouncing her as she hiccups against my shoulder.

"You looking for these?" My mother stands in the doorway, keys dangling from two fingers. Her expression is flat, her tone worse. "Honestly, I don't know that you're fit for motherhood if you can't even keep track of your keys."

I freeze, the weight of her eyes on my back. I drag in a breath before I turn to look at her, my feet leaden. I put my head down and thank her before shuffling out the door. I've turned into my brother. A doormat for her snide comments without a lick of fight in me, because maybe he was right not to provoke her.

The yard is small but it's a gauntlet, filled with grief and loss and the tiniest bit of anger underneath the rest.

When Brenda opens the front door instead of Chris, I break. Tears slip free before I can stop them. She takes one look at my face and pulls us both into her arms. Her hand smooths gently down the back of my head, and my whole body shudders at the softness.

Chris is on the steps in the house. He stares at me, and the dam cracks. The longing to run into his arms and let him sweep me away from every bad thing going on makes my knees tremble.

But I don't give him the chance.

I don't let him reach for me. I don't give him the chance to walk through the doors of my heart again. I don't let myself lean on him, even for a moment. If I do, I won't leave.

And I have to. I have to learn how to stand, without anyone holding me up again.

I press Savie into Brenda's arms and step back. Step away from him, away from everything.

By the time I close the car door, he's made it to the porch. Looking like everything I want and everything I can't have. My hands shake on the steering wheel. But I do nothing as I pull away from the house. I don't even look back.

Guilt digs deep. It burrows under my ribs, nests in my throat.

By lunchtime, dread joins it while I look for ways out. I'm on my third call to daycares, and I'm about to reach out to the places I had originally passed over when I finally catch a break. One day care will have room in the next week. One of the kids is headed to kindergarten, and their parents are pulling them out early to have a vacation. A spot. Just what we need.

When I arrive to pick up Savie from Chris after work, the weight of everything presses so heavily I can't even meet his eyes. Still, he pulls me close, his arm tightening around me. I let him, and just for a moment, I let myself sink into the warmth of him.

When his lips find mine, all the ache and longing I've tried so hard to bury comes roaring back.

"Stay," he whispers against my mouth, and the plea in his voice nearly undoes me. My heart falters, splintering with the cruel hope of it. I want to stay, more than anything. God, how I want to.

"I can't." The words barely make it past my lips as I pull away, shaking with the effort of resisting everything he offers. If I let him hold me even a second longer, I'll stay and lose myself all over again. I can't afford that, not when the future is already slipping through my fingers. Not when I know he's leaving, and I'll be left behind.

"I promised my mother we would have dinner together," I add, the excuse tasting bitter and thin.

He sighs, the sound heavy and low. It rolls over me like a storm cloud, threatening to break and drown me. Before I can say anything else, Savie barrels down the hallway and slams into my legs.

My smile trembles, brittle and unconvincing, as I force it onto my face. The concern from both Chris and his mother settle over me like a weighted blanket. I scoop Savie into my arms, clutching her close.

"Ready to go, sweets?" I whisper, pressing a lingering kiss to her soft cheek, inhaling the scent of summertime ending, drying grass and tree leaves, clinging to her hair.

She nods, lighting with enthusiasm, and starts her typical daily run-down of activities. I hear all about the playground they went to and the new friends she made. Each word slams into me with aching force, and I swallow the pain, stretching my smile wider, trying to shield her from the storm brewing inside me.

We return home to silence.

I look around, and there is no sign of my mother. I breathe a little easier, set Savie down, and start dinner. It's halfway done when I hear her. I run a critical eye over her. She looks fine, not angry, not drunk, not any sort of dangerous emotion.

But I still tense.

I watch her head towards the living room. Savie's little voice starts its familiar singsong rundown, and for a heartbeat, I let myself pretend everything is okay. I turn back to the stove. The scent of dinner wafting over me, but my hands shake as I plate it.

A cry breaks through the quiet. It's small at first, then sharper. It's a sound that slices straight through me. My body moves before my mind can catch up, the plate I was holding crashes to the floor as I run.

When I enter the room, she's there, looming over my baby. Her fingertip right in Savie's face.

Savie's cheeks are wet, and her lip trembles.

"Stop being a baby," my mother hisses, venom curling off her tongue. "Your mother spoils you. That's why you're like this."

I snap.

I don't hesitate.

I'm across the room in a breath, scooping Savie into my arms. My free hand flies out like a weapon as I back away with it out in front of me.

My voice shakes, but it's all steel. "Don't. Don't you ever talk to my daughter again."

Her smile is scarily familiar. It's the one I grew up dreading. It's a ghost of my childhood nightmares made flesh.

"Don't think you can tell me what to do in my house," she says, the silk is gone from the knives in her voice as it drags along my skin.

"That's it." I hiss, the words tasting like blood in my mouth. "We are out. I'm going to pack a bag for the night, and I'll be back to get our things before the weekend. Don't contact me again."

Savie clings to me in silence as I rush through the house, throwing toys and clothes into a bag. Her tiny heartbeat thuds against mine. I whisper apologies into her hair, over and over, as if words could undo this moment.

"I'm so sorry, sweetheart. I'm so, *so sorry.*"

I grab Trixi's leash and a small bag of dog food before I turn to head out of the house, keys in hand.

My mother's voice follows us, sharp as broken glass. "You want her to end up like you? Weak? Keep treating her with kid gloves like this, and she will."

I dare to look over my shoulder. She's standing there, arms folded, watching us leave like it's a game she's already won. The light from the porch halos her, but it sinister, casting a glow over the sharp angles.

I don't answer. I just buckle Savie and Trixi into the car and peel out of the driveway, my hands white-knuckled on the steering wheel.

"Call Brandon," I rasp at my phone. My voice cracks, unfamiliar. The tears come when the line connects.

"Tiff?" Brandon's voice slices through the chaos, urgent, trembling with worry when I don't answer right away. "Tiff, are you there?"

"Brandon." His name is a gasp strangled by sobs. My words unravel. All I can do is cry. "Can we come there? I- I need..."

"Oh, honey, yes of course you can." His voice wraps around me, warm and solid, promising safety as we flee.

I glance in the rearview mirror. Savie isn't crying. She's silent, gripping Trixi's fur with desperate little hands, her fingers white from holding on so tightly.

We don't speak, but my best friend stays on the phone the entire drive. When I pull into his driveway, he's already outside, wrapping me in his arms while Shawn lifts Savie from the back seat and leads her inside with Trixi padding after.

They feed us, and Shawn tucks Savie into their guest room. After years of half-truths and careful omissions, I shatter into tiny little pieces, and I tell them everything. I spill out every terrifying detail of my childhood. Every wicked detail of my life.

For the second time in my life I tell someone the horrible full truth.

And Brandon just holds me. At one point his tears land on my hair, but I'm shaking too hard to do anything about it. Behind my eyelids, the scene plays over and over– my mother's face as she towered over my daughter

I can't stop thinking I caused this.

I let this happen. I swore I'd never let it happen again, and I did.

This time it wasn't just me. This time, I handed my little girl into the same darkness I thought I'd escaped.

Chapter 33

Chris

FROM THE PORCH, I watch her car disappear into the twilight. The tires bite at the pavement, taillights glowing like the last embers of a fire I can't keep lit.

I know something has happened.

My hands shake as the reality sinks in. She didn't come to me. Not when it counted. Like, I'm not her safe place. Like I never was. No matter how desperately I want to be.

I want to be the arms she runs to. The steady hands Savie clings to instead of Trixi. I want to be the man who makes their chaos a little less unbearable. The man who makes them feel held.

Instead, I'm standing in the wreckage of the hope for us, watching the taillights vanish.

And then I'm running into the house. Frantically looking for my keys.

"Chris?" Mom's voice cuts through the hallway. I yank open a drawer, rattling its contents. "What's going on?"

"Something happened." I can't elaborate because I don't have any answers. "I have to go. I have to follow her."

My eyes fly over every surface of the kitchen. I rip open another drawer, my fingers useless. "Where are my keys?"

I'm untethered, my hand shaking as I try to find my keys.

"Chris, slow down." Mom tries to place a calming hand on my back, and I flinch. I don't want to be calm. I want *them*. "What is going on?"

My shoulders rise and fall with the deep breath I take as I try to do as Mom asks.

"I don't know, Mom." I turn to look at her, stumbling slightly. "She just...she ran. Her mom's back, and Tiffany left with a bag and Savie and the dog, and—" My words break apart like glass on concrete. "I think something happened."

I draw in a ragged breath and try again. "I *know* something happened."

Now I know what happened in that house when we were younger. I know I shouldn't have let her pull away from me. I should have made them come here.

I have to find them.

I have to help.

"Chris," her tone is firm. The worry's still in her eyes, but she's not budging. "You'll scare her if you don't calm down. Tiffany is so strong, if she needed help, she would ask for it."

I try to bite my words off before they escape. I don't want to snap at my mom.

"No." I snap anyway. "No, she wouldn't. For years, no one helped her, and she never asked for help. I know Jake talked to you about what was going on in that house. He told me. You told me. You said that you and Dad had suspicions. Well, turns out everyone was right, and she never asked for help."

My voice cracks. "Because that's what she does. She *never* asks for help. Not once. Even when she's drowning."

But I'm the one drowning. I can't breathe. Can't think. My fingers haven't stopped shaking since I watched the two people I love most in the world drive away. I'm just spinning in place, and I can barely keep hold of my phone when it buzzes.

Brandon

> **She's here. They're here.**

Brandon

> **Safe.**

The word sucker punches me. My knees hit the kitchen tile. *Safe, safe, safe.*

252

Chris

Are they okay?

Brandon

Physically, yes.

Brandon

Give her time.

Chris

I can do that.

Chris

Please let me know if I can do anything.

Brandon

We will.

I read the thread over and over again. Like if I stare at the word *safe* long enough, it will slow the tremor in my chest. But it doesn't. Not really.

"They are safe." I choke out. "At Brandon's."

My mom's arms wrap around me from behind like I'm six years old again and the world is too big. "They're safe," she whispers. "That's all that matters."

But it isn't.

Because *safe* doesn't mean okay.

She sends me upstairs to relax, and I go because I don't know what else to do. I stretch out across my bed and stare at the ceiling, my phone clutched to my chest like a lifeline for hours. Debating. I promised Brandon I would give her time, and I will.

But I still send the text anyway.

Chris

I love you both. Give Savie a good-night kiss for me.

The reply comes quickly.

Tiffany

I will. Good night.

It's not much. But it's more than I've had in days.

I scroll through my camera roll, finding picture after picture from this summer. Savie's curls, Tiffany's tired smile, Trixi's goofy grin. Savie and Tiffany are everywhere in my photos this summer. Every memory feels like a life I almost got to keep. I pretend they're just brushing teeth. Just tucking in for the night.

That any second now, I'll hear the soft pad of feet and the dip of the mattress as they crawl into bed beside me. That I'll wrap my arms around them and the world will make sense again.

I fall asleep waiting for them.

And the next morning, I'm on the porch by seven, coffee in hand, heart wide open. Waiting.

I'm ready to see my girls again.

By eight, the coffee's cold, and so am I. There's no car in the driveway, no curly-haired little girl flinging herself into my arms, no Tiffany with that tired, guarded smile that softens when she looks me.

They're not coming.

I check my phone again. No texts. No missed calls. Nothing but the deafening silence.

Making my way inside, every step heavier than the last, and sink onto the couch with my head in my hands.

I don't know how long I sit here just agonizing over what my next move is. All I want to do is go to them.

I don't hear the door. Don't hear the boots. I don't know he's there until his weight shifts beside me, the couch dipping under my brother.

My head snaps up. Charlie's hazel eyes meet mine. He's steady, always has been, but now he's serious. *Too* serious for the brother who once duct-taped me to a trampoline in the middle of winter.

"Mom called," he says softly.

That's all it takes. The dam breaks. The words come spilling out of me. I tell him about Dawn showing up, and Tiffany bolting down the driveway like she was escaping a burning building. Me, standing there like a fool, useless and helpless.

I tell him everything.

"I don't know what to do, Charlie."

Charlie listens. Not a single joke, not a single jab. Just him being here.

"You love her." It's not a question.

But I answer anyway.

"I do." My throat tightens. "I love them both."

He leans into me, arm looping around my shoulders like he used to do when we were kids, and the world was too much.

"What good is Boston," he murmurs, "if everything you love is falling apart here?"

My chest tightens and all I want to do is escape from what's looming in front of me. Escape from the one thing I've used to looked forward to.

"What do you mean?" I ask, though I think I already know.

"What I mean is," He pauses to take a deep, bracing breath. "Are your reasons for going back to Boston more important than staying here? Is being around to love Tiffany and to be a father to Savie less important than a job? A good job, no doubt, but still just a job."

I swallow. My voice comes out rough over the lump that doesn't quiet disappear. "I don't know if I *can* get out of it."

He shakes his head. "That's not what I asked."

I'm quiet for a long time. The weight of his question is suffocating. Not because I don't know the answer, but because I do.

"I -" I want nothing more than to keep them, always "No. It's not more important."

"Good." He claps my back and stands. "Call Junior first to have him or his lawyers review your contract before you call Dan. Don't ride this wave blind. Don't let someone else write the ending for you."

And I do.

For hours, I'm on the phone with my older brother, combing through clauses and fine print, searching every inch of my contract for a loophole.

Charlie and Jake already have their relator buddy texting me about housing around here. My phone pinging repeatedly in my ear as Junior and I talk the logistics of my contract. I send him the houses I had favorited what had seemed like months ago but was barely more than a week. He says he'll get started right away and he does.

Other houses start rolling in before I can finish up with Junior.

When I finally hang up, it's nearly seven-thirty at night. The day has slipped through my fingers, but the ground is steadier under me and my whole family is rallying around me to help me make this thing work.

I call Dan.

And I tell him.

Everything. My idea. My fallback. Every loophole Junior and I found, every term I'm willing to fight on. I don't lie. I don't bluff.

And to his credit, he listens. And for the first time in weeks, there's a path forward. Not some idealistic fantasy, but a *real* possibility. One where I don't have to choose between *who I love* and *what I do*.

One where I get to stay.

"Dan, I don't care what I lose there, if I can stay here. I want to be very clear. If I can't get a trade to Ohio, I'm out. Retired. Walked away. Whatever way you want to spin it, I'm done."

Chapter 34

Tiffany

THE MORNING LIGHT FILTERS through unfamiliar curtains, pale and watery. For a moment, I don't know where I am. Savie's weight is curled into my side, her breath warm and even, and Trixi pressing tight against her back like a guardian as I gain my bearings.

Brandon and Shawn's.

Reality sets in like a bruise. It's dull, tender, and spreading.

I smooth Savie's curls back from her forehead and kiss the soft skin there. She stirs but doesn't wake, and I let her be. I slip out of bed, Trixi's eyes following me as I leave the room to head toward the kitchen.

I'm just about to round the corner when their voices grow low and serious. They're talking about me. Discussing what to do about me.

I freeze.

The hollowness comes fast and sharp, like someone sucked all the air out of my lungs.

Once again, I'm a burden.

I don't need to listen to any more. I steel myself and step into the room. Both men jolt, caught mid-sentence, guilt flickering behind their expressions.

"You don't have to worry about me," I say, voice tight. "I have a plan."

Brandon raises his perfectly manicured eyebrow in my direction. "Oh yeah?"

"Yes." I swallow. "Well, I'm not sure it's a good one, but I've got one."

"And what is your plan?" Shawn leans against the counter, arms crossed. His tone isn't unkind, but disbelief colors it, and he's right. I don't actually have a plan.

"My dad's dead," I nod, grasping at words. No matter how casual I try to sound, my voice still shakes. "Which, I guess, is convenient because his house is empty. I don't think Jason will fight me on staying there. At least not until we sell it."

And the more I talk, the more solid my plan becomes. I talk through logistics I haven't truly considered. Even if I am pulling all the words out of my ass.

By the time I'm done, they both nod, serious and supportive.

But that was the easy part.

There's something else I need to do. This next part, though, I know they're going to have a problem with.

I open my mouth before hesitating.

It takes me a few tries to get the words out. "First, I need you to watch Savie for me, and I need to go talk to Chris. Break things off."

Brandon frowns, but he doesn't interrupt.

I press forward, my voice hollow and raw. "I got Savie into daycare. I have a start of a plan. And he has Boston."

They're both quiet.

They want to say something. Their words are hidden in the tightness of Shawn's jaw, the flicker of protest in Brandon's eyes. But they don't. Maybe they know better than to argue with someone who's already at rock bottom.

And as much as I would love for them to find any reason not to let me do this. To let him keep us. That's not real life.

"What do you mean?" Brandon ask, moving closer.

His hand cups my chin to turn my face in his direction. My chin wobbles and tears threaten my eyes. I plead with him to understand the feeling I don't understand myself.

"I don't understand." His body scoots closer to mine, his knees brushing my thigh.

"I have too much going on here. And we're not part of his plan."

"Oh, Hun. I don't think that's true, but I want you to think about something. No answer required."

I dip my head, hesitant.

"Someday, whether it's Chris or someone else. You might have to let someone in. For both of your sakes. You deserve the best of everything, and I want that for you. You don't need a man to be whole. I've seen you do this all on your own. But, girl, a life without love is not what I think you want. That's definitely not the life I want for you."

I choke on a watery laugh, wiping at the tears falling for real. "I don't get happy endings."

He exhales the sadness in his eyes, but they agree to watch her.

It's a relief, but only for a moment. Because the second I walk away, it morphs into dread. It's slow and suffocating, curling in the pit of my stomach like smoke. The plan is in motion, and there's no stopping it.

Back in the guest room, I gently rouse Savie. She blinks at me, sleepy and safe, and my chest aches at the thought of what I let happen to her. That I let my mom hurt her.

I eye the bruises in the shape of fingers as we get dressed in silence. She knows everything is different, and I don't know how to tell her it's over with Chris, so I don't.

Once she's settled with Trixi and a plate of breakfast in front of her, I text Chris.

I expect an immediate reply. But hours pass. Hours. And finally, his name brightens my screen.

Chris

Can we meet tomorrow?

Not what happened, or are you okay? Not what I was expecting. I stare at the message longer than I need to.

Tiffany

Yeah. The park?

Chris

I'll be there.

I call out of work, using the estate as an excuse, which isn't really a lie. It's just a convenient truth covering the timing. I distract Savie with sidewalk chalk, with blanket forts, with cookies we bake and burn because directions are suggestions for her. But the whole time, my heart is somewhere else. It's suspended, waiting, counting down the hours.

Tomorrow, I'm going to break my own heart.

Chris looks like something out of a dream as I walk the path toward him, sunlight catching in his hair, his shoulders squared like he's been waiting for me. He rises the second he sees me, a smile blooming across his face, and for a heartbeat, my chest caves in under the weight of wanting him.

When his arms wrap around me, the world stills. He smells like home. I could stay here forever, folded into his chest. But reality presses in, sharp and cold, and I pull back before I can forget why I came. His smile falters.

"Let's sit," he says, gesturing to the weathered bench behind him.

He turns toward me as we settle on the rough wood, his fingers brushing my hair behind my ear with a gentleness that undoes me. It's too much. My eyes flood before I can stop them.

"Darling, what happened?" His warm hands slide over mine.

But there's nothing but cold.

A shiver races up my spine. I slip my fingers out of his.

I can't think when he's touching me. "Chris, this thing between us. It's got to be over."

He goes stock-still, not a muscle moving.

"What are you talking about?" His confusion sharpens, then hardens into something else. His refusal. "We're not over. We can't be over. Please. We can figure this out if you'll just try."

"Try?" My laugh comes out bitter, broken. "We agreed, remember? Casual. And casual ends. Our time together is over, just like the summer is over. Hockey season is rapidly approaching, and I won't be the reason you give up what you've worked for."

"You're not the reason," he says fiercely. "And I'm not sure I have to give up anything."

He reaches for my hands again, but I shift away, the space between us stretching like a wound.

"You just think that Savie and I are going to pack up and follow you?" I shake my head in the performance of angry disbelief. "That's not going to happen. Not now. I'm not going to add any more disruption to Savie's life. There has been enough upheaval as it stands."

"No," he says. "Of course not. But what if—" His words stall. His face screams the heartbreak we've both been trying to outrun. The heartbreak I have to ensure stays there.

"What if, what?" I scoff at him; the deathly quiet tone in my voice makes me flinch. "I'm all sharp edges and dark spaces living in that house. I'm just trying to hang on to the tiniest spark of light I can find each day to make sure Savie doesn't know that. I don't have energy for anything else. You can't honestly expect me to uproot my life for you to chase your dreams. I've already given up everything for people who don't care. I have nothing left to give anyone else. Savie deserves better, and I'll do everything in my power to make sure she gets it. So that means there can be no what ifs."

I want nothing more than to let him wrap me in his arms and tell me everything is going to be okay, but it won't. Not with him leaving. Not with us staying.

I swallow hard, knowing my next words will cut him.

"Savie deserves stability. Not someone with one foot out the door like you. I have to start thinking about what's real. What's permanent. And Chris," My voice cracks. I turn away so he won't see how much this hurts me, too. "You aren't permanent."

We both sit in quiet disbelief. I turn to look at him, and all the words he wants to say fill the space between us. I'm thankful he keeps them to himself because if he pushed too hard, all of my walls would fall. I watch his hands clench and relax over and over. But this is the best thing for him. He doesn't need this, all this baggage, my messy life.

I put myself in front of the metaphorical bullet for people I love; this time will be no different.

Because I *do* love him.

Finally, he stands. Not angry. Just resigned. "Okay, Tiffany. I understand."

He turns, murmuring, mostly to himself, "This isn't over. You think I'm running away, but I've been running toward you this whole time. I just need a little more time."

I don't know if he means for me to hear it. It doesn't matter anyway. My heart is already splintering.

I sit there as he walks away, his footsteps fading. Every part of me wants to scream for him to stop, to take me with him, to promise we'll figure it out.

I sit there until the sun dips low, until I'm all cried out. Until there isn't any red left in my eyes. Until the mask I learned to wear as a child settles back into place, heavy and familiar.

Chapter 35

Chris

IT TAKES DAYS, TO slog through everything I'm tearing down to get what I want.

The meeting this morning is almost a week from when I asked to be released from my contract. Coach and management took it about as well as it could. They - and their high-priced lawyers - tried to get my to kowtow and it took me threatening to go public for them to agree to release me. We spent the rest of the morning detailing the costs I have to reimburse them to wrangle free from Boston.

Now Dan's in a meeting Ohio management hoping to shop me to them with my newly free agent status.

And I have nothing to do but wait.

The rower squeals beneath me, the chain grinding like it's weary of me too. My legs burn, arms tremble, lungs scrape raw with every pull. But I don't stop. Not yet. The rhythm is the only thing that keeps me from unraveling.

The room smells of sweat and metal. My hands slip on the handle, the calluses rubbing raw. I'm rowing against a tide of waiting. Waiting for a phone to ring, for a voice on the other end to tell me what comes next.

Dan.

Tiffany.

Anyone.

And finally, my phone rings.

I slow the rower, letting it coast to a stop. My chest heaves. Sweat stings my eyes as I drag my forearm across my face.

"Brother, what are you doing?" Pasha's accented voice crackles through my phone on speaker, laced with disbelief as I answer the phone. "Coach just told us that you requested a trade? To Ohio?"

"Yeah," I say, voice rough. "I think it was always leading here. Ever since Tiffany walked back into my life."

I laugh, but it's not exactly joyful.

It's a sound dragged out of exhaustion. "I've been on a collision course. I just didn't want to admit it. I used to think hockey was everything. And now –"

I trail off, unsure how to finish.

I braced myself for anger, for desperate words trying to change my mind, but instead, I'm met with amusement. He lets out a laugh, unexpected, the kind that rattles through the quiet and leaves me off balance.

"I saw it. The moment it happened." Pasha says. "We were flying to L.A., and your phone pinged with that nonsense text from Savie. I knew. You got that stupid-ass grin on your face like someone handed you the Stanley Cup."

"Yeah." I smile, but this one real. "That was the beginning of the end. Or maybe the start of everything."

"Still can't believe it's Ohio," he mutters, weights clinking in the background.

He's probably in the gym with everyone else, still working.

And I'm here. Drenched in sweat. In my parents' exercise room with a rower. Choosing a different future. One that might give me everything I want.

"Ohio's not where I thought I'd end up." I sigh, admitting it. "I still might not end up here, I guess, but I had to be honest with Coach. Dan is talking with Ohio. Their captain, Zaitsev, is retiring next year, I guess, and that leaves them with an open center. I might ride the bench this year, but it would be what I need to build the family that I want with Tiffany."

"Oh, you're serious, serious." The soft thud of a barbell being racked rings with finality. "What happens if you can't get the trade? What's your plan then?"

"Then," I slap my hands against my thighs as I stand, sweat cooling on my skin. I leave my work out behind. "I guess I walk away. Technically I'm a free agent now so I'm not obligated to do anything."

"Shit, man." There's a sharp inhale on his end, followed by a long whistle through the gap in his teeth. "You've never done things by half. So, I suppose I shouldn't be surprised that you're all in."

"Always have been," I say, pressing a kiss to my mom's cheek as I pass her in the kitchen. "Just didn't know where to aim it until now."

Silence stretches between us. Years of friendship resting in the quiet. We're both smart enough to know this will change things. We'll probably be duking it out on the ice next time we meet. But for the first time in a long time, it doesn't scare me. But hopefully I'll have my girls by my side, and that will make everything worth it.

Pasha finally breaks it. "So, what now?"

"Well, now, I wait to hear back from Dan." I drop onto my bed, rolling to look out the window. "I'm house house because there is no way I'm staying in my parents' house – as much as I love them – for the whole season. I want something halfway between here and the rink that will make a reasonable commute for me and Tiff. And once all that is squared away, I get my girls back."

There's a pause. "Wait. Get them *back*? I thought you had them?"

I hesitate. Tiffany's pain isn't mine to air out. But I owe Pasha *something*. We've been through too much to play this like just another trade and he hasn't been my best friend for years.

"She pushed me away," I whisper. "She's scared. She's been through more than I can even begin to explain. And she thinks letting me go is protecting her daughter, protecting me. So, I'm giving her space. But I'm not walking away."

"You sure?" he asks, no judgment in his tone, just the weight of a friend who knows what sacrifice looks like. "This isn't just some fairy tale. Family's not a trophy you win once and hang on the wall."

"I'm sure," I say. "I'm not trying to win her. I'm trying to stay for the long haul. And if I have to prove that a thousand times over, I will."

Pasha exhales, and when he speaks again, it's softer than I expected. "I hope Ohio knows what they're getting. Because if they don't take you, they're idiots."

"Thanks, man." My chest loosens a fraction. "I'll miss having my brother on the ice with me."

He laughs, a full belly laugh. "Yeah. We're gonna kick your ass, though. The Cup is ours."

I grin despite myself. "With me on the team? No way that Cup is going anywhere but Ohio."

The joke presses against the ache. The game we love, the life I'm trying not to lose, and the hope of finding a middle ground.

My phone beeps, sharp in my ear, and the sound slices through the lightheartedness.

Dan. I miss half of Pasha's next barb while I thumb the screen. "Gotta go, Pash. It's Dan."

"Go get your girl, brother," he says, and there's an unexpected steadiness under the teasing. "Call me if you need help with a plan."

I tuck the phone between my shoulder and ear, stare at the darkened window as if I might glimpse the shape of everything I've risked. Everything I'm still trying to hold on to.

"Will do," I tell Pasha.

I hit the keypad and answer.

"Bart," Dan says, his voice all swaggery and victorious. "I did the impossible."

My pulse stutters, kicking hard, like a puck slamming against the boards. "You got me the trade?"

"I did more than that," he says, a grin practically vibrating through the line. "I got you the trade. I got you more money. And I salvaged two-thirds of your endorsement deals. We lost the shoe deal though. They didn't want to risk it. "

Relief cracks open in my chest like thunder. For the first time in days, my breath doesn't feel like it's scraping out of me.

"Dan, that's –" I laugh as excitement fills me. "God, that's amazing."

"Well, kid," he says, and the tone shifts, just a shade. "There are a few things."

Of course there are. I stand, suddenly too antsy to stay still. My legs eat up the length of my room as I pace. "Okay. Lay it on me."

He runs through the conditions. Each one is exactly what I expect, and I sit down on my bed, the magnitude of it all crashing into me.

I'm staying, and this could work.

"I won't screw it up," I promise.

"Good," Dan replies, softer. "Because I just stuck my neck out for you in ways I shouldn't have. You're one of the best I've ever represented, Chris. Don't waste this."

I stare at my hands. They're rough, calloused, bruised from years on the ice. But they're still hands that can build something new. That will hold Tiffany on her hard days. Hands that will carry Savie's future.

"I won't," I say. "Not this time."

The rest of the week blurs into a cycle of driving to the new rink, juggling calls with my doctors from Boston, Bernedette, and the new doctors and physical therapists from Ohio.

I get scanned, x-rayed, and have blood drawn. My body's poked and prodded like a rocket they're trying to clear for launch. I go where I'm told, lift what I can, bend, stretch, and skate until everyone on the Ohio team is happy.

And when I'm not with the doctors I'm out looking at houses.

I haven't seen Tiffany or Savie in days. And there's a hollow ache I can't get rid of. Like I'm waiting for a limb to reattach. I'm not the only one who's feeling the loss of those two.

Mom worries about me, about them. And the weight of it sits heavily on her face, making every line etch deeper.

Mom comes with me. Not because I need her to, but because *she* needs to. It gives her something to do, something to hold on to. And I can't begrudge her that. It's her way of staying strong. She sits in the corner of every room, listening as doctors talk about me like I'm not there and never saying a word.

Each time a test comes back clean or we get a positive response, the hope rises a little higher in my chest. A flicker, at first. Then a steadier flame. It's in my mom, too. In the way her shoulders loosen, the color that's come back into her face.

When the last test clears, the paperwork is done, and the final meeting with Dan closes, I'm officially traded.

But still every day without Tiffany and Savie grinds a little heavier in my chest. The planning helps; it keeps my hands busy, my mind from spiraling. But with only a few weeks before my schedule gets hectic again, I'm running out of time. I've put an offer in on a house, the cash from my savings was more than enough to buy the well loved brick ranch style house.

And Saturday afternoon, I'm holed up in my room, half-sulking as I scroll through every social media that Tiffany has, staring after them willing myself not to reach out until I can confirm the house is mine.

"Whatcha doooing?" Charlie sing-songs as he flops onto the bed beside me, snatching my laptop as if it belongs to him.

"Did you do the thing?" he presses, jostling my shoulder. "Tell me you did the thing."

"I don't know what you're talking about," I say, though the laughter's already breaking through.

"You *did*! I *knew* you would!" Charlie whoops, throwing his arms around me and shaking me like I just scored the game-winner. "Now let's get your girl back."

"I want to have the house part figured out first. She needs a safe place and I'm going to give it too her."

The kitchen fills with noise and motion as family dinner gets underway. Mom barking cheerful orders, dishes clattering, the smell of garlic bread in the air. Dad's got her in his arms, swaying to a tune only they can hear. The chaos is familiar. But beneath the laughter, there's an undercurrent of something sweeter. Relief, pride, maybe hope.

Dinner is loud, messy, and perfect.

Mom disappears into the kitchen for dessert, and a hush settles over the table like dust after a storm.

Jake leans in, his voice a low tremor. "Why? Why give up everything for her?"

He can't face me, can't meet my gaze. His eyes are fixed on the table, fingers twisting at a napkin, searching for meaning in the patterns on the wood. "I just don't understand."

I stare until he finally looks at me.

"I'm not giving up anything," I confide. "It's a trade. One team for another. I might be losing some brand deals and, yeah, that means some streams of income get smaller, but I'd do that a million times over for things that matter more. I want to get them back."

Jake searches my face like the truth will change if he stares long enough. Dad and Charlie exchange knowing looks, quiet pride flickering between them.

Junior is smirking when our eyes meet. It's only how fast his expression falls that tells me there is someone unwelcome behind me.

I turn, following his gaze.

Jason stands in the doorway, eyes dark and unreadable.

"What are you doing here?" My voice comes out sharper than I intend.

"Jake invited me." He doesn't move. Doesn't blink.

I'm on my feet before I know it, chair scraping hard against the floor. Jake steps between us, hands raised, but I don't give him time to say anything.

"Why are you here instead of being with your sister?" My voice is shaking with anger I don't bother to hide. "Your mom showed up last week. Moved back in. And, she ran out of that house, clutching Savie to her chest with Trixi in tow."

Jason stumbles into Jake's back.

"I didn't know," he murmurs, voice cracking. "She never said anything."

"Don't you wonder *why*?" I demand as I lean toward him, finger pointing in his face. "Why she doesn't call you when she's not safe? Why she doesn't call anyone?"

The words are coming too fast, heat pounding through my veins.

"It's because no one – not one single person in your family – ever protected her." My hand begins to shake as I throw out my accusation. "Never treated her with the care she deserved. She had to learn to protect herself. And she's so strong. *So strong* now because of it, but she shouldn't have to be. You isolated her because you were afraid. But of what? Of being safe?"

He flinches, sputtering, and my brother turns to face him. Jake's hands bracket his face, holding him steady as Jason grips the shirt at his waist like it's tethering him to the ground. My words land, but I can't stop. "I was just trying to protect her."

"Your mother and father are to blame, but you were complicit. And while you were looking away, hiding your head in the sand, she was breaking apart. I don't know if it's because it was easier to hide than to face the truth, but you kept her isolated. Alone. She had no one. And that could have killed her."

He gasps, his eyes meeting mine, tears shining in the blue depths.

"She told me," I confess as my hands flop helplessly against my side. "She told me that she wanted to back then. That she had a plan."

"Chris, that's enough," Jake hisses at me.

I don't look at him, because he's wrong. It's not enough. It'll never be enough.

"She loved you," I say, softly. "Loved you so much she walked straight into the fire for you. You saw the smoke. You just didn't want to believe it. And she doesn't blame you, Jason. God, she still loves you. She just doesn't have the words left to say it."

He breaks. Not turbulent, not visible. It's just a shudder, a tremor that empties the room of air. The acknowledgement she still loves him. Despite everything.

"I just don't understand," I whisper as I drop back into my seat. My family sits quiet around us, listening.

"Why didn't you try to save her? Why keep her so alone? Who did that protect? Not her." I shake my head. "And certainly not you."

I gesture to him, the way he's clinging to my brother like a lifeline.

"She's not alone. Not anymore, Jason. You don't get to isolate her anymore. She told you that the other day, but I'm saying it again. She gets to choose her own life. And me?" I take a breath that feels too big for my chest. "I plan to be there for every bit of it, if she will let me."

He finally looks at me, and I pour out the truth inside me. In front of him and my family.

"I love her," I say, my voice unsteady but clear. "I love *them* both. And if I can convince her to stop hiding and let me in. You don't say one more word about it. Your shitty attitude? That's done."

"You're right. I'm sorry" His voice is rough, but there's no fight left in it. "I should've done more. I should've done *something.*"

I nod once. "Don't tell me. Tell her."

He studies me for a long moment, before he whispers, "You're good for them."

He's still holding on to Jake's waist, knuckles white, and for a heartbeat, my mind stutters. Stuck on the way he's gripping him, on the memory of how Tiffany used to hold me when emotions got too heavy to stand upright. The ache of missing her hits like a bruise that never healed.

"I try," I manage.

Jason finally releases Jake and steps forward, extending a hand. I meet it halfway, our palms locking in a firm shake. My other hand finds his shoulder, squeezing. It doesn't erase anything. But it's a lot like understanding.

I turn and lock eyes with Dad. The pride shining in his gaze. It's fierce. Brighter, heavier than I've ever seen it. For a moment, the world slows, letting warmth settle deep in my bones.

I catch sight of Mom; she's pressed a trembling hand to her mouth, but her smile bursts through, luminous and unchecked, as tears slip down her cheeks. Tears spun from joy so raw they shimmer.

There's a feeling in me that tells me to have hope.

That Savie and Tiff will be mine again.

Chapter 36

Tiffany

A WEEK PASSES IN dad's house, and my father's funeral inches closer. Savie's finally in daycare, but mornings have become battlegrounds. Each one a small war, both of us raw and losing. One of us always ends up in tears, and this morning is no different.

"Savie, sweetheart," My voice cracks as I crouch, eye-level with her stormy little face. "Please, work with me here. Mommy has to get to work."

I'm begging her, but I wish I could bargain with the universe instead of my child. I'd give anything to make her less sad, to take away how much she misses him.

She kicks off her shoes, flopping onto her back with a thud that echos in the narrow hallway. "No! I want Chis!"

I tip my head back, blinking hard, fighting the tide swelling behind my eyes.

"Savie, sweetheart, Chris is at home. He had to go to Boston for work, remember?" The lie is brittle in my mouth, like glass about to shatter.

It might not be a lie for much longer, I remind myself. *If he isn't already gone, he will be soon.*

"No!" she screams again, her small body trembling. Tears streak her flushed cheeks, her sobs jagged, wild, and bottomless.

I reach for her, desperate, but she twists away, her little legs flailing. Her grief fills the hallway. Thickening the air and drowning out reason.

"Savie," I croon, voice trembling, "You like daycare, right? You have new friends. You told me about the tea party you had with your teacher yesterday –"

"No!" She sobs harder, her sorrow spiraling, breaking me apart with each hiccupping sound. Trixi settles in with a whine, her little paws reaching out for Savie. "Want Chis!"

My knees buckle, and I collapse onto the dusty floor, surrendering to gravity and grief.

"Everything's different, sweetheart." My voice is just a whisper. "I know. But different doesn't mean it will always feel this bad."

I whisper the words to her, each syllable as much a fragile promise for her as a desperate reminder for myself, clinging to hope while the world shifts beneath our feet.

"Don't want different!" she howls, throat hoarse.

Each plea is a blow, splintering me a little more.

The tears finally overflow, hot and silent, streaking down my face. I swipe at them, trying to hide them.

"Mommy has to go to work." The words sound hollow, a plea not just for her cooperation but for mercy. From this day, from this relentless ache. "Please, Savie."

I scan my father's empty home. It's all boxes and dust motes swirling in late morning light. The ghost of his presence haunting every messy corner. It's all a ruin: his life, packed in half-labeled boxes; mine, splintered and scattered, held together by little more than hope and exhaustion.

"No, no, no. No!" She tries to scramble away, but I draw her close, my back pressed hard against the wall, seeking some anchor in the chaos.

She thrashes in my arms, legs kicking, fists pounding, every jagged sob is a tremor that rattles through both of us. I clutch her tighter, pulling her in as if I could shield her with my own trembling body. We unravel together, grief and fury pouring from us in a tangled mess of tears and shuddering breaths. I cradle her, rocking back and forth, but the motion is desperate and empty, offering no comfort. But I try anyway.

"I'm sorry," I breathe into her tangled hair, my voice raw. "So, so sorry. I wish I could make everything better for you."

Nearly forty-five minutes crawl by in a haze of begging, pleading, and apologizing before we finally stagger out the door. My nerves are lit like raw wires. I thank God my boss has the patience to see past my chaos, because I'm late.

Again.

The guilt gnaws as I wheel into the parking lot, and my phone vibrates, sharp and insistent.

My mother.

The dread stirs in my chest. I want nothing more than to let the call ring into silence, but most of my things are still hostage at her place. I clench my jaw, bracing for impact.

"Hello," I manage, my voice hollow, stripped of anything soft. "I'm at work, so make it quick."

"Geez, I don't know what I did to deserve a daughter who's so ungrateful, I said I was sorry" her words slither out, meant to sting. "Well, listen. If you're done playing sleepover at Brandon's, I'm headed back to Frank's, so you'll have the whole house to yourself again."

"No you didn't Mother," I grind out, each word jagged. "I'm not moving back into your house. Not after what happened."

"I don't know what you're talking about." Frank's voice echos in the background, a ghostly intrusion. Her tone turns brisk, dismissive, hurrying me off as if I'm the inconvenience here. "Anyway, I've got to go. I'll lock up when I leave, but the house is yours again. Bye."

The line clicks dead, and I stare at the screen, hollowed out. And once again I'm floundering. I know I shouldn't go back to that house. Every instinct in me screams to stay away. But maybe a little bit of comfort would do her good. Make life a little easier for the both of us.

I'd bear any amount of pain for her peace. But this? I don't know if I can do this. Going back is too close to what we almost had. Too close to him.

And yet... maybe it's a place where her memories of Chris can breathe without breaking her apart every morning.

I spend the entire day arguing with myself about what's right. To go back or not. Maybe moving into Dad's place *is* the best thing. At least until I can find us a real home.

But I can't stop wondering what it'll cost Savie. What will it cost me?

I still don't know what to do by the time we arrive at Savie's new daycare. The parking lot is nearly empty, the late sun flattening everything into shades of gold and gray. I hurry inside, cutting it close to closing time.

"Tiffany," her teacher says, pulling me aside. Her smile is kind, but tight around the edges. "I know you told me your dad passed recently, but is there something else going on? Savie keeps talking about a man named Chris. Was that your father?"

I close my eyes at his name.

"No," I manage, forcing a small, practiced smile. "He's a friend. He watched her for a while before you guys had a spot open up. She got..." My voice catches, splintering. I have to swallow hard to finish. "Attached. He had to go back home recently, and she misses him."

The teacher hums in understanding, the sound warm but sticky. Her sympathy clings, and I hate how it makes my skin crawl.

I can tell she wants to ask more questions. Maybe she's a Chris fan, maybe she's put two and two together.

Or maybe I'm just seeing ghosts where there aren't any.

Either way, I'm grateful when the aide rounds the corner with Savie before the teacher can say more.

"Mommy!" she shouts, barreling toward me.

I sweep her into my arms, holding her tight, and hurry us out with only the briefest goodbye. She clings to me, her little fingers digging into my coat. By the time I buckle her into her seat, she's gone quiet.

The car hums softly as we pull away, the world outside already fading to dusk. In the rearview mirror, I watch her shoulders sag, her energy leaking out in slow collapse as we drive back to my dad's empty house.

"Savie, my love?" My voice is barely more than a whisper. The decision is made for me. "What do you say we get Trixi and our stuff, and head back to the other house?"

She looks at me, eyes wide and wet, and for the first time all day, she smiles. The way she brightens tells me everything. This is the right choice. No matter how heavy it already is for me.

It's thankfully dark by the time we get to my mom's house. Streetlights bleed weak gold across the driveway. Chris's car is gone. My heart sinks.

I swallow the ache and unbuckle Savie, her small body limp with exhaustion as I scoop her into my arms. Inside, the house exhales around us. Familiar, and yet wrong. Every corner still carries traces of him. His warmth lingers like sunlight caught in dust, but beneath it, the old shadows stir. The ones my mother left behind.

Savie slips from my arms the moment Trixi scampers up the stairs, both of them vanishing toward the bedroom without a word. No coaxing, no crying.

For the first time in days.

I stand in the hallway, coat still on, staring at the empty space where Chris's smile used to greet me after a long day. It's too quiet.

A thick, heavy quiet that hums in my ears.

I move through the house, half-expecting something awful to be waiting. But there's nothing. Just the ghosts of ordinary life. Toys scattered across the living room. A mug on the counter, ringed with old coffee. The blanket he used to cover us as we cuddled, still draped over the couch.

I follow the trail upstairs and find Savie and Trixi already asleep in her bed, tangled. Sleeping off the weight of everything changing. I don't have the heart to risk waking her to put her pjs on.

My feet drag me to my room. I drop onto the mattress and surround myself with the memory of him.

And I break.

We finally get the call from the medical examiner, the day after I move back into my mom's house. My father's body is ready for his funeral. It only took eleven weeks for him to die, and three weeks to get him back, and in that time, it feels like Savie and I have lived lifetimes.

It's fitting I'm here when the call comes. This house holds all the sharpest versions of my grief. And Chris is the memory I use to combat the grief of all the loss we've had.

We're still waiting on the official results, but the examiner sounds certain. A complication from long-term ventilation. A blood clot.

Who knew death could be so ordinary? So painfully mundane.

I text Brandon, just the facts. The time and place for the funeral. The new arrangements for Savie and me.

He replies immediately, his concern bleeding through every word. He's worried. He doesn't understand why I moved back here. I tell him I'll call him.

I won't.

I don't have the time. Or the words. Or the strength to explain this.

We make it through the day somehow. Thankfully, it's quieter. Savie's easier this morning, peaceful. Like being in the space that reminds her of Chris is enough to settle her.

Brandon meets us back at the house at the end of the day.

He lifts Savie from her car seat before I can even reach for her, his movements gentle but heavy with worry. His eyes trace the shadows under mine.

He doesn't say a word. He doesn't have to.

He ushers us into the house and sets Savie down to play. She wanders off with Trixi, padding close behind.

"Why?" Brandon's voice is low but steady.

I wave him off and head for the front room. He follows, his worry sitting heavy on my shoulders. He sits beside me on the couch and pulls me in before I can resist, his chest solid against my cheek.

"Okay," he murmurs. "You're talking to me. No avoiding it. Why are you back here?"

"Bran—" I start, but my voice cracks. I shift away, rubbing my hands hard over my face, trying to scrub the ache out of it. The tears fight their way forward, hot and stubborn, and no matter how hard I try to hold them back, they spill over.

"Because it's familiar," I whisper. "Because she sleeps here. Because she can breathe here, even if it hurts me."

The words tear at me.

Still, I keep going. "Everything I have done since the day I found out I was pregnant has been for her. And if I have to rake myself over hot coals to do so, well, then, that's what I'll do."

"Oh, Tiffy." Brandon exhales my name, pulling me back against his chest. His hand trails steadily over my back, shushing me while I cry. "You can't keep breaking yourself apart for everyone around you or you'll have nothing left."

My face is buried in his shirt, my tears soaking through the fabric, when the front door creaks open. Shawn's voice fills the hall, soft and warm as he greets his husband.

I lift my head, vision blurred, as Savie's small feet slap against the carpet. She races into the hallway, breathless with hope, and falters when it's only Shawn standing there.

Her shoulders sag.

She turns to me, eyes glassy with disappointment. "Is Chis come to see me 'gain?"

"Oh, sweetheart." I open my arms, and she folds herself into me, her little body trembling against my chest. "We'll see Chris again someday. We can watch him on TV when he's working, remember? We told you about his job?"

She nods, slow and uncertain, her eyes tracing my face like she can read the lie written there. Her little face, so much like my own, softens before she presses it into my neck.

"Tiff," Shawn says gently, kneeling in front of us. "Let me take Savie out for dinner. We'll be back in plenty of time for you to do bedtime."

I barely manage a nod before he carefully lifts her from my arms. She goes without protest, her fingers lingering in my hair until she's fully gone.

Shawn straightens, meeting Brandon's eyes. One look between them says everything they don't want to say in front of me. They're worried.

About her.

About me.

About the way grief and anger still lives in this house.

Brandon turns back to me, his hands cupping my face, firm but gentle. "You love him."

I freeze, the air leaving my lungs in one sharp exhale. My eyes lock on his before they blur under tears again.

I fold in on myself, arms wrapping tight around my waist like I can keep everything from spilling out. I sob out the truth.

"Yeah," I whisper, nodding through the ache. "I do love him. For so many reasons."

A sad smile cracks through my tears. "He's so good with her. With me. He did things for me that no one ever realized I needed. He saw me. He *really* saw me. And when my dad died, he stepped in, took charge, held Savie together when I couldn't."

"Tiff, why are you still here?" Brandon releases my face, brushing my curls out of my eyes. "I don't mean this house. I mean *here*. Why not follow him to Boston? What's really left to do here?"

I open my mouth, but he cuts me off with a look.

"Of course, Shawn and I want you to stay, don't get it twisted. We love having you here, and I know Jason does, too, in his own constipated way. But you aren't happy." His voice softens. "And neither is she. So, I'm asking again, why stay?"

"I can't move her again." The words come out as a whisper before my body gives out. I sink into the couch, muscles trembling with fatigue. "I can't quit this job and chase a man across the country. I can't uproot her life one more time. I can't be like her."

"You could, though." His voice is quiet but firm. "Not be like your mom, you'll never be that, but chasing what you want? You could do that. Savie deserves to have a happy mom."

"Brandon." My warning is soft, frayed at the edges. I can't take any more pushing tonight. Not when I'm seconds away from caving. From driving straight to Boston, from calling him to find out if he meant it when he said he'd drop everything.

But I don't.

Because he loves me.

And using that love to get what I want would be selfish.

Brandon must sense the shift because he lets it go. He puts on trashy TV and just holds me. Let's me fall apart against him, steady as a wall while I come undone.

True to his word, Shawn comes home with Savie just before bedtime. He looks hesitant, his eyes darting toward the crumpled paper clutched in her hands.

"Mommy!" she calls, barreling toward me. I gather her close, breathing her in, my arms tightening around her small frame.

"Whatcha got there, munchkin?" I ask, pressing a kiss to her messy hair.

She holds out her drawing with three uneven blobs that vaguely resemble people and one that might be a dog, all in a wild green crayon. "This is our family, mommy."

Her chubby finger taps each shape. "This Mommy, and Savie, and Chis, and Trixi."

She looks at me proudly, her eyes bright with certainty.

My smile wobbles, trembling at the edges as I brush her hair back from her forehead. "I love it, sweet pea."

I lift her into my arms, her paper still clutched tight between us.

"Let's put it on the fridge," I whisper. "So, we can see our family every day."

Brandon and Shawn help me through our nighttime routine. We get Savie tucked in, her breathing evening out as her head hits the pillow.

The three of us drift down the stairs, the house settling around us.

"You know you've got a hole in your shirt, right?" Brandon says, his tone deliberately light, like he's trying to carve out one small happy memory before they go.

"Well," I drawl, rolling my eyes, "if I were trying to impress someone, I might be worried."

We all laugh, but it's hollow. It's the laughter you hold on to just to prove you still can. For a moment, the following quiet feels like acceptance. Like maybe this forced lightness is just what the new normal looks like.

Chapter 37

Chris

Brandon

Funeral 10 AM Saturday at the funeral home in town.

Brandon

You know the place?

Chris

Yes.

Chris

I don't know why you're helping me but thanks.

Brandon

I'm not helping you. I'm helping her.

Brandon

She's ready to give up. She needs a reason not to.

Chris

I'm staying for her. I've got it all figured out.

Chris

Just don't tell her yet. I have a few more things to get in order.

Brandon

I know

Brandon

I knew the first time I saw you look at her.

Brandon

And I don't mean since you've both been back.

MY PHONE BUZZES WITH Brandon's last message. I read it again, once, twice. He's right, I've always been hers.

I look at the house in front of me, checking the listing one last time. It's smaller than I imagined, and older too. But it's right. Like a place where things can finally come together.

Forever.

There is so much potential. The kind Tiffany and I could build into something real. Four bedrooms, two and a half baths worth of hope. The siding's weathered, the shutters hang a little crooked, but I can already picture it—sunlight spilling across the porch, Savie's laughter echoing through the fenced-in yard, her tiny shoes kicking up grass near the swing set. Tiffany is barefoot in the kitchen, pretending not to notice me staring at her as she cooks by the granite countertops someone already loved enough to update.

It's not perfect, but it doesn't need to be. It just needs to be ours.

My family ... hopefully.

If she opens that door, I'll spend the rest of my life proving I belong on the other side.

After my realtor walks me through the house, I can't deny it anymore. This is *our* home. I put in the offer, heart pounding, and step back out into the cool afternoon air.

I'm heading toward my future.

Toward my girls.

Saturday comes, and my whole family comes to support Tiffany and Jason. We dress in traditional mourning colors, quiet shades of respect and loss. I clutch the flowers tighter than I mean to, the stems slick in my sweaty palms as we pile into a couple of cars and make our way to the funeral home.

Nerves take flight in my stomach as I step through the doors. The hum of quiet conversation fades.

The whole world narrows to two people.

Tiffany.

Savie.

They're standing together across the room, and for a moment, I can't move. Tiffany holds Savie close, her arms wrapped tight around her daughter as if she's the only thing keeping her upright. They both look exhausted. The kind of tired that lives in the bones, and all I can think is how desperately I want to carry the weight for them.

I just stand there, staring, until those gorgeous whiskey eyes lift and lock with mine. They hit like I've been checked into the boards by the toughest defenders in the league. All I want to do is run to her, pull them both into my arms, but I know it won't be welcome.

Not yet.

I drag in a deep breath, steadying myself before I take a step forward. Then another.

I'm halfway across the room when Savie finally notices me.

She wriggles in her mother's arms, pushing at her chest, her voice too excited to be hushed. Tiffany tries to hold on, but she doesn't stand a chance.

The grin breaks across my face before I can stop it.

The second Savie's feet hit the floor, she bolts. Straight to me. I drop to one knee just in time to catch her, lifting her, little arms winding tight around my neck.

I press my nose into her curls, my eyes closing as I breathe her in, the scent of crayons and shampoo hitting me square in the chest.

My little girl.

"Hey, little one," I murmur, holding her close for one perfect heartbeat before leaning back to look at her. Her wide, blue eyes are bright with pure joy, lighting the dim room around us.

Her hands cup my cheeks, soft and certain. "Chis, you come'd for me."

My throat tightens as the tears sting.

I nod, my voice rough. "Of course I came."

And I melt, my voice softer for Tiffany. The woman I love who has finally reached us. Who's standing just close enough that the tremor in the air between us washes over me.

"I promised I'd always come when you needed me."

I stand, lifting Savie higher against my chest, her small arms looped around my neck. With my free hand, I hold out the flowers. My fingers tremble, hovering in the space between us.

"These are for you, darling." My voice catches, soft and unsteady. My eyes trace over her face, memorizing every detail I'd forgotten how to breathe without. "Today isn't the day for our conversation. But I have things to tell you. Things have changed."

She stiffens, her shoulders curling in, her guard rising just like I knew it would. The sight of it nearly undoes me. I want to reach for her, to pull her in and hold her until the world steadies again. I want to wrap myself around her and never let go.

Instead, I swallow hard, clearing my throat, trying to force my voice into something steady. The nerves flutter in my chest like they're trying to tear through me.

"Can we meet later this week?" I ask, begging her with my eyes. "Before I leave for Boston."

Her eyes lift to mine, wary and uncertain, and I rush to explain before she can mistake my words.

"I'll be back in two weeks," I add, tripping over the words. "But I'd like to talk before I go."

"What's the point, Chris?" Her voice sounds small, worn thin by grief and exhaustion. "Things can't have changed that much."

"I promise I'll explain everything. I—" I stop myself before I can say too much. She has enough to carry without adding me to the list.

I lift the flowers a little higher, and after a pause, she finally takes them. When my hand is free, I draw her gently toward me, pressing a kiss to her forehead. I hold her there, just for a moment, before passing Savie back into her arms.

"I'll explain everything when you meet me," I whisper. "But today... Today, let me be here for you." My eyes flick toward Savie. "For her. At least for this."

A thousand emotions flicker across her face. Disbelief, longing, fear, something dangerously close to hope. And, finally, she gives in. Her head dips in a small nod before she leans into me.

A breath I didn't realize I was holding shudders out of me. I sway them both gently, memorizing the weight of them in my arms before I let go.

When I step back, I guide her toward the receiving line, staying close behind her for the rest of the day. Sometimes my comfort comes in quiet words; sometimes in the brush of my hand at her back. Savie drifts between us, never far, as if she knows this moment, this fragile peace, is temporary. Like she's trying to soak it in before it slips away.

For hours, I stand sentinel.

I watch my brother do the same for his best friend. Jason's wary every time his eyes find me, like he's still turning over the words I said. He doesn't comment, and for that, I'm grateful. There are years of strain between him and Tiffany, years of trauma. And though we've reached an understanding of our own, I can't help them mend that. Not until she lets me back in.

People drift by with condolences, their words blurring together until only a few manage to break through, my family - Mom mostly. And people who share her father's sharp jawline or her soft hazel eyes.

Family.

And her mother.

The bright colors she wears slice through the sea of black. Openly defiant and deliberate. Tiffany flinches when Dawn folds her arms around her, but she doesn't pull away.

Doesn't make a scene.

Savie does, in her own small way. She presses herself tighter against my leg, refusing to move closer. Dawn's face pinches, the flash of irritation smooths over as others approach.

I almost don't hear the words she leans into whisper, but I catch enough.

"I'm sorry you lost your father. Is that how you convinced him to come back?" She hisses. "Because he deserves better than you."

Tiffany goes rigid. Her expression empties, shutters coming down hard and fast. She murmurs a thank-you, polite and distant, ignoring the accusation.

What surprises me is Jason, he shuffles closer, standing almost shoulder to shoulder with me.

"Mom, stop."

His words are hissed through clenched teeth, and his hand lands on Tiffany's shoulder. Her body sags into his support, and she turns to stare at him, her eyes wide and maybe a little wet.

Dawn tuts and tetters off.

I press my hand against Tiffany's back again, a steady pressure, and she leans into it.

And once again, I'm in awe of her strength. Of the quiet, relentless way she endures the people who should have loved her most.

By the end of the wake, the crowd has thinned, and the air is heavy with everything left unsaid. I walk them out to Tiffany's car, ignoring the buzzing phone in my pocket. The sky is bruised with evening, and the parking lot hums with low, polite conversation as people drift away.

I pull them both into my chest. Pressing a kiss to Savie's forehead before Tiffany sets her in her car seat.

I tug Tiffany back into my arms. She doesn't resist when I lean in, my lips brushing her cheek, lingering there just a moment too long. We stay like that, breathing the same air, until she finally pulls back.

And then, she's gone again.

I stand there in the fading light, helpless, watching their taillights disappear down the road until they blur into the dusk. My hands fall uselessly to my sides, the echo of them still warm against my chest.

Before I turn toward the car, I finally check my phone.

A single message lights the screen.

The house is yours. Come sign the papers

A breath leaves me in a rush, I didn't realize I'd been holding. Relief floods through me, dizzy and fierce.

The house is mine.

Ours.

Chapter 38

Tiffany

MY CHEEK TINGLES WHERE he pressed his lips to my skin. As much as I want to leave this chapter behind, as much as I want to let Chris move on, I'm so grateful he came. His quiet strength kept me from falling apart.

This isn't over. You think I'm running away, but I've been running toward you this whole time.

His words from the park echo through me, just like they have every day since I walked away from him, from us. No matter how hard I try to push them away, they find me in the silence. They find me when the house goes still, when Savie's asleep, when the world is too big, and I'm too small.

And even though I want to stay strong, to stand firm against the pull of what we were, against the weight of loneliness, I can't stop the flicker of hope.

Because he showed up.

Just like he promised.

He's everything I've always wanted. And I love him.

The day after we bury my father, I tuck Savie into bed. It's been a long day—daycare, dinner with Brandon and Shawn, laughter that's borrowed from a life I used to know. Their voices still drift from downstairs while I smooth the blanket over her.

"Okay, sweets," I murmur into the quiet room. "Time for you and Trixi to sleep now. Mommy will be here when you wake up."

She nods and curls into the rottweiler's side. Trixi's tail gives a slow, sleepy wag as they both sigh in unison.

"Mommy?"

I brush a curl from Savie's face. "Yes, my love?"

"When we see Chis again?" The yawn that splits her words gives me a heartbeat to collect myself.

"Well," I say softly, stalling, hoping the right words come to me. "I don't know, sweetheart. Chris has to work. So he's busy right now."

She seems to accept my words, eyelids drooping. I rise from her bed and head for the door when her voice catches me again.

"I miss Chis," she whispers.

My steps falter. The air leaves my chest, and I have to clutch the doorframe to keep from sinking to my knees.

I pretend I don't hear her, flicking off the light and closing the door halfway. For a moment, I linger in the hallway at the top of the stairs, collecting what's left of my breaking heart before I force myself to move.

Brandon's worried face comes into view as I descend. He's half-leaning into Shawn's arms, their quiet closeness so natural it almost hurts to look at.

I pull in a steadying breath and move toward my best friends. Settling on the couch across from them, I take the glass of wine Brandon offers. I take a sip, borrowing courage from its warmth.

"You okay?" Brandon asks.

I shrug, nodding despite the heaviness pressing in on me. "As much as I can be."

"Want to talk about it?" He leans back into Shawn, who wraps an arm around him. My eyes catch on every detail of their domesticity. The small gestures between them. The way Brandon fits easily into that space, like it was made for him.

"Not really," I sigh, "but I know you won't drop it until I do."

He's been so much more careful with me since I told them everything.

"If I thought you could get better without talking about it, I'd let it go." Brandon's tone is gentle, but there's a quiet warning in the way Shawn squeezes his shoulder. Brandon glances at him, then back to me.

"So," he says softly, "where do you want to start?"

"Nowhere," I admit. "So, you tell me where *you* want to start."

Brandon doesn't miss a beat. "Let's start with Chris, then. What's happening there?"

"He left. Or—" I pause, tracing my thumb along the stem of my wine glass. "He's leaving. He wants to meet before he goes to Boston."

Brandon and Shawn exchange a look. One of those loaded, wordless exchanges that makes my stomach twist.

"Tiff..." Brandon shakes his head, jaw tightening the way it does when he's holding back. "Don't you think him showing up for your dad's funeral means *something*?"

He's the only one whose frustration rises, sharp enough to sting.

"It doesn't mean anything," I snap, too tired to soften it. "I don't know how many times I have to say it before you get it. He's *already* left us. Just because he showed up this weekend doesn't mean he's staying."

Brandon exhales hard, leaning forward with his elbows on his knees. "You keep saying he left," he huffs, "but he's still here. He stayed. That's not nothing, Tiff."

Before I can fire back, Shawn's voice cuts through the tension. It's steady, quiet, the kind that settles instead of shakes.

"You keep waiting for someone to prove you right," he says softly. "That they'll leave. But maybe - maybe he's trying to prove you wrong."

"There's nothing to prove." I shake my head, biting at the words.

"Tiffany Anne Samson." Brandon's tone snaps through the air, all steel and affection. "That man loves you. Give him a chance. Go meet him. Don't give up on something that might actually give you your own happy ending."

I close my eyes, but the tears slip free anyway, hot and unrelenting despite how tightly I try to hold them back.

"Oh, Tiffany," Brandon whispers

Two sets of arms wrap around me, holding me together while I fall apart.

I don't open my eyes. I can't. My voice breaks through the silence, small and trembling.

I'm fraying at the edges. Everything inside me is unraveling, one good shake away from collapsing completely. Dragging all of us down into a dark abyss, I'm not sure we'll ever climb out of it.

Brandon exhales, the warmth of his breath brushing against my hair. When he pulls back, his thumb catches the tears still tracking down my cheeks. His blue eyes lock with mine, steady and sure.

"Okay." My voice is hollow. "I'll do it."

I'm still not sure if I mean it. The words feel like paper promises. Thin, fragile, maybe already torn.

Brandon doesn't let me hide behind them.

"Text him now," he says, firm but kind. "Set it up while we're here, so we can make sure you have someone to watch Savie."

My phone sits on the coffee table, still buzzing every few seconds with new messages, condolences, sympathy, words I don't have the energy to read.

My stomach twists as I stare at the screen. I'm staring down a decision that could break me all over again. But I reach for it anyway.

My vision narrows on it, my whole body rebels against the idea. Like I'm opening myself for more hurt than I am ready to face. It takes me less than a few heartbeats to reach forward and grab my phone.

I swipe the notifications away, clearing the clutter. My hand shakes, and Brandon steadies it, a silent anchor at my side.

Tiffany

When do you want to meet?

Chris

Can you do dinner, tomorrow?

Chris

I have something to show you.

Tiffany

Sure.

Brandon watches the exchange play out, offering a small, knowing smile.

"Well," he says, leaning back against Shawn with a sigh. "We'll be here."

They leave and the silence settles around me like dust.

I'm alone in this house again. The same walls that used to echo with my mother's anger, the same rooms that Chris once made feel safe.

Almost like a home.

I move through the space on autopilot, cleaning up stray glasses and folding blankets, shutting it all down for the night.

And I miss him.

I miss his dumb jokes, and bad dancing.

It makes meeting him tomorrow that much easier.

Chapter 39

Tiffany

"Please, Mom, stop. Please."

"I'll stop when I'm good and ready." *Her voice like metal raked over gravel as she yells, as dry and as ragged as her breathing. Like her fury's eating her alive.*

Tears run down my face in heavy sobs as I try to choke them back. She finally shoves me and stops. "Pack your shit. I want you out."

She turns around without a second glance at my damaged body. Slamming the door behind her.

I lay there unable to move until her tires squeal as she rips out of the driveway. I lay there, curling tighter, shaking with pain and something colder than fear. Emptiness.

When I finally uncurl, I roll to my back, sucking air through clenched teeth as the carpet scrapes my skin. Darkness threads around me, through me, and numbness blankets my body. My whole body pulses with agony, but it's the numbness that scares me most.

I shuffle over to the bathroom and stare at my reflection. The redness from her hand on my cheek has faded. No blood. No swelling. I can pass for fine.

But my eyes. They are dead. Not scared. Not angry. Just... dead.

Pain crashes through my body, through my soul, eating at any hope I thought I had left. Something inside me folds in on itself.

I head outside, tears still burning my cheeks, steps unsteady. But before I can reach the sidewalk Mrs. B calls out to me, stopping me in my tracks. "Tiffany, dear."

Shame crashes through me, sharp, regret thrashing against my chest.

Her voice is warm as she begins to walk toward me, barefoot in her lawn, kindness etched into every line of her face. "Are you okay?"

Sniffling, I shrug, my feet frozen to the pavement.

"I saw your mother peel out of here. Did you have a fight again?" Her face is creased with concern.

I try to lie, but I nod instead and a sob tears through me. It bubbles out of me without my consent. First one, and then I can't stop. She pulls me to her and wraps me up in her strong arms, like something I didn't know I needed until it wrapped around me. Her warmth floods me and pulls out a wave of gut-wrenching pain as I continue to sob in her arms.

"Tiffany, I know it's hard now," she whispers into my hair, "but life won't always be this way. Someday you will find everything you ever needed. Some mothers just don't know how to love the right way, especially when their daughters grow up into strong young women. I promise, dear girl. Don't let her get you down. You're a good girl and you have so much going for you, it's just a small chapter in your story."

I nod again, unable to form any words as I soak in her comfort. Her hand strokes my hair, and the dam inside me shatters. She pulls back, cupping my face.

Sadness is bright in her pale blue eyes, and I can't help but wonder if she knows more than she lets on. And for a second, something soft flickers in my chest. Something that feels a whole lot like hope.

"We will always be just next door. If things get too hard. We are here for you." She wipes at the tears, whispering. "Don't let her win, sweetheart. Don't let her, okay?"

I clear my throat, studying her and an understanding passes between us.

"Thanks, Mrs. B." I manage, stepping back.

A text comes through my phone, Brandon excited about this or that but the message is clear, he can't wait to show me something.

And another struggling flicker of hope fills my chest.

"See, there's more out there than this. And people who want to share the joy of it with you." she says, her palm soft on my cheek as she smiles at me.

The memory fades. My Brenda's voice dissolves into silence, replaced by the faint hum of my ceiling fan.

The same little flicker of hope fills my chest again. I don't know why I never noticed before, but somehow the Bartkowski's have always been able to help me see the sun through all the darkness in my life. A smile struggles to my face.

Then I hear little feet in the hallway.

"Mommy?" Her voice is still threaded with sleep.

I roll over, reaching out to cradle her face, just like Brenda did in my memory. "What's wrong, baby?"

She lifts her arms, and I gather her to me, curling around her tiny body, like a shield.

"Did you have a bad dream?" I ask.

She shakes her head but burrows closer, holding on to me like a lifeline. I rub her back gently and soak in the peace I find with her in my arms. It's something I've only been able to find in one other place, Chris's stalwart arms.

We are quiet for a while, and I can feel her fighting the sleep she desperately needs.

Savie's little nose is pressed deep into my chest when I hear her mumble out the thought that must be keeping her awake still. "When can we see Chis again, Mommy?"

"Soon." I whisper into her hair. Like Mrs. B did for me so long ago. "I hope really soon."

I close my eyes, pressing a kiss to her hair and lay down with her in my arms. I breathe her in, cuddling her close as I try to breathe more oxygen into the flickering hope, because I hope Brandon and Shawn are right. I hope him being there yesterday means something good. I know he loves, and I love him too.

Maybe that *can* be enough.

"Let's go back to sleep and everything will be different tomorrow."

The next day moves, jumping forward and dragging its feet. The clock can't make up its mind and my thoughts keep circling the same pointless question.

What's changed?

By four o'clock, with less than an hour left in the workday, my phone buzzes with a message from Chris. Just an address. Thirty minutes outside of town.

When I look it up, my stomach twists. It's out past the city limits, where the roads thin out and neighbors are few and far between. The quiet kind of Midwest country living that's peace to some and isolation to others. The kind of country living that's barely outside of suburbia.

I text back to ask why there. But he just tells me to be there, and he'll explain everything.

And a moment behind the first, another text comes through telling me to bring Savie and Trixi, and that he'll have dinner ready for both of us.

Just like before everything fell apart.

Chapter 40

Chris

THE HOUSE IS OFFICIALLY mine.

Having the cash ready helped with the quick turnaround, but standing in it now, I realize how little that matters. This place isn't just about money. It's about rebuilding something worth keeping. It's about making a home for the family I hope to build.

Pasha and my brothers came after the funeral to help me, Derek popped in for a little while too. Fixing holes, painting walls, laying flooring that still smells faintly of sawdust and glue. There's plenty left to do, but the house is already starting to *feel* different. Less abandoned, more alive. More like a home.

Moments after I text Tiffany, telling her to meet me here, I shoo the guys out. They don't question it. They just slap me on the back, crack a few jokes, and take off down the gravel drive. I'm so thankful for these men who show up, no matter what. Even Pasha, who isn't my teammate anymore, still came.

By the time their taillights disappear, the house is quiet again. But it's a hopeful quiet.

Paint swatches cover the kitchen counter like fallen leaves, dinner's ordered, and my nerves are live wires at the crunch of gravel under tires again.

My hands are streaked with pink paint. I thought I'd have time to change, but I don't mind.

She needs to see me like this.

Messy.

Because that's what I've been since they left.

Before I know it, I'm moving.

We reach the door at the same time. She doesn't even have a chance to knock before I've got it open wide, heart pounding in my chest.

Savie bounces in Tiffany's arms, excitement bubbling over as she waves at me. I grin back at them, the sight alone loosening something tight inside me. Tiffany steps over the threshold, eyes sweeping the room, and her voice comes soft but edged with caution.

"What is this, Chris?" She sounds curious and wary. Like she's afraid to hope again.

My gaze follows hers around the room, trying to picture it through her eyes. It's a mess with paint cans, tools, and a stack of pizza boxes, but somehow, there's a warmth to it. A heartbeat. It's all coming together.

I shrug, searching for the right words.

"Well," I turn back to meet her eyes. "It's my new house."

Her brow furrows, a question caught behind her lips. I nod toward the half-finished walls and scattered paint swatches.

"It's safe enough if you want to let Savie explore," I say, scanning the space again. Yeah, the walls are still tacky in places, but she should come away paint-free. "There's a swing and playset in the backyard. Completely fenced in so it's safe."

Tiffany studies me for a long moment before she nods. She sets Savie down, and before I can blink, the little girl launches herself at me. I catch her easily, her laughter echoing through the quiet house.

When I set her back on her feet, she takes off toward the backyard, Trixi barking excitedly as she joins in the chase.

I watch them for a long moment — Savie's laughter, the rhythmic squeak of the swing, the way the last bit of sunlight spills across the yard.

I turn to Tiffany, and for a second, I forget how to breathe. Having her here, in this space I'm building for them, and every piece of my world finally fits.

I gesture for her to follow me out to the porch, where we can watch Savie play.

"So," she says, folding her arms, cautious but curious, "are you going to tell me why you have a house in Ohio now?"

"Well, I'm staying—" I try to explain.

She cuts me off, sharp but trembling underneath. "What do you mean, you're *staying*? Your job's in Boston. Did you quit?"

"Well, no –" She cuts me off again, and the warmth of affection wells within me. I bite back a smile at her frustration with me.

"Then why?"

I can't help it; a quiet laugh slips out. "If you let me explain."

"Sorry, please explain." Her lips twitch despite herself, just the barest hint of a smile.

"Okay," I say, smiling as I reach out to brush a strand of hair behind her ear. My fingers graze her cheek before settling at her waist. "I'll be quick, because I know you're going to have a million questions. And I promise I'll answer every single one of them."

She nods, eyes locked on mine, waiting.

"I asked to be traded to Ohio," I tell her. "Both teams agreed. I got the final clearance a couple days before your dad's wake. I put a cash offer in on this house a week ago, I got the keys just after the funeral and the guys drove straight over and helped me put even this much together in the last three days."

Her lips part, but no words come out.

"They'll announce the trade next week," I continue. "I start with the team here in three weeks. That's why I have to go back to Boston. To pack up the penthouse, close everything out."

Her voice is small when it finally comes. "I don't understand. Why?"

I take a step closer, my pulse thundering in my chest.

"Do you really need to ask that?" I try to smother a smile, and fail. "I love you, Tiffany. I love you both."

She gasps softly, my hand drifts back to her cheek.

"I want this to be *our* home," I tell her. "And if you decide you hate it, I'll find somewhere else. Whatever it takes. I just want to build a life with you. I want to be your shelter through every storm. I want to raise Savie, and maybe," I pause, smiling faintly, "maybe some more babies, with you."

"Chris, I—"

I cut her off with a gentle kiss. Her hands clutch at the fabric of my shirt, and I steal one more kiss before I speak again.

"Shh," I whisper against her lips. "You don't need to decide right now. I want to show you around the house and if you need more time, well, then take it."

I untangle her hand from my shirt, threading our fingers together.

"I'm staying," I promise. "For as long as you will let me."

I'm about to lead her through the house when a knock sounds at the door. I hurry to answer it, pay the delivery guy, and unload everything across the messy counter. We use paper plates and have a picnic in the empty dining room on the newly replaced flooring.

We talk about nothing important as we eat.

Mostly, Savie fills the silence, telling me about daycare, her new friends, and how much she misses Granny B. Her chatter fills the house, wrapping around us like a promise of normalcy.

Savie finishes first. Trixi helps her clear her plate, and they take off back outside to play again.

Tiffany clears her throat, but when I glance up, there's a gleam in her eye as we finish our dinner. The air between us is weighted with potential, but not uncomfortable.

I take the trash from her and stand, offering my hand to help her to her feet. She slips her fingers into mine without hesitation. We check on the girls through the back door before I lead her down the hall.

The first room I open hasn't been started on yet, but I show her it anyway. Sunlight spills across the room's potential. The old paint peeling, and the flooring scuffed with the years of love that this house has known.

"This one's a spare," I say, nodding toward the open room across the hall with chaos spilling out. "Same with the one across the hall. These two are about the same size. My brothers and Pasha have been helping me get things ready. I'll probably have to hire someone to finish once the season starts."

She hums, smiling softly. "That's very nice of them."

I guide her farther down the hallway, pointing out the bathroom before stopping at the last two doors. I open the one on the right.

Her breath catches. The room glows in the fading light, the soft pink walls warm and inviting against the new flooring.

"This will be Savie's room," I tell her, my voice brightening with each word. "Jake said he'd have his friend, who's an artist, come by while I'm out of town next week to paint a mural. Stars, spaceships, princesses, all of it. I found a princess bed that'll still work when she outgrows this phase. And these cute little princess-themed plug covers with matching switch plates."

"You've put a lot of thought into this," she says softly.

When I turn to look at her, Tiffany's eyes are wide, glassy with tears.

I don't take a moment to consider the ramifications if this doesn't go my way, I just pull her into my arms and sway her gently.

"Hey," I whisper against her hair. "What's wrong, darling?"

Her smile breaks through her tears, brilliant and hopeful. "Nothing. It's perfect."

I drop a kiss on her lips, soft and lingering. She wraps her arms around my neck and deepens it, just for a heartbeat, before she pulls back.

"Show me the last bedroom," she says, her voice a mix of excitement and apprehension.

I lace our fingers again, and we cross the hall to the last bedroom.

When I open the door, she stops short. The room glows in the soft light filtering through the curtains. Pale beige walls. A king-sized bed fills the space, dressed in deep navy bedding. The best I could find on short notice and dark enough to hide the inevitable mess of kids and dogs.

Matching nightstands flank the bed, each already set with small comforts on top: plugs, device holders, and a book light. The walk-through closet opens into a decent-sized master bath. Functional for now. But one day, I hope, it'll reflect her touches too.

She's quiet as she takes it all in, lingering through the space. I stay back, leaning against the door jamb, watching her trail her fingers along the bathroom counter.

"This is our room," I say softly.

Her hand stills. She turns toward me, her eyes finding mine. I expect the same spark of wonder from Savie's room, but what looks back at me is different. Hesitation. Fear. And hope, maybe, buried deep under years of self-protection.

Chapter 41

Tiffany

I can picture it; I can see a life full of us and Savie. A full, messy, beautiful life. But nerves run rampant through me. Brandon's voice in my head, urging me to give in, to let this happen.

But deeper still, I hear my mother's voice, sharp and cold, whispering I don't deserve it.

Chris's warmth at my back makes her easier to ignore, for now.

I turn back toward the bathroom, toward the gorgeous, if slightly outdated, finishes that make this room feel lived in. Loved. I can see the vision. I know exactly what I'd do with this space if it were mine.

If I let myself take hold of this.

When I turn back to him, that same hopeful look is on his face. It's patient and steady. I fight the fear every step I take toward him.

"Our room?" I ask softly.

A grin pulls at his mouth, rising higher with every inch I close between us.

He nods, his hands finding my waist as I reach him. My palms rest against his chest before sliding over his shoulders, wrapping myself around him.

"I'm terrified," I whisper.

His thumb moves in slow circles along my lower back. "Me too."

"No, you don't understand, Chris." I shake my head, my fingers curling into the back of his neck. "I'm afraid she's right. That I don't deserve this."

"Baby girl," he murmurs, pressing a kiss against my forehead. "She's never been right about that. You deserve care and love and everything you didn't get growing up."

He leans back just enough to meet my eyes, his voice breaking a little on the next words. "Even if it isn't with me, you deserve the world."

I have no hope of stopping the tears that fall from my eyes. "You're the only one I would trust enough to try with."

He brushes his thumb under my eyes, catching the tears. "The scars other people left on you don't define you. I know how to be patient. I think I've been waiting for you since we were kids."

"I don't want you to wait for me." My voice trembles as I tighten my arms around his neck. "I don't want to be afraid anymore."

I pull him down to my lips, and the world falls away as we move together backward through the closet and into the bedroom. Chris sinks onto the edge of the bed and tugs me into his lap. My knees bracket his thighs, my hands bracing against his chest as his heart hammers beneath my palms.

I break the kiss just enough to speak, my lips still brushing his. I want to say it. To tell him I love him too. To give the words shape at last.

"I... I lo-" He cuts me off with another kiss, deeper this time, his hand sliding to the back of my neck.

"Chris," I breathe against his mouth.

He pulls back, his forehead resting against mine, his voice thick with restraint.

"If you say it, I won't be able to stop myself. And our little girl is just outside that door." His thumb grazes my jaw, soft and sure. "She could interrupt us, and I want to hear it when we have all the time in the world to celebrate it."

I smile and press my lips to his again. "Come home with us?"

"I wouldn't miss it for the world." He lifts me off his lap, setting me gently back on my feet before kissing me once more as he stands.

I lace my fingers through his and lead him toward the backyard. Savie and Trixi are still tearing across the grass, both of them skidding to a stop when I call out. Chris lifts Savie into his arms as they race toward us.

I press a kiss to her cheek and lean into the open space against Chris's chest. "Hey, sweets. What do you say we head home?"

"No." She wraps her arms around his neck, clinging tight. "Stay with Chis."

"Savie-girl." I can't fight my smile, and Chris's widens against my hair. "Chris is coming home with us."

She bounces in his arms, her laughter spilling out like music. It's contagious; before long, Chris and I are both laughing with her.

"Okay, ladies," Chris says through a chuckle. "Let's head home and get this little one to bed."

He walks us out to the car, settling Savie into her seat before jogging back toward the house. Through the windshield, I watch the lights flip off one by one, and then he appears, locking the door and running to his car.

He follows us all the way home, Savie chatters from the backseat until her words slow, her yawns taking over. Her eyes are fluttering, half asleep as we pull into the drive. Chris parks behind me and is out of his car before I can even open my door.

He slips Savie from her seat and carries her toward the house as I grab Trixi's leash. I open the door, and Chris has Savie up the stairs before I even get Trixi unleashed. His low voice drifts down the stairs as he murmurs in her ear. I can't quite catch what he's saying until I find myself standing in the doorway as he settles her into bed.

"I'll be here when you wake up, little one." His voice is gentle as he tucks her blankets around her.

"Chis, you go 'way,'" her voice is thick with sleep, small and accusing. "I missed you."

The words pierce straight through me. They're meant for him, but the ache of them settles deep in my chest.

Chris smooths her hair back, his voice steady and warm, full of sincerity. "You're right, but I'll always come back for you and your momma," He promises.

When he looks at me, his eyes say the same thing his words do. His promise hits me harder than I expect. It doesn't quite ease the guilt, but it softens it. Turns it hopeful. Like it's just a small mistake we can fix.

He stands as Trixi jumps onto the bed, pressing one last kiss to Savie's forehead before stepping toward me. His strong arms find my waist, electrifying me as he guides me from the room, flicking the light off and pulling the door halfway closed behind us.

He walks me backwards toward my room, the air between us charged with everything not yet said. The door latches, soundless as it shuts behind us. And the world shrink to just this. His breath, our racing hearts, and the quiet promise of starting over. Of moving forward.

He tilts my chin, and when his lips meet mine, it's not urgency that fills the space but something deeper and more sure.

And for the first time, since I pushed him away, I let myself lean into it. Into him. Trusting maybe this time, home doesn't have to hurt.

He begins his slow seduction, his lips pressing more urgently against mine. He trails them over my cheeks, my eyelids, and down my neck. Every touch is a vow. His hands slide to the small of my back, drawing me closer before they work up the back of my shirt, and lifting it from my body.

"Say it now," he pleads, his voice is wrecked with restraint.

My head drops back, feeling the tremor of his breath on my skin, the reverent warmth of his lips brushing along my jaw. My confession floats out on a shaky exhale. "I love you."

A sound breaks from him, a low, aching exhale. As if my love mends the holes I left in him when I ran away.

"Again."

"I..." My voice trembles as I draw his face away from my body and cradle it in my hands, staring deep into his hazel eyes. My thumbs brush away the tears that begin to gather at the corner of his eyes. "Love you, Christopher Michael Bartkowski."

He closes his eyes, the tears finally spilling over. My thumbs brush at the tears dripping onto his cheeks. His eyes open to greet me as I kiss him gently.

"I've been waiting to hear that," he whispers, his voice barely audible. "I love you, Tiffany Anne Samson."

He leans in again, pressing his lips to mine in a kiss that sears me. A kiss that sparks, lighting our desire on fire. A kiss that tastes of tears and promises of our future. Our hands begin to roam, relearning the familiar landscape of each other's bodies, peeling away the layers until there's nothing between our skin.

When we are finally free of our clothing, he lays me back on the bed, settling into the cradle of my hips. The heavy heat of his cock pulses against my thigh as his lips leave mine, carving lines of desire into my neck.

His lips trail reverently down my body, stopping to kiss at the peaks of my breasts, lingering. Teasing my nipples until they harden beneath his touch before he continues memorizing my body. He kisses every mark pregnancy left on my stomach, every scar I carved into my body, worshiping each one as a part of what made me who I am.

Kneeling between my thighs, he presses a chaste kiss on each one before lifting his gaze. His eyes simmer with heat.

"Say it again," he murmurs, voice thick with need.

"I love you, Chris." My breath shudders out, chest rising and falling with the force of my desire. It's raw and consuming.

Our eyes lock, the moment stretching taut with anticipation before he leans into me. His mouth descends, tongue lapping gently at my cunt, a fire burning into each nerve. My eyes slam shut, overwhelmed, and my hand slaps against my lips, stifling the desperate moan that tumbles free as he consumes me, savoring each trembling response his touch ignites.

"That's right, baby girl." His voice is a molten whisper, vibrating against my clit. Each word sends shockwaves through me, threatening to rip another moan out of me. "Quiet, we don't need any interruptions. You're just for me tonight."

He lingers, savoring the exquisite tension between us. He's in no hurry to throw me over the edge of release. Bringing me to the brink, then retreating, trailing kisses along my trembling thighs, coaxing me back to him.

My hand stays clamped firmly over my lips, trying to stifle my moans as I struggle to follow the commands mumbled against my skin.

"Such a good girl for me," he whispers, each word adding to the molten heat. After the third time he lets my release ebb away. "This time, I'm going to let you come. Hard and fast. I want to feel you unravel in my hands."

True to his promise, he presses into me with a renewed intensity that steals my breath. His tongue and teeth working in a relentless rhythm, sending sparks through me. Two fingers slip inside, curling gently, stroking the sensitive walls already fluttering with anticipation. His fingers are incendiary, each stroke drawing me closer to the edge of exquisite ruin.

It takes him only moments to roll me over the edge of the most intense release, my entire body arching into a storm of sensation. Sparks bursting behind my eyelids, my teeth clenching against my hand to stifle the cry that threatens to escape. His fingers pull from within me as my body continues to jerk, tremors coursing through me.

My unfocused eyes open as he nestles back between my thighs, settling his weight on top of my sweaty body.

A languid, satisfied smile pulls at my lips as I reach with unsteady hands to softly brush away the shimmering evidence of my arousal on his lips. My fingers trail down to trace the curve of his jaw.

"Hi," I whisper, breathlessly.

"Hey, baby girl." He grins, the warmth in his eyes unmistakable. "Got one more for me?"

I nod as he presses inside me. His hand slides down, rough and possessive, hitching my thigh high around his hip as he buries himself as deep as he can into me. He pauses with a guttural groan against the hollow of my throat, breath searing my skin, every inch of him trembling with restraint.

My hands wrap around his shoulders, digging my fingers into his hair, desperate and greedy as I tug him closer.

"Chris." I whimper into his ear, my tone flooding with need. "Move. Please, baby, move."

"I'm going to fuck you so good, baby girl. Make you fall apart in my arms, over and over." His voice is wrecked as he rasps against my skin. "I just need a moment, or it's going to be over too quickly."

"Please, I need you. Don't stop." My voice is ragged, desperate.

"Let me savor you, this, just a moment longer," he growls, his lips hovering above my flushed skin before claiming my mouth in a kiss that burns with hunger and need. "If I don't, I'll lose myself in you before I'm ready."

He finally starts to move, unhurried, withdrawing before slamming home again with a force that steals the breath from my lungs. A gasp escapes me before I seize his mouth in another hungry, desperate kiss.

Every time he pulls back, it's tormentingly slow, and every return is a fierce, possessive thrust that sends shockwaves through me. The air between us crackles with heat, his body slamming into mine, and our breaths mingling.

My entire existence shrinks to the rhythm of his hips, the searing press of his lips on mine. His relentless grip is possessive, branding me with his touch. Every caress, every deliberate motion, sends desire spiraling higher and higher, flames licking hungrily at every nerve until I am utterly consumed.

He devours every moan I offer, and I drink in the rough, frantic groan torn from his throat, our bodies tangled together as his thrusts turn into the smooth rhythm that he is always so good at. Pushing me closer to release.

After a long moment, he tears his lips from mine, his voice cracked. "Oh God, you feel so good, baby girl."

"Chris," I gasp, my fingers clawing desperately at his back. "You feel so good, baby. So big. I'm going to come."

He groans, gripping me tighter as he lifts my other leg, plunging even deeper. His words are like gravel in my ear. "Come for me, baby girl. Come now. I want to feel you lose control."

And I do.

I shiver apart in his arms, wildfire races along my nerves, sweeping me under.

He continues to move against me, slowing just enough for me to stop shuddering. To catch my breath.

The aftershocks still rippling through my body as he surges forward again, relentless and desperate.

"Just one more," he pleads, "Give me one more, baby girl."

He settles back into the smooth, relentless rhythm, thrusting and retreating, building the heat between us a third time. His hands roam over my body, no longer frantic but burning with an insatiable hunger. My fingers glide along the lines of his back, tracing over the welts and crescents I left there.

It doesn't take long for me to start climbing toward the peak again, every muscle in my body wound tight, primed from the echos of my earlier releases. My feet brace against the bed, lifting me toward him, desperate to close the distance between us, to challenge his pace within me.

"Chris," I breathe out his name, trembling. It's the only word I'm able to say as my body quivers against him.

"I know, baby girl." His forehead presses to mine, his breath hot and teasing across my lips. "I know."

He slips his hand between us, fingertips dancing against my clit, sending flames across every nerve. His fingers push me over the edge, my release crashing through me like a tidal wave. He captures my mouth as a cry bursts from me, devouring the sound.

He loses himself within the heat of our kiss, his hips stuttering against mine, swelling inside me as he comes. Wet warmth floods my body as our we slow.

The warmth of his breath mingles with mine, his forehead pressing to mine, trembling in the quiet. "I love you, Tiffany."

"I love you too," The words find their home against his lips.

"I'm going to keep you forever," A shaky laugh escapes him, lips curving into a smile against my skin. "If you'll let me. I want to marry you."

My breath catches, tears stinging my eyes as his words settle between us. He kisses me again, and a promise is sealed in the space between heartbeats.

His thumb runs under my eye, finding a tear and brushing it away. "You can't just ask me that," I whisper, my voice breaking into a quiet laugh. "Not when you're still inside me."

His smile is radiant, filled with boyish charm, as another tear slips free as his thumb brushes it away.

"Then I'll keep asking," he murmurs. "Every day, until you say yes."

I close my eyes as he slips from my body and gathers me against his chest. I snuggle into him, into the safety of his arms, and let the weight of his words sink into me.

For the first time, the idea of forever doesn't scare me anymore.

It's a lot like peace.

Chapter 42

Chris

I WAKE UP ALONE, and for a moment, my chest tightens, panic wrapping tightly around my ribs as I blink against the haze of sleep. My hands drag over my face, rubbing at the grit in my eyes.

When my vision clears, I'm met not with the sleek lines of the penthouse or the newly painted walls of my home, but the faded wallpaper of Tiffany's room at her mother's house.

The tension drains from me all at once, and I let out a slow breath, sinking back into the pillows. I reach over to the nightstand, grab my phone, only to find it plugged in and charging. This quiet act of care has me fighting a smile as I check the time.

Six thirty.

Early.

Early enough that Tiffany should still be tangled in the sheets beside me.

But the space is cold.

I sit up, a low thud sounds against the covers, and a wet tongue drags across my hand. Trixi, cheeky as ever, thumping her tail against the mattress like she's proud of herself.

"Hey, girl." I scrub at her ears, chuckling. "You're supposed to be guarding a much smaller bed."

When she just wags harder, I sigh, pushing to my feet. My jeans are in a pile near the foot of the bed, but my shirt's gone. I pull on what I can find and head out to look for my girls.

Savie's room is empty when I check it.

I turn and head downstairs, the boards creaking under my feet in the quiet. The faint smell of pancakes and coffee draws me toward the kitchen, and there I find my shirt.

It hangs off one of Tiffany's shoulders, soft fabric brushing the skin of her thighs, the morning light catching in her hair.

For a second, I just stand there, taking her in.

I move closer, sliding my arms around her waist, fitting my chest against her back. She melts into me easily, her warmth seeping through the soft cotton. I press a kiss to her bare shoulder, breathing her in.

Her hand finds its way back to me, fingers threading into the hair at my neck, scratching lightly and sending a well of sensations shivering down my back. The small sound that escapes me is half sigh, half growl.

"You look good in my clothes, darling," I murmur against her ear, my voice rough with sleep. I sway her hips gently, dancing her in my arms. "Look better out of them."

She laughs lightly, swatting at me.

My hands sway her hips more dramatically, running her ass over my groin, before turning her into my arms. We start to dance around the kitchen, one half of my heart in my hands.

It's not as lively as the dance my parents have perfected over the years, but its a start. It's our *real* start. There's no music but we don't need it. We move to the rhythm of love beating out of our chests. She tilts her head back, letting her chin rest on my chest.

I open my mouth to tease her — maybe tempt her away from breakfast and back into bed — when a tiny body hits my leg and two little arms wrap around me.

"Chis!"

I look down to find a tangle of curls and a grin that nearly knocks the breath out of me. This, this messy, beautiful chaos, is what the rest of my life looks like, and I'm ready for it.

I scoop her up, her small body warm and solid in my arms, pressing a kiss to her temple. "Hey, little one."

She studies me for a beat, then pokes my bare chest with a tiny, serious finger. "Chis, you naked."

Tiffany's laugh bursts out first, bright and unrestrained, and I can't help joining her. "You're kind of right, little one," I say, grinning. "I had a sleepover with mommy, that okay?"

Savie tilts her head, thinking it over.

She nods solemnly and rests her head on my shoulder. "You could sleep over every night. Mommy so sad when you went away."

The words hit like a quiet punch, soft and honest and heavy with everything we almost lost. I glance at Tiffany, and her smile falters just slightly before she hides it behind the rim of her coffee cup. The ache in my chest spreads, but it's warm this time. Hopeful.

I press my lips to Savie's curls and whisper, "I'll always come back. I promise."

She sighs against my shoulder, and for a moment, the whole world spins a little slower.

It's everything I didn't know I wanted before I met them.

I lean down, brush a quick kiss across Tiffany's lips, and carry Savie to the dining room, settling her in at the table. "Alright, little one, you stay here. I'm going to help Mommy finish breakfast."

Back in the kitchen, Tiffany hands me a spatula without a word, a faint smile playing at her mouth. We move together easily, falling into a rhythm that feels practiced.

It's so seamless.

This is how it's supposed to be.

Before long, we're all seated at the table, clinking forks and Savie's chatter filling the air.

"So," I say, glancing between them, "what's the plan for today?"

Tiffany arches a brow, her lips curving. "Well, I've got work and Savie's got daycare. Isn't that right?"

Her bare foot slides up my leg beneath the table, a small, teasing reminder of last night, and I have to fight not to grin.

"What about you?" she asks.

"I'm going to work on the house." I reach down and catch her ankle, keeping her there just a moment longer. "This weekend, I'll head out to the penthouse to pack. Maybe you two could come with me. See if there's anything you want us to keep."

Her eyes flick to mine, unspoken words passing between us. The look that says *we're really doing this.* Building something for us.

A family.

I nod, because we are really doing this, and her eyes soften. I follow her upstairs after settling Savie in front of the TV, her giggles fading behind us.

"Savie could stay with me," I say. "Or Mom could watch her. She misses her."

There's a tug-of-war behind her eyes. Her desire to give in and accept everything, and her fear of what's been true her whole life.

"Tiffany," I say, taking her hand. "I'm all in. I want you both. I want a life where this, us, isn't something I have to leave behind at night. I want you in my bed, matching bands on our left hands."

I pause, brushing my thumb across her knuckles. "My family wants you too."

I pull her back against my chest, pulling my shirt off her body.

She exhales, her eyes shimmering with relief and disbelief.

I draw her closer until her back rests against my chest, feeling her heartbeat sync with mine.

"We don't have much time," I murmur, my breath catching in her hair. "But we've got time enough for this, for me to remind you how much I want you."

I drop to my knees and turn her body to face me, lifting her leg over my shoulder and making quick work of proving my point. The space between us dissolves, and everything else falls away, leaving only the quiet certainty that this, whatever *this* is becoming, is home.

Tiffany's got a pretty pink flush on her cheeks when we reach the bottom steps. I can't help myself. I pull her back against me, stealing one more plundering kiss before I turn her toward the door.

"Don't worry, darling. I've got Savie. I'm going to drop her off with my parents until lunchtime, and we will go back to the house until we meet you back here for dinner. I'll also call the movers and have them swing by here on their way from the penthouse. That means packing whatever you unpacked here."

She arches a brow, half amused, half wary. "Chris, we haven't even talked about moving in together."

"This is the same as asking you to marry me," I breathe against her lips, grinning when she rolls her eyes. "I'll ask you every day until you say yes."

Her laugh is soft and incredulous. "So, are you asking me to marry you or move in with you?"

"Both," I grin.

"Okay, Casanova." She rises on her toes and kisses me, playful and sweet. "Let's start with moving in, and you keep working on that proposal."

"Well, one out of two ain't bad." I kiss her again, a final promise pressed against her lips. "I love you."

I turn toward the living room, calling out, "Savie, come say bye to mommy. We have a date with Granny B!"

Squeals echo through the house, followed by the slap of little feet on carpet. Savie barrels into Tiffany's arms, plants a wet kiss on her cheek, wriggling free and bolts toward the door.

"Whoa there, little one." I catch her mid-run, spinning her toward the stairs. "Let's get dressed first."

She laughs the whole way, Trixi bounding after her in happy chaos.

I glance back at Tiffany, catching the soft curve of her smile. "I've got this, darling. We love you."

Her smile deepens, tenderness sparking in her eyes.

Epilogue

Tiffany

This morning – the morning of game 7 of the playoffs - sunlight filters through the gauzy drapes, painting the room in a soft gold. From the hall, Savie's giggles float through the half-open door, followed by Chris's low rumble of laughter.

The smell of cinnamon wafts in, warm and sweet, and I know exactly what they're making. Those giant cinnamon rolls Chris insisted we buy from the bakery last weekend. And I have a feeling that another proposal is headed my way. Just as unserious as every one of them before today.

He's proposed every single day, just as he promised, in increasingly ridiculous ways. Written in the steam on our mirror, a sticky note on my steering wheel, and even on those generic flower cards stuffed in a bouquet of roses.

I slip out of bed, tug on one of Chris's shirts to hide the love bites he left on my body the night before, and pad down the hall.

When I reach the kitchen, I stop, my hand caressing the small bump our baby has created between my hips over the last 16 weeks.

They're both standing by the counter, Savie on her stool, helping Chris drizzle icing over the rolls. It's chaos. The icing is getting everywhere, clinging to her sticky fingers as laughter continues to spill out of them both.

I'm about to step in when Savie's laughter fades. Her little brow furrows as she looks at him.

"Chris," she says softly, "are you gonna be my daddy now?"

The question hangs in the air, fragile and heavy all at once. I press my fingers to my lips, holding back a gasp. I can't move. I want to hear what he'll say. Chris crouches so he's eye level with her, his voice gentle but steady.

"Well, little one," he says, "We're a family now. And maybe, someday, if you decide you want me to be your daddy, that would make me the happiest man in the world."

Savie studies him for a long moment, turning his words over in her head. And I realize they've talked about this before. She's not confused, just thoughtful. And it makes me wonder how many quiet mornings like this they've shared, just the two of them, stitching our lives together when I wasn't looking.

Chris smooths back her curls as she wraps her arms around him. "Chris is my daddy."

My heart stops, then takes off into a sprint. His eyes, already shining with joy, brim with tears as he pulls back and presses a kiss to her forehead.

"Yeah, little one," he murmurs. "I'm your daddy."

And he is. The best one she could have asked for.

"I'm glad you're my daddy now." She presses her sticky hands to his cheeks, smearing icing over his face.

That's when Chris catches me, right as I lift my fingers to swipe away the tears threatening to spill. There's a smile tugging at my lips, one I couldn't stop if I tried. His answering grin lights his whole face, that familiar, steady warmth radiating through the room. He leans over to whisper something in Savie's ear, and her eyes go wide before she spots me.

"Mommy!" she squeals, launching herself off the stool. Trixi bounds after her, intercepting before I'm completely tackled by sticky fingers. Savie's giggles fill the kitchen while Trixi's tail wags furiously, her tongue cleaning the sticky icing. The whole moment is so *us*. It's chaotic, warm, and full of love.

When I look over, my gaze finds Chris again. He's this steady presence. And I can't imagine my life without him.

"Ask me again," I whisper.

He cocks an eyebrow. "What?"

"Ask me again." The tears finally slip free, warm trails down my cheeks. "Ask me to marry you."

His grin widens, boyish and brilliant. "Yeah? You sure?"

I nod, laughing through the tears. "Yeah."

"Okay, hang on." He darts out of the room before I can say another word, and Savie dissolves into giggles watching him go.

I scoop her up, her little hands finding my cheeks, smearing icing across my skin as she presses her forehead to mine.

"Mommy happy?" she asks softly.

"So happy," I whisper back, kissing her sticky curls.

Chris skids back into the kitchen, slightly out of breath, his grin impossibly wide. He drops to one knee in front of us, pulling a small velvet box from his pocket.

"Tiffany Anne Samson," he says, voice thick with emotion. "From the moment I first saw you, I knew my life would never be the same. You and Savie are the best things that ever happened to me. You're my whole heart. My whole world. You're everything I never dared to dream of. Make me the happiest man on earth. Let me spend the rest of my life loving the three of you. Marry me."

He opens the box, and nestled inside is a ring that takes my breath away. A stunning oval diamond, framed by a line of smaller stones, all set in platinum, that catches the morning light just so.

"Yes." I nod, tears streaming freely now. "Yes, of course."

Chris lets out a soft, shaky laugh as he stands, lifting Savie gently out of my arms. He pops the ring from the box and slides it onto my finger, pressing his forehead to mine.

"I love you," he whispers. "I love all three of you."

Savie crashes her forehead against ours, and we both burst out laughing.

"Ow," I giggle, leaning into her as she squeezes between us.

Chris kisses me, sweet and unhurried, before he presses another kiss to Savie's curls. One hand drifting to rest against our baby.

"You kind of ruined my plans, darling," he teases. "Savie and I had everything all worked out. Breakfast in bed, a sleepover with Granny B. I was going to ask you tonight. When we win the cup. With the ring and everything."

"No. This was exactly right." I shake my head, smiling through fresh tears

I reach for his phone on the counter. "Hold still."

I make him pose, his larger hand holding mine with Savie's pudgy little finger pointing proudly at the ring over our cinnamon rolls, the icing everywhere in the photo. We take one more, Savie's head resting on his shoulder, my hand brushing her curls back, the diamond catching the morning sun against her dark hair.

I type out a group text to his family and Jason.

It's simple. Just the photos and one line.

Chris

She said yes!

His phone starts buzzing, and I'm sure mine is too, but we ignore them both. We move through the rest of breakfast as we do on any other day. With sticky fingers, shared smiles, and hearts that feel impossibly full.

SIGN UP FOR MY AUTHOR NEWSLETTER

Be the first to learn about Tegan E. Armstong's new releases and receive exclusive content!

WWW.TEGANEARMSTRONG.COM

Acknowledgements

I want to take a few minutes to thank those that helped this book – and me – to the other side. After many, *many,* attempts at finishing a manuscript, this story finally came to life. It's a story that is both near and heartbreakingly dear to me. This story came in a season when my family was navigating more heartbreak and hardship than we probably deserved, and writing it became both a refuge and a release.

So, I want to thank my friends who held me together this year. Thank you for being the sounding board for my sometimes overwhelming amount of rambling, venting, spiraling and dreaming. Your kindness made the hard days easier.

First, I want to thank my very best friend, Melissa, who has somehow always managed to be by my side even when we lived miles and miles apart. You are the reason I stay sane somedays. And thank you for not judging the outrageous amount of TikToks and memes I send you. (It's my love language. Sorry!)

To Katie and Emily, thank you for being the first people to read my book and for supporting my crazy dream of writing it. Your grace and encouragement mean more than I can say and I'm thankful for the years of friendship you've offered me.

To DJ, thank you for keeping me laughing – and reminding me I'm old. Your perspective grounds me in all the best ways. You make me a better person. I'm thankful that I got to be your boss once upon a time and even more thankful to call you a friend.

And lastly, but most importantly, I have to thank the non-readers in my life – also known as my motley crew. To Ellie and Samson, thank you for the endless cuddles, drool and enthusiastic games of fetch. You sat with me through every long night of drafting, editing and lots of reading out loud. To Styx, Monster and Jib, thank you for carrying the weight of my emotions and being my rocks in the hardest years of my life. You make flying without wings feel possible. I wouldn't know who I am without the five of you carrying me through everything that's been thrown our way.

Finally, I want to take just a few seconds to remember the furbabies that left before for I ever got a chance to finish a story. Frostie, Baby Dos, Uno, Blossom, Theo, Dreamer, Rhea, Stryder, and Khan. I've been luckier than most to be loved by so many cats, dogs and horses.

You are the heart of me and this book.

www.ingramcontent.com/pod-product-compliance
Lightning Source LLC
Chambersburg PA
CBHW050009120726
47903CB00006B/1699